the
right
kind
of
fool

Books by Sarah Loudin Thomas

The Right Kind of Fool
When Silence Sings
The Sound of Rain
A Tapestry of Secrets
Until the Harvest
Miracle in a Dry Season

the right kind of fool

SARAH LOUDIN THOMAS

BETHANYHOUSE
a division of Baker Publishing Group
Minneapolis, Minnesota

© 2020 by Sarah Loudin Thomas

Published by Bethany House Publishers
11400 Hampshire Avenue South
Bloomington, Minnesota 55438
www.bethanyhouse.com

Bethany House Publishers is a division of
Baker Publishing Group, Grand Rapids, Michigan

Library of Congress Cataloging-in-Publication Data
Names: Thomas, Sarah Loudin, author.
Title: The right kind of fool / Sarah Loudin Thomas.
Description: Minneapolis, Minnesota : Bethany House, a division of Baker
    Publishing Group, [2020]
Identifiers: LCCN 2020028878 | ISBN 9780764234019 (trade paperback) |
    ISBN 9780764237843 (casebound) | ISBN 9781493428144 (ebook)
Subjects: GSAFD: Suspense fiction.
Classification: LCC PS3620.H64226 R54 2020 | DDC 813/.6—dc23
LC record available at https://lccn.loc.gov/2020028878

Unless otherwise indicated, Scripture quotations are from the King James Version of the Bible.

Scripture quotations labeled RSV are from the Revised Standard Version of the Bible, copyright 1946, 1952 [2nd edition, 1971] National Council of the Churches of Christ in the United States of America. Used by permission. All rights reserved worldwide.

Cover design by Kathleen Lynch/Black Kat Design and Paul Higdon

Author is represented by Books & Such Literary Agency.

20 21 22 23 24 25 26   7 6 5 4 3 2 1

For Larry Phillip Loudin
AUGUST 1941–APRIL 2020

———————

Thanks for the stories, Dad.
I'll take it from here.

Let a man meet a she-bear robbed of her cubs, rather than a fool in his folly.

Proverbs 17:12 RSV

one

The day's heat lay close to Loyal like a quilt he couldn't push back. He imagined the cool, dark current of the Tygart River. But Mother would never let him go swimming by himself. He loved diving deep, feeling the pressure of the water press against his face and ears so that he heard a whooshing thrum. At least that was what he thought he heard. He could almost remember . . .

But Mother never let him go anywhere alone. He'd been home from school for weeks and weeks, and she rarely let him leave the house without her. He wasn't a baby. He'd turned thirteen back in May, was well on his way to fourteen. He'd be a man before long. Like Father. He bet Father would let him go swimming. If he were here.

If he were ever here.

Mother was at one of her church meetings. He glanced at the tall clock wagging its tail behind glass. She'd be gone another hour at least. And while she told him not to go any farther than the back garden with its rows of corn, beans, and tomatoes,

7

the thought of disobeying seemed less and less terrible as the airless day hemmed him in. He grunted. He would do it. It was time he acted his age.

Delphy pushed a strand of damp hair back from her face and sighed. Did they really need to discuss plans for decorating the church for Christmas in such detail this far in advance? The discussion as to whether or not to have a "greening of the church" service or to simply put the decorations up on the Saturday after Thanksgiving was grating on her nerves. Didn't they have more important things to discuss?

"Delphy, will you supply the cedar branches?" Genevieve Slater laid a cool hand on her arm. How was her hand cool in this heat?

Delphy pushed a smile up from the place where she stored manufactured emotion. She'd been forcing smiles since the town realized her husband spent more time on his beloved Rich Mountain than he did with his family. He still came down to see them but only on his own indecipherable schedule. Maddening. "Of course," she said. As if she had the only cedar trees in Beverly. Yet it wasn't worth pointing out. She'd learned to save her energy for battles that mattered. And goodness knew the battle she was fighting to convince the town that her family was intact required the bulk of her energy.

Genevieve smiled and turned to a discussion of the Christmas pageant and the timing of the Christmas Eve service. Delphy spotted one of the funeral home fans tucked behind a hymnal and began stirring the thick air. At least no one had made a pointed remark about whether or not Creed would help cut the cedar and bring it to church. She supposed she should be grateful for small blessings.

The cool water was every bit as delicious as Loyal had imagined. His clothes lay piled on the bank next to a piece of toweling he'd found in the ragbag. If he didn't stay too long, Mother would never know he'd been gone. The sheer joy of being alone—of being free—washed over him. It was even more refreshing than the water. He dove again, then surfaced drawing air deep into his lungs. He could smell damp soil and moss. He floated on his back and let the sun bake his face as he watched a few puffy clouds drift through the washed-out sky.

A movement on the far bank drew his attention from the blissful river. He treaded water, watching. It wouldn't do to be caught by someone who would tell Mother. There. A flash in the trees. He moved closer so he could crouch in the edge of the river among water-worn stones where the water lapped at his legs. The figure looked familiar . . . Michael Westfall.

Loyal ducked lower, grateful that Michael was rushing along a path and paying no attention to the river. The older boy had teased Loyal more than once, made fun of how he talked with his hands. Loyal wondered why he was in such a hurry on this hot day.

Michael paused, looked over his shoulder, and beckoned someone on with a *hurry-up* gesture. He glanced around wildly and then stuck something in a rotted-out stump. As he straightened, a girl with russet hair sped into view. It was Michael's sister, who was the same age as Loyal. They would be in the same class too, if Mother would ever let him go to the school in town. He had always found Rebecca to be her brother's opposite. Kind, still, peaceful—always ready with a smile and a wave for him. Plus, she was pretty.

Now, though, the girl was gasping for breath. Her hand pinched her waist as she ran after her brother. She glanced over her shoulder, fear in her eyes. Loyal glimpsed another movement—higher up the mountain—but before he could focus on it, he saw the older boy's hand motions get bigger and his lips move. Loyal saw the word *hurry* take shape over and over. What was wrong? Michael grabbed his sister's hand and tugged her forward, then released her and rushed ahead. Rebecca looked back again and paused, panting. She closed her eyes and bowed her head. When she lifted her face, she turned toward the river, and Loyal had the notion she saw him. Her eyes were full of something . . . a secret maybe? He rose up just a little, and her eyes widened. He lifted a hand the way he would when signing *your*. She lifted her hand in the same way, and he understood that something terrible had happened. Then she turned and sprinted after her brother.

Creed headed out to the only spot near the cabin that got good sun. He planned to pick a mess of beans where they climbed the stalks of corn he'd planted in his garden patch. He wished for Delphy's good pork roast with sweet potatoes, but he'd eat his beans and be glad for them. As a boy there'd been more than one lean year and he knew even now folks in cities were going hungry. The country was in a pickle, and he wasn't so sure President Roosevelt was going to get them out of it.

There'd been rumors in town about some homestead project Eleanor Roosevelt was championing. They were talking about setting one up on mostly empty land out near the Westfall place. Word was, they'd pay good money, but there were plenty of folks who valued their land more than empty government promises. And Hadden Westfall was one of them.

Creed felt an ear of corn to see if the darkening silks were telling the truth about it being ripe. He grunted and added the ear to his galvanized bucket. He might even dig a few early potatoes. He ought to leave them to grow until the tops frosted and the tubers hardened off, but they'd sure be tasty cooked with the beans and a piece of salt pork.

Pausing, he peered down the mountain through the trees to

where he could glimpse the Tygart twisting along the wide valley below. He stretched his back and took in the view. It was a good place—the valley shaped like his grandmother's long wooden dough bowl. The bottomland was gentle and rich, softly curving up to the steeper hillsides, offering plenty of room for a man to make a life if he were so inclined.

Creed turned back to his garden. Some days it was lonesome up on Rich Mountain no matter how much he appreciated the peace and quiet. No matter how many times he told himself his family was better off with him up here.

The mountain was where he could keep an eye out for ginseng to dig each fall so he could sell enough to pay Loyal's tuition. No one could accuse him of depending on his wife's inheritance. Then, in the spring, he'd gather the morels folks were happy to trade for, and he could always sell a mess of fish if he needed to buy the boy some new shoes or books for that special school he went to.

Not such a boy anymore. The thought flicked through his mind as he went back to gathering his supper. Loyal had turned thirteen a few months back. Some places he'd be considered a man already, but Loyal was different. He was special. Creed didn't know what was going to happen to him, what he was going to be. Maybe, if he learned enough, he could be a teacher at that school he went to. He was plenty smart—at least Delphy said he was. Creed hadn't much learned how to shape the boy's language.

He broke off another ear of corn and dug out those potatoes, then strode to the cabin to set everything to cooking. Who'd have thought he'd be the chief cook and bottle washer in his own house? When he married Delphy, he'd supposed she would do that from then on. And then Loyal came along and Creed took his own father's advice too much to heart. Pushed the boy too far. Demanded too much. And now . . . well, it wasn't worth dwelling on. Dad wasn't here to see how far he'd fallen, and that was a relief.

Creed started nipping his beans and breaking them into a pan. They'd need to cook the longest. He lost himself in the rhythm of the simple task, thinking about how many times his grandmother had done the same. She'd stepped in when his mother died bringing him into the world, and she was the only person Creed had ever seen stand up to Dad. He smiled at the memory of the petite woman in her perfectly starched apron, dressing his father down. She'd laugh to see Creed doing women's work now.

No, he thought, she'd fuss. She would not approve of a married man baching it up on a mountain while his wife and son lived just a few miles away. He made a point of going into town to attend church with them most weeks and he even spent the night now and again, but mostly he felt more at ease here on his mountain and suspected Delphy and Loyal were more at ease once he was gone. Still, it might be nice if . . .

Movement along the path leading to the cabin caught Creed's eye. He noticed a puff of smoke rising from the path and jerked to his feet. Had some fool started a fire?

Setting his pan aside, he laid a hand on the rifle leaning against the doorjamb. He cradled the long gun in the crook of his elbow and watched to see what—beyond the smoke— had drawn his attention. Not many ventured this high up the mountain without having a purpose in mind.

When he saw it was a boy, he relaxed. Then he recognized Loyal and every sense went on alert. Delphy never let the boy wander on his own, and she rarely set foot on the mountain. What in the world?

Loyal got close enough to make Creed out, and his eyes lit with fire. He hurried on, sticking his hand straight out in front of him and flapping it—the funniest-looking wave Creed had ever seen. He formed a fist with his right hand, the thumb sticking up in the air, and smacked it into his left palm. He did this several times, moving both hands toward his chest, eyes pleading with Creed.

"What's the matter, Loyal? What's wrong?" Creed spoke slowly, locking eyes with his son.

Loyal made a sound of frustration. He fanned the fingers of his right hand, touched the thumb to his forehead, and lowered it to his chest. Then he held both hands flat in front of him, one palm up, the other palm down, and flipped them both over to his left as though turning pages.

Creed felt his own frustration rise. He'd never taken the time to understand what Loyal was saying. He knew the boy could understand him by watching his lips, but how to make sense of what Loyal wanted to tell him? He was clearly upset, and Creed realized the boy's hands were shaking as he made those motions over and over, as if Creed would suddenly grasp what they meant.

"Where's your mother? What are you doing here alone?"

Loyal screeched and stomped his foot.

Creed held up both hands toward his son. "Wait," he said. "I know what." He patted the rough boards of the porch. "Sit. I'll be right back."

Loyal groaned and slumped onto the porch as if carrying the weight of the world on his shoulders and expecting his father to relieve him of his burden. Creed might not know sign language, but he knew body language and it tore at his heart to see his son unable to communicate with him.

He darted inside and grabbed several sticks of kindling. Back outside, he crouched down and smoothed a patch of mountain dirt. Loyal brightened and grabbed a stick. He knelt down beside his father and began to mark in the earth.

M-A-N

He made the motion with fanned fingers and thumb touching his forehead, then chest again.

"Right, you want to tell me about a man."

Loyal nodded and looked serious. He made the flipping motion with one hand and then scratched some more.

13

D-E-A-D

Creed felt his eyebrows shoot up into his hairline. "There's a dead man?"

Loyal nodded like his life depended on it.

"Are you sure he's dead?"

The boy dropped the stick and made the flipping motion some more, frowning and shaking his head. Creed tried the motion himself, and Loyal nodded solemnly.

"You'd best show me where," Creed said.

two

The house was quiet when Delphy finally got back. She sagged against the sink, wetting a cool rag to wipe her neck and chest, her arms. It felt delicious. She closed her eyes and sighed, trying to think what they could have for supper that wouldn't heat up the kitchen. Maybe she'd just make sandwiches and take Loyal down to the river, so he could swim and she could dip her feet in the cool water.

Smiling, she started through the house, looking for Loyal to tell him she had a treat planned. He wasn't on the front porch, so she checked his room. Not there either. Frowning, she made her way out back to the bottom of the yard where Loyal often played in the shade of the sought-after cedar.

No freckled, brown-haired boy tossing a ball in the air.

She chewed her lip. Surely he wouldn't have gone anywhere after she'd specifically told him not to. The town was safe enough, but for a boy like him . . . it was worrisome. She considered walking down the street to see if Sheriff White was in his office, but she hated to be thought of as the sort of mother who panicked at the least provocation. People already talked about her plenty enough as it was.

She made her way back to the house and picked up one of Loyal's shirts that needed mending. She'd give him until suppertime to turn up before she went asking for help.

Loyal hurried ahead of his father, reveling in the fact that he'd communicated with him. Father had even mimicked his signs. It made him feel grown up and he was trying not to enjoy it. Someone was dead after all. And there was more he ought to tell, but this at least was a start.

He led Father down to the edge of the river where he'd discovered the man with a hole in his chest and one in his arm. It felt like hours since he'd struggled to pull dry clothes over wet skin while his mind ran a hundred different directions. Then the idea of going to his father came to him, and it had filled him with relief. He'd only been to the cabin on Rich Mountain a few times when Mother had taken him there for a visit. The visits had always been short, his father clearly uncomfortable and eager for Loyal and his mother to go home again. But he'd found it. He'd walked all that way and he'd not only found the cabin but had also made Father understand that someone was dead.

He stopped suddenly when the body came into view, and his father nearly ran into him. He felt a large hand settle on his shoulder. It steadied him. He sensed a slight rumbling and craned his neck to see if Father was speaking. He was, though Loyal had missed most of it.

". . . here while I take a look."

His father made a "stay" motion. While it wasn't the right sign, Loyal understood regardless. He stepped into the shade of a maple tree where he could watch and wait.

Creed felt like the wind had been knocked out of him. Sure enough. Loyal had brought him straight to a dead man. He knelt down and looked without touching the man. He wasn't anyone Creed knew right off, and he knew pretty much everyone—especially the folks who lived on the mountain. One shot had winged the man's right arm, while the second did him in. And quick, too, from the looks of it.

"Guess we'd better go tell the sheriff." He turned to look at Loyal, who was watching a bird high in a nearby tree.

Creed waved to get his son's attention. Loyal raised his eyebrows, lifted his hands, and shrugged his shoulders. Even Creed understood that one. This time he made sure Loyal could see him as he spoke. "We need to tell the sheriff."

Loyal nodded his head while also making a fist with his right hand and bobbing it up and down. Creed mimicked the motion, and Loyal grinned.

"That means yes?"

Loyal smiled wider and made the motion again.

"Well, I'll be dogged. That's not too tricky."

They grinned at each other until Creed remembered the dead man and sobered back up. "Right. Let's get this over with."

As they walked back to town, Loyal fingered the fancy little hair comb in his right pocket. He was pretty sure he'd seen Rebecca wearing it at church the Sunday before. He'd found the comb near the dead man and pocketed it before he'd really thought it through. He supposed he should show it to Father now. It might be evidence. He glanced at the strongly built dark man beside him and saw he was lost in thought. Loyal shoved the comb deeper in his pocket and took the opportunity to look more closely at his father. He wore his hair cropped close over his ears and a little longer on top with something shiny keeping it smoothed back from his forehead. Loyal guessed it wouldn't move even if there were a breeze. He had a thin mustache, kind of like the one Loyal had seen Errol Flynn sporting in a movie magazine. Father wasn't overly tall, but he took up space all the same.

Loyal touched his upper lip and drew his shoulders back to match Father's posture and stride. It felt good to be walking together toward town with serious business to conduct. Maybe now that he was older, Father would spend more time with him. Maybe he would even learn some more signs so they could talk. And even if Father didn't want to learn, Loyal figured he could read lips and write things down. They'd do fine.

He was almost sorry when they arrived in town—he could have walked a hundred miles beside his father—but it was important they tell someone about the dead man. He felt a pang of guilt about the comb. What if Rebecca could tell the sheriff something about what had happened? The dead man was likely what she and Michael had been running away from. He wrinkled his nose and guessed he should probably tell about seeing the Westfall kids. Maybe they should fetch Mother so she could talk while he signed. Loyal reached out to tug on his father's shirt, but Father saw Sheriff White standing outside Rohrbaugh's Store talking to someone and stepped away without noticing Loyal's touch.

The sheriff turned and grinned. "Well, if it ain't Creed Raines in the flesh. What are you doing down off the mountain? Come to make sure I'm still sheriffing right?"

Creed seemed to have forgotten him, so Loyal hung back, angling so he could see what the adults were saying.

"Afraid it's bad news, Virgil. I've come to report a shooting."

The sheriff's face went all solemn. "Those Hacker boys at it again?"

Father rubbed his chin and grimaced. "Don't know who did it, but there's a man out there where the Tygart takes a sharp bend. He's dead as mutton, and recently too. Got a couple of bullet holes in him."

Sheriff White's shoulders sagged. "Who is it?"

"Don't recognize him. He might not be from around here."

Virgil nodded and looked toward Loyal. "Your boy with you when you found him?"

Father glanced at Loyal and frowned. "Yes, but he doesn't know anything more than I do."

Loyal lifted his hands to say he saw the Westfall kids, but Father patted the air in a way Loyal took to mean he should keep his peace. It's not like they would understand him anyway. He'd need paper and pencil or Mother to translate if he was going to tell them much of anything. He gave an exaggerated shrug and stuck his hands back in his pockets. His fingers closed over Rebecca's comb and he hesitated, then grasped it tighter. He'd show it to them later.

The two men turned away and continued their conversation. Loyal craned his neck to see what they were talking about, only he couldn't make it out as they were leaning close together. So he turned his attention to the store window, where Folgers coffee cans were arranged in a pyramid next to a sign for Coca-Cola. He was thinking about how good a cold soda would taste on this hot day when the sheriff touched his shoulder.

"Come with us," he said, his lip movement exaggerated. Loyal wanted to tell him he could understand him better if he talked regular but knew it was no use.

He and Father started after the sheriff, who was climbing into his car along with one of his deputies. Loyal felt a surge of excitement. Not only was he going to ride in an automobile, but it was a black-and-white police car with a star on the door. Father had been sheriff once, but that was a long time ago—when he was little. He climbed into the back with Father and ran his hands over the smooth seat. He could feel the car jump to life, vibrating beneath his body. Then they were moving with air streaming in through the open windows.

Father jerked and looked at Loyal, and he supposed he must have made a sound. Sometimes he did that when he got excited and it would surprise people. It was funny, just because he didn't talk, people tended to think he didn't make any noise at all. They'd even taught him to speak at school, though he didn't like to do it. It was hard, and speaking seemed silly when he could say so much more with his hands.

It felt like mere moments until they pulled off the road as close to the place where the dead man lay as they could get. Loyal fell in beside his father as they retraced their steps. Nearing the spot, Father placed a hand on Loyal's shoulder and looked straight into his eyes.

"Stay here." He made the sign for "your," but Loyal guessed he thought it meant "stay." Loyal stuck the thumb and pinkie out on each hand and pressed his hands down to show he understood. Father looked surprised and mimicked the sign, the ghost of a smile playing across his lips.

Loyal sighed and sat down. "Good boy," Father said, and Loyal tried not to feel like a well-behaved dog.

After situating Loyal, Creed led the sheriff and deputy over to the dead man. It tickled him that he'd managed to talk to his son with those hand signs not once but twice today. He'd never really tried to do much with them before. He made signs of his own sometimes but hadn't felt the need to learn the ones Loyal used. For the first time it occurred to him that those were signs other deaf people used, too. His son spoke a whole other language. Now, wasn't that something?

Delphy was a whiz when it came to talking with her hands. She and the boy would "talk" with their fingers flying a mile a minute. He figured even if he did know the signs, he could never keep up with how fast they went. So, if he needed to tell Loyal something, he let the boy read his lips or got Delphy to sign for him.

But today was different. He realized he hadn't been alone

with his son since . . . well, he couldn't remember the last time. Probably not since he got so sick and the fever went to his ears. But Creed didn't want to remember those days when he thought it was important to be somebody—to make sure his son grew up to be somebody. Now he saw Loyal on Sundays or special occasions, and Delphy was always there to smooth the way between them. But managing to communicate without her . . . he was surprised to realize he was enjoying it.

"He's dead alright," Virgil said, interrupting Creed's thoughts. "And you're right. It's recent." He waved the deputy closer. "Recognize him?"

The younger man crouched down and squinted at the figure as if that would make him more recognizable. "Can't say as I do."

Virgil snapped his fingers. "Say. We got word on Monday that some federal workers were in the area looking at land for that homestead business of Eleanor Roosevelt. It's the deal where they're supposed to build whole towns with schools and churches and stores for folks who're down-and-out." He cocked his head and looked harder at the body. "You don't reckon he's a government worker?"

Creed didn't have the least notion. He was more than a little skeptical of those "self-sustaining communities." Plus, he hated to see this land he loved built up with houses and businesses and who knew what else? He hoped they'd at least stick to the rolling land along the river and stay off his mountain.

"Guess he could be," Creed said. "Can't think why anybody'd shoot him, though."

"Can't you?" Virgil said. "Plenty of folks don't want the government meddling in their business. Who knows what sorts of people they'd bring in." He shook his head. "Course, could be he just come up on the wrong feller out here by himself."

This time Creed knew just what the sheriff meant. He'd been the sheriff once himself. Not everyone on Rich Mountain was honorable. There were liquor runners, poachers, and the sorts of ne'er-do-wells that avoided being seen in town. Creed knew most of them, and while he wasn't afraid of them, he guessed they might not be partial to a stranger nosing around.

"You need help getting the body to the funeral home?"

"I will. But first I'm going to make sure we've looked around real sharp." He tapped the deputy on the shoulder. "Bud, you go back into town and send Gerald out with the hearse. Me and Creed will look the area over real close. By the time you get back, we should be ready to move this poor fella."

Once the deputy was gone, Virgil took his hat off and rubbed his bald head. He looked Creed up and down. "Anybody asks, I deputized you. You know this mountain and stretch of river better than anybody. And while I know you don't fancy being a lawman anymore, you've got the experience. Ever since that Black Tuesday business back in October, everybody keeps talking about belt-tightening. I'm short-staffed and I've got Bud spending most of his time up in Elkins. This"—he waved a hand toward the dead man—"might take some legwork. You up for pitching in?"

Creed glanced back at Loyal, who was watching them as if he could read their movements the way Creed could read the mountain. He saw an eager expectation there and swallowed hard. He'd sworn off taking responsibility for just about anything once he'd finished ruining his son's life, but maybe it was time to take a step back into the world. If only to look out for his boy. He nodded. "Sure thing. Ginseng won't be right for digging for another month or more. I guess I can spare the time."

"I might be able to pay you a little something, but don't count on it," Virgil said.

"I won't," Creed said, and the two men began to make a slow search of the area.

three

Delphy folded Loyal's mended shirt, straightening every seam and smoothing every crease. Once this task was complete, she would go out and search for her son. She wet her lips as she set the shirt aside, smoothed her hair, and headed out the back door. She'd begin with Sheriff White and then she'd walk every street, every road, and every mountain trail until she found that boy. And then she just might strangle him.

She tried not to think about the river. The water wasn't high, and Loyal was a strong swimmer.

As she rounded the corner of the house, she saw them. Not just Loyal, but Creed too. Had the boy been with his father all this time? Astonishment and anger battled inside her. Realizing her fists were clenched at her sides, she flexed her fingers and signed, *Where have you been?* Her hands felt jerky, her fingers stiff.

Loyal ducked his head and clapped his fists together before pointing at Father. Creed laid a hand on the boy's shoulder, and Loyal stood straighter, looked at his father with something almost worshipful. It sent an arrow straight into Delphy's heart.

It was how a son should look at his father, but God forgive her if she didn't think Creed had earned such a look.

"The boy's had a hard day, Delphy. How about we go inside and tell you about it?"

Delphy felt her lips turn down in a deep frown that was beyond her control. She waved for them to follow her inside. As she turned she saw Loyal reach out and grasp his father's shirt as they walked toward the back door. It was something he'd done when he first lost his hearing—grasped the clothing of the parent closest to him as though afraid he'd lose them if he didn't hold on. It nearly broke her heart and filled her with anger all at the same time. She was going to have more than Loyal's whereabouts to sort out in her mind this evening.

Once inside, she motioned them to the kitchen table and set sandwiches in front of them. She'd gone ahead and made the picnic, telling herself Loyal would turn up any moment. She served them in silence, words tumbling over themselves inside her head. Which should she fling at her husband and son first?

Creed cleared his throat. "Delphy, will you sit?"

For no reason she could understand, tears burned her eyes at the gentle request. She didn't trust herself to speak but simply sat.

"Loyal found a dead body this afternoon."

She gasped, and her hand flew to her mouth. She darted a look at Loyal, but he was focused on his supper, clearly hungry. "What are you talking about?" The sound of her voice here in the kitchen surprised her. She rarely spoke when it was just her and Loyal.

"A man's been shot—no one we know—over at the bend in the river. Loyal found him and came to tell me."

Questions assaulted Delphy. Why had Loyal been at the river? Why hadn't he come to tell her? How did he remember the way to Creed's cabin? And how was it that she suddenly felt like the outsider in the room when Creed was the one who'd left?

But when she found her voice, it wasn't a question that emerged. "You must have known I would be worried." She signed as she spoke partly for Loyal's benefit and partly out of habit.

Creed watched her hands intently as if he could make sense of their dance. "We had to see to the body once I told Virgil." His eyes darted around the room. "And Virgil might've wanted to ask Loyal some questions."

Delphy felt anger tighten her voice. "And how did you suppose Virgil would do that? Has he learned sign?" She stopped signing and clasped her hands together as though forcing them to be still. "Or perhaps you were going to translate. Oh, but you don't know sign either. And here I sat imagining the worst."

"There was a dead man, Delphy. What you were or weren't thinking wasn't my main concern."

Delphy froze and let her hands fall to the table, settling like fallen leaves. "It was foolish of me to think you'd spare me a thought. Why start now?" She stood and took Loyal's empty plate, pushing her lips into a smile she knew fooled no one. She tousled Loyal's hair and set the plate in the sink before signing, *Wash and get ready for bed. We'll talk about why you were at the river later.*

Loyal grimaced and looked at his father, who was staring down at the table in front of him. Delphy could see the longing in the boy's eyes—could see how badly he wanted his father to stay with them. He tapped Creed's arm and, when he looked up, signed, *You stay* with his eyebrows high and a hopeful look.

Creed furrowed his brow, then his expression cleared. He pointed at himself and made the sign for "stay" with a question in his own eyes. Loyal nodded, rising from his seat with excitement.

"Delphy, I think the boy wants me to stay."

She frowned. "Did you just use sign?"

"Did I?"

"That was the sign for 'stay.' Where did you learn that?"

A slow smile spread across Creed's face. "Loyal showed me."

Delphy pressed her lips into a thin line. She did not want to let her anger go, and yet it was good to see this man she still loved in spite of herself making an effort to connect with his son. "Well, that's a start." She looked from man to boy, opened her mouth, then closed it again. She sighed. "Stay if you want to."

Loyal clapped his hands, and she made a shooing motion—one he didn't need to know sign to understand. It was bedtime, and she'd had all she could stand for one evening. Loyal kissed her cheek and then kissed Creed's, as well. Delphy could tell the gesture had taken them all by surprise. But then what was one more surprise in a day like this one?

Creed wanted to press his fingers to the spot where his son had pressed his lips, but didn't dare while Delphy watched so closely. Something had shifted in his world today. His son had come to him for help. And then they'd communicated. Not just with lip-reading and words scratched in the dirt, but with Loyal's own language. Before today, Creed hadn't given much thought to the fact that there were other people in the world who used that language. It wasn't just something Loyal made up. He watched Delphy, her back stiff as she tidied up the kitchen, knowing he wasn't welcome here. Eventually, he headed up the stairs to his son's room. Loyal, brown hair spiky from a quick wash, had changed into striped cotton pajamas and was about to climb into bed. He must have sensed someone coming, because he turned and raised his eyebrows.

Creed froze. He felt ridiculous. But no, it had been good to use his son's language. He spoke carefully, shaping the words with his lips. "Show me your name."

Loyal frowned. He pointed at himself, then stuck out the first two fingers on each hand and brought the right-hand fingers down on the left all while looking a question.

"Does that mean *name*?" Creed repeated the motion and pointed at his son. "Show me."

The boy's face lit up like Christmas morning. He began moving his right hand much too fast for Creed to follow.

"Whoa there. Slow down and show me again."

Loyal nodded, taking a deep breath. He slowly moved his fingers into a series of shapes, most of which Creed saw looked like the letters of his son's name—especially the *L*. Creed tried it, and Loyal made a sort of clicking sound. Creed figured that meant he was pleased. He did it several times until he was sure he could remember. He licked his lips, trying not to feel foolish. Pointing at himself, he made the correct sign with both hands again while saying, "Now show me my name."

Loyal crowed, and Creed flinched, then managed to smile and laugh a little. "Guess you like that," he said.

Loyal nodded and grabbed his father's hand. He began to move it into shapes that again made sense except for the *r*. He couldn't think why twisting his index and middle finger together made an *r*. He repeated the motions until Loyal seemed satisfied with his performance. He thought to ask how to shape *Delphy* but decided not to.

"That's enough for tonight," he said. Loyal smiled and slid between the bedsheets. Creed reached out and smoothed the boy's hair where a cowlick made it stick up in back. It felt good, being with his son at bedtime. He swallowed hard and turned, pressing the button for the electric light as he moved past the door. He heard Loyal sigh and rustle under the covers. He paused to listen, marveling at the gift of being able to hear, as well as the gift of being able to communicate with someone who couldn't.

He eased down the stairs, noticing every creak and groan of the old wood, along with the sigh of the wind outside an open window and even a voice somewhere down the street. Sounds of Delphy finishing her chores came to him as well, and he realized that it all made a melody he hadn't listened for in far too many years.

Stepping into the kitchen, he had the urge to take his wife in his arms but stopped himself. He doubted she would welcome his embrace. Not after the tensions of the day. Not to mention the years. He drew nearer and heard another sound—a gulp and a sniffle.

"Are you crying?"

She swiped at her eye with the back of her wrist. "I am, and I don't expect you to do a thing about it, so don't let it worry you." She wrung out her dishrag and hung it on a hook. "You know he disobeyed me by going to the river. He should never have been there in the first place. And then when he got into trouble, who did he go to? His father." She turned away from him and snatched up a basket of laundry, folding shirts and britches like they'd done her wrong.

Creed stepped closer and grasped her wrist, stilling her angry motions. "I'm sorry."

She snorted, but it sounded weak. "Sorry for what?"

"Everything."

She jerked away and picked the basket up, holding it between them like a shield. "Well, that's not enough," she said and marched toward the stairs. "You're welcome to sleep on the sofa. I'm sure Loyal will be glad to see you in the morning." She snapped off the lights as she went until Creed was left alone in the dark, keenly aware of the soft sounds of the house settling . . . and his wife weeping.

He knew he'd handled himself all wrong. He'd been so excited by his sudden connection with his son that he'd thought all sorts of past hurts were on the mend. He flopped down on the sofa and worked his boots off, then flipped an embroidered pillow over so he wouldn't risk getting the needlework dirty.

Settling back, he stared at the ceiling trying to think what he needed to do to fix his family.

Then he lifted one hand into the air so he could see his fingers by the shaft of light coming through the front window and shaped his son's name over and over until sleep swept him away.

four

When Loyal woke, he wanted to rush downstairs to make sure Father was still there, but as he swung his feet to the floor, he saw the comb he'd left on his bedside table. He picked it up and examined it more closely. It was a swirly brown color with gold in it, and there were flowers carved along the top edge. He'd seen his mother wear combs to keep her hair back and out of her face. He flipped the comb over and noticed an *R* and a *W* scratched into its back. For Rebecca Westfall? Was this proof that she'd been there when the stranger was shot and killed?

Loyal slowly moved around his room, folding his pajamas and getting dressed. He'd planned to show his father the comb and tell him about seeing the Westfall kids. But the more he thought about it, the more he was afraid he'd get them in trouble. He didn't mind so much about Michael, but he liked Rebecca. Finally, he dug out a pair of itchy wool socks, pushed the comb into the toe of one, and buried them in the back of a bureau drawer. Maybe, if Father stuck around, Loyal would ask him what to do. For now, though, he'd keep the comb to himself.

The house smelled like cinnamon and yeasty bread. Loyal

scrambled down the stairs and swung into the kitchen where he saw Mother pulling cinnamon toast from the oven. She was alone. He let his shoulders sag. If Father had stayed, he hadn't stayed long. Mother smiled and nodded toward the table. Loyal dropped into a chair and propped his chin in his hands. Then Mother glanced over his shoulder, and Loyal whirled around to see Father stepping out of the lavatory, his face moist and freshly shaved. He jumped from the table and threw his arms around Father, breathing in the woodsy smell of him laced with Mother's soap. He threw his head back in an exaggerated laugh to show his delight. Father looked alarmed, so Loyal immediately stopped. Of course, Father would prefer that he act like boys who could hear. He pulled back and nodded gravely, then slipped into his chair hoping Father would join him. After a moment, he did.

Loyal guessed that Mother was still angry about his going to the river since she'd stopped smiling. She set the hot bread slathered with butter and a sprinkling of sugar and cinnamon on the table and then sat herself. His parents stared at each other. Loyal considered reaching for his favorite treat but sensed there was an unspoken conversation going on. He was good at those. So, he waited.

"Want me to say a blessing?" Father finally asked.

Mother bit her lip and nodded.

Father bowed his head, then looked up, brow furrowed. "But the boy can't hear me pray."

Mother signed as she spoke, "There's no rule that you have to close your eyes to pray. Loyal can read your lips while I sign what you say."

Father got that wild look in his eyes again. He took a deep breath and nodded once. "Okay. Well then. Here goes." He looked around the table, closed his eyes, opened them again, then started. "Father in heaven, we give thanks for this food and for the hands that have prepared it." He relaxed as he got going. Loyal alternated between watching his mother's hands and his father's lips. "Guide the sheriff in his investigation and be with the family of the man who died. We pray that they find peace and comfort in you." His glance flicked around the table. "Please bless Delphy and watch over . . ." He lifted his right hand and spelled L-o-y-a-l. There was a long pause, and Loyal could see that his parents' eyes were locked on each other. His mother's hands dropped into her lap as Father signed. Her teeth worked her lower lip and her eyes looked wet. Finally, Father swallowed, his throat moving. "Thank you, Father, for your many blessings. Amen."

Loyal smiled and took a piece of bread, sinking his teeth into the rich, buttery sweetness, but his parents just sat there. At last, Mother lifted the platter and offered Father a piece. Loyal couldn't think why she'd do that since Father was sitting plenty close, but whatever the reason he could feel the heaviness in the room lift. He smiled and grabbed another slice.

After breakfast, Creed walked to the sheriff's office. Loyal wanted to come with him, but he made the boy stay at home. The more he could keep his son out of this mess, the better. He'd let Virgil think they'd found the body together. He didn't want Loyal to be put on the spot. No, better to keep things simple. Anyway, it wasn't as if Loyal knew any more than Creed did.

As soon as he stepped through the door of the old Beverly courthouse, Virgil started talking. "I was about to come hunting you. Afraid you'd gone back up the mountain already."

"Not yet. Thought I'd better see if you need anything. And I'll confess to a measure of curiosity about that fella we found."

Virgil ran a hand over his bald head. "You mean like who in tarnation he is? Well, turns out he *is* working for the government. Or was. Name's Eddie Minks. His partner turned up here this morning hunting him. He's over at the diner now getting himself a cup of coffee. He was real shook up about what happened."

Creed propped a hip against a heavy wooden desk. "Why weren't they together? Seems like it'd be smart to travel in pairs when you're poking around hills and hollers where you don't much know what, or *who*, you might run into."

"Earl Westin—that's the other fella's name—said they usually do, but he wasn't feeling so good yesterday." Virgil got a cagey look. "You ask me, he was sleeping off a drunk. Anyhow, Eddie went out without him and never came back, so Earl started looking."

"And he's sure the body we found is his partner?"

"Walked him over to the funeral home and let him have a look. Thought he was gonna throw up on my shoes. So I sent him to get a cup of coffee and maybe a biscuit to settle his stomach." Virgil craned his neck to the side. "Here he comes now. Stick around—might make him feel easier if there's a *civilian* hangin' around the place. He won't know about your checkered past as a lawman."

Creed gave his friend a lopsided grin and watched as a fellow who looked like he was in his late forties stepped through the door. Although, on closer inspection, he might be in his early forties and living hard. He had deep lines around his mouth like he smoked a lot and bags under his eyes. His rumpled shirt wasn't tucked in evenly, and one pocket of his pants had been torn and sewed back with the wrong color thread.

"Sheriff, I been thinking and can't see why—" He stopped and looked hard at Creed. "Who're you?"

"This here's Creed Raines. He's helping me with the investigation." Virgil smiled and looked at Creed from the corner of his eye. "He's what you might call a plainclothes policeman. Knows his way around Rich Mountain."

Earl shifted from foot to foot and ran a hand through his salt-and-pepper hair. "If you say so. I've been thinking about what you asked—about who might want Eddie dead. And I can't come up with anyone. He might not've been the most popular man around, but nobody was mad at him or out to get him that I can think of."

"What about women troubles?" Virgil asked.

Earl shrugged. "I think he's got a girl up in Pittsburgh. He's always been pretty tight-lipped about his personal life."

Virgil sat in his swivel chair and leaned it back until it groaned under the strain. "Creed, I don't guess you'd have heard if the Hacker boys were up to anything? And by *anything*, I mean the kind of anything they might not want someone from the government to stumble upon."

Creed shook his head. "I don't think so. Clyde's running his usual operation, but it's over on the other side of the mountain. Can't think why any of those boys would've been down near that part of the river." He kept an eye on Earl as he talked. The man was getting paler by the minute, and sweat was beading his brow, even though the day wasn't all that warm yet.

Virgil grunted and put his feet up on the desk. His chair protested. He turned his attention back to Earl. "The pair of you been in the area long?"

The man started looking even twitchier. "About a week. This area looks real promising for a self-sustaining community. Several folks have signed on to sell their land—we just need that Westfall tract and maybe one other to finish it out."

Virgil dropped his feet to the floor. "That land's been in Hadden's family since before the War Between the States. He gonna sell?"

Earl buried a hand in his hair again. "We haven't gotten that far in negotiations. Eddie and I were scouting the land first."

"Did Hadden know you were out there poking around?" Virgil sat up straighter.

"We, uh, sent a letter letting him know the, uh, approximate dates we'd be around."

Virgil shuffled his feet and stood. "Which is to say you were trespassing on Westfall land."

Earl braced his hands on his hips. "Now, hold on there. We've got governmental authority to be on that land. Sending a letter was a courtesy."

Virgil shook his head and looked at Creed. "That's like pitching a rock into a beehive to let the bees know you're coming after their honey." He hooked his thumbs in his belt. "Son, you and your partner just may have aggravated the wrong landowner." He sighed. "Creed, will you come with me to talk to Hadden? He might not shoot me right off if there's a witness present."

Now Earl's eyes were so wide they looked mostly white. Creed kept a straight face. Virgil was mostly just scaring the government man, seeing how he'd react. It would've been funny if there hadn't been a dead man involved. "Be glad to run out there with you. Want me to come armed?"

Virgil snorted and gave Creed a sideways look. "Guess not. Might give ole Hadden the notion we want a fight." He squinted at Earl. "Where you stayin'?"

"Hotel just this side of Elkins."

"Fine. I'll be in touch."

Earl wet his lips. "What should I do until then? I've got to report this, but I'm not sure what to say."

"As little as possible would be my recommendation," Virgil said as he waved Creed to follow him out to his car.

five

Mother was watching him like she was the warden and thought he was about to make a jailbreak. Loyal lounged in the swing on the front porch, tossing a baseball in the air and catching it over and over. He'd bounced it against the wall for a while, but Mother made him stop "that racket." He smiled. Maybe sometimes it was good not to be able to hear. While he'd been hoping Father would take him along wherever he was going, he'd made the sign for *stay*. And he'd used the right one.

Now it was Saturday afternoon, and he was a prisoner on the front porch. He saw someone walking along the street and sat up. It was Reverend Harriman, the pastor of their church. Loyal slouched again. If he was headed to their house, it was almost certainly to see Mother.

As he drew nearer he waved at Loyal, who gave a halfhearted wave back. Church was usually pretty boring. The singing was okay—he could feel the vibrations of the old organ—but watching the pastor talk and talk and talk took focus and concentration and usually wasn't worth the effort. At least he waved his arms around some.

Reverend Harriman turned in at their gate and stepped up onto the porch. He waved again, as though he needed to make sure Loyal was looking at him. "Is your mother at home?" He spoke slowly, shaping each word. Loyal was almost willing to bet he was yelling. A lot of people thought they had to talk slow and yell when you were deaf.

He nodded and pointed inside, but before the pastor could get the door open, Mother was there and stepping outside. She smiled and waved the reverend over to a rocking chair. She settled into one beside him and talked animatedly, clearly happy to see the man. Loyal stopped paying attention, returning his focus to tossing the ball.

Then he saw movement out of the corner of his eye. Mother was trying to get his attention. He made the sign for *what?* She tightened her mouth and signed. *Sit up straight and pay attention when the pastor is here.* She smiled. *You're being invited to a church activity for youth.*

Loyal raised his eyebrows and signed, *What activity?*

Mother gave her head a little shake. *If you were watching, you'd know.*

He looked chagrined, made a fist and circled it in front of his chest twice. He'd apologize a hundred times if it meant he might get to set foot off the porch.

Mother nodded at the pastor, who turned to Loyal and began that painfully slow way of speaking, which actually made it harder to understand him. "The school is allowing us to use the gymnasium for youth activities. Would you like to join us for a volleyball game?" He nodded and raised his eyebrows, miming the motion of serving a volleyball.

Loyal nodded his head while making the sign for *yes.* Mother managed to look pleased and worried at the same time. *You'll be okay?* she signed. *You don't have to go.*

Loyal cocked his head and looked up as though pondering the invitation. He grinned and jumped to his feet. Mother bit her lip, then gave him a hug that wasn't altogether welcome. He wished she'd treat him like the other boys. Most of their mothers were probably glad to get their kids out of the house.

Mother talked earnestly to the pastor for a minute or two, then hugged Loyal again and waved him off along with Reverend Harriman.

Though the school wasn't far, Loyal could tell the pastor wasn't altogether comfortable walking with him. He'd run into this before. Hearing people liked to talk and talk, which meant his silence often made them feel awkward. Harry Davidson—one of his buddies at school—had explained it to him. Harry said it was fun to make hearing people uncomfortable. *They do it to us,* he'd signed. Yet Loyal didn't see the fun in it. Nor did he know how to make people more comfortable. It's just the way life was, he guessed.

At the school, there were already a dozen or so kids milling around. Loyal had seen most of them at church but didn't interact with them much. He only saw them when he was home from the West Virginia School for the Deaf, and they usually didn't pay much attention to him. Unless it was to make fun of him, like Michael Westfall often did.

As if the thought conjured the boy, Michael stepped into the gymnasium with his sister, Rebecca, close behind. Michael strutted out toward the volleyball net and began talking and waving his arms around. Reverend Harriman quickly stepped up and took charge, apparently making Michael the captain of one of the teams. He chose another boy for the other side, and they each picked five players to round out their teams.

Loyal didn't get picked. He sighed and leaned against a wall where he could watch. It had probably been a dumb idea to come here. It was only because he'd been so bored at home that he'd done it. Probably the best he could hope for was that no one would make fun of him.

Rebecca was on the team playing against her brother. She

gave Loyal a hesitant smile and a small wave. He wondered if she really had seen him that day at the river. He wished he could ask her about that, along with the comb still hidden in his sock drawer. Today she wore her long hair in braids over each shoulder. No combs.

Lost in thought, Loyal almost missed seeing the ball come flying his way. He caught it and tossed it back to Rebecca's side. She smiled at him again, and he began to think about how he could ask her a question. If only he had paper and a pencil.

Michael's team started jumping up and down and slapping each other on the backs, so Loyal assumed they'd won. Reverend Harriman lifted a whistle to his lips and puffed his cheeks. He waved his arms around, and the teams broke up, then began reforming with different players. This time, Loyal got picked and Rebecca was left along the wall. Loyal took his place in the front row near the net. He liked being on the outside corner because it was easier to see what was happening. He hit a ball to a teammate, and they got a point.

Then he shifted to the front center position. He hated this spot. Since he couldn't hear what was happening behind him, he had to twist back and forth to try to see everything. The server hit the ball, and he craned his neck to watch it go over the net. A tall boy on the other side leapt into the air to spike the ball, and Loyal dove to keep it from hitting the floor. Instead, he crashed into one of his teammates who was trying to do the same thing. They ended up in a heap with the ball bouncing away.

As he stood, Loyal could tell the boy he'd crashed into was mad and he chose not to read his lips. He swiped at his own lip and realized it was bloodied. Reverend Harriman was suddenly there handing him a handkerchief and waving him toward the door and the boys' lavatory. Loyal shuffled after the pastor and obediently washed his mouth out and then pressed the folded handkerchief to his lip. The reverend looked worried.

Loyal guessed he was already imagining what Mother would say. Which made Loyal smile. Which hurt.

Reverend Harriman leaned down and looked into his face. "Do you want to go home?"

Loyal shook his head *no*, not bothering to make the sign. The pastor looked relieved. "Okay, just sit down until the bleeding stops." He made a little squatting motion as though to help Loyal understand what "sit down" meant. Loyal nodded and made his way to the wall where Rebecca sat cross-legged watching the game. He tilted his head as a sort of question. She smiled and patted the floor next to her. Loyal flopped down, letting his shoulders fall. His lip throbbed, but at least he wasn't bored anymore.

Now if he could just figure out how to talk to Rebecca.

She touched his arm, and he turned toward her. "Are you okay?" she asked.

He pulled the handkerchief away and touched his lip with the tip of his tongue. The bleeding had stopped. He nodded and gave her a lopsided smile, trying not to stretch the injured spot.

He could tell she laughed, and the strangest longing to hear that laugh hit him. He'd always wished he could hear his mother's voice—thought he could almost remember it—and he was pretty sure it would be nice to hear music, but this feeling was different. He looked away.

She touched his arm again.

"You saw us at the river yesterday." He could tell it was a statement. Not a question. He nodded. Tears welled in her eyes, but she blinked them away. "That man is dead." Another statement. He nodded again. "Will you tell on us?"

Loyal widened his eyes. Then he wrinkled his brow and let his shoulders rise and fall once.

"You know about what, but thank you for acting like you don't."

Loyal was astonished. She'd understood exactly what he

meant even without words or signs. He lifted his hand to make the sign for *who* when the ball bounced over and struck him in the leg. He tossed it back toward the game, and Michael caught it. The older boy paused, the ball propped on his hip. "Rebecca, about time we headed home."

She made a face and clambered to her feet. She gave Loyal a rueful look and said, "See you later. I'm glad we got to talk."

Loyal watched the pair leave the gymnasium. *Glad we got to talk.* She'd said it just like he was a regular person.

As Creed and Virgil climbed out of the car, Hadden's man Otto limped around the side of the massive brick house. Otto took care of Hadden's prized hunting dogs. When he showed up in Beverly, folks had been suspicious of his German accent and his bum leg, but Hadden—not known for acts of generosity—took the boy in. Now he was devoted to his employer and treated the hounds like they were royalty.

Virgil called out to him. "Otto! Is Mr. Westfall to home?"

"Yes, sir. He is inside the house using the telephone. I will tell him you are here." The boy's accent was less pronounced than when he first arrived, but Creed supposed with all that was happening in Europe these days, even a hint of an accent would make folks suspicious. He felt sorry for the young man.

"Naw, that's alright. We'll find the way." Otto looked skeptical but didn't appear to be willing to contradict the sheriff. He just continued on his way toward an outbuilding, glancing back at them as he limped along.

Creed and Virgil peered in through the screen door on the wide front porch. The house sat on a hill overlooking a rolling valley and the Tygart River—one of the prettiest spots in the county. They could see Hadden standing in the hall, receiver in hand. He waved them in as he finished his conversation. He had long been high up with the Baltimore & Ohio Railroad, and now he was involved in building an airport, of all things. Creed was a little bit in awe of this man, who seemed to have his finger on the pulse of Randolph County but tried not to let it show. Virgil just acted like he did around everybody, as if he were a country bumpkin playing sheriff. Creed—and most everybody else—knew it was an act.

Hadden dropped the receiver into its cradle with a clatter. "I'm betting you're here about the dead man you found down along the river." He waved them into a fancy sitting room, and Creed dusted the seat of his pants before perching on a velvet settee.

"You know anything about him?" asked Virgil.

"Not a blasted thing beyond who his employer is. And it's almighty inconvenient for him to get shot on my property. Shouldn't have been there in the first place."

"So you knew he'd been poking around?" Virgil settled into a wing-back chair and crossed his legs like a dandy.

"Two of them have been poking around. They already have terms for the adjoining land, and I've been working directly with the government office in Washington, D.C." Hadden poured clear liquid from a crystal decanter and slugged it back. "If, and I stress the word *if,* there's going to be an agreement, I won't be making it with two ne'er-do-well flunkies parading around Randolph County." He sat in a chair that matched the one Virgil selected. "There was no reason for either one of them to be out there."

"So, you do plan to sell land for this Roosevelt community."

"Not unless those idiots offer me what it's worth. They think just because the country is in this ridiculous downturn, they can pay half the value." He snorted. "They don't realize who they're dealing with."

Virgil nodded his head. "Guess Eddie didn't realize either."

"You've got that . . . Hold on. What do you mean by that?"

"You have a reputation for flying off the handle now and again.

42

If you got fired up and tried to scare off a trespasser, I can see how a shot might go awry."

Creed braced himself for a burst of anger from Hadden. Instead, a slow smile spread across his face, and he relaxed back into his chair. He propped his elbows and steepled his fingers. "Virgil, I sometimes forget you're not the fool you try to make people believe you are. No, I did not take a shot at one of those government flunkies and kill him by accident." He smiled wider. "Nor did I kill him on purpose."

Virgil winked. "That's good to hear. Don't guess you'd have any notion who might have done it instead?"

Hadden shook his head. "No, I do not. I haven't seen the Hackers over this way since I ran them out of the hollow down there near the old home place. Although I hear the government is after their land, too. Only other person I see out here is Creed." Creed tensed the muscles in his legs almost involuntarily. Like he might need to run. He forced himself to relax. "But since he's tagging along with you, I assume you've eliminated him as a suspect."

"Not entirely," Virgil drawled. Creed felt his eyes go wide. Virgil winked again. "He found the body, though, and if he has a motive, I can't think what it'd be."

"I, on the other hand, have a plausible motive. If I am indeed wrangling to either keep my land or sell it for a higher price, those government men might have gotten in my way."

"I was thinking something like that," Virgil said.

"When was he shot?"

"Yesterday—probably around noon."

Hadden stood and dusted his hands. "Well and good. I was in Elkins, meeting with the engineer about the new airport." He raised his eyebrows. "Can I show you gentlemen the door?"

Virgil let one side of his mouth tip up. "Sure. You mind if we poke around the crime scene one more time?"

"Not at all, although I suppose since it's a crime scene it wouldn't matter if I did mind."

Virgil shook Hadden's hand, and there seemed to be a moment when each man was trying to best the other. Virgil let go first and gave his hand a shake. "You've still got it, Hadden. Guess being a man of business hasn't made you go soft."

"That it has not," Hadden said as he opened the front door.

six

Virgil parked as close as he could to the spot along the river where Eddie Minks breathed his last. Creed got out of the car and followed the sheriff along a path near the water's edge. Humidity hung heavy in the summer air, and he felt sweat prickle under his arms, even though it was an easy walk. The only sound was the rush of water to his left and their footsteps. No birds sang, and the air was as still as a tomb.

As they approached the place where river grasses were mashed down, Creed saw that the earth had already absorbed the worst of the bloodstains. Nature was like that. Quick to reclaim anything man tried to change. He crouched down and examined the place where the body had lain.

"Did you see footprints or anything like that when you first got here?" Virgil asked.

"Sure. Deer tracks, turkey, grown men, kids, probably a raccoon or possum. This trail is used by all sorts of warm-blooded critters. Killer's tracks could easily have been here, but I don't know how you'd tell 'em apart."

Virgil grunted and circled the area looking high and low.

He finally stopped near a small stand of river oaks. "Remind me which way the body was laying." Creed closed his eyes to picture it and pointed.

"So, the killer was probably standing opposite this spot if Eddie fell when he was hit." The sheriff scratched under the edge of his hat where beads of sweat had formed. He let his gaze swing around. "Or Eddie might have staggered a few steps . . . Here we are!" He flipped open a pocketknife and jabbed the blade in a tree trunk. "Slug. Probably the one that winged Eddie in the arm."

Creed stepped closer to see what Virgil had found. "Could be. Or it might be an old slug from a hunter."

"This looks fresh. Not many folks hunting in July."

Creed nodded. It was too hot for deer hunting, and the game wasn't good this time of year. "If it is the bullet, what good does that do you? Lots of folks around here have a gun that caliber."

Virgil worked the slug out and dropped it into his breast pocket. "There's this new science called 'ballistics.' They say they can look at a slug under a microscope and match it to the gun that fired it. We already got the bullet that was lodged against Eddie's spine, so we can test 'em both." He shrugged. "If nothing else, I'd like to see how it's done."

Loyal sat between his parents in church the next morning. It was boring, like always, but he didn't mind as much when Mother and Father were with him. It made him feel like part of a regular family. He leaned against Mother as they stood to sing so he could feel her voice.

After Reverend Harriman finally raised, then lowered his hands at the end, they all filtered out into the airless day. Men clustered under a tree, smoking cigarettes and tapping their toes. Loyal knew they wished their wives would stop talking and go home to get dinner on the table, and he sympathized with the women. If he could talk freely like that, he'd do plenty of it.

Across the yard, he saw Rebecca standing near her father. He noticed that she had her hair pulled back with mismatched combs. They were both the mottled brown, but one was plain and the other carved like the comb in his drawer at home. So it really was Rebecca's. He frowned, considering what that—along with her earlier comments—meant. She and Michael must have found the body before he did. But why had she asked if he would tell on them? His eyes widened. What if they had killed the man? Michael had brought one of his father's pistols to the Fourth of July picnic. Loyal had seen him showing it to some older boys. Why would kids shoot a grown man they didn't even know? It was the kind of notion Mother would tell him was the result of an overactive imagination.

Loyal stared at his shoes, so deep in thought he didn't sense someone approaching from behind. Suddenly he felt something cold and wet slither down the collar of his Sunday shirt. He arched his back and jerked the tail of his shirt out, shaking it and high-stepping until he was sure whatever it was had fallen out. He turned to see Father holding a crawdad that must have come from the creek below the church. Loyal realized everyone in the churchyard was staring at him—including Michael and his buddies, who were bent over laughing.

He felt his face go hot as he tucked his shirt back in. Father walked over, and together they strode down to the creek where they put the crawdad back in the water. Father kept his hand on Loyal's shoulder the whole time. When they got to the creek, backs to the crowd, Father looked earnestly into his eyes. "Any fool can play a trick. Courage is holding your head high when they do." Loyal nodded, fighting a prickling of tears. "Show me how to shape *courage*."

Loyal looked to his father. Was he asking for the sign? He lifted his hands to his shoulders and made a motion as if he were plucking something from his shirt and holding it tight in his fists. Father imitated him. "That's you," he said, pointing at Loyal. "Courageous. Brave." He made the sign again.

Loyal still wanted to cry, only now it was a different kind of feeling.

Delphy tried to slow the whirl of her mind as she ladled stewed chicken into a tureen. Even when it was just her and Loyal, she liked to serve a proper Sunday dinner. And this morning Creed had offered to wring the neck of the old rooster that had taken to crowing well before dawn. She'd been meaning to do it herself but was grateful to let someone else put an end to the old fellow. A secret smile quirked her lips. She'd save her neck wringing for Creed Raines. He'd spent a second night so they could go to church together, and her conflicting emotions were keeping her up at night. While she was grateful to see Creed taking more of an interest in Loyal, she was afraid he was setting the boy up for disappointment.

She settled the stew on the table next to a pea salad and angel biscuits. Creed spoke even before she could sit. "I need to get back up the mountain." She felt every muscle in her body tense and darted a look at Loyal. The boy was perched on the edge of his seat, watching them intently. Oh, but he could see so much more than people with two good ears.

"I'm surprised you stayed this long." She didn't sign the words. Loyal would likely follow along, but at least he couldn't hear the way her words twisted between them. She wished she could tell Creed that he broke her heart every time he came home and left again. If he'd left all at once and stayed gone, maybe it would be different. Instead, he'd drifted away from them in bits and pieces. Still was. Although each time he came home, some foolish part of her dared to hope he would stay.

Delphy suspected he blamed himself for taking Loyal on that

fateful trip that ended in a fever, an ear infection, and . . . she looked at her son. A wave of fierce protectiveness washed over her, and she realized that maybe she blamed Creed, too. For the first time she considered that maybe she'd played a role in Creed's slow abdication of his family.

"Maybe . . ." Creed sat and spooned some peas onto his plate. Something took flight in Delphy's heart. As if his *maybe* were echoing her own and they might finally talk about what stood between them. "Maybe I should take Loyal up on the mountain with me this time."

Her heart turned to stone. "Absolutely not," she said as she pushed her plate away.

Creed broke open a piece of bread and buttered it. "Might be good for both of us." He ducked his head, then looked up again. "I didn't realize we could . . . communicate. I'd like to try more of that." He turned toward Loyal. "You want to come up on the mountain with me?"

She didn't mean to do it. Didn't know she was going to until her plate of stew crashed to the floor, spattering bits of food and making Loyal jump. While he couldn't hear the crash, she knew he could feel the reverberation.

"Come with me," she said to Creed and marched him out the back door into the yard. She could feel her cheeks heating and knew tears stood in her eyes. Loyal did not need to witness what she would say next.

When Delphy returned to the kitchen, she saw that Loyal had cleaned up her mess. He was such a good boy. For a split second she wondered if she should let him go with his father. Boys needed their fathers, didn't they? But no. The last time the two of them went somewhere alone, it changed all of their lives. And while she knew this was different, her mother's heart couldn't bear the notion that something even worse might happen up on the mountain where help was simply too far away.

She forced a smile and began to sign. *I'm sorry I got angry. Your father doesn't realize what he's asking. You . . .* She paused and looked toward the ceiling. *You're special, not like he was at your age. He doesn't understand what you need.*

Loyal clenched his hands and shook his head. *Where's Father?* he signed.

She gritted her teeth and signed, her movements sharp. *Gone to his mountain.*

Loyal stomped his foot. *I'll go, too.*

No. She made the sign twice. *Not safe.*

I don't care. Now Loyal's motions were choppy, uneven. *You don't understand. I want to go. I will go.*

Delphy gave her head a shake. *We can talk later,* she signed. *When we're calm.*

Loyal formed both hands into claws facing his chest and flung them up and out. He stamped one foot, turned, and ran out of the house. Delphy ran after him but stopped when she saw he'd gone only as far as the cedar tree, where he kicked at the trunk, grunting and screeching before leaning against the far side, arms crossed tightly over his chest. Frustration filled the air, and she longed to go to him, to soothe him, but knew she couldn't comfort him right now.

She'd seen him get like this in those early days—when he'd suddenly been thrust into a world of silence. He hadn't learned to read yet when he lost his hearing. The gap in time between the loss and his learning sign language had been deeply frustrating. For a child used to communicating through words to suddenly be robbed of them meant tantrums were a daily occurrence. She suspected that was when Creed began to leave them behind in his mind. What would he do up there on his mountain if Loyal acted like this?

Biting her lip and fighting tears, she went back inside to finish cleaning up the kitchen. And what if, up there on Creed's mountain, Loyal no longer felt the need to act like this?

Creed had never been so glad to be by himself in his cabin as he was that evening. He'd eaten some questionable leftovers without even warming them, and now he sat on the front steps sharpening a hoe. He was alone and grateful for it. At least that was what he told himself. Being with Delphy and Loyal for several days had been good—he should probably do that more often—but he needed to keep up with his work on the mountain. And it wouldn't do to get used to the comforts of home.

He'd really wanted to bring Loyal with him. He could teach the boy some things and maybe he could learn some more of that hand-talk himself. But Delphy had always been overprotective and that hadn't changed one iota. They'd argued about it plenty when Loyal first lost his hearing. Creed wanted to let the boy fend for himself, to spend time with kids his own age. But Delphy could hardly stand to let the boy out of her sight. It was another reason he'd come up on the mountain. When a man's wife didn't trust him alone with his own son, it got hard to stay married. And he'd been raised to stay married.

Of course, Delphy wasn't the only one who didn't trust Creed alone with Loyal. If he were honest, it had been a relief when he realized she wouldn't let him make such a devastating mistake with their son ever again.

He took the sharpened hoe out to the garden and began chopping weeds with a vengeance. He'd go check his ginseng patches in the morning. It was still too soon to harvest, but he could make sure no one else had dug the valuable roots and double-check how many were likely for digging. Lost in thought, he jerked his head up when he heard something foreign to the sounds of the mountain all around him. Might have been a deer or a bear, but he suspected the sound was human. He'd left his rifle in the cabin, and while he doubted he'd need it, his fingers itched to hold something more threatening than a hoe. He continued working but kept his eyes on the leafy trail leading to the cabin. Soon the figure of a man emerged from the poplar and rhododendron.

It was that Earl fella from the sheriff's office. He was huffing and puffing as he climbed the trail. Creed guessed scouting land for the government must not require the man to walk very far or fast. He leaned on his hoe and watched.

As Earl topped the trail, he rubbed a forearm across his sweaty brow then wiped it on his shirt, leaving a dark smear. He looked up and spotted Creed, his weary eyes brightening. "Man, I'm glad to find you. Wasn't sure I was on the right trail." He plodded toward the porch and flopped down. "Got any water?"

Creed propped his hoe against the corner of the porch and fetched a bucket with a dipper. Earl scooped up some water and gulped it down. Then he dumped another dipperful over his head and slung water like a dog. "Man, that feels good. Didn't realize you were so high up."

"What brings you all this way?" Creed asked, crossing his arms.

"I was hoping you'd listen to me better than that sheriff down in Beverly. I don't think he's taking my partner being killed near as serious as he should."

"Sheriff's a friend of mine. Always seemed to me he listened real good."

"Yeah, that's because you're not an out-of-towner here to *change* things." He emphasized the word as if they were all heathens afraid of innovation.

"Virgil embraces change just fine," Creed said. He thought to mention the ballistics business but decided that might be giving something away. "What have you got to say that he's not hearing?"

Earl slicked his wet hair back. "He's not pushing people hard enough. It's like he doesn't understand how important it is to find out not just *who* shot Eddie, but *why*."

"Virgil's been doing a fine job for almost a decade now. I'm betting he knows more about how to handle folks around here than you do." Creed wasn't sure what this fellow thought he could—or should—do.

"Thing is, I've reported this to the home office, and they might send a man out here to look into things." Earl started cracking his knuckles one by one as if he didn't realize he was doing it. "I'd hate for them to think things weren't being handled right and decide to take over the investigation." He shrugged. "That'd be embarrassing for your friend."

Creed couldn't get a read on this fellow. First, he didn't think Virgil was doing a good job, and then he suggested he wanted Virgil to look good for whoever the Feds might send.

"Virgil can handle whoever shows up. And if they did take over the investigation, seems like that'd be taking things serious enough."

Earl stood and moved back and forth, head down, kneading his fingers. "You don't want those federal boys messing around in your business, trust me. Virgil needs to turn up some answers and quick." He stopped and glared at Creed. "Seems like if you really were his friend, you'd be down there helping him, not up here hiding out."

Creed jerked his head back a notch. "I'm not hiding out. Virgil didn't need me anymore. Anyway, I've got work to do."

"Yeah, well, if it had been someone you knew who got killed, I bet you'd still be down there doing everything you could to figure things out."

Creed wet his lips and picked up his hoe. "Reckon it's time for you to leave."

Earl eyed the hoe and raised both hands. "Yeah, yeah, I'm going. Hope you rest easy up here on this mountain where you don't have to worry about anybody else's troubles." He headed back toward the trail. "Just remember there's a man *dead* before you lay your head on your pillow tonight."

Creed watched him go, then kicked the water bucket, making it slosh. He still didn't know what the man had been playing at, but when he accused Creed of hiding . . . well, he might have been closer to the truth than Creed cared to admit.

seven

Loyal was still angry with Mother, but he knew that if he ever wanted to leave the front porch, he'd better get on her good side. So he did all his chores without being asked and even pulled the push mower out of the shed and began trimming the patch of yard in front of the house. He liked watching the whirling blades slice through the grass, making it spin and fly through the air. There was a rhythm and satisfaction to making the plot smooth and pretty.

He'd just finished and was standing back to admire his work when Michael slouched down the street with Rebecca a few paces behind. The older boy's posture straightened when he spotted Loyal. He waited for his sister to catch up, then jerked his head toward Loyal. "Look, it's your deaf boyfriend. Bet he talks worse than you." He threw his head back and laughed.

Rebecca ignored her brother and smiled at Loyal. She approached the picket fence and admired the yard with its abundance of late-summer flowers. "Your yard sure is pretty," she said.

Without considering that she didn't know sign, Loyal fanned his fingers and touched his thumb to his chin. She cocked her

head and wrinkled her brow. He licked his lips, focused on form-
ing the word *mother* with his mouth and voice. He rarely spoke,
but everyone at school had learned to do so, and he could do it
if he needed to. Something about Rebecca made him want to
talk to her any way he could.

Her eyes lit up. "You can talk!" Loyal shrugged.

Michael butted in. "I was right. He talks worse than you.
You two can stand here making noises at each other, but I'm
going on into town." He stuck his chest out. "I've got business."
Rebecca rolled her eyes and turned her back to her brother. He
waited a beat as if expecting her to follow, then swatted at the
air and continued on his way.

Rebecca looked at Loyal, mimicking the sign he'd just made.
"This means *mother*?" she asked. "She grows the flowers?"

Loyal nodded as he reached out to adjust her fingers a little
until it looked right. She smiled, and it was blinding. "Show me
father." He did, then moved on to brother, sister, family, and
finally she asked for the sign for *friend*. Loyal hooked his index
fingers together, flipped the position of his hands back and forth,
released and then re-hooked his fingers. "Oh, like your fingers
are hugging." Rebecca repeated the sign. "I like that one." She
eyed Loyal intently. "Can we be friends?" she asked, hooking
her fingers and holding her hands between them.

Loyal said yes as he raised his fist and moved it like a nodding
head. He also smiled almost as big as Rebecca. He had plenty
of deaf friends at school, but not many hearing friends. Well,
none really, and he liked Rebecca a lot.

They were quiet and still for a moment, just admiring the
flowers. Rebecca tapped him on the arm, and he turned to
her, eyebrows raised. "I talk funny," she said. "I guess you can't
hear it, but kids make fun of me sometimes. My brother does
all the time."

Loyal furrowed his brow and tilted his head to the side.

"I have a lisp," she said. Loyal didn't even know what that

was. He guessed you had to be a hearing person to understand. He smiled and shrugged, lifting his hands in the air.

She laughed. "I guess you don't care since you can't hear it." Her smile softened. "And when I'm with you, I don't care either."

They stood there quietly for a moment, smiling at each other. Loyal hadn't realized a hearing person could understand him so well without sign. He wondered if it was just because no one else had ever cared enough to try.

Virgil sent Bud up the mountain to fetch Creed later that week. Creed didn't much want to go back to town. Didn't much want to be caught up in this mess over a dead man he didn't know, but since Loyal was involved, he went regardless. He didn't want Virgil or anyone else putting his son on the spot, questioning him or pressing him for information. He remembered how his own father had always been pushing him. *Do more. Try harder. Always have the right answer ready.* The man was never satisfied, even after Creed worked his tail off to become sheriff. His dying words for Creed were to make sure his grandson—then almost two years old—turned out better.

Well, Creed had messed that up, too. He sure wasn't going to let anyone else make things worse.

Virgil had his bald head bent over a stack of papers. His free hand worked across his shiny pate in circles as though rubbing it helped him think. He flung his pen down and stood when Creed came in.

"I've gotten twenty-eight calls from Washington, D.C."—he dragged out the *D* and *C*—"since you went and turned up Eddie Minks's body. Now they want me to fill out all these *forms* like that's gonna help them more than me getting out there and figuring out who did it."

"Guess Earl informed his superiors," Creed said.

"He didn't exactly rush to do it, but it's done now and they're planning to send an investigator down here to help me 'resolve the issue.'" Virgil rubbed his head some more. "All they'll do is slow me down. That's why I sent for you. I need someone who can *actually* help." He glared at Creed. "Which I thought you were going to do before you ran back up the mountain without a word to me."

Creed held his hands up. "Figured you were done with me once we found that slug. I've got work to do."

Virgil shook his head. "Why somebody with a good-lookin' wife and a boy at home wants to be up on that mountain is beyond me."

Creed hardened his jaw. "Maybe it's not for you to understand. Maybe I'll just go back up there so I don't have to deal with people like you sticking their noses into my business."

Now it was Virgil's turn to hold up his hands. "You're right. I crossed the line. Your family's your business." He braced his hands on his belt. "But I sure could use someone with brains and common sense, not to mention experience, if you're willing to stick around awhile."

Creed felt like a dog letting its hackles fall. He shook out his neck and took a breath. "You said Earl didn't hurry to report his partner's death. You got any idea why he might've waited?"

Virgil perked up. "No, but I did think it was almighty strange. You got any ideas?"

"Well, he came up the mountain to see me the other day. Said he'd reported the murder and seemed plenty anxious for you to solve the case before anybody else showed up. Seemed to think I could hurry you along."

Virgil narrowed his eyes. "You probably could. That fellow's been turning up here twice a day to ask if there's been any progress. Have I found any new clues? Who's my prime suspect? Finally told him if he didn't leave me alone, I'd never get anything done."

"Guess he's upset about his friend," Creed said.

"That's just it. I've dealt with more than one killing over the years, and nobody's ever acted like this one. Shoot, if Maxine over at the motel hadn't sworn Earl was there when Eddie must've been killed, I'd say he'd make a fine suspect." Virgil drummed his fingers on the desktop. "He's just too . . . anxious. Nervous."

Creed nodded his head. "I noticed that, too. Like he can't make up his mind how to feel about his buddy getting killed. One minute he talks like he didn't think much of you, and the next he's worried about your looking bad. Double-minded that way."

Virgil snapped his fingers. "That's the word for it. Makes me wonder what his angle is."

"What about Eddie?" Creed asked. "What's his story?"

"A gal in the office he works out of gave me the particulars from his employee file. He doesn't have any family that they know of. Been contracting with them for almost a year, doing this land-acquisition work. Gal kept saying his work was marked 'satisfactory.' Guess that means he wasn't great, but he wasn't terrible either." Virgil had been ticking the facts off on his fingers. "And that's about it. Listed an address in Pennsylvania."

Creed chuckled. "Well, not to sound like Earl, but *do* you have any suspects?"

Virgil frowned. "Hadden Westfall's the only one so far."

"And he's got an alibi. Guess that checked out?"

"Talked to the secretary over there at the engineer's office. She said Hadden was there sure enough. She saw him arrive around eleven in the morning and leave after four. Takes a good hour to drive up there, so unless we're way off on when Eddie was killed . . ."

"What about the engineer? What'd he say?" Creed asked.

A slow smile crept over Virgil's face. "You trying to catch me out on not being thorough? I left a message for Gordon Shiloh to call me—he's the one in charge. I expect he'll confirm what the secretary said, but you can't be too careful."

"Sounds like you've got everything covered. What was it you needed me for again?"

Virgil laughed and slapped his hat on his head. "We're going to talk to the Hacker boys."

Creed groaned. He didn't have anything against the Hackers, but he didn't seek them out either. Rough as cobs, every one of them. "Alright then. What you gonna take 'em so they don't run us off?"

Virgil reached under his desk and pulled out a paper sack. He winked. "Got me some conversation starter right here."

When Delphy heard voices out front, she headed for the door to peek outside. Loyal must have company, though she couldn't think who . . . Ah-ha. The Westfall kids. She saw the older boy—she couldn't remember his name—sauntering off as Loyal and . . . Rebecca—that was her name—engaged in conversation. She watched for a moment, reveling in the sight of her son and a young lady communicating with each other. It made her heart swell. She gave them a few moments before pushing open the door.

Rebecca turned toward her, cuing Loyal to do the same. She smiled so big it almost hurt. "Rebecca, what a treat! Won't you join us for luncheon?" As she used the more formal word for the noon meal, she saw Loyal roll his eyes. She stifled a laugh. *Boys.* He and Rebecca exchanged a look that did her mother's heart good.

She ushered them inside and fed them from the garden— buttery corn on the cob, slices of deep-red tomatoes, green beans with streak o' lean, and golden biscuits with the strawberry jam she'd made earlier in the season.

Humming to herself, she pulled out cloth napkins and adjusted the jar of black-eyed Susans she'd set in the middle of the table that morning for no reason. She wanted to laugh at her son, who was clearly confused by all the fuss. Much as his father would be. That last thought sobered her. When they married, she'd assumed they'd have lots of children. She'd even thought she was pregnant about a year before Loyal lost his hearing, but it had been a false alarm. And then, when Creed brought their boy home so sick and the fever left him deaf . . . well, suffice it to say they hadn't tried for another child after that. Thinking back on those dark days, she wasn't sure whose choice it had been—hers or Creed's?

Watching the children there at her table, she felt a pang of regret. Maybe it wasn't too late . . . No. She would not torture herself that way. If Creed wanted to put his family back together, he'd have to do a great deal more than spend a few nights and learn a few signs.

Forcing a smile, she set a plate of cookies on the table and tried to be satisfied with the blessings in front of her.

Once they'd eaten and Rebecca helped with the dishes, Mother suggested they go for a walk. Loyal squinted at her. Just that morning she'd acted like she wasn't going to let him leave the house except to go to church. And now she was practically pushing him out the door. He shook his head. People were complicated.

The house sat on the outskirts of town just beyond the Beverly cemetery. He and Rebecca strolled along past Cemetery Lane and onto Main Street. Loyal was gawking at the display in the window of the Beverly Market when Rebecca bumped his arm and tilted her head toward the old courthouse catty-corner to where they stood. Although the county seat had moved to Elkins before Loyal was born, the sheriff still kept an office in

Beverly in the brick building with its double doors flanked by windows.

Loyal spotted his father climbing into the sheriff's car. He lifted a hand to flag him down, but the car was already pulling away from the curb and Father didn't turn toward him. He wished he could yell or whistle—shoot, he knew he could—he just wasn't quite sure how to manage it properly. He longed to know where the two men were headed and wished he was going with them. Then Rebecca poked him again and pointed to the public square, a grassy area on the corner across from them. This time he saw Michael standing near a tree, watching the sheriff's car as if he were a spy.

Rebecca tugged on his arm and motioned for him to follow her. They crossed the street and walked toward Michael. He jumped as they approached. Loyal guessed he didn't hear them coming. He knew how that was.

"Where'd you two come from?" the older boy snapped.

Loyal didn't see how Rebecca answered but could tell she was being sassy. Loyal bumped her and made the sign for *what*, then gestured toward Michael.

"Yeah, what are you doing?" she asked. "Were you hiding from Sheriff White?"

"No." Loyal could see the annoyance in Michael's eyes. And when he glanced at Rebecca, he noted caution in hers.

"Then what?"

Michael shrugged and slouched onto a nearby bench. "Just seeing what I can pick up around town."

"What do you mean?" Rebecca asked.

Michael darted a look at Loyal and jerked a thumb at him. "He can't hear, right? Like he has no idea what I'm saying?"

Rebecca looked at Loyal out of the corner of her eye. "That's right. Deaf as a post." Loyal tried not to frown. He hated that saying.

Michael leaned forward. "I'm trying to figure out what the

sheriff knows about—" he paused and glanced around them—
"you know. That day on the river. What happened."

"Do you mean, like, has he figured out it was us?"

Michael's eyes darted all around as he patted the air as if
tamping down dirt. "Yeah. Exactly like that."

A look of alarm spread over Rebecca's face. "What if he
thinks the wrong person did it? What if someone innocent gets
into trouble?"

Michael gnawed at his lip. "Best-case scenario, it just goes
unsolved."

"But what if—?" Michael stood abruptly, cutting Rebecca off.
"I don't want to talk about this. You and your *boyfriend* go on
now," he said with a sneer. "I'm going to see if I can't find some
stuff out." He stuck his thumbs in his pockets and sauntered
down the street in an exaggerated way that Loyal supposed he
thought looked casual.

A soft touch drew his attention. Rebecca was looking at him
with tears welling in her eyes. "How much did you see that day?"

He hesitated, then shrugged, not sure how to tell her he'd
just seen them running.

"You saw everything?"

Loyal thought for a minute. The sign for *running* might not
make sense to her. He pointed at her and then moved his arms
as if he were pumping them to help him run.

"You saw us running away." He nodded. "But you didn't
see . . ." She ducked her head, and when she looked at him
again, a tear trickled down her cheek. He reached out to gather
the moisture on the tip of his finger and shook his head.

"It was awful," she said. Loyal wanted to comfort her but
wasn't sure what to do. Hug her? That seemed awkward. Although he also thought it might be kind of nice. While he was
still trying to decide, Rebecca pushed a smile onto her face.
"Thank you for being my friend," she said and made the sign
he'd taught her earlier.

Loyal put his flat hand to his chin and moved it forward and down. Then he managed a smile of his own. He pointed toward the horseshoe pits in the square and raised his eyebrows.

"Okay," Rebecca said, "but my aim is terrible."

Loyal waggled his eyebrows and rubbed his hands together. He was delighted to see Rebecca's posture relax. He'd think more about what Michael had implied, later when he was alone.

eight

The road to the Hacker family cabin was barely wide enough for the police car as they bumped over its many ruts and gullies. Creed considered that if they needed to leave in a hurry, they likely couldn't do it by car.

"What is it you plan to talk to Clyde and his boys about?"

Virgil flicked him a look. "Whatever they want to tell me. You know there's not much use in asking 'em anything straight out."

"Yeah," Creed agreed. "Although they might tell us something straight out. Like 'get off my property and don't ever come back.'"

Virgil laughed. "I thought you and Clyde were friends."

"If by *friends* you mean he won't shoot me on sight, then yeah, I guess we're friends." He paused. "At least I think we are. You, on the other hand . . ."

"Don't go trying to make me feel overconfident," Virgil said as the car broke through the trees and came out in a bare patch leading up to a surprisingly grand cabin that looked as if it had taken root and was now flourishing in the protected mountain cove. The Hackers might be backwoods, but they were also craftsmen. The two-story cabin boasted a stout front porch and railing made from rhododendron branches polished to a sheen.

A hound bayed from under the front steps, and Clyde himself stepped out onto the porch. He was unarmed, but Creed knew there was bound to be a rifle or shotgun close to hand.

As Creed climbed out of the car, he lifted his arm in greeting. Clyde braced his hands on his hips. "You bringin' the law here for a reason?" he called out, making his long white beard jump.

Creed shot a *stay here* look at Virgil and stepped closer to the porch. "I'm helping Virgil look into that shooting over at the bend of the river." Clyde's eyes narrowed. "A body can't hardly stir on the mountain without you'uns knowing about it. We're hoping you might've seen or heard something."

Clyde spit. "Or done something?"

Creed shook his head. "Don't have any reason to think that."

Clyde stood motionless for too many breaths, then seemed to come to a decision. "You fellers come in the house. Don't have much of anything to tell you, but we can sit a minute since you come all this way."

Creed let out a gusty breath and waved for Virgil to follow him. The front room of the cabin was as handsome as the outside. The stone fireplace was a work of art with chunks of quartz worked in and polished until they gleamed. Clyde waved his visitors to chairs that were clearly handmade with skill and precision. Creed wondered if Clyde might trade him one to give to Delphy for Christmas.

Now, what had made him think such a thing?

"Heard about that government man getting shot down," Clyde said, refocusing Creed's attention. "Neither me nor my boys were over that way, but word gets around."

"You have any dealings with him?" Virgil asked.

"Him and his partner sent word the government might like to buy up some of our land." Clyde grinned. "Guessed they couldn't find their way to the house to ask in person."

"You selling?" Virgil asked.

Clyde got a cagey look. "Well now, that'd be between me and whichever one was doing the buying."

Virgil laughed. "Guess so. Main reason we came out here was because I was thinking you might get word that wouldn't necessarily come to my ears."

Clyde cackled and stroked his beard. "I can see how being sheriff might make folks what you'd call reluctant to spread their tittle-tattle." Virgil smiled and waited. Clyde got a philosophical look. "Thing is, I'd expect whoever done it to brag a little and ain't nobody said nothing."

Virgil nodded. "So maybe it wasn't anyone from around here."

"Maybe. Maybe not. You asked that partner of the dead man if he done it?"

"He has a solid alibi."

"Bet Hadden Westfall has one, too," Clyde said. He leaned forward enough that they could see the tobacco stains in his beard. "Easier for some folks to come up with an alibi than others."

"You say that like you know it for a fact," Virgil said.

Clyde settled back in his chair. "What I know for a fact is that money solves a whole passel of problems. 'Specially in these hard times. Maybe you oughta talk to somebody who's got some."

Virgil nodded slowly. "Brought you a little something," he said, passing the jar he'd shown Creed to Clyde. The old man took it and set it on a side table crafted from a section of tree that looked like it had been at least fifty years old when they cut it down.

"Thank ye." Silence descended, and Creed knew they were done here. He stood. "Good to see you, Clyde. Hope your boys are well."

"Fine as frog hair and ornery as a bear woke before spring," he said. "If ever I did sell this land, it'd be for them. Reckon you'uns can see yourselves out."

Creed nodded and followed Virgil out to the car. As they walked across the yard, he got an itchy feeling like someone was watching them. Maybe more than one.

"I'm betting there are at least two rifles pointed at our backs," Virgil said in a low voice.

"More likely three by now," Creed said.

Virgil huffed a laugh. They climbed in the car, and Creed didn't fully relax until they hit the paved road.

When Creed's silhouette blocked the light coming in the back door, Delphy was annoyed to feel a thrill of happiness. After she'd told him in no uncertain terms that Loyal would not be accompanying him to his cabin on Rich Mountain, she thought she might have run him off once and for all. Now her traitorous heart reminded her that she still loved this stubborn, damaged man.

"Got enough supper for one more?" he asked.

She pushed a hank of hair off her forehead with the back of her hand and leveled a look at him. "How hungry are you?" she shot back.

A smile quirked the corner of his mouth, but he subdued it. "I already ate once today so I'm not too starved."

She fought her own smile. "Come on in then. Loyal will be glad to see you." He looked like he was about to tease her some more but thought better of it. Instead, he stepped into the lavatory. She could hear him washing his face and hands. She could say that much for him—he'd always been clean and respectful. The memory of how he always washed himself before coming to bed took her mind in a direction she didn't want it to go. She wrestled her thoughts back to the here and now. No need to borrow heartbreak.

After supper with a clearly delighted Loyal, they all went out to the front porch to enjoy the evening breeze. Delphy sat in her favorite rocking chair, breathing in cooling air that promised rain. Creed settled in the swing and patted the spot next to him for Loyal to sit. The boy wedged himself in sideways so he could keep an eye on both parents.

Delphy let her head fall back and closed her eyes. Creed set the swing into motion. The creak of the chains made a soft music, and soon the autumn smell of smoldering tobacco filled the air as he lit his pipe.

"Looks like it might rain," Creed said.

Delphy lifted a hand and made the sign for *yes*. She did it without thinking about Creed being hearing. She peeked at him and saw that he accepted the sign without comment. "I guess you're here because of Virgil," she said, signing for Loyal's benefit.

"That's not the only reason."

"But it's the main one." She let her hands drop.

"We went out to see the Hackers this afternoon."

Delphy rolled her eyes. "Well then we're lucky you came back at all. You think Clyde had anything to do with that shooting?"

"No. He wants us to think Hadden Westfall had something to do with it, though." Delphy noticed that Loyal froze and watched his father intently. Hadden's name interested him. She smiled. Maybe that had something to do with the man's sweet daughter.

Delphy stilled her rocking. "I can't see Hadden being involved. Clyde just doesn't like him."

"Probably. Anyway, he was in Elkins."

"That's good," she said. "It's hard enough, Hadden losing his wife and raising those two children on his own. He doesn't need idle talk and rumors circulating."

Creed frowned, which pleased Delphy. She'd been hoping to remind him that Hadden once courted her. Before a certain mountain man stole her heart.

"I'm surprised the church ladies haven't married him off," Creed grumbled.

Delphy smiled. "They probably have, he just hasn't realized it yet."

Creed pushed the swing harder. "Oh yeah, who do they have in mind?"

She shrugged and lifted one hand to her forehead and flicked it out—the sign for *don't know*—and then she remembered to speak the words. Loyal giggled, apparently pleased to have taken priority with her signing.

Creed opened his mouth, then closed it again, his eyes straying to the street. Delphy turned to see what drew his attention and saw Fred Rohrbaugh, owner of Rohrbaugh's Store, hurrying toward the house.

He waved at them and hollered, "Virgil says come quick as you can!" Creed stood and looked a question. The portly man stopped outside the front gate, with beads of sweat on his brow in spite of the cool evening air. "He said something about making an arrest and told me to send you over if you were to home."

Creed stood and moved toward the steps, speaking in a low voice. Fred darted a look at Delphy, and Loyal then answered too softly for her to hear. Loyal jumped to his feet to follow, but she snagged him by the collar and shook her head firmly.

Loyal gave her a pleading look. She signed *no* emphatically and stood, tugging him through the front door. She aimed him toward the stairs and swatted him on the behind, pointing to his room. Loyal heaved a sigh and dragged up the steps. Delphy watched him go, eyes narrowed. Then she went to the window and watched her husband disappear toward the sheriff's office. She heaved a sigh of her own and went to the kitchen to see what she could make for breakfast, assuming her husband spent the night. She might not be sure where they stood right now, but she'd feed him just the same.

70

The handful of people in Virgil's office all seemed to be talking at once. One of them—a man in a good suit—was a stranger. He sat in a chair looking pale and swiping his face with a handkerchief. Creed sidled over to the sheriff, who leaned against his desk, arms crossed. "What's going on?"

"I'm arresting Hadden Westfall."

"You're doing what?" Creed saw that Hadden was in the corner, shaking a finger in Deputy Bud Wallace's face—which was bright red. Bud kept saying, "I don't care." Fred Rohrbaugh was trying to add his two cents to the one-sided conversation consisting mostly of Hadden explaining how Bud and Virgil were going to be out of work and generally hated by everyone in the county for the rest of their lives. The stranger had the look of a man who'd been on a week-long drunk.

"That engineer up in Elkins, Gordon Shiloh—he said Hadden left the meeting early. Said the secretary probably saw everyone else leave late in the afternoon and just assumed Hadden was with 'em."

Creed gave a low whistle. "Pays to be thorough."

Virgil looked pointedly toward the men gesticulating wildly and talking on top of each other. "Does it?"

"Whyn't you put a stop to it?"

"Waiting on you. Plus, I expect you know it can be useful to just let people blow off some steam for a while. You never know what someone might say in the heat of the moment." He glanced at the pale, sweaty fellow. "And with the federal government's man showing up this evening sicker than a dog, I can use all the help I can get." The man patted his forehead and closed his eyes.

Virgil heaved a sigh, stood, and whistled loud enough for Delphy to hear back at the house. "Alright then," he said when the men jerked their heads toward him. "Hadden, this doesn't give me an ounce of pleasure, but until we sort things out, we're going to have to make you a guest of the Randolph County Jail up in Elkins."

"The devil you will," Hadden said. "I told you I was in Elkins when that man was shot."

"So you did. Unfortunately, I haven't been able to corroborate your story."

"I thought Miss Gillespie confirmed that I was there."

Virgil nodded. "She did. But then I asked Gordon to confirm that." Creed saw hot color rise up Hadden's neck. "Seems you left the meeting early."

Hadden clenched his fists. "There's an explanation for that." He darted a look around the room. "One that I don't care to share in present company."

"Good," Virgil said. "But until we get your explanation sorted, you're going to be our guest." He took a few steps closer and motioned Hadden to join him. "Now, if you'll agree to cooperate, you, me, and Creed are gonna ride up to Elkins while Bud keeps an eye on things here."

The government man started to stand, then thumped back down in his chair. "Here now. I should be the one going with you," he said in a thin voice.

Fire filled Hadden's eyes, and Creed saw Virgil motion toward Bud, who held a pair of handcuffs. But before the younger man could make a move, the door opened and Hadden's man Otto stepped inside. Every head turned to look at the young German who grimaced and limped into the room.

"I have come to confess," he said. The government man bolted for the door and deposited his dinner in the street.

nine

Loyal counted to one hundred before scooting out his window and shimmying down the porch trellis. It was risky, but he was too curious to just sit in his room wondering what the sheriff wanted with Father. Now he stood outside the open window at the side of the sheriff's office. It was hard to tell what was going on, with people moving around and turning their backs to him. But their body language told him most folks in the room were angry, and it sure looked like Bud was about to put handcuffs on Mr. Westfall.

Then Otto stepped inside, and Loyal had a clear view of him when he said he'd come to confess. Loyal felt his eyes go wide. Confess to what—shooting that man? He'd thought Michael and Rebecca were mixed up in it, but he hadn't seen Otto that day. And Otto moved slow, couldn't run like the Westfall kids had.

Loyal stood on tiptoe and craned his neck to try to get a better view of the room. One of the men—a stranger—suddenly ran for the door and threw up in the road. Before he could think what to do, Father was outside. He laid a heavy hand on his shoulder. Loyal looked up, fear in his eyes.

73

Father gave him a squeeze. "Your mother will have a fit," he said. "But I'd rather you were with me than out here." He motioned for Loyal to follow him back inside. The sick man came with them, dabbing at his mouth and looking green in the face.

When they entered the room, the sheriff was making a *time out* sign, which most everyone seemed to understand. "You all need to settle down," he said. "Otto, how about me and you step into the back room?"

"*Nein.* I mean, no thank you. I will say my confession for all to hear. It was I who shot the man on Mr. Westfall's property."

Loyal thought the adults looked like they were playing a game of Simon Says, frozen in place until Otto uttered the key phrase.

"Now hold on, Otto." The sheriff was the first to find his tongue. "That doesn't make sense. Why would you shoot someone?"

"He was trespassing on my employer's land." Otto looked nervous. "I thought he was a . . . how do you say, poacher? I hoped only to frighten him."

Loyal had to really focus on Otto with his different way of speaking. Which meant he missed it when someone else must have spoken. Otto shrugged. "I was in too much hurry. I regret it now."

Everyone started talking at once, and Loyal couldn't keep track, his eyes darting from one mouth to another trying to understand what was going on. He finally zeroed in on Mr. Westfall, who just stared at Otto, his eyes asking a question Otto seemed to understand. The young German gave a little nod and clenched one fist in a motion that spoke of strength to Loyal. Was Otto telling Mr. Westfall to be strong, or was he saying he himself was strong?

Then all the mouths stopped moving, and everyone looked toward the sheriff. He stood with fists on his hips and fire in his eyes. Loyal guessed he must have yelled at them all to be quiet. "I'm clearing the room," he said, and the way his face moved told Loyal he'd said it very loud. People began drifting toward the door, looking at each other and then at the floor. "Otto, you stay. Hadden, I'll follow up with you shortly—don't go any farther than across the street. Creed, I want you as witness. Mr. Mason, you ought to lie down somewhere. Bud, escort everyone out and guard the door." The sheriff's eyes landed on Loyal, and he rubbed his shiny head. "What in tarnation is that boy doing here?"

Father laid a hand on Loyal's shoulder. "I'll run him on home."

"Doggone if you will. I need you here." The sheriff looked Loyal up and down. "I'm betting he found his way here without help. Can I trust him to get home the same way?"

Father bent down and looked Loyal in the eyes. "Son, I need you to go straight home and stay there." He made the sign for *stay*, maybe without even realizing it. "Will you do that?"

Loyal let his shoulders slump and looked as disappointed as he knew how. Father squashed a smile. "I know. But will you promise me?"

Loyal nodded while making the sign for *promise*. Father imitated the sign, then reached out like he was going to tousle his hair but stopped. Instead, he took Loyal by both shoulders and squeezed. "You're a good boy—almost a man. I'm glad I can trust you." The disappointment Loyal felt over having to leave was replaced by a swelling pride. A man—his father thought he was a man. Hearing that was almost worth his missing whatever was about to happen. He nodded at the sheriff and tried not to stare at Otto as he left the room and made his way home.

Creed watched his boy go. He was grateful he'd realized he could communicate with his son more easily than he'd thought possible. He just hoped he wasn't messing things up for the boy. Was it good to expose him to whatever was happening with the investigation? He'd long thought Delphy too protective, but he sure didn't trust himself to do any better. Now the fact that he had the care of Loyal in this situation made the sweat pop out on his forehead. What if the boy didn't make it back home? What if a car were coming and he didn't know it was there until too late? Why hadn't he considered how dangerous the world was before taking the boy on that hunting trip all those years ago?

Virgil slumped into his chair and waved Otto into a beat-up folding chair nearby. "Take a load off. This might take a minute." He looked at Creed. "You might as well get comfortable, too."

Creed forced his mind back to the task at hand. "Reckon none of us are what you'd call comfortable."

"Ain't that the truth," Virgil said. He put his elbows on his desk and leaned toward Otto, who was perched on his chair like it might give way beneath him. "What are you aiming at?"

Otto looked at Creed, then back to Virgil. "I do not understand Herr White." He paled. "Mr. Sheriff." He shook his head. "I am not saying this correctly."

Virgil groaned. "It doesn't matter. What I want to know is why you've come in here with such a tall tale?"

Otto wet his lips. "Tall tale?"

Virgil rolled his eyes. "I don't believe you, son. Why would you say you shot Eddie Minks?"

Otto brightened as though he'd finally gotten a handle on the question. "Because I did this thing. I shot him."

"Alright. We're going to try something different." Virgil drilled Otto with a stare. "Where's the gun?"

Otto flushed. He looked up and to the right. "I threw it in the river after I had done this terrible thing."

"Why would you do that?"

"So no one would know."

Virgil leaned in. "And yet here you are, ready to tell the whole town you did it. What's changed?"

Otto leaned in, as well. "Mr. Westfall must not be blamed. He did not do it, and I owe him a great deal. I cannot let him

76

take the blame for what another man has done." Otto lifted a hand and let it fall. "And so I have come to tell you. Now you will leave my employer alone."

Virgil eyed Creed as if inviting him to offer his two cents. Creed held his hands up. He had nothing to add at the moment. "Fine. Sounds to me like you're taking the fall for Hadden."

Otto shook his head. "Falling is what caused this," he said, thumping his bad leg. "I have not fallen lately."

Virgil heaved a sigh. "Are you saying you shot Eddie because you think it will keep your boss out of trouble?"

"Nein. I tell the truth so you do not punish an innocent man."

"Innocent." Virgil crossed his arms over his chest. "I doubt any of us are innocent, least of all Hadden." He sat silent for a minute, apparently deep in thought. "Alright. I've got a temporary cell we can put you in if you're so all-fired determined to be arrested. But I'm not done with Hadden quite yet. There are a few more questions I'd like answered before we call this case solved." He turned to Creed. "Let's take a walk."

Loyal clambered back up the trellis and slipped into his room. He rarely thought much about being able to hear, but at times like this he could sure see how it would come in handy. As it was, he'd have to peek out into the hall to see if Mother had any notion he'd been gone. He stood at his closed door a moment, hoping he might feel the boards shifting if Mother were walking by. He was just reaching for the knob when the door opened. He jumped and so did Mother.

What are you doing? she signed. *I was coming to say good-night.*

Loyal bared his teeth and used his index finger to make a brushing motion. Mother rolled her eyes and made a *go on* gesture. Loyal grabbed his pajamas and scampered downstairs to the lavatory where he quickly finished his bedtime preparations. Mother caught his arm as he started past her and turned him to face her.

I know you wanted to go with your father, she signed. *I want you to stay safe.*

Loyal nodded. *It's okay. Do you think he'll come home soon?*

Mother made a face and shrugged. It was obvious she didn't want to talk about Father's comings and goings. *Good night. I love you.* Then she gave him a quick kiss on the forehead that he didn't have time to duck. He made a face of his own and acted like he was going to wipe the kiss away, then grinned and rubbed it in. She laughed and gave him a swat.

Alone in his room, Loyal closed the door and lay with his head at the foot of his bed so he could catch any breeze coming through the open window. He'd read about night sounds— hooting owls, distant train whistles, howling coyotes, and chirping crickets—and wondered what it would be like to hear all of that. Or better yet, to hear Father tromping up the porch steps and through the front door. He almost thought he could remember such a sound from when he was very small . . .

Rebecca could hear all of that. He wished he could tell her what he'd seen at the sheriff's office. It was obvious she and Michael knew plenty about the murder of that man. He'd told Rebecca he saw them running away, but he hadn't known how to get her to understand that he'd also seen Michael hide something. Or to tell her that he still had her comb found beside the dead man. He would have just given it to her, but it was still in his sock drawer. He stood and fetched it out, tracing the cool curve of it with his fingers.

Had the Westfall kids seen Otto shoot the government man? And if so, where had Otto gone? He moved slow with his bad leg, and it hadn't taken Loyal long to find the body. Surely he would have seen Otto. He thought back to that day and remembered how he'd glimpsed something higher up the mountain. A fleeting something flashing in the sunlight.

A chill swept through him. What if Otto had been hidden on the mountain, watching his every move? The notion that a murderer had been peering at him from the trees made Loyal's stomach feel funny. Did Otto know Rebecca and Michael had been there, too? Had he confessed because he figured the kids wouldn't let their father go to jail for something he hadn't done? But that made him wonder why the Westfall kids hadn't told already.

Loyal rolled over, trying to find a cool spot on his pillow. None of this made sense. He needed to talk it all over with Father. He drifted off hoping both parents would be there come morning.

Creed followed Virgil not much more than a block to the Odd Fellows Hall on Main Street. Although membership in the organization had dwindled, the building with its stamped metal sheathing and false front remained a point of pride for many in the town. Apparently, Hadden was a member, and from the way Virgil walked in like he owned the place, Creed guessed the sheriff must be a member, as well.

Hadden sat at a table to the side of the long, narrow room. A cup of coffee sat in front of him, and he was reading a copy of the *Randolph Enterprise*. He lowered the paper, folded it, and set it on the table. He crossed his arms.

"Appreciate you sticking around," Virgil said.

"I'm saving you a trip to my home. I hope you appreciate that."

Virgil grunted and pulled a chair over near Hadden. "Could have gone ahead and locked you up. Then I wouldn't have needed to cross the street."

Hadden turned his attention to Creed. "We could use some new members here. Have you ever thought of becoming an Odd Fellow?"

Creed laughed. "Guess I'm odd enough without joining a group to prove it."

Hadden dismissed him with a wave. "You'd have to come into town with more regularity. I suppose if a wife and child aren't reason enough, I can't expect a fraternal organization to tempt you."

Creed clenched his fists and took a step forward. Virgil stood and grabbed another chair, shoving it toward Creed. "Here you go. Take a load off." He looked pointedly at the chair. Creed shook his hands out and sat. He'd never much liked Hadden and decided he wasn't going to change his opinion anytime soon.

Virgil sat back down. "So, what's your man Otto about?"

"Perhaps he shot that fellow and is feeling guilt-stricken over it."

Virgil heaved a sigh. "You know that's almost as likely as you winning a popularity contest around here."

"Oh, I don't know, I'm popular in certain circles."

"Circles of hell maybe," Creed said under his breath. Virgil's mouth quirked, though he didn't look at Creed.

"You going to let that boy take responsibility for something he didn't do?"

Hadden stood and paced a few steps, hands clasped behind his back. "Since you asked, I honestly would rather he didn't." He shook his head. "Still, I don't know why he'd lie."

"Don't you?" Virgil said.

Hadden frowned at him. "I know you want to believe I shot that man, but I didn't."

Virgil leaned in. "How about you give me that explanation for leaving your meeting early. You know, the one you didn't care to share in 'present company.'" He jerked a thumb at Creed. "And I'm not giving you a choice about this company."

Hadden rubbed the back of his neck and frowned at Creed. "Is this confidential?"

"Sure," Virgil said. "Right up until one of us has to testify in court."

Hadden snorted. "Well, let's hope it doesn't come to that."

He sat back down and paused as though ordering his thoughts. "There's a woman." Virgil raised one dark caterpillar of an eyebrow but didn't speak. Creed leaned back in his chair and stretched his legs out, crossing them at the ankles. Seemed like he might as well get comfortable. "She's, uh, separated from her husband." Now Virgil's other eyebrow joined the first. "It would be . . . difficult for her if word got out that we were . . . seeing one another."

"I can see how that might be the case," Virgil said. "Is her reputation worth more than your hide?"

"Like I said, I would hope it doesn't come to that."

"Reckon you might give me her name just in case it does?"

Hadden grimaced. "Bridgette Henderson."

Virgil whistled. Creed guessed he knew the woman.

"She can vouch for you?" Virgil asked.

Hadden nodded. "Although, as I mentioned, I would rather she didn't have to."

"Yeah, well, I'd rather I didn't have to investigate the murder of Eddie Minks and find the real killer before that federal investigator lying down on a cot in my back room feels healthy enough to tell me how incompetent I am."

Hadden ran a hand through his thick hair. "I can't imagine that Otto did it."

Creed felt like it was high time he did something other than listen. "Who *can* you imagine did it?" Virgil shot him an inscrutable look.

"One of the Hacker boys? Maybe Sam or Glen."

"We already talked to their daddy," Virgil said. "With that family anything is possible, but they don't look good for it." He squinted and rubbed his head. "Anyone else likely to be upset about one of those communities moving in around here?"

Hadden shrugged. "Businessmen I've talked to aren't thrilled. There are concerns about what it might mean for a 'self-sustaining' community that doesn't need any of our local services to come barreling in." He gave a smug laugh. "But I've been saying it will take a while for those folks to become self-sustaining, and that puts local businesses in a fine position to meet their needs until then."

"And when they don't need you anymore?" Creed asked.

Hadden grinned. "Oh, I'd be surprised if that ever really happens. I'd say the idea is more than a little pie in the sky. And when it fails, the people who have been taken in by the idea will need all sorts of services. Which I'll be more than happy to help provide."

Virgil furrowed his brow. "So why then are you opposed to selling them your land?"

Hadden waved a dismissive hand. "Like I said, I'm not opposed to the idea, but I do intend to get a good value." He leaned toward Virgil. "Which is why I have no reason to kill Eddie Minks. I've been negotiating directly with his superiors." He furrowed his brow. "Although that does raise the question as to what the two of them were doing on my land—there really wasn't any need for them to be scouting it."

Virgil got a faraway look on his face and fell into a long silence. Creed finally cleared his throat. "I ought to be getting on home."

Virgil startled and looked around as though he'd forgotten he wasn't alone. "Right. Me too. Hadden, I'd just as soon you didn't leave the general area until we get this sorted out. We'll keep Otto in the temporary cell in my office—no need to involve the county jail at this point." He slapped his knees and stood. "We'll talk more later." Then he turned and walked away.

Creed watched him go, then turned to stare at Hadden. The other man shrugged, gulped the last of his coffee, and left as well. Creed shook his head. He was more confused than ever about who the murderer might be. For now, he'd go back to Delphy and Loyal and do some more pondering.

ten

Delphy was reading the same paragraph in her book for the third time when she finally heard Creed come through the kitchen door. She read the same words a fourth time—still not knowing what they said—as she waited for him to find her. He stepped into the room and slumped onto the sofa that had become his bed. Delphy stuck a finger in her novel and waited.

"Virgil planned to arrest Hadden, but doggone if Otto didn't show up claiming to have pulled the trigger."

"Otto? The German boy?"

"That's the one."

Delphy frowned. "I don't know much about him, but I would have said he wouldn't hurt a fly. Why in the world would he shoot someone?"

Creed blew out a breath and rubbed his neck. "I don't think he would. Neither does Virgil. Best guess is he's lying to protect Hadden."

"That would be quite a sacrifice." Delphy stuck a slip of paper in her book and laid it on a small piecrust table. "Guess

Otto feels like he owes Hadden for taking him in when no one else would."

"Not sure the debt's that big." Creed leaned forward and began unlacing his boots. Delphy started to rise to help him, then pressed herself back into her chair.

"Didn't Otto and your father have dealings when the boy first showed up?"

Creed froze. Delphy knew he didn't like to talk about Harold Raines, but she frankly didn't care right now. She'd always wished her husband would root out the pain his father inflicted—expose it to the light of day. So, tonight she'd push a little. What did she have to lose?

"He worked for Dad briefly when he first turned up in town." He tugged off one boot and then the other, lining them up at the edge of the sofa—as though for a quick getaway if need be.

"Why briefly?"

Creed flinched. He rubbed both hands over his face, then ran them through his hair making the perfectly groomed strands shoot out at odd angles. Delphy suppressed a smile. Creed always had been vain about his hair.

"Guess you never did hear that story," he said at last. Then, almost to himself, "Guess I never told it to anyone." He licked his lips and stared at the ceiling. "Otto rode the train into town. Kind of a hobo, I guess. He was looking for work, but nobody wanted to take on a German—not even one who was little more than a boy. Finally, Dad offered to let him cut and stack firewood. He did a good job, so we fed him and let him sleep out in the shed." Creed shuddered but didn't take his eyes off the ceiling. "It was cold that night. I assumed Dad would have given him some blankets, but when I went out to fetch him for breakfast, he'd made a nest of old feed sacks." He blew out a breath. "Even so, he was chipper and raring to go. Dad told him he could have breakfast as soon as he finished stacking everything he'd cut the day before." Creed finally lowered his gaze to meet Delphy's, and there was a hollowness behind his eyes. "It went on like that for a week or so. Dad kept giving him more work—harder work—constantly pushing him. God help me but I was just glad he was giving someone else a hard time for once. I suppose I piled on, too." Silence hung in the air, like a rain cloud ready to burst.

"What happened then?" Delphy almost whispered the words.

"He fell and broke his leg." Creed spoke the words simply, as if it were the only logical next thing to happen. "Dad had me help splint it up and insisted Otto could keep working." He laughed, but it sounded empty. "It was Hadden, of all people, who saw what Dad was doing and took Otto home with him. Said he wouldn't treat a mule like that, much less a man. Of course, Otto's leg never was right after that, so Hadden gave him the dogs to take care of. I think, at first, he did it just to spite Dad as much as anything else."

"Lucky for Otto," Delphy said.

"Yeah. Lucky."

"So maybe Otto *would* feel like he owed Hadden that much of a debt."

Creed stood and looked out the window without seeing. "Yeah. Wish there'd been somebody for me to owe." Then he turned and disappeared down the shadowy hall.

Father was there when Loyal woke in the morning. Mother made sweet rolls for breakfast with cinnamon and a sugary icing. Loyal ate three, which seemed to please both parents. They were talking quietly to each other, and Loyal kept forgetting to watch what they were saying. But the main thing was that they were all together.

He looked up as he washed down the last bite of roll with sweet milk. Mother was frowning but in a way that made it look like she was thinking rather than unhappy. "I'll need to stick around until everything's sorted out," Father said. He looked uncertain. "Will that be alright?"

Mother nibbled her roll and managed a smile. "Of course it will. I just . . ." She darted a look at Loyal. "It's easy to get used to something like that." She stood suddenly and began clearing the table. Father reached out and laid his hand over one of hers. "Delphy, I—" he stopped, looked from one to the other of them, and removed his hand—"I guess I'd better check in with Virgil this morning. Loyal, you want to come with me?"

Loyal leapt to his feet, nodding as hard as he could.

Mother opened her mouth, then pressed her lips into a tight line. Finally, she said, "Keep him safe."

Father winked and kissed her hard and fast on the mouth. She flushed and gave him a shove, but it looked like she meant it in fun. Loyal didn't know if it was watching his parents together or the notion of stepping into town with his father, but a sense of well-being washed over him, and he thought he could almost be glad something terrible had happened if it meant his family would be together like this.

"Come on then, son. Let's get out of here before your mother changes her mind." He winked again—at Loyal this time—and they headed for Main Street.

As they walked along, Loyal wrestled with what he should tell his father about the Westfall kids—as well as how he would tell it. He figured it was important that they'd been there that day and whatever Michael hid might be important, too. He was pretty sure he could find that old stump again. He was tempted to slip away and go there by himself to see what it was—Father would be easier to get away from than Mother. But something told him it would be wise to have someone with him. He was still pondering when they arrived at the sheriff's office.

"Virgil, you need me today? I figured that man from Washington could help you out and I was thinking of taking this boy fishing." Father pantomimed casting a rod and reeling the line back in. Loyal grinned as big as he could to let the men know he thought this was a fine idea.

The sheriff looked like he'd rubbed coal dust under his eyes, and his clothes were wrinkled. He gave them a weary smile. "Shoot, I might just throw in the towel and come with you. Mr. Mason has taken to bed with a bucket handy. I don't expect much help from him, which suits me fine."

He stood to pour himself a cup of fragrant coffee. "Want some?" he asked Father, who shook his head. Then the sheriff eyed Loyal and pointed at the coffeepot with raised eyebrows. Loyal felt a laugh bubble up inside but tamped it down since sometimes people looked at him funny when he made sounds. He smiled and shook his head no.

"Suit yourself," Virgil said. "Julia should be here soon with breakfast for me and Otto. I'd be grateful if you'd let me run a few things by you while I wait."

"Sure," Father said, settling into a chair and fishing his pipe out of a pocket. "We're in no hurry." He clamped the pipe between his teeth but didn't fill it. Loyal had the notion it helped him think. Maybe he should get a pipe for thinking, too.

"Had a long talk with Otto last night," Virgil said at last. Loyal kept his eyes pinned to the two men. He didn't want to miss a word. "There are too many things that don't add up." He rubbed both hands over his face, hiding any additional words.

Father shifted his pipe. "You mean other than the fact that it would take him all morning just to walk out there, much less walk back?"

"Yeah," Virgil said. "That's just the beginning. He said he tried to scare Eddie off and accidentally killed him. Now, let's ignore the fact that you'd have to be a pretty terrible shot—which Otto isn't—to aim over a man's head and shoot him in the chest. The harder question is why Eddie was shot *twice*." He held two fingers up.

Father took his pipe out of his mouth. "Maybe Otto's first shot hit Eddie in the arm, then the boy got scared and fired again?"

"Weak but plausible. The problem is, Otto didn't know Eddie had been shot twice. Came as a real surprise to him. Flustered him pretty good."

Father frowned. "I guess a fellow could be so rattled he'd shoot twice without realizing it."

"Maybe. Or maybe Otto didn't spend enough time thinking his story through before he turned up here to confess to something he didn't do." Sheriff White tapped an index finger against a stack of papers on his desk. "Plus, Bud went back out there and found a cartridge. It was .44 caliber, although just the one. Otto doesn't often carry a gun, but when he does it's a .22 rifle. Hadden, on the other hand, had been bragging about getting ahold of a Colt Peacemaker that fires that very caliber."

Father pulled out some tobacco and filled his pipe. "I'm getting the feeling you might have another kind of fishing in mind for me today."

The sheriff leaned back in his chair. "Maybe if you and the boy went out there to the Westfall place for a friendly visit, you could ask after that gun of his. He might be more willing to talk to someone who only used to wear a badge." He nodded at Loyal. "Your boy knows those kids of Hadden, doesn't he?"

Father looked at Loyal with his eyebrows raised, and Loyal realized he didn't really know the answer to the question. He wanted to explain that it was mostly Rebecca that he knew. Instead, he just nodded his head.

Virgil looked at Loyal with an expression of . . . what? Admiration maybe? "Reads lips real good, doesn't he?"

Father smiled, and this time Loyal felt certain that what he saw was pride. "He sure does. Smart as a whip." He reached out and squeezed Loyal's shoulder. "Knows how to read lips, and he can talk with his hands."

Virgil got a thoughtful look, but before he could say anything else, his wife, Julia, came through the door with a basket of food. And then Loyal and Father were out the door and on their way to the Westfall place.

Deep in his bones, Creed knew that Delphy would not approve of his taking Loyal along on this visit. And while he thought she was overprotective of Loyal, he wasn't altogether sure it was a good idea himself. Virgil had implied it would make the visit feel innocuous to have the boy along—as if they were just stopping by so the kids could get together. But he was going to ask about a gun, for Pete's sake, and Hadden was no fool. Creed glanced at the boy trotting along beside him. He was smart knowing two languages. Creed used to think hand-talking was just a way to show, word for word, what people were saying. Now he was beginning to realize it was a lot more nuanced than that. And what you did with your face was almost as important as what you did with your hands. He decided he'd learn more, but first they'd see to this business with Hadden. And hope to goodness Delphy didn't find out.

Though the Westfall place was nearly three miles outside of town, Loyal had no trouble keeping up. *Smart and strong*, Hadden thought. They followed the river for a ways before veering onto a road that led up a wide valley.

Creed noticed the sky hanging low and heavy up ahead. Curls of fog and cloud swathed the mountaintops and crept down through the trees as though coming to meet them. Loyal pointed and gave him a quizzical look. Creed shrugged. "Maybe it'll rain and cool us down," he said, earning a smile from the boy whose hair was stuck to his sweaty neck.

As they approached the Westfall place, Creed admired how Hadden had built his big brick home on a rise that gave him a good view of the river below, with a mountain behind the house to protect it. Which meant if Hadden was watching, he'd see them coming for a long time.

Loyal grabbed Creed's shirt and jerked. He pointed across the fields. A hawk had burst from the mountain mist and swooped down on something. There was a short struggle, and then the bird took to the air again, a snake dangling from its claws. Loyal made some excited gestures with his hands, and Creed wanted to understand but honestly he had no idea what the boy was trying to say. He wrinkled his brow and shook his head, then shrugged and held his hands up in an exaggerated way. Loyal began to laugh, and Creed flinched at the strange, overly loud sound. Loyal immediately stopped and looked at his shoes.

Creed reached down and tapped Loyal on the shoulder. "How do you say, 'I'm sorry'?"

Loyal slowly lifted a fist to his chest and circled it there. Creed imitated the motion, looking deep into his son's eyes. "You laugh all you want. I like to hear you laugh." A small smile eased the look of hurt in Loyal's eyes. Creed made the motion again. "I'm also sorry I don't understand what you're saying with your hands. I'd like to learn more." Now his son's eyes lit up. He pointed at himself, pinched his fingers together like a crawdad's claws, held them at his temples, and moved them toward Creed like he was taking information from his own head and putting it in Creed's.

Creed laughed. "Does that mean *teach*? You'll teach me?" He slapped Loyal on the back, and they covered the remaining distance to Hadden's front porch.

This was way better than fishing. Loyal wouldn't have thought it, but discovering a dead body—as awful as it had been— seemed to mean Father was going to be around a lot more. While he felt sorry for that poor man, he sure was glad to be going places with his father.

As they approached the house, Loyal saw Rebecca standing at an upstairs window. She gave a little wave before ducking behind the curtain. Mr. Westfall himself opened the door as they stepped up onto the wide porch with its fancy pillars. "Virgil not in the mood to come himself? It's not often you and I have the chance to socialize."

Loyal frowned. He might not be able to hear, but he could read the scorn rolling off the man standing in front of them. Father hooked his thumbs in his pockets and rocked back on his heels. He looked almost devilish with his grin and narrow mustache. "Is that how it's going to be? Well then, let's cut to the chase." He raised one hand and pointed at Mr. Westfall like a kid pretending to have a gun. "We're here to see that fancy Colt Peacemaker of yours." He mock-fired his finger pistol.

Mr. Westfall tensed all over. "My gun collection is none of your business. Virgil should have the courtesy to do his own dirty work."

Father held his hands up. "True enough. But if you show me the pistol, me and Loyal can get to fishing and you won't have to mess with Virgil today."

Acting put upon, Mr. Westfall opened the door wider and waved his arm as though ushering them inside. "Let's get this over with." He led them down a hall and must have said something because Father made a face.

Loyal looked up the grand staircase and saw Rebecca peeking down at him. She grinned and motioned for him to come up. Father was a few steps ahead by now, and Loyal supposed it would be all right to go to his friend since this was her house. Seeing the men turn into a room at the end of the hall, he scampered up the stairs.

Rebecca led him onto a sort of upstairs porch that overlooked a garden and barn, where the Westfalls' automobile was parked. There was an outside staircase leading up to a third floor or maybe the roof. They sat on the bottom step.

"Michael's acting strange," Rebecca began. "I'm worried about him."

Loyal signed *Strange how?* before he realized Rebecca wouldn't understand. But then she nodded, imitated the sign for *strange*, and kept talking. "He's always been kind of"—she scrunched up her mouth—"hard to get along with. But lately he hardly talks to me at all, and last night he said that if I ever told anyone about that day at the river . . ." She stopped and looked around. "Well, he said he'd make me sorry." She looked down and then met Loyal's eyes again. "He scared me."

Loyal noticed that she moved her hands in a way that was almost the sign for *scared*. He made the sign; she nodded her head and repeated it correctly this time. He looked at her and shaped the words *Do you know sign language?*

"Are you asking if I can talk like you do?"

Loyal felt his eyebrows shoot up. He nodded. She smiled and gave his shoulder a little push. "No, silly. It's just kind of obvious." Loyal shook his head. No one else seemed to think his hand movements were obvious, unless they'd learned sign language. Still, it was nice to be understood.

"Hey," Rebecca said, "want to see something?" He nodded. She reached in the pocket of her skirt and pulled out a little notebook with string tied around it. She undid the string and handed it to him. "I found it when we were running away that day. It was just lying there along the trail. I don't know why I stopped to pick it up, but it has some nice pictures in it."

Loyal thumbed through the book. There were tiny drawings of flowers and the river, one of a bird perched on a fence post. He guessed they were pretty good. Other pages had names and numbers written on them. Some of the names seemed kind of familiar . . . maybe people his parents knew?

Rebecca sat up straighter and glanced toward the door. She grabbed the book and scooted away from Loyal, which made him realize just how close they'd been sitting. And how sorry he was that she'd moved.

The door popped open, and Father stood there. "Loyal. We need to go." Loyal could feel the urgency. He jumped up and hurried after Father. They marched downstairs and left the house without seeing Mr. Westfall, although Loyal did see Michael standing at a window, watching them with narrowed eyes and clenched fists. As they strode away from the house, Loyal turned back and saw Rebecca at her window, waving at him. He waved back and hoped Michael wouldn't give her any more reasons to be scared.

eleven

Loyal watched Father's face as they hurried back to town. He was clearly upset, which made Loyal feel uneasy. What had the men talked about? Did it have anything to do with the gun they'd gone there to ask about? He knew he should tell about seeing Rebecca and Michael that day of the killing. The fact that Michael had threatened his sister weighed heavy on him. He couldn't see his way clear to do anything about it, but Father . . . well, maybe he could help. And while he still wasn't sure exactly what had happened, it must have been bad if Michael was that worried about Rebecca talking to anyone about it.

As they neared town, Father slowed. Loyal tugged at his shirt. His father stopped and looked at him like he'd forgotten they were together. "Sorry, son, am I walking too fast for you?"

Loyal shook his head. He lifted his hands but then wasn't sure how to proceed. How to make Father understand? He supposed he could try speaking, but it was much harder than signing and what if someone else heard? Maybe he should write everything down. Father's expectant look had shifted to something more like concern.

"What is it?" he asked.

Loyal shook his head in a *never mind* gesture. He'd write it all down when they got home. Father started to speak again, then snapped his mouth shut and glared over Loyal's shoulder. Turning to see who or what had drawn Father's attention, he saw a stranger staring at them. He jerked a thumb at Loyal. "That your boy?"

Father stepped forward, putting himself between Loyal and the man. Which also put his back to Loyal so he could no longer read his lips. He craned his neck, but Father held up an arm to keep him back. After a moment, the man spoke again. "He was there when you found the body, right?"

This time Father turned and bent down to look Loyal in the eye. "Go home. I'll see you there." Loyal frowned as hard as he knew how and shook his head. Father gripped his shoulder tight enough that it hurt. "Do it." Loyal considered refusing, but Father's expression changed his mind. He let his shoulders slump and headed toward home dragging his feet. He looked back once and saw Father jabbing the man in the chest. He hoped Mother could tell him who it was.

"You leave my son out of this." Creed hadn't much cared for Earl from the first time he laid eyes on him, and his interest in Loyal made him even less likable.

"He's a witness. He's in it whether you like it or not."

Creed lowered his voice. "The boy's deaf. He can't tell you anything. You may as well think of me as the one who found the body, because my son can't help you."

Earl curled his lip. "He must communicate some way. Is he simple?"

Creed balled his fists. "Smarter than you and me put together.

He talks with his hands." He started to add that Loyal could read lips but decided this fellow didn't need to know any more details.

"You understand that hand-talking?"

Creed swallowed hard and flexed his fingers. "Some of it." That was barely the truth—another thing Earl didn't need to know.

"So, I'll ask the questions and you translate for me."

"No."

"But I've got the right—"

Creed cut him off. "You been to talk to Virgil today? I'd assumed you were here because he got a confession." Earl paled, which was not what Creed expected.

"Who confessed?" The question was little more than a whisper.

"Let's go talk to Virgil. He can tell you." Creed took a few steps toward the sheriff's office, then paused. "Or not." Earl followed him like an obedient dog. Creed almost felt sorry for him. His partner had been murdered, and the man who confessed to the killing seemed unlikely to have actually done it. He didn't envy Earl's position.

Virgil looked like he'd just walked into the office himself, hat flung on his desk and sweat beading his forehead. And he didn't look happy to see Earl trailing in after Creed.

"Figured you'd turn up eventually," he said to Earl. "I made my report to your *superiors* just a little while ago. Word must travel fast."

"Creed told me somebody confessed." Creed flinched at the thunder in Virgil's eyes. He might have some explaining to do. "You have the murderer?" Earl asked.

"I have someone who says he's the murderer. The truth of that confession remains to be seen."

"What the devil does that mean?"

Virgil thumped into his chair, making the swivel mechanism

squeal. "Just what I said. Sometimes people lie when they say they didn't do something, and sometimes they lie when they say they did." He smiled tiredly. "And once in a blue moon, they tell the truth."

"Let me talk to him," Earl said.

Virgil barked a laugh. "That's not gonna happen."

"Well, why don't you believe him?" Earl was almost whining now.

"Creed, why did you bring this man here? To torment me?"

Creed grimaced. "Sorry, Virgil. He followed me like a hungry pup."

Virgil snorted. "After you gave him scraps from your plate." He turned to Earl. "Call your boss. He has my report to this point, and he can choose what to share with you. Or you can go by Mrs. Gibbs's boardinghouse and see if Fred Mason has rejoined the land of the living."

Earl looked like he was going to stomp his foot and throw a fit. "Who in tarnation is Fred Mason?"

"The federal investigator they sent down once you reported the shooting. Unfortunately, he's been sick as a dog since he got here and hasn't been much help." Under his breath Virgil added, "Or much hindrance."

Earl steeled his jaw, spun on his heel, and stormed out the door. Virgil glared at Creed. "I thought you were helping."

Creed sighed. "Sorry about that. He was set on questioning Loyal, and I had to distract him."

"Hunh. Wish you'd tried something else, but at least I managed to run him off." He gave Creed a dark look. "I sure hope you have some information for me to make this day worthwhile."

Creed blew out a breath and pulled up a chair. "As a matter of fact, I do."

Mother wasn't home. Loyal found a plate with some cookies under a cloth on the kitchen table, making him realize it had been a long time since breakfast. There was a note saying she was helping one of the neighbor ladies who'd just had a baby. He ate two oatmeal cookies, downed a glass of milk, and picked up a third cookie to munch as he wandered out into the backyard. The weather had finally cooled, and butterflies made Mother's zinnias look alive. Loyal guessed if he had to give up one of his senses, he was glad it wasn't his sight. He polished off his cookie. Or his taste.

Feeling bored, he had a notion to pull weeds in the vegetable patch out back but couldn't quite convince himself to do it. He wished Father would come home so he could teach him more signs. He brightened. Of course. He'd write down what he knew about Michael and Rebecca for Father.

He jogged back inside, found some paper, and went out on the back porch to get to work. He balanced a book on his knee, chewed the end of his pencil for a minute, and began writing. Loyal was so focused he didn't feel the flooring of the porch bounce under the weight of another person until Michael Westfall was looming behind him. He startled and dropped his pencil. Michael snatched the paper from Loyal. "You saw? You were there?"

Before Loyal could react, Michael grabbed a fistful of his shirt and jerked him to his feet. "Who have you told? Why are you writing this stuff down?"

Loyal shook his head and tried to free himself. Michael gave him a push. He stumbled backward and fell hard, banging his elbow. He frowned and scooted away from the older boy. Michael looked crazy. His eyes had red veins showing in them, and his hair stuck up in back like he hadn't combed it since he slept last. Plus, his shirttail was halfway untucked.

Michael snatched up the fallen pencil, turned the paper Loyal had been writing on over, and scrawled something there. He held the page up so Loyal could see. *Have you told anyone?*

Loyal shook his head.

Michael wrote some more. *Are you going to?*

That was a trickier question. He was planning to tell Father. But he was afraid of what Michael would do if he knew that. Loyal slowly stood. He looked Michael in the eyes and shook his head again. He wasn't going to *tell* Father. He was going to *show* him.

"Yes, you are!" Loyal was pretty sure Michael was shouting. "That's why you're writing it down." He looked at the paper, quickly reading it over. Loyal had gotten as far as seeing the two kids running but hadn't written down the part about seeing Michael hide something. Michael glared at him. "Where's the rest of it? How much else do you know?"

Loyal looked at him blankly. Michael began scribbling on the paper in his hand and finally held it up with *How much do you know?* scrawled across it. Loyal held his hand out, and Michael stared at it. Loyal mimed writing, so Michael handed him the pencil and shoved a fresh piece of paper toward him.

That's all, he wrote. *I saw you running away.*

Michael crumpled the page in his hand. "I don't believe you." Loyal just looked at him. Michael rolled his eyes and wrote *Who were you going to tell?*

Loyal considered, decided there was no harm in the truth, and wrote *Father* on his own page.

Michael began to pace back and forth, making it hard for Loyal to see what he was muttering. He saw *sheriff* and *trouble* and *Rebecca.* None of which comforted him. Finally, Michael glared at him and wrote *If you tell anyone, you'll be sorry.* He gave Loyal's shoulder a hard push and shook a fist in his face. Then he ripped the paper into shreds and sprinkled the pieces over Loyal's head before stomping away.

"Are you saying he couldn't show you the gun or that he wouldn't?" Virgil paced from desk to window like a bear Creed had once seen in a cage. He felt almost as sorry for Virgil as he had the bear.

"He tried to make out like he wouldn't, but when he opened that cabinet of his, he was sure enough surprised at whatever he saw there."

"Or didn't see," Virgil added. "Do you think he was acting? Trying to make you think he was surprised that the gun—which could be the one used to kill Eddie—was missing?"

Creed tried to ignore his growling belly. What he wouldn't give for a tomato sandwich about now. "It's possible that he was putting on a show. But if he was, it was the best show I've seen in a long time."

Virgil stopped and stared out the window. "Or maybe Otto did take the gun."

"That thought occurred to me, too. If it was Otto, he must've been out there waiting on Eddie. Maybe set up a meeting with him for some reason."

Virgil cursed. "Which would make this a premeditated shooting instead of an accidental one. Doggone it. None of this feels right."

"You think Otto was trying to do his boss some kind of favor?" Creed slouched in his chair as if relaxing might drain some of the tension radiating from the sheriff.

Virgil shook his head. "I don't know, but I'm going to do my best to track every move that boy made the day of the shooting." He slapped his hat on. "I was hoping to avoid putting Hadden on the defensive, but there's nothing else for it. I'm going to have to ask a lot of questions of a lot of people. And I'm starting with the Westfall family." He strode toward the door, then looked back at Creed. "I might need you tomorrow or the next day. You willing to hang around?"

Creed thought about Loyal. And then he thought about Delphy. "Don't guess I mind." Virgil nodded and left Creed to hunt up a late lunch—maybe one he could share with his son. Or his wife.

twelve

Loyal was as happy as a hog in mud. Father had been home for a week now. Though he claimed he was sticking around to lend Sheriff White a hand, he mostly spent his time around the house. They'd worked in the garden, and even though it was a task that fell pretty far down Loyal's list of favorite things to do, hoeing weeds with Father was all right. They'd also done little jobs like fixing a door that wouldn't open all the way because it scraped the floor. Now Loyal knew how to take a door off its hinges and shave the bottom with a plane. They'd even gone fishing, and Mother had fried the perch they caught to a golden brown. And Father learned some more signs. Loyal guessed he was about as happy as he'd ever been.

At least he was so long as he didn't think too much about Michael and Rebecca, and poor Otto who was still locked up. Loyal hadn't written another note for Father, not so much because he was worried about what Michael might do to him as because he was worried for Rebecca. He didn't want to bring her any more trouble. Still, when he let thoughts of the murder and Otto—who might not have done it—linger, the itch to tell his father what he knew grew stronger.

It was the first week of August when Father announced that he needed to go check on the cabin—to see if the critters had left anything in the garden and just to make sure everything was all right. Mother frowned.

"Now, don't get that look, Delphy. I'll be back for supper." He stroked his mustache and winked at her. "Might even bring you something special I tried growing this year."

Mother looked at him sideways. "It's been good having you here. I suppose you just reminded me that it's not a permanent situation."

Father puffed his cheeks. "Well, when the ginseng comes in, I'll sure enough have to go back up on the mountain." He glanced at Loyal. "But maybe I won't need to stay too awful long."

Loyal saw a light in his mother's eyes he'd never noticed before. Maybe it was because they were wet, like she was caught between crying and laughing. "I'll be praying that it's so," she said.

Can I go? Loyal signed.

Mother shook her head and spoke as she signed back. *No. I'm going over to help Mildred with her new baby, and I need you to clean out the root cellar.*

Loyal dropped his shoulders and threw his head back to exaggerate his exasperation. Cleaning the cellar when he could be up on the mountain. Father grinned and gave him a gentle punch on the shoulder. "At least it'll be cool down in the cellar." Loyal rolled his eyes.

The cellar dug into the hillside out back was cool. It was also full of empty jars that needed to be tucked into crates and hauled back to the kitchen, so Mother could wash them for her canning. And there were some potatoes that had clearly rotted. Loyal made a face. He might not be able to hear, but he sure could smell. He set to work, figuring that if he did a good job he might at least earn some praise from his parents.

It was on his fourth trip across the yard that he saw two strangers on the back porch. One was peering through the screen door. He stepped closer and saw that one of them was the man who'd talked to Father the day they came back from the Westfall place.

When the first man saw Loyal, he waved and signed *Are you Loyal?* Loyal was so astonished, he nearly dropped the crate. He set it down and stepped closer. He hesitated, then signed *Who are you?*

The first man smiled, signing *My name is Tom. Nice to meet you.* He pointed at the second man. *This is Earl.*

I'm Loyal. Then he froze. He had a dozen questions for this man who signed so smoothly. But he didn't know where to begin. The man seemed to sense his hesitation. *We're here about the man you found. Earl thought it would be easier for you to talk to me.*

Loyal frowned and made a rolling motion in front of his mouth with his index finger to ask if the man was hearing. He signed *yes*, patted his chest, and echoed the motion.

What do you want to know about the dead man? Loyal signed. Tom pointed to a bench on the back porch. *Can we sit?* Loyal guessed that would be okay. He shrugged and sat. Tom sat next to him, angled so he could sign more easily. Earl leaned against a post and watched. He made Loyal uneasy.

Tom launched into an explanation of how he'd been brought in to talk to Loyal as part of the investigation because it would be hard for the sheriff to ask him questions. Tom said it was important that they get Loyal's firsthand account of what he witnessed that day without any barriers to communication.

Loyal darted a glance toward Earl. *Who's he?* he asked.

The dead man was his friend. He's very concerned. Loyal felt a niggling doubt. Why hadn't the sheriff come? Wouldn't his father know about something like this?

Why isn't my father here? Or Sheriff White?

Tom smiled. *They're busy. But it's okay. I'm here, and Earl will be our witness.*

Loyal could see that Tom was speaking as he signed—for Earl's benefit, he supposed.

I think I should wait for Father, he signed.

Okay. We can talk about other things. Do you like to fish?

Loyal hesitated. It had been so long since he signed with anyone other than Mother. Soon he found himself telling Tom about fishing, his favorite subjects in school, how he wished they had a dog but maybe it was better they didn't since he was away so much of the time, though it would be nice for Mother to have company, too.

Tom signed fluidly, asking questions, watching Loyal's hands fly. Without meaning to, Loyal shared about Rebecca and how, even though she didn't sign, she seemed to understand much of what he wanted to say.

That's good, Tom signed. Then he got a sly look. *Is she pretty?*

Loyal felt his face flush and ducked his head. He shrugged and signed *I guess so*.

Tom winked. Then he looked serious. *Is she Hadden Westfall's daughter?*

Yes.

And it was their land where that man was killed. It must have been awful to find a dead body.

Without pausing Loyal agreed that it had been. *I'd never seen a dead person before.*

Tom signed *And he'd been shot. Terrible.*

Yes, he'd been shot twice. Loyal pointed to his own body to show the locations of the wounds. He gave an exaggerated shudder. *Rebecca saw the man, too.*

What else did you see? Who else? Tom signed, an urgency to his motions.

Loyal had forgotten Earl was there. In his mind he was back at the edge of the river on that hot July afternoon. Until this moment, he'd forgotten the smell of the blood. Now it came back to him sharp and unexpected. He had seen fat bottle flies buzzing around and landing on the dead man, their metallic blue-and-green bodies flashing in the sun. The man had been so pale, and his eyes were wide open. Loyal squeezed his own eyes shut as if that would block the images in his mind.

He raised his hands and signed *I saw—*

He didn't sense anyone approaching, just felt the boards of the porch shudder as Father ran toward them and grabbed a handful of Tom's shirt, yanking him to his feet. He didn't try to follow what anyone was saying but knew without a doubt they were all angry—Tom, Earl, but most of all, Father. He shrank back on the bench, hands clenched in his lap, and waited for the fury to die down.

After Tom and Earl scurried from the yard, Father knelt in front of Loyal. It was only then he realized his face was wet. He was crying. Father held his arms out, and Loyal crashed against his chest. He was afraid Father was angry with him for talking to those men, but more than that he was shaken by how vivid his memory of finding the dead man was. He'd been so focused on his parents, on the joy of having them both under one roof, that he'd pushed what he'd seen to some dark place where he didn't have to look at it. Tom, with his signing and his interest, had flung the door to that memory wide open. And now Loyal felt sick.

Father eased him back just far enough to look into his eyes. "Are you okay?" Loyal tried to nod, but the tears fell faster, and he thought he might throw up. Father drew him close again. He smelled like pipe tobacco and sweat. It helped to drive the memory of the smell of blood from Loyal's nostrils. Father patted his back and eased to a sitting position on the bench, pulling Loyal in tight beside him. It was too hot to sit like this. Loyal could feel sweat prickling his skin where they were pressed close. But he didn't care. The only thing that would be better is if Mother were pressed equally close on his other side.

Father reached down and tapped Loyal on the knee so that he looked up. "Those men aren't working with the sheriff. They were hoping you'd tell them something more than Virgil has." Father firmed the line of his mouth. "It makes me think Earl has something to hide." He eased away a notch. Loyal felt his face drying, even in the August humidity. "You don't have to talk to anyone you don't want to." He frowned. "Even if they can talk with their hands like you do."

Loyal gave a jerky nod, his neck hitching. He hadn't particularly wanted to tell Tom about the murder. It had just been so wonderful to sign with someone new. He felt tears starting to rise again but quickly pushed them back. He squared his shoulders and managed a small smile. Father slapped him gently on the back. "That's my boy. Now, what say you and me put some supper together and surprise your mother?"

This time Loyal managed a grin. That sounded like a fine idea.

She was later getting home than she'd hoped, but Mildred had been desperate over the way her baby would hardly nurse. Spending so much time by herself with Loyal at school and Creed up the mountain had left Delphy time to become, well, not a midwife exactly, but an expert on caring for infants. Seemed like there was always a new mother in need of her help for one thing or another. She'd longed for more children, but after what happened with Loyal . . . As she thought back on those days now, it occurred to her that the way Creed acted, it was almost as if he didn't trust himself to be a father ever again. She wondered if she could convince him otherwise.

She wiped the back of her sweaty neck with a handkerchief

as she hurried on, steering her thoughts toward home. Supper would be late—that was what she should be thinking about.

But when she stepped through the back door into the kitchen, she saw her husband and son at the stove with aprons tied around their middles. Creed turned toward her with a shy smile while Loyal beamed—although there was something in his eyes . . .

"Thought we'd go ahead and rustle up some grub," Creed said. "We fried up some cabbage along with taters and onions."

Delphy smiled and undid the top button of her blouse to let the air reach her neck. She saw Creed's gaze stray there and was surprised to feel a flush that had nothing to do with the day's heat. "Smells good," she said. "Just let me wash up."

She ruffled Loyal's hair and kept an eagle eye on him while keeping her tone light. Something wasn't sitting right with her boy. In the lavatory she peered at herself in the small glass. She looked tired and no wonder. Splashing water over her cheeks, she took her hair down and rewound it into tidy damp strands. Not that she cared how she looked. Oh, who was she trying to fool? No matter how frustrated she got with that man standing in her kitchen, she still hoped he thought her pretty. She gave herself a stern look in the mirror before returning to the kitchen.

"Now, before we sit down to this fine feast, I have a surprise!" Creed had one arm behind his back. He whipped it around with a flourish and showed them a melon with a dark green skin. He winked at Loyal and whacked the fruit with a butcher knife, splitting it open with a crack to expose its glistening red flesh. "Watermelon!"

Loyal clapped his hands, and they all dove in, enjoying the sweet fruit and getting their fingers and faces sticky. It was a delicious surprise, but Delphy could see that as much as Loyal was enjoying it, he was quieter than usual—more still. They ate supper, and Delphy praised her son and husband mightily for how delicious it was. Finally, she sent Loyal off to bathe and change into his pajamas. As soon as he left the room, she turned on Creed.

"Are you going to tell me what's going on?"

"How about I make us some coffee?" he said.

She pierced him with a look. "Talk while you do it."

Creed took a deep breath and began adding ground coffee to the percolator. "Earl—the partner of the fella that got killed—found someone who talks sign language. The two of them paid a visit here today and got Loyal to tell about the murder."

She stood from her chair at the kitchen table. "And you let them?"

"No, I did not. They showed up when he was here alone."

Tears sprang to her eyes. "If you think you're going to blame me for not being here, I don't want to hear it. You're hardly ever here and I was only gone—"

Creed stepped closer and put his hands on her shoulders. "I would never blame you. You're the best mother in the world to Loyal." His words were an unexpected balm. "I tend to think Earl would have found a way to talk to the boy alone regardless." He gently massaged her tense shoulders, and she felt the muscles ease. "At least I came along before too much damage was done."

She sank from beneath his hands, limp now, and collapsed back into her chair. "Damage? What kind of damage?"

Creed sat as well and took one of her hands in his, gently kneading her fingers and palm. She tried to stifle the delicious shiver that coursed through her body. "I think it brought that day back for him a little too clearly. He was pretty upset when I showed up." Creed sighed and laced his fingers through hers. "He was never really questioned by the sheriff. I let Virgil think I was the one who found the body—just never corrected him. I thought it would be better if Loyal didn't get pulled in too deep."

Delphy tried to sort through what she was feeling. Anger that those men had upset Loyal. Sadness that she hadn't been here to stop it. Delight to be sitting hand in hand with her husband. And desire for this man who was trying to take care of them . . . at last. She slipped her hand from his—finding it all too much at once. "Loyal can hold his own. He's smart and strong." She bit her lip. "He's had to be."

Now it was Creed's turn to read into her words. "And I haven't been around to protect him."

Delphy began folding and refolding a cloth napkin. "There's some truth to that." She gave a dry laugh. "Of course, I probably try to protect him too much." Thank goodness Creed had the sense to keep his peace. "Do you think Earl and the sign language interpreter will be back?" she asked.

Creed stroked his mustache. "Not here I don't think. But I wonder if they might try to get Virgil to really question Loyal. And if they get the federal boys involved, it might make Virgil look bad—him not having done it sooner." He stood and lit the stove under the percolator. The smell of sulfur and coffee perfumed the air. "What if I took him up on the mountain for a while?"

Delphy stiffened. Not this again. "What do you mean *take him up on the mountain?*"

Creed pulled mugs down from the cabinet, his back to her. "You know, spend some time up on Rich Mountain. We could do some fishing, pick the garden. Shoot, I could even teach him to hunt ginseng with me." He set the mugs on the counter and glanced at her, hope glowing in his eyes.

"Would he be safe?" Her voice sounded so small.

Creed stepped closer and knelt beside her. "Safer than here, I think. Safe as I know how to make him." She could see it cost him to admit that he couldn't absolutely guarantee their son's well-being. "I need to do better by him. I'm finally realizing that."

She turned her face away from him. "Why didn't you realize it sooner?" She didn't mean to chastise him but couldn't help herself. "We've needed you for so long, and now you're going to take Loyal away from me."

Creed reached up and tilted her face back toward him. "You could come, too," he whispered. She could see the longing in his eyes—the desire that matched her own. She began to lean into him, pulled by a force she'd felt since she first set eyes on him. Then she stood, making the chair jump and stutter against the floor.

"Take him. You're right. He'll be safer up on the mountain with you." She moved to leave the room, then spun around and looked at him as if she were offering a condemned man one last chance at redemption. "At least he'd better be." Then, tears in her eyes, she hurried up the stairs to the room that had belonged to her alone for a long time now.

thirteen

RICH MOUNTAIN

Loyal woke to the smell of bacon frying. Mother only made bacon on Saturdays, but this was a Wednesday in August. He grinned. He guessed Father liked bacon as much as he did. He scrambled up from the pallet Father had made for him in the corner of the cabin's bedroom. There were really just the two rooms—a main living area with a sofa, a table with two chairs, and the stove, and this room with Father's bed and a chest of drawers. There was a privy out back, and a shed that he had yet to investigate.

Having slept in his shirt and underwear, all he had to do was shimmy into his britches and he was ready to face the day. He hurried into the main room just as Father was cracking eggs into bacon fat in a big black skillet.

"Show me how you say 'good morning.'" Loyal smiled and showed Father the two-step sign. Father imitated it. "Like the sun rising," he said to describe the second part of the motion. Loyal signed yes, and they just stood there grinning at each other, until Father whirled back to the stove and scooped eggs out of the pan. As they ate, Loyal could have sworn everything tasted better up here in the cabin without Mother watching and fussing over him.

Father got his attention before speaking. "Wish we could just fish and play today, but I need to get after that garden. You want to help me or would you rather explore?"

Loyal realized he'd let his mouth fall open. Was Father offering to let him go off on his own? He stuck his index finger in the air and circled it with a question in his eyes. Father tilted his head and squinted his eyes. "Hang on." He went in his room and dug in the dresser, then came back with a pad of paper and a pencil. He handed them to Loyal, who wrote *Go alone?*

Father furrowed his brow, then nodded. "Guess your mother doesn't much let you do that." He rubbed a hand up the back of his neck, ruffling his short-cropped hair. "Still, you're welcome to poke around so long as you don't go too far or stay away too long." He gave Loyal a lopsided smile. "Although I'd sure enjoy your company while I work."

A feeling like getting exactly what he wanted for Christmas washed over Loyal. He made the sign for *stay*, and Father thumped him on the shoulder. "Good. Let's get some tools and see how much we can get done."

Creed was grateful Loyal hadn't taken him up on the offer to go poking around the mountain on his own. When he'd suggested it, he hadn't really thought the idea through. What if the boy got lost? He couldn't holler to call him back to the cabin. And he wouldn't be able to hear if an animal—or a person, for that matter—came up on him.

He'd never thought about it before, but there were quite a few clues he listened for in the course of a day on the mountain. It might be distant thunder or a rising wind alerting him to a change in weather. Or the sudden hush of birds telling him someone was coming. Loyal wouldn't be able to hear the howl of a coyote or the warning huff of a black bear. Shoot, there were rattlers up on the mountain as well, and the boy wouldn't have any notion of being warned off by a shimmying tail.

Creed felt sweat pop out on his brow, and it wasn't because the sun had climbed above the trees. The weight of the responsibility he'd taken on when he brought Loyal to the cabin with him was sinking in. Was this what he'd left Delphy to live with every day? Wondering and worrying and imagining ways their silent boy could get into trouble?

He watched Loyal hoeing his few rows of corn. The boy was completely focused on his work, oblivious to anything around him. If he couldn't see, smell, taste, or touch it, he wouldn't know it was there. Creed felt a familiar fear rise in him. He struggled against it, not wanting to remember, not wanting to give in. He squeezed his eyes shut and clenched his fists.

It was the same fear he'd felt when he brought this boy home so very sick from a spring gobbler hunting trip. It had been Loyal's fourth birthday, and Delphy insisted he was too young to tag along. But Creed was determined. If he was going to make something out of the boy, it wasn't too soon to start shaping him. He'd pushed Loyal, even when he seemed sluggish and listless. By the time they got home, he was running a high fever and was clearly ill. Delphy didn't fuss, just cared for the child, nursed him as only a mother could. The infection settled in his ears, and within the month Loyal had been stone deaf.

Delphy had taken it in stride and immediately started in on learning to talk with her hands and teaching Loyal to do the same. She found out about the West Virginia School for the Deaf and the Blind and made plans to send Loyal there as soon as he was old enough. Creed never felt like Delphy blamed him exactly—and yet he knew it was his fault. He'd pushed his son to please his own father, who wasn't even alive anymore. And so he let Delphy take over the raising of their boy lest he make a worse mistake.

That was when the fear began creeping in. Fear that he would damage Loyal even worse. That if they had another child, he'd make more mistakes. Creed had left his role as sheriff behind and spent more and more time up on the mountain. It was the only place he'd been able to escape the tide of terror that washed over him every time he tried to imagine what kind of life a boy who couldn't hear would have. Every time he thought about how thoughtlessly he had condemned his own son to such a life.

It had been years since he thought about the fear that made his ears buzz and the tips of his fingers tingle. But he was sure as shootin' feeling it now. He gulped a breath and opened his eyes when he felt a hand on his arm. It was Loyal, looking a question at him. He made a shape like the o for his name, then another like a pair of open scissors.

Creed swallowed past the dryness in his throat and placed his hands on his son's shoulders. "I'm okay," he said.

Light dawned in his son's face. It was like watching the sun touch the tip of a mountain and then slowly spread its life-giving warmth down into the valley. His son had known he was suffering. Without words, without a sound he'd *known*. And Creed had understood the boy's question in turn.

He felt the fear ebb. It didn't leave him completely, but he thought he could manage it now. He thought maybe it was worth the managing.

After working in the garden all morning, Father gave Loyal cold corn cakes and jam for his midday meal, then handed him a walking stick that was as tall as he was. "We'll check some of my ginseng patches this afternoon. It's cooler in the woods."

Loyal grinned. He'd seen the dried roots Father brought into town to sell, though he'd never actually seen one of the plants. Maybe he could learn to "hunt sang" as well as his father. Of course, Mother thought he should grow up to be a teacher, but

Loyal wasn't so sure about that. He sure liked it better out here on the mountain than he did in a classroom, or even their house in town. Maybe he was cut out to be a woodsman like Father.

Loyal soon learned that the walking stick wasn't just for fun. They headed into the deep woods, where trees towered over their heads and there was less undergrowth. It was also where the hills were impossibly steep. He needed the stick to save himself from sliding down the side of Rich Mountain where the leaf litter was deep and rocks jutted out as though the mountain were trying to keep them from passing. He also needed it to pull himself back up the mountain and to push through tangled laurel thickets. But there were gentler places too, where green ferns feathered against his legs and scarlet newts darted.

Father knelt beside a rotting log and waved Loyal over. He crouched beside his father and examined the plant growing there. At first he didn't think there was anything really special about it, but then he saw the crown of reddening berries growing where three stems supporting leaves met. It was kind of pretty, and yet he didn't see what the big deal was. Father tapped his shoulder and began to explain what they were looking at.

"This one is big enough to harvest since it has three prongs. They can have more, but they ought to be at least this big. While it's a little early yet, we'll go ahead and dig this one so you can see." He had a short stick with a pointed end stuck in his belt. He pulled it out and began working it into the soil in a big circle around the plant. He loosened the soil until he could work it with his fingers, pushing his hand in along the stem of the plant until he'd worked a fat, gnarled root loose. He brushed off the dirt and showed Loyal how it almost looked like a man with tapering arms and legs. "Over there in China, they think this will treat all kinds of troubles." Father shrugged. "Maybe it will."

Loyal reached for the root and held it in his hand. He looked at Father with a furrowed brow. He pointed at him, then the root.

"Are you asking if I've tried it?" Loyal nodded. "No, can't say as I have. Too valuable to waste, and I don't guess I put all that much stock in it being good for anything." Loyal nodded his head more slowly and handed the root back. He used to think there might be a cure for being deaf, but he guessed ginseng wouldn't be it. If it were, his parents would surely have tried it on him by now.

Father elbowed him and showed him how to crush the little red berries to free their seeds. Then he planted them back where he'd dug the root out. "It's important to plant the seeds so there'll be more plants in a few years." Loyal nodded to show he understood. "Think you can find one?"

Loyal nodded and began scanning the area. He was afraid he was going to fail, then spotted another plant—even bigger than the first—with that crown of berries. He pointed, and Father beamed at him.

"The Cherokee say these plants have minds of their own. Claim they only show themselves to people they favor. Guess you're favored." Loyal had to grin at that.

Father let him dig a second plant nearby and then said they'd check on a few more patches before heading home for supper. Dusk was settling by the time they returned to the cabin. Loyal noticed a light ahead, high in the trees as they walked along. He'd heard stories about a light on the mountain at night. Some said it was the spirit of an Indian maiden looking for her true love who had been murdered. Others said it was swamp gas or crazier things. He drew closer to Father, who didn't seem to notice the light. He hoped it was just moonlight, but whatever it was, it sent shivers down his spine.

At the house, Father sliced a loaf of bread Mother sent with them and laid slices of ham and big red tomatoes on top. Loyal thought he'd never tasted anything so delicious, even though he was as tired as he'd ever been. As soon as he'd eaten, he flopped down on his pallet and gazed out the window, grateful that he didn't see any strange lights in the trees. He guessed Father would send him to wash his face and brush his teeth, but maybe he'd close his eyes for just a minute first . . .

The boy fell onto his bedding and was asleep instantly. Creed guessed he wasn't used to working like this. Not that he'd shirked in the least. Loyal had toiled in the garden, hauled water, followed Creed across steep mountain trails, and had never given any indication that he'd rather be somewhere else. As a matter of fact, he'd done everything with such eagerness and passion that Creed found himself enjoying each task more than he ever had before. And the boy was a natural when it came to handling ginseng. Plus, it hadn't been too awful hot. There had always been a little bit of cloud cover just ahead of them wherever they went.

Creed whistled to himself as he filled a pipe and went out to sit on the porch as the moon climbed over Rich Mountain. He was beginning to seriously question if he'd done the right thing in spending so much time away from his family. He'd been so certain it was for the best—for him to provide for their needs from afar. Delphy inherited the house in town from her parents when she was a teenager. A descendant of one of the founding families of Randolph County, Creed had known she was too good for him, but his father approved, and he soon realized the dark-haired beauty was everything a man could want in a wife—in a friend.

And he'd provided for her well enough as sheriff. But Loyal's deafness took the wind out of his sails. He'd announced that he wouldn't run for reelection and began spending more and more time in the hunting cabin on Rich Mountain. Digging ginseng to sell had been the only smart decision he made. He had a knack for finding the valuable plant, and even with the economy taking a downturn there was still plenty of demand for the mysterious root. At least this way he was close if Delphy needed him.

But when was the last time she needed him?

Creed drew on his pipe, filling the air with a scent that always reminded him of autumn. He heard a whippoorwill call from the edge of the clearing. It was a lonesome sound, and he realized that he'd been lonesome for a long time. He guessed he hadn't noticed it until Loyal came along to show him how his life here could be different. He stood and took a step toward the edge of the porch. He suddenly wanted Delphy here, too. He wanted her here the way a husband wants his wife near when the joy of contentment needs to be expressed. Physically.

He felt like a fool. Had he thrown away his family? Was it too late to reclaim what he'd so readily given up? He remembered the day Loyal had been born. He'd held his son, who blinked up at him with the clearest blue eyes he'd ever seen. And then he'd looked at Delphy, and it was as though they were a single cord, woven together in love.

Turning, Creed went inside. He looked in on Loyal and drew the door between the two rooms mostly shut. He lit an oil lamp and pulled out the Bible his mother had left him when she died. He brushed through the pages until he found Ecclesiastes. There. He'd underlined it when Loyal was born.

"And if one prevail against him, two shall withstand him; and a threefold cord is not quickly broken."

Once upon a time, that verse in chapter four seemed like it had been written just for the three of them. How had he forgotten that? His eyes drifted to the verse preceding it, and he swallowed hard. *"Again, if two lie together, then they have heat: but how can one be warm alone?"*

He was tired of being alone, and while having Loyal here was a mighty fine start, he realized he would not be satisfied until he'd redeemed himself in the eyes of his wife.

fourteen

Morning dawned gray and wet. Creed made a simple breakfast and noted that Loyal was watching drops slide down the windows like he'd lost his last friend. Tapping him on the shoulder, he motioned for the boy to follow as he ducked out the back door.

They darted out to the shed with its boards weathered a silvery-gray. Creed flipped the wooden latch up and hustled inside, Loyal close on his heels. They both laughed as they shook off water. As he'd noted before, his son's laugh sounded too loud and out of tune, but he was expecting it this time and decided he liked hearing the boy make noise. He stood and watched as Loyal looked around the small room with its bench, open window, and sloping roof that kept out most of the rain. Loyal's eyes fairly sparkled as he looked a question at Creed.

"I'm no great craftsman, but I can knock together a table or a chair if I need to."

Loyal nodded, picked up a piece of wood, and turned it in his hands.

"Your mother's been wanting a pie safe. Thought it'd be a good project for a rainy day."

Loyal's face lit up. He made a thumbs-up sign with his right hand, planted the hand on the palm of his left, and moved both toward Creed with an expectant look.

Creed shook his head. "I'm not sure what that means. Can you say it? With your voice?"

Loyal's eyes widened and he wet his lips. His eyes darted around and settled on Creed. He wet his lips again and spoke in a low, rough voice. "Help you?" he said, making the sign again.

Creed nodded with all the enthusiasm he could muster. He imitated the sign. "Yes, I want you to help me." Loyal's answering smile was so bright, Creed thought they could probably work by it into the night. He wrapped an arm around the boy's shoulders and squeezed. Creed realized he was excited. Not only was he going to try to win his way back into his wife's good graces, he was going to do it with his son at his side.

Loyal figured life didn't get much better than this. The only thing missing was Mother, and once they gave her this cabinet they were making, he figured she'd be so pleased she'd want to be up here on the mountain with them. And maybe he wouldn't have to go back to school in the fall. Maybe instead he could learn to dig ginseng and make things to sell. He'd learned plenty from books, and now he wanted to learn what Father had to teach him.

The rain tapered off late that afternoon, with sunlight peeking through the clouds and making the wet trees sparkle green and gold. Father motioned toward the door, and they both stepped out into the clean air to stretch and walk around a bit after working at the bench most of the day. Loyal lifted his arms high into the air and felt as though he could take flight. He grinned at Father to share his joy, but Father was looking down the path beyond the cabin, squinting as if he was trying to make something out. Loyal turned and saw the sheriff approaching.

He liked the sheriff well enough, yet he wasn't sure he wanted anyone butting into his time with Father.

"Hey there, Creed." Virgil was close enough for Loyal to see what he was saying. The sheriff looked at him and nodded. "Loyal." He smiled, grateful to have been included.

"You're a long way from the office," Father said.

"Heard a rumor Earl brought an interpreter in to question your boy." The sheriff didn't look happy, which pleased Loyal. He wasn't happy about it either.

"Word does get around," Father answered.

Sheriff White stepped up onto the porch and sat on a bench. Father leaned against a post. Loyal sat on the steps so he could keep an eye on both men. The sheriff glanced at him.

"Guess I was thinking you and the boy found that body together." He waited, but Father didn't reply. "Did I get that wrong?"

"He came and got me as soon as he found it."

The sheriff's lips shaped a word Loyal knew he wasn't supposed to use. "Might've been nice to know that."

"Yeah, well, didn't seem all that important. The main thing was to let you know a man had been killed."

The sheriff twisted his body toward Loyal. "You read lips good, don't you?" Loyal nodded. "I need to know exactly what you saw that day." Loyal just stared at him, his eyes wide. The sheriff took off his hat and rubbed his head. "Creed, can you interpret what the boy says?"

"Not much."

"But his mother can. And that fella Earl brought in sure enough could. They're raising Cain. Say if I don't do a proper *interview*, they're going to sic the federal boys on me. Fred Mason finally gave it up and went home so his wife could nurse him. Now Earl's insisting Tom be present when I question the boy, so that nobody puts words in his mouth." He paused. "So to speak." He slapped his hat back on. "Not to mention the fact

Otto's trial has been moved up—supposed to start on Monday. Some folks are plenty happy to pin this killing on a German and be done with it. You've put me in a pickle here."

"Nobody's questioning Loyal." Although Loyal couldn't hear Father's words, it was like he could feel them. A rumble in his chest. It felt good.

Sheriff White stabbed a finger toward Father. "You don't get to have a say in this. I'll be questioning him, and I want you, Earl, and Tom there in the room with me when I do it. Probably bring Bud in too, since he's the only one who doesn't have a dog in this fight." The sheriff stood and shook his head, mournful, like a hound. "I'll expect you two in my office at ten a.m. tomorrow. Think you can manage that?"

Father looked like a thundercloud about to burst, but he gave a quick nod. "He can't tell you anything you don't already know."

"Good," the sheriff said. "Because if he can, we're all in a world of hurt."

That evening, Loyal could tell Father was drawn deep inside himself. He hadn't attempted to communicate at supper at all. Now they sat on either side of a kerosene lamp, Loyal punching holes in a piece of tin that would go in Mother's pie safe, Father smoking his pipe and staring at nothing Loyal could see.

Finally, Father knocked the ashes from his pipe, leaned close to Loyal, and looked deep into his eyes. "Virgil will ask you some hard questions in the morning. Is there anything I should know before then?"

Loyal swallowed past what felt like a rock in his throat. He'd been wanting to tell Father everything. He guessed now was the time. He nodded his head while making the sign for *yes*.

He saw Father take a breath and puff his cheeks out. "Hang on," he said. He fetched a pad of paper and handed it to Loyal.

Then he found a pencil and sharpened it with his penknife. He blew on the tip, then gave the pencil to Loyal. "Tell me."

Creed could've kicked himself. It was his fault he hadn't asked Loyal if there were any details he hadn't shared. He just assumed the boy would have told him anything important. But why would he? And how? It wasn't like Creed had made a point of communicating with the boy beyond a few basics. He'd been a fool, and Virgil had caught him out.

He watched his son furrow his brow in thought and then press the pencil to the pad. The scratching of lead against rough paper sounded too loud. How strange that Loyal couldn't hear that sound at all. After a minute, Loyal turned the pad so Creed could read it.

Michael and Rebecca were there.

Creed felt his eyebrows shoot into his hairline. Hadden Westfall's kids? Why would they have been there? He looked at Loyal. "When you found the dead man?"

Before. They were running away.

Oh, this was bad. Creed closed his eyes and tried to hide the emotions he imagined were scrawled across his face. Especially plain for someone as aware of body language as Loyal. "Do you know what they were doing?"

Loyal hesitated, then shrugged. He wrote, *Maybe, they saw and got scared.*

Creed smoothed his mustache while he pondered the situation. He could come up with several explanations for what the Westfall kids might've seen and why they hadn't come forward to tell. None of them were good. If they had seen their father—or Otto, for that matter—they'd definitely be afraid to tell, and for good reason.

"What else did you see?" he asked. The boy hesitated as though holding something back. Creed laid a hand on his shoulder. "You can tell me, no matter what." His stomach knotted. He really hadn't earned this level of trust with his son. Not yet.

Loyal worried his lower lip with his teeth, then plied his pencil once more. *Michael hid something in a tree.*

For the first time Creed understood what folks meant when they said their blood ran cold. What could the boy have hidden? Evidence? Virgil was going to be livid. If it was something important, then Creed had been complicit in keeping it from the authorities. "What was it?" he asked.

Loyal shrugged and wrote, *Too far away.*

"You think you could find it again?"

Loyal nodded this time. Creed wanted to go right then. Wanted to march down to the river and find out just how badly he'd messed up. But it was dark, so this would have to wait until morning. He prayed that it was nothing more than a girly magazine or a pack of cigarettes the kids had gotten ahold of. Maybe it didn't have anything to do with the murder and he was worrying himself over nothing. He forced a smile. "We'll go see if we can find it in the morning before we go into town." He squeezed Loyal's shoulder. "Now get some sleep. We'll head out right after first light."

Loyal let out a long breath, and his shoulders sagged. It occurred to Creed that the boy had been carrying the weight of what he knew around with him for a long time now. If nothing else, it was a good thing that the pair of them could bear the weight together of whatever was to come.

Loyal slept deeply and woke eager to try to find whatever it was Michael had hidden. It had been such a relief to tell Father the truth. And he hadn't been angry. Not one bit. Loyal smiled. Father would take care of everything. And if Michael or Rebecca had been involved with the shooting, Father would help them. He'd make sure everything came out all right.

After a cold breakfast, they set out for the river as the sun crept over the mountain. The morning was fresh and cooler after the previous day's rain. A fog rose up before them and didn't dissipate until they reached the trail along the river. Then, as the air cleared, they slowed so Loyal could keep an eye out for the right spot. But after an hour of walking back and forth, he still couldn't find the stump. And they were expected in town soon.

Loyal began to feel anxious. What if he couldn't find it again? What if Father thought he'd been making his story up? What if Michael had already come back for whatever he'd hidden? And maybe, worst of all, they found it and it was nothing? He wanted to find something that would impress Father, that would be important. He felt sweat break out and swiped his face with the back of his hand.

A weight settled on his shoulder, and he turned to look into Father's eyes. "Take your time, son. We can always come back if we need to."

Loyal inhaled deeply and let the air out. He nodded his head. Then he had an idea. He made the sign for *river*. Father seemed to catch on.

"You want to see if you can spot it from the water? Where you were that day?"

Loyal nodded eagerly. He hurried along the trail until he found the spot where he'd tugged dry clothes onto his wet body. Taking off his shoes and rolling up his pant legs, he waded out, picking his way over and around dark rocks. The water felt deliciously cold, but he focused on the task at hand. He had to find that stump. Turning, he scanned the river's edge, letting his eyes trace the route of the trail he knew was there. As he did, his memory unfurled, replaying what he'd seen that day. Movement. Then Michael . . . with Rebecca following behind. Michael was pressing her to hurry and . . . Wait. Loyal closed his eyes for a moment, watching the scene inside his head. There had been something else . . . some*one* else?

His eyes flew open, and when he saw the stump, he took an involuntary step forward, tripped, and plunged into the water. He came up sputtering and there was Father, slogging through the water in his shoes to help. Loyal laughed, and Father didn't flinch at the sound, just threw his own head back and laughed with him.

Then Loyal grinned and pointed, jabbing the air over and over, too excited to consider what else he'd just remembered. Father looked too and gave him an answering grin when he saw the stump that looked a heck of a lot like a bear sitting in the sun. They both made for the bank and picked their way through the scrub to stand beside the remains of a tree.

Creed had imagined twenty different reasons for the Westfall kids to hide something in a rotted-out stump. Laughing with his son over his wet shoes had been just the relief valve he needed. Now he thought he could handle whatever they found calmly. Shoot, they might not find anything. Michael could have retrieved whatever he stashed there by now. And if there wasn't any evidence, well, Virgil didn't need to know any of this. He took a deep breath and bent down to take a closer look.

And saw the barrel of a gun catch the light with a bawdy wink.

Loyal reached for it, but Creed caught his arm. He held up his other hand in a *wait* gesture. Should he go get Virgil to come see this for himself, or should he just fish it out and take the gun into town? Which option was worse? Because they were both bad. If he actually took a salary for being "deputized," Virgil would surely fire him for this.

Creed found a stick and stuck it through the trigger guard so he could lift the handgun from its resting place. Leaves and debris fell away, revealing a . . . Colt Peacemaker. Creed cursed before he could catch himself, and for the first time ever he was grateful Loyal couldn't hear him.

Turning to his son, Creed made sure the boy was reading his lips. "You're my witness, Loyal, to finding this gun here. He won't be pleased, but you'll have to tell Sheriff White you saw me fish this gun out of the stump and bring it to town."

Loyal paled, and his eyes widened. He shook his head vehemently, grunting the word "no" over and over. Creed had no idea what the problem could be. He touched Loyal's shoulder, but the boy jerked away. He patted his pockets as though looking for something, then grabbed his own stick and smoothed a spot in the dirt path. *No show sheriff*, he wrote.

"Loyal, we have to turn this evidence in to Virgil. It could be important to figuring out who killed that man. Otto goes on trial Monday morning—this could tell us whether he's guilty or not."

Loyal screeched in frustration, rubbed out his words, and wrote *TROUBLE*.

Creed nodded. "Sure, there's all kinds of trouble here. That's why we're going to turn this over to Virgil."

Loyal stomped his foot and reached for the gun, but Creed spun away before he could get it. "What are you doing?" he demanded. Bright tears stood in Loyal's eyes. He began signing so rapidly that Creed wouldn't have been able to keep up even if he knew more than a handful of signs. "Son, I don't understand."

The boy hung his head, then looked up with pained eyes. He curved the index finger on each hand and hooked them together, reversing the position repeatedly.

"I'm sorry, Loyal. I don't know why you don't want me to give this gun to the sheriff. Maybe you're afraid Michael and Rebecca will get into trouble." A tear broke free and trickled down the boy's cheek as he nodded his head. He made the sign with his hooked fingers some more.

Creed wanted to put his arm around his son, but he was afraid Loyal would try to grab the gun again. For just a moment he contemplated flinging it into the river. Then Loyal would be happy, and he wouldn't have to face Virgil. But no. He couldn't do that. One man's life had been taken and another's hung in the balance. "Loyal, they're not going to get into trouble. Shoot, they might be in danger even now with whatever they know. Virgil will look out for them." He turned and took a step toward town, then motioned for Loyal to follow. The boy came along as though headed for his own funeral.

fifteen

oyal fought tears with each step. He wouldn't break down and blubber like a baby. At least not yet. It wasn't just the fact that he'd probably gotten Michael and Rebecca into deep trouble. No, it was that he'd thought he could trust Father. He'd known whatever Michael had hidden might be bad, but he'd never guessed it would be a gun. And the way Father acted, it was probably the gun that had been used to shoot the man he'd found. And if Michael had hidden it, that meant . . . what? That he'd seen Otto shoot the gun? But why would Otto give the gun to Michael? Maybe Otto had dropped the gun, and Michael found it. But why then would he hide it? None of it made sense. And the way Rebecca had talked about what happened made him afraid . . . Well, what if Michael shot that man, and Otto was protecting him? That would explain a lot.

No matter which way he looked at it, he didn't see how Michael and Rebecca could stay out of trouble. Loyal's stomach heaved, and he nearly tripped over nothing. He felt like throwing up. More than anything he wanted Father to stop and puzzle this out before going to the sheriff. But Father was walking so fast, Loyal could barely keep up. Father acted like he didn't even remember Loyal was with him.

He considered falling behind so he could slip away to go warn Michael and Rebecca. Which would be awful. He'd have to tell them it was his fault they'd been found out. He kept trotting behind Father. He guessed it would be better if he tagged along to find out what the sheriff was going to do. He could always slip away later. Adults had a way of forgetting he was around—especially when something serious was happening.

Creed was relieved when he saw Virgil waiting for them outside the old courthouse building. He didn't want to have to give him the gun in front of anyone else. Virgil saw them coming and took a step their direction. Creed moved close, shielding the gun between them. "Can we talk somewhere private for a minute?"

"Based on what you've got hanging from that stick, I think that'd be best," Virgil said. He motioned toward the Odd Fellows Hall, and they stepped inside, Loyal trailing behind them like a starved puppy.

"Don't tell me that's the murder weapon," Virgil said as soon as the door was shut behind them.

"Can't say if it is or isn't." Creed deposited the ugly piece of hardware on a table. "Turns out Loyal did know one or two things he hadn't shared yet." He darted a look at his son, who glowered at him. "But it's my fault he didn't get a chance to tell anyone."

Virgil laced both hands over his bald head as though trying to keep it attached to his body. "I've got a roomful of people across the street waiting to hear from your boy. This right here is a whole lot more than any of us bargained for." He dropped his arms and sagged into a chair. "And durn if I want to discuss it in front of Earl or that feller he dragged in here to talk with his hands." He stared at a knot in one of the floorboards. "Alright.

I'm gonna go over there and tell them the boy's sick and the interview's being delayed until tomorrow. Here's hoping no one was looking out the window when you walked up." He stood and moved toward the door, then turned back to glare at Creed and Loyal. "You two don't move even an inch from this room. I'll be back shortly."

Once the sheriff was gone, Creed risked a look at Loyal. The boy's face was a thundercloud. He sat down on the floor where he stood and drew his knees up to his chest. He glared at Creed and then rested his forehead on his knees, dismissing his father as effectively as if he'd left the room. Creed sighed and sat in the chair Virgil had vacated. Maybe he should've just kept minding his business up there on the mountain. Getting tangled up with people was every bit as complicated as he'd remembered.

Creed pulled out his pocket watch. It had been a good twenty minutes since Virgil left them. Not long and at the same time forever. Creed guessed the sheriff was having a time convincing his audience that Loyal's questioning would have to wait. The boy hadn't moved since sitting down. Creed could almost imagine he was asleep, except that every line of his body exuded tension. He'd let Loyal down in some way he didn't quite understand. He wanted to touch him—to talk to him—but was afraid he'd make things worse. He wished Delphy were here except that she'd likely skin him alive.

Finally, the back door of the hall eased open and Virgil stepped inside. He looked like a man who'd just come from a henpecking. Creed halfway expected to see blood and bruises, but all he noted were the dark circles under Virgil's eyes and the slump of his shoulders.

The sheriff pulled out another chair and straddled it, bracing his arms across the back. He blew out a mighty gust of air. "I'd lock you up for obstruction of justice if I thought it'd help," he said at last. He glanced at Loyal. "But I guess I can understand what you've been thinking. Now tell me about that," he said, motioning toward the gun with his chin.

Creed licked his lips. "Loyal saw the Westfall kids hide it in an old stump along that trail beside the river." Virgil raised his eyebrows. "It was right before he found the body. Then he came and got me. He didn't tell me about . . . that"—he waved a hand at the gun—"until last night."

"I knew I should have hauled you two down here right away. Why didn't Loyal say or do anything before now?"

"I think he's worried about getting his friends into trouble. He didn't know what Michael hid. Didn't know it even mattered. Probably wouldn't have even remembered it if I hadn't asked him."

Virgil sighed and stood. "Well, we're going to ask him some more questions right now." He fished in his breast pocket and pulled out a pad of paper and a pencil. "He can write his answers for now. I should make you leave the room and get Bud in here, but I guess the boy ought to have a parent present. We're just going to do this informally, so I have an idea what direction to go next." He turned to Loyal, still sitting with head bowed. "Now get him on up here and let's talk."

Creed approached his son like he was sneaking up on a half-wild dog he hoped to tame. He crouched down and laid a hand on the boy's shoulder. Loyal jerked away from him without looking up. Creed started to speak, remembered it wouldn't do any good, and tried to hook a finger under his chin instead. Loyal spun away, turning his back and clamping his arms more tightly around his knees.

"Now, Loyal, we've got to do this." The words were mostly for Virgil and maybe a little bit for himself. He tried to pull the boy's arms away, but Loyal just grunted and folded in on himself like a turtle. Creed cast a helpless look at Virgil. "Seems he's not interested in talking to us."

Virgil took a step closer. "I don't care what he's interested in. This has gone on too long already. I need some answers, and he's going to give them to me. That trial starts in four days and this could change everything."

Creed felt a spurt of anger and frustration. "Give him time. This is rough on him. Let me take him to his mother, and you swing on by in an hour or so. I bet Delphy can help draw him out and she can translate, too."

"Doggone it, Creed. I've given you enough rope to hang your-self twice over. I'm not cutting you any more slack. Get that boy straightened out or I will."

Creed surged to his feet and stood nose to nose with Virgil. "The heck you will. He's my son and I'll handle him."

"You mean like you've been handling him?" Virgil's face turned red, and veins stood out on his forehead. "Like you've handled him all his life? Seems like you've been pretty hands-off up until the last month or so. I'm starting to think involving you in this business might be the worst idea I've ever had."

"You've got no right to comment on how I've fathered Loyal. That's between his mother and me. And if you don't want my help, I'll be glad to leave you to solve this murder on your own."

"Gonna run back up on the mountain and hide some more?" Virgil sneered. "Guess I'll have time to talk to the boy then, when you abandon him all over again."

Creed sucked air in through his nostrils, balled a fist, and drew back before he realized what he was about to do. He stepped back from Virgil, breathing as hard as if he'd run all the way into town. He shook out his hand like he was trying to sling something off. He spoke in a low voice. "Virgil, I've called you friend for a long time, but those are words I'd sooner expect to hear from an enemy."

The fire went out of Virgil's eyes, and he pinched the bridge of his nose. "I've got a hangover headache and haven't touched a drop. Between that and Earl hounding me about interviewing your boy, I'm feeling as ornery as a bee-stung bull." He shook his head, slow and easy. "I'm sorry, Creed. I've got no right to butt into your life like that." He sighed. "But I do need to talk to Loyal. You really think Delphy might could help us?"

Creed let the tension fall from his shoulders. "I'm sorry, too. I know I've made a mess of things, not telling you about Loyal finding the body on his own. I just didn't want him to end up in the middle of this mess. It's hard, wanting to keep him safe."

Virgil chuckled. "I guess most boys his age got a knack for getting into trouble. We sure did." He leaned around Creed to get a look at the boy. His face drained of color, and Creed turned to see what he was looking at.

Nothing.

Loyal was gone.

sixteen

Loyal stood at the back corner of the house trying to catch his breath. He was pretty sure Father and the sheriff hadn't seen him slip out and he hadn't passed anyone on the way here. All he needed was to grab a few things from his room. And fast. This would be the first place Father looked for him.

He climbed the porch trellis and slipped in through his open window. He laid a flannel shirt out on the bed and dug in his top dresser drawer. He came out with a partial box of matches, some twine he'd been using to practice tying different knots, a first-aid book his great-aunt had mailed him the Christmas before, a clean T-shirt, and a Baby Ruth bar he'd been saving. As an afterthought, he fished out Rebecca's hair comb and added it to the pile. Then he rolled it all up, tied the sleeves around the package, and used the extra sleeve length as a handle. He scurried back out the window and was on the ground in moments.

Heading through the trees behind the house, Loyal quickly made his way to the river, then followed it toward the Westfall house. It would be faster to take the road, but he'd surely be seen if he went that way. The only person he saw along the river was an old man fishing from the opposite bank. He ducked into the trees and was pretty sure he'd made it past without being seen.

When he finally saw the massive Westfall house on its knoll above the river, he was exhausted, scratched from doing battle with brambles, and hungry. He'd eaten some blackberries along the way, but they were doing little to keep his stomach from grumbling. He was tempted to eat his Baby Ruth but decided he should save it. Plus, he needed to hurry. He had to find Michael and Rebecca and get them to understand that they all needed to disappear before the sheriff came to arrest them for murder.

He looked all around before circling the house and approaching it from the rear. With Otto locked up in jail in Elkins, he hoped there wouldn't be anyone to see him from this angle. He made it to some kind of fancy squared-off bushes and was trying to figure out how to get inside when someone grabbed his shoulder and spun him around. It was Michael. His eyes were wild and filled with terror.

"What are you doing here? Are you spying on me?" Michael fisted Loyal's shirt in his hand and gave him a shake. "What do you know?" Loyal could tell Michael was screaming, which made him think his father must not be at home. Good.

Rebecca came running from the back door and pushed Michael away from Loyal. "Leave him alone."

"He's a spy. Although why they'd send someone who can't hear I don't know."

Rebecca shot Loyal a pleading look. "He's not a spy." Then she smiled. "He's my friend."

Michael sneered. "Th-py, th-py, th-py. You can't even say it right." He eyed Loyal. "Who sent you?"

Loyal frowned. He'd meant to add paper and a pencil to his supplies, but in his hurry he'd forgotten. Rebecca noticed the bundle in his hand. "Are you running away?" Loyal nodded. "Does it have something to do with the dead man?" Loyal nodded again, letting his urgency show on his face. Rebecca worried her lower lip. She looked at Michael. "Something must have happened. I think he's come to warn us."

Loyal grabbed Rebecca's arm and nodded some more. He was amazed by the way she understood him. It gave him the confidence he needed just then. He made sure they were both looking at him and held up his hand like a child shooting a pretend gun.

Michael furrowed his brow. "Yeah, yeah, he got shot. That's nothing new."

Rebecca's jaw tightened, and she looked into Loyal's eyes like she was reading something written there. She gasped softly. "Did they find the gun?"

Color drained from Michael's face as he took a step back. Loyal nodded slowly. Michael staggered to the side porch and thumped down on the step. "I knew I should have thrown it in the river." He buried his face in his hands. "I thought I'd need to put it back sometime in case Dad noticed it was gone." Then he looked up and glared at Loyal. "But your father came asking about it before I could do it. Now Dad knows the gun's missing. He asked me about it, and I told him I'd seen Otto messing around in his office, but I don't think he believed me."

Rebecca looked at Loyal. "Can they tell who shot the gun?"

Loyal shrugged. He didn't know how all that stuff worked, but as important as the gun seemed to be, he figured Father and the sheriff expected it to tell them something.

"But you wouldn't have come here if you didn't think we might be in trouble," Rebecca said. Loyal reached out and took her hand, gave it a little tug. "You think we should run away, too." He nodded.

Michael stood abruptly. "Hey. How's he know what you're saying?"

Rebecca rolled her eyes. "He can read lips."

Fire lit Michael's eyes. "So when we talked about that day on the river in front of him, he knew what I was saying?"

"Sure. So long as he could see you."

Michael loomed over Loyal, practically standing on tiptoe to make himself taller. "Which means he's probably the one who told on us."

Loyal shifted uneasily. What Michael was saying was a little too close to the truth. He was responsible for the sheriff getting that gun. Which was also why he wanted to help them get away.

Rebecca inserted herself between them once again, giving her brother a push that made him fall back. "He's come here to help us, not get us into trouble." She shot a look of understanding at Loyal. She probably guessed just how close to the truth Michael was and yet she was taking his side. A jolt of pleasure shot through him. She trusted him.

Turning to Loyal, Rebecca asked, "What should we do?"

He held up his pack and pointed toward the mountain.

She nodded. "We need to go hide out on the mountain until we can figure out what to do next," she said to Michael.

He sucked in his cheeks and looked toward Rich Mountain. He gave a curt nod. "Okay. But we'd better hurry." He looked at Loyal. "Folks'll be looking for you, won't they?" Loyal nodded. Michael jogged up the steps to the side door, then turned to face them, apparently deciding to take charge. "Only pack what you absolutely need. And get some food. Dad's in town, and Mrs. Tompkins will be having her afternoon lie-down. We'll meet back here"—he pointed at the steps—"in ten minutes." He glared at Loyal one more time. "And you'd better know what you're doing."

Delphy spent far too many afternoons alone. Once Loyal left for school and Creed disappeared up his mountain, she tended to have too much time on her hands. She'd found purpose helping new mothers, specializing in treating colic, teething, and other maladies common to infants. She'd also watched over many a babe while its mother enjoyed a few precious hours of uninterrupted rest.

But this afternoon she was actually enjoying some time to herself. Knowing Loyal was with his father filled her with . . . hope. She knew Creed's absence from the family had as much to do with his fear and guilt over Loyal's deafness as anything. Maybe if he grew brave enough to spend time alone with his son, he might grow brave enough to come home. She whispered a prayer that he would as she sliced and salted a ripe tomato and arranged it on a plate with cheese and crackers. She smiled. It was also a pleasure to have only herself to feed on this muggy afternoon.

Delphy was deep in her copy of *The Seven Dials Mystery* by Agatha Christie when Creed snuck up on her. She didn't suppose he meant to, but she was so absorbed she gave a little shriek when she realized he'd entered the room. She laughed until she saw the somber expression on his face. She stood abruptly. "What is it? Is something the matter with Loyal?" He cleared his throat and looked uneasy. "Creed? What's wrong?"

He licked his lower lip and sat down across from her. She sank back into her chair, as well. "Loyal been about this afternoon?" he asked.

Her brow furrowed. "No. Why would you ask me that? Isn't he with you?"

"He was. Until just a little bit ago. We were down at the Odd Fellows Hall, and he . . . went off on his own. Thought he might've come by here."

"Creed Raines, where is our son? You're supposed to be keeping him away from town. Keeping him safe." She could feel tears of frustration prickling her eyelids.

He inhaled deeply. "Virgil asked us to come into town so he could interview Loyal. Guess Earl made some pretty good points about how that really hadn't been done. At least not proper."

"Why wouldn't you tell me something like that? I need to

be there if someone's going to try to talk to Loyal. Who's going to interpret?"

Creed shifted like he was sitting on a jagged rock instead of a kitchen chair. "Virgil has someone who can do sign language."

She stood and wished her hands weren't shaking. "Not that man who came here and cornered Loyal?" Creed lowered his eyes and nodded. "What were you thinking? How could you?"

"We found the murder weapon, Delphy."

She dropped back into her chair. "Who did?"

"Loyal and me." Creed swallowed past a frog in his throat. "He saw more than he'd told anyone the day of the shooting. He saw the Westfall kids out there. Michael hid what might be the murder weapon along the river trail. And with Otto's trial starting on Monday . . ." He trailed off, letting the implication hang in the air.

Delphy squeezed her eyes shut. After a moment's silence, she ground out her words. "This is what you call keeping our son safe? Pulling him deeper and deeper into the worst thing that's happened in Beverly for as long as we've lived here?"

"I'm not pulling him in, Delphy. He *is* involved. I'm just trying to teach him to be a stand-up man. It's not right to hide the truth, and I'm afraid he's trying to protect the Westfall kids at the expense of Eddie Minks."

She slammed a hand down on the table with such force the lid on the sugar bowl bounced and fell. She hadn't realized she had such anger in her. "You've picked a fine time to step in and teach him how to be a *man*." She said the word like it dirtied her mouth. "Well, where is he, Creed? Where would a *man* who wanted to protect his friends go in this situation?"

Creed widened his eyes. "He'd protect his friends." He grabbed Delphy's hand and pulled it to his lips, kissing her fingers before she could jerk them away. "You're right. I haven't been a good father. But I'm going to be one." Then he rushed from the house.

Delphy watched him go, seething anger slowly dissipating in the stillness of the room. The backs of her fingers tingled where his mustache had tickled them. As she stared at the door her husband had disappeared through, replaying the cruelty of her words, it struck her that when Creed drifted from them she hadn't tried to stop him. She might have even thought her son was better off without his father pushing him to achieve. If Creed had failed to be a role model to his son, then maybe she had failed to let him.

seventeen

Michael was slowing them down. He'd insisted on bringing an oversized ax, along with a Boy Scout haversack containing who knew what. He'd fallen behind, and when Loyal risked a look back at him, he saw that the older boy was dragging the ax, sweat staining his shirt. It was a hot day, the hillside steep. Plus, they were pushing through the underbrush and thickets rather than taking the more obvious trails.

Rebecca and Loyal exchanged a look that spoke volumes between them. They waited for Michael to catch up.

"Are you sure you need that heavy ax?" Rebecca asked.

"What do you know about it?" Michael demanded. "Axes are important for all kinds of things. Chopping wood, building a shelter—shoot, we could even use it for protection if we had to." He drew up even with them and puffed his chest out. "Probably the most important thing we have out here in the wild." He sank to the ground beneath a huge tulip poplar. "Guess you guys needed a rest, huh?"

Loyal shrugged and sat down, as well. He figured even if

Father or the sheriff were looking for them, they had a good head start.

"Where are we going anyway?" Michael asked.

Loyal pointed up the mountain. Michael snorted. "That doesn't tell us anything. Do you even know where you're going?"

Loyal nodded, trying to look confident. He'd once heard Father talk about an old sheep pen near a mountain bald. Apparently there was a rock overhang, and back in the old days farmers had built a pen out of rocks and brush to create a shelter. Father had given him a rough idea of where it was, and ever since they started out, Loyal had noticed puffy clouds near the horizon that drew him on. He told himself he wasn't following the clouds exactly, yet it felt as if they were pointing him in the right direction.

"How much farther?" Michael asked.

Loyal shrugged and made the sign for *near*, holding his bent hands apart and moving them close together. Though he wasn't sure that the place was nearby, he figured it would keep Michael moving.

The older boy rolled his eyes. "What's that supposed to mean?"

Rebecca tilted her head. "I think he's saying we're getting close. Like his hands are getting close to each other." Loyal smiled and nodded.

Michael pursed his lips. "If it's close, maybe I'll just hide the ax here and come back for it later. You know, once we're sure about where we're going."

"Good idea," Rebecca answered quickly. She and Loyal exchanged a glance.

"Right, then," Michael said, standing and dusting off the seat of his pants. "Better keep moving." Loyal stood and set off in the direction he hoped would take them to their destination.

Creed lost precious time rounding Virgil up to drive out to the Westfall place. And when they got there, Roberta Tompkins, the cook and housekeeper, was the only one at home. They asked if she'd seen the kids. "Oh, they're about the place somewheres. They always turn up when it's time to eat."

"And Hadden?" asked Virgil.

"Due back anytime now." She squinted down the hill from the front porch. "Believe I see a dust cloud comin'. Probably him."

"Thank you, Mrs. Tompkins. Would you keep any eye out for Creed's boy, as well?" Virgil shifted his focus to the approaching automobile.

"The one what's deaf?" she asked. Creed bit down on a retort. She harrumphed and mumbled as she turned back to the house. "Seems like it'd be smart to keep that one to home." Creed clenched his hands and held his tongue.

They stood waiting as Hadden pulled up in front of the steps and climbed out of the car. "To what do I owe the pleasure," he said with a sneer that made clear his utter lack of pleasure in seeing them standing there.

"We're looking for Loyal and thought he might've come to see your young'uns," Virgil said.

"Why would he do that?" Hadden walked past the two men and stood with his hand on the screen door. Creed wondered how much Virgil would share.

The sheriff hooked his thumbs in his belt. "Any chance your boy might've *borrowed* that Colt Peacemaker of yours?"

Hadden's eyes narrowed. "You have a strange way of making conversation, Virgil. It's a generally accepted practice to stick with one topic until it's been exhausted. So, back to my original question, what would a deaf boy be doing with my children?"

Creed stepped forward. "That *deaf boy* is most likely trying to keep your kids out of trouble."

Virgil held up a hand and motioned for Creed to take a step back. "Hadden, this is official police business, and you can either answer my questions here on your front porch or we can go down to my office and talk there." He lowered his hand. "Shoot, we can go on up to the jail in Elkins if you want to get really serious about it."

"Are you suggesting that you're about to arrest me?" Hadden looked like he might burst into laughter. "It might be awkward having two men in custody for the same crime."

"Oh, I can probably come up with a different crime if I need to." Virgil sighed. "But I'd rather we just turn up those three kids and make sure they're safe."

"What makes you think they're not safe?" Hadden finally seemed to be taking the sheriff seriously.

"I can't tell you the whole of it, but there's some new evidence in Eddie Minks's shooting, and the kids are mixed up in it. Might be they're scared and think their best bet is to try and hide." Virgil nodded toward the house. "Roberta hasn't seen them, and I'm wondering if they might've lit out."

Creed wanted to grab Hadden by the lapels of his fancy coat and shake him until he realized that he was slowing them down. Keeping them from finding those kids. From finding Loyal.

Hadden frowned, slung open the door, and mounted the stairs. Virgil and Creed followed. Hadden entered what was clearly a boy's room—Michael's. He rummaged around a bit and turned. "His rucksack is gone. He took a fair amount of pride in that thing, claimed he was going to earn his way to Eagle Scout, but I never saw any evidence he was putting in the work." Hadden uttered an oath. "If it were just Michael, I'd leave him to learn a hard lesson on his own, but if Rebecca is with him . . ." He trailed off, running a hand through his hair.

And Loyal, thought Creed, trying not to envision all the ways his boy could come to a bad end.

The sheep pen failed to meet Loyal's expectations. And the expression on Rebecca's face told him she wasn't too sure about it either. Little more than a low rock overhang with rough stones scattered about, Loyal guessed it would be fine for sheep, but he wasn't sure he wanted to crawl up under there. The old pen was near a bald, which he supposed would have offered grazing for the sheep. And there was a stream below. While they wouldn't die of thirst, the hillside was steep. Scrambling up and down for water wasn't going to be easy.

He was surprised when Michael dropped his pack and smiled. "Time to make camp," he said. Was he actually pleased? He began unpacking his rucksack, extracting all sorts of items that drew Loyal as surely as the aroma of his mother's cinnamon rolls.

Michael knelt down and began arranging the items on the ground. There was an official Boy Scout mess kit, all the pans nested together with the handle latching them in place. Next came an equally official-looking first-aid kit. Then a canteen, a flashlight, and finally a compass.

Without consciously thinking about it, Loyal knelt beside Michael. He watched the older boy lay out each item with something like reverence. Loyal reached out and lifted the compass. It was cool and weighty in his hand. He watched the needle spin until it found North. He glanced up to see Michael watching him through narrowed eyes.

"Gather wood for the fire," Michael commanded. "And give me back my compass."

Loyal nodded, handing the treasure over. He scrambled to his feet and began gathering sticks and small branches. Michael started placing stones to create a fire ring. And he must have sent his sister to fill the canteen, since she was scrambling down the hillside with its strap slung over her shoulder.

As the sun dropped in the western sky, the three sat cross-legged around a cheery fire. Loyal's main contribution to the camp had been his matches, which Michael grudgingly admitted he hadn't thought to bring, although he assured them he could have used a flint just as easily. It was a small triumph. Rebecca had brought along crackers, cheese, some apples, and several potatoes. Michael commandeered the food and portioned it out, saying they needed to make it last until they could set traps to maybe catch some rabbits or go fishing.

He buried a potato in the edge of the fire to roast and, using his official Boy Scout knife, cut and handed out slices of cheese for each of them to add to the crackers. Michael said they'd have the apples for breakfast. They ate without conversation, taking swigs of cool water from the canteen. Loyal thought it was one of the finer meals he'd ever enjoyed. As they ate the last of the soft, floury potato, he pulled out his Baby Ruth candy bar and allowed Michael to cut it into thirds. He took the middle piece, which had less chocolate. The sweetness on his tongue was wonderful. Satisfied, he leaned back on his hands and watched the last streaks of red fade from the sky.

Soon Michael banked the fire and said they should all "get some shut-eye." Loyal could barely make out what he was saying in the flickering light of the fire. But it didn't matter. He didn't need anyone to suggest he get some sleep. The fear and excitement of the day had passed through him, leaving his spirit feeling wrung out. He folded his spare T-shirt to serve as a pillow and draped his flannel shirt over himself as he lay down near the fire. Michael and Rebecca shared his rucksack as their pillow, and she used the cloth she'd tied the food in as her blanket.

With the weariness of the day weighing down Loyal's eyelids, he smiled. He'd rescued his friends. People thought that he couldn't do much of anything just because he couldn't hear. But he'd done this. He'd led the Westfall kids out of danger. His last thought before sleep took him was that Father would be proud.

eighteen

The sun was setting in a blaze of reds and oranges by the time they'd concluded that Loyal and the Westfall kids were on the run. Creed was ready to head into the woods with a flashlight or lantern, but Virgil persuaded him to wait. It was a warm night with fine weather. "Sleeping out one night will do 'em good," Virgil said. "Make 'em feel like they've been on a real adventure."

While Creed agreed in theory, he doubted Delphy was going to be quite so easygoing. "Will you let Delphy know I'm going to spend the night at the cabin and get an early start at first light?" he asked Virgil.

The sheriff shot him a knowing look. "Not planning to brace the mama bear in her den? Yeah, I'll tell her." He gave a short bark of laughter. "And then you can tell that bunch expecting to interview your boy tomorrow."

After a fitful night, Creed headed back to Hadden's. He'd noted a trail of bent stems through the pasture beyond a barn the day before. It could have been an animal, but he felt pretty certain it was three kids headed up the mountain. He considered asking Hadden if he wanted to come too, but then decided against it. He'd move faster on his own.

Now he was deep in a laurel thicket. Disturbed leaf litter made him feel pretty sure the trio had come this way. But he was taller and broader than the kids, and sweat started running into his eyes. He paused, swiping at his forehead with a bandanna. The thicket lessened here where a poplar tree overshadowed it, pushing the laurels back with its presence. It was early yet and fog hung in the clearing, swirling like a thing alive.

Then he saw an ax. It leaned against the tree as though a woodcutter had set it down for a moment while he went for water. Creed looked all around. No evidence of anyone cutting wood. And he doubted the ax had been sitting there long—there wasn't even a hint of rust on the ax-head. Could a wayward boy have forgotten or abandoned it in his flight?

Leaving the tool, Creed pushed through the brush with re-newed vigor and the sense that he was close to finding his boy. After another thirty minutes of hot work and losing the trail once, Creed thought he heard a . . . laugh. He crept closer, not wanting to burst upon the kids and frighten them.

He circled wide and higher up the mountain, remembering there was a rock face up ahead where farmers used to pen their sheep. If he could get to the top of it, he'd have a decent view, and what he couldn't see he could likely hear. Easing out to the edge of the rock, he peered down through the leaves.

And there they were.

It was a pretty little camp. There was a well-built fire ring with a pile of sticks beside it. Looked like the kids had piled rocks and branches near the overhang so that it partially closed them in—offered some protection. There was even a mess kit stacked neatly by the fire, with what looked like blackberries in one of the tins. The kids were huddled together, and Michael was showing them how to tie knots with a piece of twine.

"This is a clove hitch," Michael explained. "If we needed to make a raft, we'd use it to lash poles together." He demonstrated, then handed the twine and a stick to Loyal. Creed felt a spurt of pride when his son got it on the first try. "Now you," Michael said to Rebecca. Loyal handed the materials over, and after a couple of tries, she got it, too. Then Loyal made a motion Creed couldn't see. Michael picked up a stick and scratched in the dirt. Loyal nodded as he made shapes with one hand. Creed shifted to see better and realized Loyal was spelling something. He saw an *l* and an *o* but didn't know the others. As the Westfall kids imitated Loyal's motions, Creed saw he was teaching them to spell c-l-o-v-e.

Slipping back from his perch, Creed sat against a tree. The kids were fine. He guessed Loyal had remembered his story about the sheep pen and they'd had sense enough to bring supplies with them. Could be Hadden was wrong about Michael not taking his Scout training seriously. One of the three knew how to make camp. And as much as Creed wished it were Loyal, he knew he hadn't taught him such and who else would have?

He eased forward and peered down at the kids again. Loyal was showing them more signs, and they were laughing. He'd never seen Loyal look so . . . free. He sighed. It was almost a shame to spoil their fun, but he guessed he'd better slip down there and . . .

Creed frowned. Why had he better? They were probably safer out here than in town. Earl and his interpreter couldn't give Loyal any trouble. And until they were sure who'd shot Eddie Minks and why, it might be better if the kids simply weren't around. The more he thought about it, the more it seemed like leaving the kids right where they were was the best plan. The trick would be making sure no one else found them in the meantime. Delphy, Virgil, Hadden—they would all want the kids brought in. He was going to have to be creative in keeping the searchers away from this part of the mountain.

Decision made, Creed melded into the trees and headed

for the trail he knew would lead him back to the river. With luck, he'd head off Virgil and be able to convince him to hunt elsewhere.

"Tell me again why you think the kids followed the river?" Virgil had driven out to the Westfall place with Bud. "Thought I saw some sort of trail out there back of the barn."

"I followed it. Must've been some deer. I saw a few hoof-prints that just sort of petered out in the woods." He pointed toward the river. "With that little girl along, I feel like they'd stick with the easier path along the river. Plus, it's cooler and they could get water. I don't think any of 'em know the mountain much."

Creed tried to relax as he watched Hadden stalk toward them. "Shouldn't there be more men? Don't tell me you three are the only ones planning to search for my children."

Virgil ran a weary hand over his head. "Yeah, we're getting more folks out to walk the river. Creed here's been looking up on the mountain and he's pretty confident they took the river trail."

Hadden crossed his arms and drummed fingers against his coat sleeve. A bright August day and the man was wearing a coat. "They couldn't have gotten far. It's not as if they have any wilderness skills."

"That's what I'm hoping," Virgil said. "Were you planning to come with us?"

Hadden pursed his lips. "Why wouldn't I?"

"Oh, I was thinking it might be good for you to stay here in case they come back this way. Maybe for food or just because they realize how foolish running away is."

Hadden looked suspicious, but he went along. "Fine. Keep me apprised of any new developments." Then he turned on his heel and returned to the house.

Virgil watched him go until he disappeared through a side

door. "Couldn't think of much worse than having him looking over our shoulders the whole time. Full of himself, ain't he?"

"Full of something," muttered Bud. The comment broke a tension Creed hadn't noticed until that moment. They all laughed a little and headed down to the river to meet the rest of the search party.

Was it wrong that he was having a really good time? Loyal popped some more berries in his mouth while they roasted the last two potatoes. Michael had rigged a fishing line and seemed confident they'd have fresh fish for breakfast. And even if they didn't, Rebecca was even now up on the bald picking apples. Those plus the berries and some chestnuts might not be meat and potatoes, but at least they wouldn't starve.

Loyal grinned. Not only did Rebecca understand him better than most, she and Michael were starting to learn sign language. While he'd never much liked Michael before, there was something about being out here in the woods that made him mind the older boy less. It was like he'd stopped trying to show off. Except now, for the first time, Loyal thought he had something to show off about. He really did know a lot about camping—he could fish, tie all kinds of knots, build a fire, make a shelter, and who knew what else? They were teaching each other, and for maybe the first time in his life Loyal felt like he fit in with hearing people.

Michael came over and settled beside Loyal. He hooked an arm around one knee and stared at the fire he'd let die down to little more than embers—just right for roasting potatoes and the handful of chestnuts he'd dropped at the edge of the fire ring.

"Guess Rebecca told you about that day by the river." He turned toward Loyal but didn't meet his eyes.

Loyal held up a hand and wobbled it back and forth to indicate *sort of*. Surprisingly, Michael understood.

"I shot that man," Michael said. His eyes landed on Loyal's briefly, then darted away. "Did you know that?"

Loyal shook his head no.

"I didn't mean to. Didn't want to. Rebecca and I went out there to shoot Dad's pistol. She didn't want to come, but I talked her into it." He turned his gaze to the dying fire. "Wish I'd listened to her now."

Loyal had to lean forward to see Michael's lips. He was less surprised by the fact that Michael had shot a man as by the fact that he was admitting it. He touched the boy's arm and, when he turned, made the sign for *why?*

"Are you asking me why I shot him?"

Loyal nodded, again surprised that Michael had understood.

"He was making fun of Rebecca." He made eye contact. "You know she talks funny, right?"

Loyal shrugged.

"Yeah, I guess it wouldn't matter to you. But people—especially other kids—give her a hard time about it." He lowered his head and must've said something more.

Loyal tapped him on the arm and pointed at his own mouth.

"Right. I said it seemed wrong that a grown-up would act like that. I got mad." He hung his head, then looked up. "The gun was in my hand, and next thing I knew I'd shot him." He shook his head. "I guess I shot him twice but I don't really remember."

Loyal supposed that sometimes it was just as well he didn't speak. He sure didn't know what he'd say if he did. Rebecca appeared with her skirt full of apples. She took in their serious expressions and came to join them after piling her bounty in the shade. "Whatcha talking about?" she asked.

"I told Loyal about the day at the river. How I shot that man." Loyal could see that Michael's eyes were wet, but at the same time he seemed . . . peaceful. Loyal was so used to him being sullen and angry, the change was startling.

"Do you think the sheriff knows?" Rebecca asked.

Loyal held his hands out, palms up, and seesawed them back and forth.

"Maybe, right?" She imitated the motion. "Except Otto said he did it. Which is a lie." She furrowed her brow. "Why would he do that?"

"He thought Dad was going to get blamed for it," Michael said. "You know he'd do anything for Dad."

Rebecca bit her lip. "So maybe we should just let him take the blame? I mean if he's willing . . ."

Michael chewed his lip. "Yeah," he said. "I guess that would be the smart thing to do."

Loyal remembered he still had Rebecca's comb. He pulled it from his small stack of belongings and pressed it into her hand.

"Where did you find it?" she asked. He made the sign for *dead man*. She furrowed her brow, then her face quickly cleared. "I lost it that day. You found it where the dead man was." Loyal nodded.

Michael took the comb from her and held it up to the light. "It's evidence, then. If the sheriff had found it, he'd know we were there." He handed it back to Rebecca without another word.

Loyal watched as different emotions played across the older boy's face. He was pretty sure letting Otto take the blame was wrong, and from what he could see in the set of Michael's jaw, his new friend might be thinking the same thing.

nineteen

Delphy was weary of being alone with her own thoughts. The notion that she might have played a role in Creed drifting out of her life—not to mention Loyal's—was weighing her down. She alternated between anger, sorrow, and frustration. She hadn't had this many emotions bottled up inside her since she'd been pregnant. And this time she wouldn't even have a babe to show for all the aggravation.

Unable to focus on chores, reading, or much of anything else, she jumped when she heard a sound at the front door. She rushed to fling it open and thought for half a moment that she'd conjured Creed Raines. But no, the worn-out-looking man with sagging shoulders and disheveled hair had brought himself to her door. Their door.

"Where is he?" She peered past Creed, hope fading as quickly as it had sprung up.

"Can I come in?" he asked.

Her jaw tightened. "It's your house, isn't it?"

"It was yours first." Well. That was true enough. He stepped inside and stood there, looking ill at ease. "Mind if I sit?" She didn't speak, just motioned toward the front room with its faded sofa and side chairs flanking the fireplace.

An unguarded look passed over his face. It might have been hope or a sweet memory, but he gave himself a shake and sat at the end of the sofa. "I want to tell you something, but you have to trust me." The words were not what she'd been expecting.

She moved closer but didn't sit, feeling too tense to relax. "Trust is a tender thing right now."

He nodded. "I know that. I'm trying to do what's best for our son and I'm hoping you'll go along with me."

She folded her hands under her chin and closed her eyes, wanting to give him the benefit of the doubt but fearing he would disappoint her again. "What if I don't agree with what you think is best?" She opened her eyes and bit her lip.

Creed rubbed his palms on his britches legs. "I guess you'll do what you think is best then." He looked deep into her eyes. "And I won't stop you."

She sank into one of the chairs. Maybe she could trust him. "I'm listening."

"I know where the kids are." She gasped and leaned forward, but he held up a hand. "I'm acting like I don't know. I'm keeping it from Virgil."

Her brow furrowed. "Why would you do that? Virgil's a good man. On the side of the law."

Creed nodded. "That's right. And he'd bring those kids in, because that's the right thing to do from the law's perspective." He drew in a deep breath as though it would give him the words he needed to convince her. "But I'm trying to do what's right from a father's perspective."

She dug her nails into her palms to keep from crying. These were the sorts of words she'd longed to hear from him. "A father is just what Loyal needs right now. I'm afraid I've . . ." Her voice faded away. How could she say what she'd been thinking?

Creed didn't press her. "It's what he's always needed. I'm

just sorry he's had to go—" Creed choked, then cleared his throat—"to go without."

Delphy steepled her fingers and pressed them to her lips, fighting for control. "Are you going to tell me where he is?"

"He's up on Rich Mountain with Hadden Westfall's kids. They're all tangled up in this shooting business." He shook his head. "I just can't help feeling like I need to figure this out before Virgil questions them."

"Are they safe?" She could feel her defenses falling and found she was relieved to let them.

Creed's lips quirked. "Hadden talks like that boy of his is no-account, but he's shown Loyal and his sister how to set up a pretty little camp." He laughed. "And our boy is teaching 'em how to talk with their hands. Shoot, I'd say they're better than safe." He reached for her hand. "They're enjoying themselves."

Delphy took in a great, shuddering breath and let it out, feeling a piece of her mother's heart yield. "It's no small thing for me, but I think, maybe, I can trust you in this." She laced her fingers with his, feeling daring as she did so. "Don't make me regret it."

Creed lifted her fingers to his lips and held them there. "I won't," he said. Then he drew her, slowly and surely, into his arms. And she went. Gladly.

The next morning, Creed rose early while Delphy slept on. Though she hadn't invited him to her bed, he'd seen a softening that made him think he had a chance to win his way back into her heart. This half-life they'd been living was no longer enough for him and he had the notion it wasn't enough for Delphy, either. He wanted his family back—in every possible way. And he figured the first step toward that was to put this murder behind them. Of course, to do that, they needed some answers. And he aimed to get them.

The cool of the morning let him make good time up the mountain to check on the kids. He approached stealthily. Michael was at the creek with several fish on a stringer. Creed shook his head. That boy's father had made some wrong assumptions about his son. Maybe that could be put to rights, too. Up the hill, Loyal and the girl still slumbered on either side of their now-cold campfire. He watched longer than he needed to, enjoying seeing his son so at ease in these woods he loved. Finally, the sun rising, he eased back down the mountain and set off for town at a lope.

Virgil was already in his office. "You ready to lead the search party?" he asked. "I need to get up to Elkins to see about Otto's trial. Might have to delay it until we find those kids."

Creed steeled himself. He was about to take a risk. Virgil was a good friend, but what he was going to ask . . . having been the sheriff, he knew he was putting Virgil in a tough spot. "What if I told you I know where the kids are?"

Virgil jerked his head up from the file folder he was sifting through. "I'd want to know why they aren't standing here beside you."

Creed's mouth felt as dry as plowed ground in August. "I might be reluctant for just anyone to know they'd been found."

"Just anyone like *who*? No. Wait. Like a particular fella who's been pushing us hard to interview your son?"

Creed nodded, unable to work up enough spit to speak. Virgil was either about to go along with him or about to arrest him and throw away the key.

The sheriff let out a long-suffering sigh. "You're worse than a woman to wear a man down." He tilted back in his chair until it groaned. "Tell me what you've cooked up."

The smell of fish cooking over an open fire woke Loyal. He stretched and rubbed his face. He was getting used to sleeping on the ground. His muscles didn't ache as much, and he'd slept without dreaming.

Michael squatted by a small fire. He had fish skewered on sticks stuck in the ground so that they leaned over the flames. Although he stared intently at their breakfast, Loyal had the notion the older boy was thinking of something else.

Rebecca stirred and stretched, finger-combing her hair and tying it back with a wilted ribbon. She smiled at him, and he suspected she was enjoying herself almost as much as he was. He glanced back at Michael and frowned. Something was troubling his new friend. He moved closer and, when Michael looked up, made the sign for *what?*

Michael shook his head. "I've been thinking." Rebecca joined them, exclaiming over the fish. Michael handed her one, and she peeled the skin back to nibble at its flaky flesh. Loyal took one and did the same. Even without salt, it was still really good.

What thinking? he signed, juggling his breakfast as he did so.

Michael moved away and sat on a rock. He didn't eat. "It's not right to let Otto take the blame for what I did."

Loyal nodded. He agreed, but he sure could understand why Michael wouldn't want to tell the truth.

"I'm thinking I should tell Sheriff White what happened."

Rebecca must have cried out, because Michael went to her and patted her like he wasn't used to doing it. "It'll be alright," he said. "I'm just a kid so probably they'll go easy on me. Plus, it was an accident." He pulled his shoulders back and stuck out his chin. "Maybe I'll only have to serve a little bit of time in jail."

Tears ran down Rebecca's face and she abandoned her breakfast. "But you don't have to," she said.

Michael bowed his head, then looked up again. "I think maybe I do. I've been trying so hard to keep anyone from finding out. But now that Loyal knows, it's kind of a relief." He rubbed at a mosquito bite on his arm. "I've been feeling rotten.

And Dad thinks I'm useless anyway. At least Otto's good for something around the house."

Rebecca protested some more, but Loyal wasn't paying close attention. He'd long thought Michael was a jerk. But out here in the woods he'd become someone different—someone he liked. And when he really thought about it, he guessed Michael was doing the right thing. He stood, drawing the attention of the other two, and made a fist with his right hand, his thumb sticking out. He pointed the thumb toward his belly and drew it up to his chest. As he did so, he wet his lips and spoke the word "proud." Then he pointed at Michael.

If he didn't know better, he'd have said the older boy looked like he was about to cry.

By midmorning, Bud was leading a handful of searchers down the river they'd searched up the day before while Virgil and Creed were on their way to Elkins. Earl was staying in a boardinghouse there, and Creed had some questions for him.

"You sure it's a good idea for you to do this on your own?" Virgil asked for the third time. "Might be better if any questions were what you'd call official."

"Earl waves that word *official* around like a cattle prod." Creed smoothed his mustache. "I'm thinking it's time to have a regular old man-to-man conversation."

Virgil gripped the steering wheel with both hands. "You gonna get me into trouble with this? And by trouble I mean worse than I'm already in?"

Creed felt sweat prickle under his arms. Truth be told, he wasn't all that sure about his plan. He just knew he needed to extricate his son from this mess and he was willing to try just about anything to do it. "My plan is to get us all *out* of trouble."

Virgil grunted. "We all know what the road to hell is paved with. Just try not to build too many more miles." He pulled in at the county courthouse in Elkins, saluted Creed with two fingers to his forehead, and went inside. Creed understood that sign well enough—it said *You're on your own now.*

Well and good.

Creed ambled down the street, considering what he knew. Eddie Minks had been shot twice while scouting for a government homestead project. Hadden Westfall might or might not have been willing to sell his land for the new community, which meant he might or might not have had a reason to shoot Eddie. The fact that he'd lied about his alibi sure didn't look good. Otto, on the other hand, had confessed, except his motive and ability to commit the murder stretched credulity. And then there were Michael and Rebecca who had surely been at the scene that day and had ended up with the gun that was likely the murder weapon—but how?

Creed kept circling back to the same notion. If he wanted to know who shot Eddie, he needed to come up with a good reason why someone wanted him dead. And Earl seemed the likeliest candidate to point him in the right direction.

Swinging up onto the porch of the boardinghouse, Creed lifted a hand to knock. But before his knuckles hit the wood, the door jerked open. A woman stood there, eyes wild and hair coming loose from its twist. "Who're you?" she blurted.

"Creed Raines. Up from Beverly to see Earl Westin."

She pushed out onto the porch and eased the door shut behind her. "Do you know anything about what happened to Eddie?"

Creed wet his lips. Who was this woman? "That's what I came to talk to Earl about."

She took his arm and turned him down the steps. "Come with me," she said. Although mystified, Creed had the sense this woman might be someone he should talk to. She led him several houses down and then turned onto a side street adjacent to a small park. She plopped down on a bench, looking back the way they'd come.

"Sorry son of a gun won't tell me anything." Tears stood in her eyes. "Me and Eddie was getting married soon as he'd earned enough to set us up. I came down from Pittsburgh to see Eddie got buried proper." She dashed away a tear that had escaped. "And to claim what's mine. Eddie said everything he had was mine as much as his—just needed a marriage license to prove it to the world." She laid a hand across her stomach, and Creed realized it was rounded more than might be expected. "But that ornery cuss Earl says I've got no claim and should leave him alone." She turned deep blue eyes on Creed. "What happened? Who killed my man? The way he's acting, I'd almost think Earl done it."

Creed debated what to say. "Well, the sheriff's investigating Eddie's death as a murder, and there's a fella who's confessed to doing it." She put a hand to her mouth, eyes wide. "He says he thought Eddie was trespassing on his boss's land and was just trying to scare him off."

"Why wouldn't Earl tell me that? He acted like it was all a big secret."

Creed shrugged. "Most folks know that much. The fella's trial is supposed to start on Monday."

Her eyes took on a steely shine. "You say that like there's more to know."

"Maybe. Hey, can you tell me how long Eddie's been working for the government?"

"'Bout two and a half years. But he just started this scouting business when Earl talked him into it. He had a nice comfortable office job before." She rubbed along the side of her belly as though something ached there. Creed remembered Delphy doing the same thing when she was pregnant with Loyal. He felt a pang for this woman and her grief. "Eddie said the job paid a whole lot better and we could get married that much sooner." She sighed. "And I believed him when he said we'd be wed by now." She ran a hand over her belly again, sorrow cutting lines at the corners of her mouth.

"Don't guess I ever thought about government jobs paying all that well," he said. "Steady work, sure, but not the sort of thing that'd make you rich."

"Yeah, me neither. But Earl, he flashed money around and got Eddie excited about it. They used to meet up of an evening and 'make plans' as Earl called it. Never did understand why they couldn't do that on regular work time. Took Eddie away from me many an evening."

The combination of easy money and off-the-clock planning made Creed think he might have hit on something important. He just wasn't sure what it was. "Can you think of anyone who would've wanted Eddie dead?"

"No," she said, tears rising again. "He might've aggravated somebody now and again. He had a wicked tongue when he let it get the best of him or when he'd been drinking. But I don't think he ever made anybody *that* mad." She gripped Creed's arm. "Do you think he suffered?"

Creed pictured the hole in the man's chest. "No. I think it was quick."

She nodded and released his arm. "Why'd you want to talk to Earl anyhow? You the police? You think he knows something important?"

"I've been giving the sheriff a hand, but I'm not the police." He patted her arm. "We're going to figure out who did this and why."

"Can I have Eddie's things?"

"What things? Do you mean his suitcase from the boarding-house?" As far as Creed knew, Virgil still had the small bag with its toiletry kit and a change of clothes. Maybe it was sentimental to this woman.

"I mean his gold watch that belonged to his daddy and that little notebook he carried around." The ghost of a smile softened the lines in her face. "He mostly used it for work, but he did these little sketches for me sometimes—flowers, animals, things he saw when he was out looking for property. He could draw the purtiest pictures."

"I, well, I guess I can let the sheriff know you'd like to have them. Say, what's your name?"

"Christine Mankin." She shook her head. "Wasn't going to be hard to switch from Mankin to Minks. Now . . . well, I don't know what I'll do."

"I'm real sorry for your loss," Creed said. "I'd best be getting back, though. The sheriff will wonder what happened to me."

She nodded and shrank back against the bench. "You go on then. I'll leave my forwarding address at the boardinghouse when I go. The lady what runs it let me use Eddie's room since he'd paid in advance, but that runs out on Monday."

Creed felt like there should be something more for him to do for this woman, but he couldn't think what. He stood and took a step away, then turned back. "We'll find who did it."

"I hope you do," she said. "'Course my knowing won't put food on the table."

Creed bit his lip and headed back the way they'd come. He guessed there were harder things than having a son who couldn't hear.

twenty

Creed didn't go back to the boardinghouse. Instead, he went to the courthouse. He wanted to hash out what he'd learned with Virgil. But the sheriff was in a deposition, and the petite woman with bobbed hair at the desk said he couldn't be disturbed. But she said it with a warm smile and a look that made Creed feel warmer than even the August afternoon suggested. He settled himself on one of the ugly chairs and mulled over what Christine had told him.

"Say, maybe you could help me—" he glanced at the little nameplate on the woman's desk—"Mrs. Wilkins." She looked up from her typing and raised her eyebrows. "Do you happen to know what kind of pay somebody scouting for one of those homestead projects might expect to get?"

She looked at him through her eyelashes and smiled. Rolling her chair back, she stood and walked with small, precise steps to a filing cabinet in the corner. "It just so happens I have a federal pay scale in my files." She ruffled through some folders and plucked one out. She flipped the folder open, licked a finger, and ran through pages until she came to the right one. Then she minced over to where he sat and perched on the chair beside him. She leaned forward farther than seemed necessary—especially considering the cut of her blouse—and held the folder open to a neatly printed page. Her arm brushed his as she ran a painted nail down the column of numbers. "There you go," she said. "That would be in the vicinity of starting pay for a position like that."

Creed read the figure. It was decent pay, but Eddie must have been making peanuts before to think this was a big increase. "Guess it pays better than a desk job," he said.

She laid cool fingers across his wrist. "I suppose if you were entry level it would. Someone with tenure, though, could certainly make more." She ran her nails along his arm like a splash of unexpectedly cold water. He forced himself not to recoil. "Are you looking for employment?" The way she said the word made him think she meant something other than government work.

A door opened and voices burst into the room. Creed stood like he'd been scalded and took a step away. Mrs. Wilkins snapped her folder shut, returned it to the file cabinet, and resumed her seat.

Then Virgil was standing in front of Creed with a look like he wanted to bust out laughing. "You done *investigating*?" he drawled.

"Sure enough," Creed said with a croak. He cleared his throat. "Picked up some interesting tidbits."

"So I see." Virgil turned back to the other man and shook his hand, saying he'd see him soon.

Stepping out into the August sunlight made Creed feel as though he'd come up for air even with the heat and humidity.

Virgil chuckled. "She's a doozy, ain't she?"

"Who?"

"Mrs. Wilkins. 'Course nobody's ever known of a Mr. Wilkins, but I guess it keeps her respectable."

"I'm not talking about her," snapped Creed.

"Sure enough. You two didn't seem to hardly be *talking* at all."

"Aw, cut it out, Virgil. I think I might've found out something important."

Virgil sobered and appeared ready to listen. "You talk to Earl, then?"

"No, I ran into somebody way more interesting." He looked around and drew Virgil into the shade of a nearby building. "Eddie was getting married. His girl's in town and she's . . . well, she's going to have a tough time without a man to help take care of her and the little one on the way." Virgil let out a low whistle. "She was hoping to get ahold of Eddie's personal effects—she mentioned a watch and a notebook."

Virgil nodded. "He had a watch on him. It's back in my office. Can't give it to her until after the trial, but if no one else claims it I don't see why she couldn't have it." He swiped at the back of his neck with a handkerchief. "As for a notebook . . . I don't know anything about that. We packed up the contents of his room—which wasn't much—and I didn't see any notebook. Why'd she want it?"

"She said he used it for work mostly but that he also drew pictures in it—drawings of flowers and such. I guess she's sentimental about the pictures." He shrugged. "Maybe Earl will have it."

"Maybe." Virgil stared at the ground like he was trying to puzzle something out. Then he looked up at Creed. "Anything else?"

"She said Eddie took the homestead job because he was supposed to be piling up money for them to get married on." He made a face. "That's what Mrs. Wilkins was showing me—a federal pay scale. Unless she's way off, the amount Eddie was making wasn't all that impressive."

Virgil nodded, looking thoughtful. "Are you suggesting Eddie was piling up money some other way—under the table maybe?"

Creed tried not to get too excited. "If he was doing something shady, that might be a reason for him to get killed."

Virgil pursed his lips. "Could be. Or he could've been string-ing that poor woman along."

Creed felt like Virgil was letting the air out of his tires. "Yeah. I guess so. But seems like it's worth looking into."

With a sigh, Virgil started walking back to the street and turned right. "You sure do have a knack for making more work for me."

"Nobody can say we don't need you around with all this work to do." Creed grinned. "I'm just making sure you stay employed."

Virgil rolled his eyes. "Wish I could say thanks, but until we round up Earl and nail some of this information down, I'm going to withhold my appreciation."

"We going to talk to him now?"

"No time like the present." Virgil shot him a dark look. "But let me do the talking." Creed made a motion like turning a key at his lips and smiled.

Loyal and Rebecca persuaded Michael to wait until eve-ning to turn himself in. He'd promised to show them how to use the compass he had in his pack. The plan was to use it to find Father's cabin. And if Father was there, he could take Michael into custody. If he wasn't, they'd just walk on into town and go directly to the sheriff. Michael wasn't hard to convince—he seemed relieved by the idea of telling Creed what he'd done before he told the sheriff. Loyal could see how his father would be easier to talk to than someone wearing a uniform and a badge.

Michael explained how the compass worked, made what he figured was a good estimate of the direction they needed to go to find the cabin, and the trio set out. They took turns carrying the compass. Loyal liked the feel of the cool metal against his palm. It fit nicely and it was fun to try to keep the needle pointed in the right direction. He was so focused on the dial that he didn't realize Michael and Rebecca had stopped. He turned when he realized they weren't keeping up and froze.

Two men with untrimmed hair and stubbly chins stood on either side of his friends. They carried rifles and wore serious expressions. One pulled a twig from his shirt pocket and began to chew it. Rebecca's eyes were wide and darted from one man to the other. Michael had his arms crossed over his chest, and while his expression was stern, Loyal could tell he was scared. Rebecca motioned for him to come back to them. He debated running away—he was pretty sure he could find his way back to the cabin and his father—but the thought of abandoning his friends felt wrong. He closed his hand around the compass and moved closer, keeping a wary eye out.

Neither man spoke, but one of them motioned toward a trail Loyal hadn't noticed before. While the two men didn't point their guns at them, Loyal felt like they might if the three of them didn't go along. Loyal forced a smile for Rebecca, who managed one in return. He signed an *o* and a *k*. She nodded. Michael must have been watching, because he nodded too and made a *come on* gesture.

They started down the trail with the two men following behind as if this were all part of their plan for the day. Loyal pretended to stumble and dropped the compass on the ground. Maybe someone would come looking for them.

When they knocked, Earl flung the door open. "I thought I told you—" He stopped talking and narrowed his eyes. "What do you two want? And where's that boy of yours? Tom can't stick around forever waiting to do this interview."

"I've got a couple of follow-up questions for you. Want to come down to the parlor and talk?" Virgil peeked into the untidy room. "Or we can step inside here."

Earl looked like he was chewing the insides of his cheeks. "Give me a minute and I'll meet you downstairs."

The woman who kept the boardinghouse asked if they wanted some lemonade, but they declined. "Won't be cluttering up your parlor but a few minutes, ma'am," Virgil said as Earl slunk down the stairs and into the room. Virgil escorted the landlady out and eased the door shut on her disappointment.

They took seats as far from the door as they could get and motioned for Earl to join them. "What's this about?" he asked.

"I don't suppose you'd know what happened to your partner's work notebook?" Virgil said. Eddie paled, and beads of sweat popped out on his forehead. Could have been the closed-up room, but Creed doubted it.

"Wh-what notebook do you mean?"

Creed started to speak when Virgil shot him a look that he thought might have been fatal if he'd taken it full in the face. He clamped his lips.

"Eddie's betrothed seemed to think he kept a notebook for work details. Didn't find it on him or in his room. Thought you might know something about it."

Earl went from pale to ruddy. "Oh. That. Yeah, he used to doodle in some little book of his. Haven't seen it since he got killed. Guess he must've lost it." He swallowed audibly and coughed. "Why?"

Virgil shrugged. "Oh, probably nothing. Just being sure to follow up on all the details. Say, I guess working for the government pays pretty good."

Earl choked and thumped his chest. Once he regained his breath, he glared at Virgil. "I wouldn't say that. Better than a lot of jobs these days, but it won't make me rich anytime soon."

Virgil nodded and pursed his lips. "Right you are. Guess if you wanted to get rich, you'd have to figure something else out." He stood and smiled. "Me, I guess I'll stick to sheriffing. Doesn't pay good, but at least when somebody shoots at me, I know why."

Earl laughed weakly, like he wasn't sure he was supposed to. Creed took a breath to speak but got cut off by another look from Virgil. He rolled his eyes and headed for the door.

"We'll be seeing you around, Earl. Hoping to get that trial under way next week."

Earl surged to his feet. "Not until we interview that boy of his," he said, jerking a thumb at Creed. "When's that gonna happen?"

"Oh, me and the judge are gonna do that interview on Monday," Virgil answered. "Just had a nice visit with him and it's all taken care of. We'll have an interpreter and everything." He grasped the doorknob. "I guess that means old Tom can go on home." He grinned at Earl. "There's some good news you can share."

Creed trailed the sheriff out of the house, feeling like he was going to burst if he didn't speak. "Why didn't you ask him about Christine, and what do you mean 'the judge is going to interview Loyal'?"

"Now, Creed, don't give yourself apoplexy. You're just gonna have to trust that I've questioned one or two folks over the years and know what I'm doing. As for talking to Loyal, that's something we have to do, and I would've thought you'd rather Judge Kline asked the questions."

"Well, I would. I just wish you'd talked to me first."

Virgil gave him a withering look. "You haven't exactly consulted with me on several decisions you made. How's it feel?"

Creed grunted. "Fine. I guess I can see what you're up to. You think that notebook is important? Maybe Earl's lying about knowing where it is?"

"I do think it's important, and I'm afraid our man in there is telling the truth when he says he hasn't seen it. And I'm pretty sure he's hoping we don't see it, either."

They walked in silence until they reached the sheriff's car. "You need to go fetch those kids now, Creed. We can bring 'em into Elkins. The judge said they can stay with him, so they'll be safe." Virgil looked pleased with himself. "His wife is real partial to young'uns, and their own grandchildren live all the way in Tennessee. I reckon this might even be fun for 'em."

Creed didn't know about that, but he realized Virgil wasn't going to let him call the shots this time.

twenty-one

Creed stared at the remains of the kids' campfire. It had been carefully extinguished—raked for any embers and doused with water. Sweat ran down the back of his neck and it had little to do with the heat of the day. He'd searched all around, thinking they'd be down at the creek or up on the bald. Nothing. No sign of them. Or rather, lots of sign, yet all of it pointing to their responsibly breaking camp and moving on.

But where?

He went to his cabin next, hoping maybe they'd gone looking for him. Nothing. Frustrated and maybe even frightened, he backtracked. That was when he saw something glint in the light filtering down through the trees. He stooped to pick it up—a Boy Scout compass. It seemed like just the sort of thing a boy like Michael would carry with him. Had he dropped it by accident? It was clean and dry like someone had just set it down for a minute, planning to come back. He opened his mouth to holler for the kids, then snapped it shut. Loyal couldn't hear, and the Westfall kids wouldn't know whether or not he could be trusted.

Creed began to make a careful search in widening circles. Pushing aside branches, he spotted a narrow trail leading around the mountain at a slight downward angle. Might be a critter trail. Then again . . . He pocketed the compass and set out to see where this trail might lead.

It was getting dark as Delphy sat at the table, her Bible open before her and a cup of cold coffee sitting forgotten. When she heard Creed thump onto the back porch, she forced herself not to leap to her feet and meet him at the door. As soon as she laid eyes on him, she knew something wasn't right.

"Where's Loyal?" she whispered. "When are you bringing him home?"

He licked his lips. "Got any hot coffee?"

"On the stove," she said, pointing with her chin.

He poured himself a cup of coffee and sat next to her at the table. "Judge Wendell Kline up in Elkins is going to interview Loyal. Me and Virgil found out some new details about Eddie Minks that might shed light on him getting shot. Earl could be mixed up in it somehow, so the judge said the kids could stay with him."

"So Loyal's with Judge Kline in Elkins?"

Creed slurped his coffee and sucked in air. Good. He'd probably scalded his tongue. "Well. No. Virgil sent me to fetch the kids from their camp and take them up there."

Delphy wanted to scream. "Creed Raines, stop giving me unnecessary details and tell me where our son is!"

He took another swallow of hot liquid—and flinched when it hit his already-scorched tongue. "I don't know."

"What?" She could hear a buzzing in her ears and laid both hands on the table to ground herself.

He cleared his throat and spoke louder. "I went to their camp and they were gone. Looked like they'd tidied up after themselves, so I guess they made plans to move somewhere else. I found a compass and thought I might've hit their trail, but it petered out."

She didn't know what she intended until she heard her coffee cup shatter against the wall and saw coffee run down, staining the wallpaper. How many times was Creed going to make her lose her temper like this? She didn't speak, didn't trust herself to form words past the shaking of her whole being. Creed lifted a hand as though to comfort her, then drew it back.

"Find him." She ground the words out through clenched teeth. "I don't want to lay eyes on you again until you've found our son." She stood and took two steps toward the hall, stopped, and turned back to pin him to his chair with a look. "And I'm not altogether certain I want to see you then." She knew she should stop. Should measure her words before unleashing them, but she couldn't. Or maybe wouldn't. She'd had such hope . . . had trusted this man . . .

"Maybe this farce of a marriage has gone on long enough. I thought . . ." She choked on a sob. How could she tell him that she'd thought he still loved her? Still wanted her. That they still had a chance to be a family. "It doesn't matter what I thought. What matters is that you find Loyal and return him to me." Her face crumpled. "I trusted you," she cried, then turned and ran upstairs.

Creed had rarely spent a more miserable night. Virgil had been almost as mad as Delphy. He'd left him to spend the night in the makeshift cell that had recently held Otto. Creed tried to blame his sleeplessness on the narrow cot and thin mattress but knew it was fear that haunted him. Had he lost his son? Had his desire to keep the boy safe caused him to repeat his past mistakes in a new way?

He tossed and turned, then finally heaved himself to his feet and walked out into the night. He stood on a street corner, taking in the town sleeping all around him. Stars pricked the sky, and he could smell the damp of the river. He stared into the darkness until his eyes adjusted and he could make out the silvery outlines of buildings and trees. Now if only he could make out his own motives.

When he'd argued in favor of leaving the kids on their own, had he really thought them safer? Or was he still trying to keep Loyal tucked away from the world? He'd vowed never to pressure Loyal to do or achieve anything again. The trial was the talk of the town—every bench would be filled, and Loyal would be front and center. The pressure would be enormous. And while a judge like Wendell Kline would treat him with kindness and compassion, what would other folks do? What kind of questions would Loyal be asked? Could he handle being in the spotlight like that? Creed had long thought of Loyal as fragile—easily broken—and while recent days had shown him how strong and resilient the boy could be, he didn't want to risk pushing him too far.

Truth be told, he'd hoped that if Loyal and his friends stayed hidden away, something might happen to make Loyal's testimony at a trial unnecessary. Truth be told, Creed was just stalling.

A mourning dove started its melancholy call down near the river. He thought about how Loyal would never hear such a sweet, sorrowful sound. And then it occurred to him that Loyal probably wasn't wasting much time wishing he could hear something he didn't even remember. No. His boy had been busy learning to talk with his hands. To understand more with his eyes than most people did with their ears. And even now, he was out there, somewhere, standing by his friends.

Creed ran determined fingers through his hair and turned toward the first hint of light showing in the east. He wasn't going to waste any more time, either. He'd find Loyal, and he knew no matter what happened next, he'd be there for his boy.

At first, Loyal figured pretending he wasn't scared might keep him from really being afraid. Now he was just too interested in what was going on to be afraid anymore. They'd followed the men for miles and miles until they popped out in a clearing with the best-looking cabin he'd ever seen. It was two stories tall with an attic window on top of that. A porch wrapped around three sides of the house with a railing made from rhododendron branches polished until they gleamed. There was a row of rocking chairs on the wide porch. An older man with a long beard stepped outside and looked them up and down.

"You Hadden Westfall's young'uns?" he asked Michael. His lips were hard to read with the whiskers growing around them. The older boy nodded and jammed his hands in his pockets. Because they were shaking, Loyal saw.

The man eyed Loyal. "And you belong to Creed Raines." He looked thoughtful and pointed at his ear. "The one what can't hear." Now it was Loyal's turn to nod. "You can tell what I'm saying by watching me, can't you?" Loyal nodded again. The man threw his head back and laughed. "If that don't beat all. I can think of one or two uses for something like that." He hooked a hand in the screen door and jerked it open. "Come on in then. Bernie will get you fed."

Now they were sitting at a table cut from a single piece of wood that was at least three feet wide and ten feet long. The edges were still covered in bark that, like the porch railing, had been rubbed to a silky sheen. Loyal guessed this was how God's furniture would look—like the thing it came from, only better.

A woman with long gray hair in a single braid down her back bustled around and set plates of food in front of them: green beans and new potatoes cooked with bacon, thick slices of bread, fried squash, sweet pickles, baked apples, and a pitcher of milk. Although Loyal had thought they were doing fine feeding themselves out in the woods, they all three fell on the food like they hadn't eaten in days. Rebecca was carrying on a steady conversation with the woman, who looked tickled to have someone to talk to. But Loyal didn't pay much attention. He was too busy shoveling food into his mouth.

Then he saw a word—*notebook*. His fork paused on its way back to his plate, and he watched as Rebecca pulled the little notebook she'd showed him from her pocket. He'd forgotten all about it and wondered why she'd brought it with her.

"It's got nice drawings. And there are still plenty of blank pages," Rebecca told the woman. "I thought I might try to draw something, too."

The oldest man who'd been eating with them held his hand out for the book. He flipped through the pages one by one, then nodded, a grim smile emerging from the depths of his beard. "I'll be dogged," he said and looked at each of them in turn. "You'uns need to stay here for now. It ain't safe for you to go back to town. And with a coyote on the loose, you don't need to be sleeping outside."

Loyal missed what he said, but Michael must have asked about the coyote. The man's mouth tipped up in a lopsided grin. "This coyote's got two legs." He turned to Loyal. "Sam will fetch your pa, let him know you'uns are safe and welcome to stay here as long as need be." His eyes shot sparks. "Best way to catch a coyote is to wait for him in the last place he got a good meal. Ain't never had much for 'em to eat round these parts."

Loyal wasn't quite following all the talk about two-legged coyotes, but if one of the men was going to get his father, well, then everything would be fine. Now that Michael wanted to tell the truth, Father would know what to do. And until then, the food here sure was good.

twenty-two

It was past noon and Creed had been walking for hours. He'd started at the kids' camp and planned to search all of Rich Mountain if need be. Then he'd search all of Randolph County. Shoot, he'd search the entire state if that was what it took. Of course, Virgil would probably string him up before then. He hadn't told the sheriff his plan—just started walking as soon as he could see to put one foot in front of the other.

Stopping to rest in the shade of an oak tree, Creed nearly jumped out of his skin when someone spoke. "You huntin' them kids?"

Jerking his head around, he saw the man step out from the shade of a huge rock. "Where'd you come from?" he asked. If he wasn't mistaken, this was one of the Hacker boys.

"Been watching you awhile now." He spoke around a sassafras twig he was chewing on. "Thought I might have to go all the way to town after you. Glad you was out here stumbling around."

Creed frowned. He was a better woodsman than most and didn't appreciate this not-so-subtle criticism. "You know where my boy is?"

"Sure enough. Pa sent me to tell you your boy and them other two are at the house."

"I guess your pa would be Clyde Hacker."

He nodded, removing the twig from his mouth. "I'm Sam. Don't guess we've run into each other in a while."

"You boys aren't what you'd call well known for socializing."

Sam grinned. "That's so. You want to follow me on back to the house?"

"If the kids are there, I do."

"C'mon then." He started down a nearly invisible trail and then glanced back over his shoulder, a glint in his eye. "I'll try not to get shut of you between here and there."

Creed gave him a sour look. He guessed he could find the Hacker family home just fine. A heavy gray cloud blew in as they started out. Sam looked at it like he was suspicious of it, while Creed hoped it might cool them as they moved through the trees. It never let go any rain, though, and an hour later he'd changed his mind about being able to find the Hacker place. He had a suspicion Sam was taking him on a circuitous route, probably so it would be harder for him to find the place on his own next time. He was aggravated not only by the lack of trust but also by the loss of time. He was about to suggest that Sam quit leading him in circles when they popped out behind a massive barn. As they walked around it, Creed noticed there weren't any windows, and the doors were shut up tight. Which would be a misery for any animals inside. But then he doubted that was what the silvered wood hid from prying eyes.

Clyde sat on the porch, legs crossed and fancy carved pipe dangling from his lips. He took the pipe out of his mouth and pointed the stem at Creed. "That boy of yours makes up for what he can't hear with what he can see. And I don't just mean with his eyes." The old man stood and waved Creed toward the door. "He's inside, learning my woman to say her alphabet with her fingers." Clyde shook his head. "He's a wonder."

As much as he wanted to go in and check on Loyal, Creed paused and eyed Clyde. "You think so?"

"Don't you? Any fool can hear what folks say—that boy can *see* what they mean." His beard waggled as he shook his head. "Beats all I've ever seen. You must be right proud."

Creed swallowed hard. "I am," he said, surprised by the hoarseness of his voice. "Now, why in the world did you bring him here?"

Clyde ran fingers through his beard. "Whyn't you come on in the house and we'll talk through it." Creed frowned but didn't see much other choice. He followed Clyde through the door.

It tickled Loyal how hearing people wanted to watch him say things with his hands. Like he could do some kind of special trick. Rebecca had picked up enough that the two of them were able to carry on a simple conversation while the woman with the gray braid—Bernie was her name—tried to guess what they were saying. They were all smiling now. Even Michael looked like he was having a good time.

Loyal was signing *Rebecca is my friend* when he sensed someone coming up behind him. The presence felt familiar and he turned to see his father standing there. He felt such a surge of joy it lifted him from his seat, and he flung his arms around Father's waist. After a moment's hesitation, he felt arms settle around his shoulders, and for a heartbeat it was just the two of them. Then he felt the rumble of Father speaking and looked up.

". . . looking after my boy." Father released him and tousled his hair. "But it's time I got all these young'uns back to town."

The older man moved to the door and crossed his arms. "I think there's something you need to see before you do anything so foolish as that," he said. Loyal had to really focus to read his lips with all the hair blurring his words.

Father bristled. "What do you mean?"

"We'd been hearing those three out there in the woods and thought to let 'em be. But then I got to thinking about what's going on with that government feller getting killed. Heard his partner's been asking lots of questions." The man narrowed his eyes. Loyal shifted closer and watched his lips intently. "It come to me he might be trying to tangle these kids up in that mess."

Father looked surprised, then confused. "There might be some truth to that, but how would you know it?"

The man's veiled lips curled in a sly smile. "We listen real good and see almost as much as that boy of yours." Loyal smiled at that. It was nice to be noticed.

"Alright, what is it you want me to see?"

The man waved at Bernie, who tucked her head close to Rebecca's so Loyal couldn't see what she said. When she raised up, Rebecca handed her the little notebook they'd been looking at and passed it to the bearded man. He held it with something like reverence. No, that wasn't quite right. He held it the way he might a rotten potato he was trying to get rid of without spreading the stink. He flipped it open, found a page, and handed it over.

Father ran his eyes down the lines written there. Loyal had glanced at it before. He remembered names and numbers, but it hadn't meant anything to him. Mostly he'd looked at the sketches that had captured Rebecca's attention.

Father's lips moved, but Loyal suspected he wasn't actually making sound, just shaping the names and numbers he saw lined out. Finally, Father looked up. "Is this what I think it is?"

"If you think it's a list of folks working with them fellers to get the government to buy up their land for more than it's worth, then yeah, it's what you think."

"But, how do you know that's what it is?" Father looked upset. Like he didn't want what they were saying to be true.

The man nodded toward the book. "We might not sit beside them folks in church of a Sunday, but word gets around. Who needs ready cash. Whose land don't yield what it once did." He waved his hand toward the window. "'Course, we own more than a few acres, and that Earl feller sent word—he knew better than to come himself—that he wanted to talk turkey." He grinned. "And I was willin'. Thought it might give my boys a way out of this holler. I was expecting those government fellers to come around the day that one got shot." He chuckled. "Kept my name out of that there book anyhow."

Father began ruffling the pages faster as though desperate to find something.

"You won't find Hadden Westfall in there," the bearded man said with a nod. "I ain't saying he's what you'd call an upstanding citizen, but I guess he's not the sort to deal with the likes of them."

"Which means just about everyone in here has a better reason for shooting Eddie Minks than Hadden does." Father furrowed his brow. "But that still doesn't explain why Otto would claim to do something I'm pretty sure he didn't."

As Loyal watched, everyone's head jerked in one direction—toward Michael. The young man stood beside the table, back straight, arms stiff at his sides. He looked directly at Father. "You heard me. I said I shot that man."

Creed wished he could just tell everyone to sit down, be quiet, and let him think. Too many pieces of information were flying at him from all directions. Clyde Hacker seemed to think he was doing them all a favor by keeping the kids here. Rebecca had a notebook that sure seemed like the one Christine said Eddie carried with him, which included the names of landowners who were apparently working with Eddie and Earl to cheat the government. Now Hadden's boy was claiming to be the killer. Questions darted around inside his head like birds trapped inside a house. He wanted to fling the windows open and let them all out, but tried to capture just one or two instead.

He stepped over to Michael and laid a gentle hand on his shoulder. "Son. Are you telling me you killed that man?"

The boy's stoic expression slipped a notch and his eyes glistened. "I didn't mean to."

"What happened?"

Rebecca stepped forward and put an arm around her brother's waist. "Michael had Daddy's gun. He told me he'd show me how to shoot it, so we went way down there along the river where no one would see or hear us." Creed noticed the girl had a lisp. He'd never paid enough attention to her to realize it before. "That man must've been taking a nap in the shade. As quick as we shot the gun, he jumped up and started yelling at us to get out of there." She worried her lip and glanced at her brother, who gave a small nod. "Michael told him it was our land and he was the one that needed to go away. He laughed and said he was meeting someone." She took a deep breath. "I tried to explain that it was alright for us to be there, and then he . . ." She ducked her chin.

Michael picked up the thread. "He started making fun of how Rebecca talks. Started acting like he couldn't say his words right, either. And he just laughed and laughed. I told him to stop, but he wouldn't." One tear escaped his control, and his hand shot up to scrub it away. "I had the gun in my hand and I just shot it before I had time to think."

Creed's blood thrummed in his head. Of all the possibilities he'd considered up to now, this was the last and probably the worst. He'd felt sure Otto hadn't pulled the trigger, but for it to have been a boy defending his sister . . .

"I appreciate your telling me the truth," he said. He reached out and squeezed Michael's shoulder—a man-to-man gesture that wasn't lost on the boy. He lifted his chin and squared his jaw.

"We were on our way to tell you and then the sheriff when

Mr. Hacker found us and brought us here. Guess we oughta go on into town now." He cleared his throat. "Can't let Otto take the blame for something he didn't do."

Clyde stepped forward. "Whyn't you leave these ones here with us." He nodded at the notebook still in Creed's hand. "You and Sam take that on to the sheriff. If that government feller figures out you know what he's been up to, ain't no telling what he'll do." A slow smile parted his beard. "But I'd be willing to bet he ain't gonna show his face around this house." He grunted. "Coyotes are sly, but they ain't dumb."

Sam argued with his daddy about taking Creed into town, yet Clyde won out in the end. Now Sam ghosted through the trees with a scowl etched on his face. The man had an endless supply of sassafras twigs, and the sweet smell trailed along after him. Though Creed had been reluctant to leave the kids at the Hacker place, he was equally wary of exposing them to further danger by marching them back into the middle of town. And while he expected Hadden would bluster about being able to keep his own children safe, Creed wasn't altogether certain how the businessman would handle hearing his son had killed a man with a gun he wasn't supposed to have.

It was a mess.

And he still needed to fill Delphy in.

When they arrived at the sheriff's office, Hadden was there berating Virgil. He looked as if the words Hadden was pouring into his ears were hitting like physical blows. He kept flinching. And the smudges under his eyes looked like bruises. Creed guessed he might prefer being beaten up to the tongue-lashing that was under way.

Then Hadden spied him and Sam standing in the open door. He whirled on them. "Where in the blue blazes have you been? And where are my children?"

"Clyde Hacker's looking out for 'em." The look of utter shock on Hadden's face was almost worth it. He sputtered and acted like he was revving up for another round of verbal warfare when Virgil stood.

"Enough!" the sheriff roared. "I want every last one of you to plant your hindquarters on a chair and seal your lips until I give you permission to speak."

Hadden opened his mouth, but Virgil drew his pistol and pointed it at him. "I said *sit*." He waved the pistol at Creed and Sam. "You two do the same."

Creed saw Bud peek into the room, then duck back out. Smart man. They all sat, Hadden glowering, Sam wearing a bemused expression, and Creed wondering in what order he should share all the information swirling around in his head.

Virgil holstered his gun and used both hands to rub his head like he was trying to get something sticky off of it. "I'd just as soon run you all on up to Elkins and lock you up until Judge Kline and those attorneys can do whatever they want with you." He blew out a breath and closed his eyes. "They went ahead and started picking a jury for Otto's trial." Creed raised up and opened his mouth when another look from Virgil silenced him. "The judge knows as well as I do there's more to this story than what Otto says, but there's pressure from all sides—the Feds, locals scared about a murder, even that woman who says she was engaged to Eddie. Only one who wants to slow things down is Earl, and Judge Kline doesn't put any more faith in him than I do."

He let silence fill the room until it pushed at them, yet no one dared speak. "Now. Creed. Would you care to explain why your boy and Hadden's young'uns are at the Hacker place instead of here, in this room, with us?"

Hadden opened his mouth, then snapped it shut, choosing to glare at Creed instead. Sam tilted his chair back on two legs and stared at the ceiling. Creed tried several explanations out in his head, but none of them seemed like they'd satisfy Virgil. So he pulled out Eddie's notebook and handed it to the sheriff. He took the book and began going through it, page by page, absorbing every notation.

"Rebecca found that the day Eddie got shot. His fiancée—Christine—can most likely identify it as his. I think it might shed some light on why Earl is so fired up about figuring out who wanted to shoot his partner."

Virgil's eyebrows climbed his forehead. Creed let him continue his perusal in silence. The sheriff finally looked up. "Even if this doesn't tell us who committed murder, it'll tie a few knots in some important tails around here."

"Including Earl's," Creed said.

"What is that?" Hadden asked. "I demand to see it."

Virgil laughed. "Demand all you want. This is evidence and it's got nothing to do with you." He shook his head. "Which you can be almighty grateful about." He shifted his gaze back to Creed. "'Course, it doesn't appear to have anything to do with Otto, either. Gives a passel of folks a mighty fine motive, but not the one who claims to be the killer."

"About that," Creed said, suddenly finding his chair particularly hard. "Turns out Otto might've been covering for somebody."

Hadden threw his hands in the air. "Not this again! I told you I didn't do it."

Virgil moved like a cat, standing inches from Hadden in a flash. He jammed a finger in his face. "Well, once we get that ballistics report back, I'm betting we'll know it was your gun that did it. Now the only question is, who pulled the trigger—you or your man?"

Clearly taken aback, Hadden shrank back into his chair. "I explained how it wasn't me."

"I think he's telling the truth," Creed said.

Virgil looked at him with surprise. "You're taking up for Hadden? You really think Otto did it?"

"No. I . . ." He darted a look at Hadden. "Maybe we should talk in private."

"You're not leaving me out of this," Hadden said. "I want to know who you think could've taken my gun and used it to kill that man."

Creed paused, noting a cruel smile tugging at Sam's lips. "Michael confessed to the shooting, and Rebecca backed him up."

Hadden stood, took two steps toward Creed, and slugged him in the chin.

twenty-three

Delphy hadn't been able to stand the waiting another minute. She finally repinned her hair, smoothed her skirt, and marched down to Virgil's office. Not many women went in there other than Virgil's wife, Julia, but Delphy didn't care. She heard voices as she approached and felt certain one of them was Creed's. She raised a hand to knock on the doorframe just as she saw Hadden leap to his feet and strike . . . her husband.

Delphy flew to Creed's side, barking at Virgil to bring her a wet cloth. Astonishingly enough, the sheriff obeyed and without saying a word. Delphy knelt on the floor to bathe Creed's face with the cool rag. She was about to ask Virgil to help her roll Creed onto his side when he flinched and blinked up at her. She bit her lip and watched a look dawn in his eyes that she knew well. She felt her cheeks flush in response, and her breath hitched. He lifted his hand, grazing her cheek with his knuckles. She froze and it was as if the room fell away around them and she was only aware of his look of love washing over all the dry places in her soul.

"Might be worth getting knocked on my hind end if I can

wake up to you," he whispered. She flushed and pulled back, reminding herself that they were not alone. He grabbed her wrist, tugged her back toward him. "I'm sorry," he said. "For everything."

She fought tears. "Might be worth your getting knocked on your hind end if you wake up with good sense," she said.

"Is he awake?" Virgil asked. Delphy snapped back to attention and moved away, eyes still locked on Creed's. He sat up, rubbing his jaw as Virgil stepped closer and held a hand out for Creed to grasp. "I've got Hadden settled—now tell us what you meant when you said Michael shot Eddie Minks."

Delphy stared up at the sheriff. *Michael? Hadden's son?* Creed stood and staggered once before dropping into one of the hard folding chairs. Delphy moved close and laid a hand on his shoulder. He glanced up at her. "How long have you been here?" he asked.

"I stopped by to see if Virgil had heard from you—or Loyal. I arrived just in time to see you laid out on the floor." She managed a smile in spite of the dozen or so questions buzzing through her mind. "I guess seeing you like that made me realize I'm not quite ready to be shut of you yet." He reached up and grasped her hand where it rested on his shoulder. And she let him.

Something tender passed between them then, and Delphy had the notion—for the first time since Creed came home with a fevered boy on that fateful spring day—that they were on the same side of whatever battle was being waged. She looked up and saw Virgil waiting none too patiently for Creed to speak. Hadden stood in the corner, arms crossed, and . . . well, there wasn't actual steam coming from his ears, but there might as well have been.

Creed cleared his throat and gave her hand another squeeze. "Michael was on his way into town with his sister and Loyal to turn himself in when Sam and his brother waylaid 'em and took 'em to their place." He glanced at Sam, whom Delphy hadn't noticed until now. The taciturn fellow showed no indication that he wanted to add any details. "Clyde seems to think they're safer with him, and I tend to agree." He nodded at a notebook on Virgil's desk. "If Earl had known they were carrying that around, I think he might've tried real hard to get it from them."

Hadden strode forward and, even though Virgil gave him a warning look, loomed over Creed. "What do you mean Michael was on his way to turn himself in? If he's claiming he shot that man, then he's simply trying to prove something to me. Foolishness. Pure foolishness!"

Creed ran his tongue over his lip, and Delphy noticed a cut there. "Says he took that fancy pistol of yours and planned to teach his sister to shoot it. They happened upon Eddie, and he gave your girl a hard time about the way she talks." Hadden flushed. "Michael said he didn't really mean to do it—just fired without thinking it through."

Again Hadden slumped into a chair. "Why would he do that?" He seemed to be talking to himself.

Virgil tapped the notebook on his desk. "I'm gonna have to tell Wendell all this, and quick." He glanced at the clock on the wall. "Late as it is, I'll phone the judge and see what he wants to do. I need everyone to clear this room, but I don't want anyone to go any farther than the end of the street." He went and opened the door and hollered toward the back room. "Bud, I know you're hiding back there. I need you to keep an eye on this rabble while I make a telephone call."

Bud shuffled out with a sheepish look on his face. Virgil waved a hand at the ragtag group. "Don't let 'em outta your sight." He narrowed his eyes. "And don't let 'em eavesdrop, either."

Bud waved everyone together, marched them outside and toward the park on the corner. They all stood, looking first at each other, then the ground. Bud positioned himself on the sidewalk, resting a hand on the butt of his pistol. Hadden paced back and forth while Sam lounged on a bench, watching them like a vulture watching a dying squirrel. Creed reached out and took Delphy's hand. Her breath caught and she hesitated, then laced her fingers through his. He tugged her closer until they stood hip to hip.

"Loyal's alright?" she asked.

"He is." Creed gave a soft laugh. "As a matter of fact, I'd say he's having a fine time. He's been teaching everyone he sees how to do sign language. And even Clyde Hacker noticed how smart he is."

She let a smile lift her lips. "He did?"

"Said he's a wonder."

The smile grew and she bumped him with her hip. "He surely is that."

Creed gripped her hand tighter and lowered his voice. "Hey, remember that day I first talked to you at Rohrbaugh's Store? You were digging through bolts of fabric like there was gold buried in there somewhere."

She laughed and angled toward him. "You were determined not to pay me any mind just because your daddy thought we'd be a good match. Stubborn, that's what you were."

"Still am," he said. "Sorry to say." He tucked a stray curl behind her ear. "But that day—I don't know what it was. Maybe the way the sun hit your hair. Or the way you didn't give up looking until you found just what you wanted—"

"Blue roses," she said, the memory dawning. "That fabric had the prettiest blue rose print."

"Right, focused is what you were. And I couldn't resist."

She laughed and looked at him from under her eyelashes. "Well, I could."

"Not for long," he said in a low husky voice. A shiver of pleasure ran through her, and she barely had time to remind herself that she should be thinking about Loyal and Michael and what was going to happen next when Virgil stepped out onto the street and waved them all back into his office. Creed kept a firm hold on her hand as they walked back. And she let him.

Back in the office, Virgil looked like a man who just got word the bank was foreclosing on his farm. "Judge says every last one of us is to report to his chambers at nine o'clock tomorrow morning. He wants the kids there, too. Bud and I will drive out to the Hackers' and pick 'em up early." He glared at them all as if they'd eaten the last piece of his fried chicken. "You bunch get to spend the night right here."

"Now, hold on—"

Virgil raised a hand to cut Hadden off.

"Don't think for one minute that I'm looking forward to hosting overnight guests. We don't exactly have what you'd call appropriate accommodations. But we're all gonna have to make do. Judge Kline doesn't want to give anyone a chance to blab about what's going on until he's got the right of it, and Bud and I have been given the job of keeping a thumb on all of you."

"Are you saying we're all under arrest?" Hadden asked.

"No, but if that's what it takes to keep you here, it can be arranged." Virgil turned his attention to Delphy. "Ma'am, I'm real sorry about this. There's a cot back there in the holding cell—that's yours. The rest of us will make do out here."

Delphy gave Creed's hand a squeeze and released it to step forward. "Virgil, if it's acceptable—" she paused and glanced at Creed—"and if my husband agrees, you'd all be welcome to stay at the house tonight. I'm sure you and Bud could keep an eye on us there just as well."

Virgil raised his eyebrows and looked to Creed, who shrugged. "If Delphy's game, then it's fine with me."

The sheriff turned to Sam and Hadden. "Can I trust you two not to slip out a window?"

Hadden swatted his thigh with the hat he was carrying. "If you'll give my boy a fair shake, I'll put up with whatever you say."

"I hope you know I will." Virgil sighed. "Last thing I want

is for a boy to be the one to take the blame." Hadden gave a curt nod and slapped his hat on his head. Virgil turned to Sam. "What about you?"

"I ain't got a dog in this fight. And sure as shootin' I'd rather sleep in a house than on this plank floor."

"Alright then," Virgil agreed with a weary puff of breath. "Mrs. Raines, if you'll lead the way . . ."

"Why do you think Otto said he did it?" The three kids sat in a circle in the room Bernie had given them. There was one huge bed, and Loyal guessed they'd all sleep there, which made him feel kind of funny. He'd never shared a bed with anyone and wasn't sure he was supposed to share one with a girl, even if her brother was right there, too.

Rebecca elbowed him. "Why would Otto lie like that?"

Loyal shrugged, but then he thought about it some more. He signed, *Did Otto know?* Rebecca squinched her face and made the sign for *again* that he'd taught her. He slowly spelled O-t-t-o and then touched his flat hand to his forehead while raising his eyebrows.

"Oh, you're asking if Otto knew that Michael shot that man." She looked to her brother. "I don't think so."

Michael shook his head. "I don't see how. He was at the house messing with Dad's dogs that afternoon. Maybe he really did think Dad did it and he was trying to save him."

"Will he be in trouble for lying?" asked Rebecca.

"Maybe," Michael said. He looked miserable. Loyal raised his eyebrows and signed *scared*, something he'd shown Rebecca weeks ago. She remembered and nodded.

Moving closer to her brother, Rebecca tucked her arm through his. "The main thing is that you decided to tell the truth." She smiled and looked at Loyal, then made the sign for *proud*. "Loyal already told you he's proud of you, and so am I."

Michael ducked his head and almost smiled. "Thanks. I'm just hoping since I'm a kid and I didn't mean to do it, whatever they do to me won't be too bad." He looked Loyal in the eye. "I sure am sorry I did it. I don't think I'll ever shoot a gun again for as long as I live."

Loyal nodded. Seemed like a good plan to him.

twenty-four

Virgil and Bud camped out in the living room, saying they'd take turns staying awake just in case anyone took a notion to do anything foolish in the night. Delphy gave Hadden the guest room, which she always kept tidy and pristine. Sam got Loyal's room. That only left one place for Creed to spend the night since she didn't have a doghouse to put him in.

Creed eyed his wife. She set her lips in a firm line and motioned for him to follow her. "You know the way," she said. The room had once been theirs, but when they were inside with the door closed, Creed realized there was little of him remaining. The quilt was the same, though she'd added embroidered pillowcases, and there was a vase of zinnias on her dressing table. The chest where he used to lay out his shaving things and tin of Brylcreem now held a lacy doily with a china figurine centered on it.

He cleared his thick throat. "You've changed things."

"And why shouldn't I?"

"I'm not saying you shouldn't. Just, well . . ." He ran a hand through his already-messy hair. He hadn't had time to groom it

197

properly in days. "Doggone it, Delphy, I don't know what to say or how to act. I know you don't want me here."

The tenseness in her jaw softened and she settled on her dressing table bench like a bird fluttering down from a branch. "I've always wanted you here, Creed." She twisted her hands together in her lap. "I've never stopped wanting you. Even when I acted like I didn't." He saw a flush paint her cheeks. "You're the one who went away."

He wanted to kneel at her feet, to wrap his arms around her waist and rest his head in her lap. But he didn't deserve to do that. What she said was true. "You're right," he said. He bent down to remove his boots, then took a blanket from the chest at the foot of the bed where, thankfully, she still kept extra bedding. He folded it and laid it out on the floor. "I'll sleep here."

Her hand covered her mouth, but she didn't speak. Just stood, blew out the hurricane lamp on her bedside table, and lay down on her bed in the dark. He waited to hear her breath grow gentle and even but must have finally fallen asleep. He never did hear the soft whiffle of breath he still remembered from before.

Virgil drove Sam and Creed out to the Hacker place at first light. Now that he'd hiked in with Sam, Creed realized the house was positioned so it was almost impossible to reach except by the road. The path they'd come in on from behind was likely known only to the family. Creed was pretty sure he couldn't find it again. That Clyde was fox smart.

As the car pulled into the clearing in front of the house, Clyde stepped out onto the porch with the three children. It was like he'd known what time they were coming. Michael stood tall beside the wiry old man, while Rebecca and Loyal stood in front of him, his hands resting on their shoulders. Creed felt a jolt at how comfortable and right they all looked there together. Loyal fit right in—there was nothing to set him apart. So why was it Creed persisted in thinking of him as different?

"You going to keep these young'uns safe?" Clyde asked. He had an unlit pipe clenched between his teeth.

Creed stepped forward and met the older man's steady gaze. "Do you have any doubt?"

Clyde chuckled and lifted his hands to fish a kitchen match from his breast pocket. He flicked it into flame with his thumbnail and held it to the bowl of his pipe. Once he had a nice plume of smoke going, he nodded. "Nary a doubt in this world." He patted Loyal on the shoulder. "This one'll go far if you don't hold him back."

Creed felt regret rise like the smoke from Clyde's tobacco. "You're right about that," he said. Then he smiled at Loyal and held his arm out so the boy could tuck in at his side. "You ready to talk to a real-life judge?" he asked. Loyal grinned and signed yes. "Let's do it, then."

Virgil and Creed sat in the front of the car while the kids piled in the back where they were unexpectedly quiet. As they bumped over the rough road, Creed waved a hand in front of his face. He'd carried Clyde's tobacco smoke with him—a little puff of haze hung there. He blinked and rubbed his eyes. Or maybe his vision was going funny. Goodness knew he hadn't slept well on his pallet on the floor last night.

Shaking his head, he turned to Virgil. "What's the plan?"

Virgil glanced back at the kids. "Let these kids tell Wendell what they know." He sighed and massaged the back of his neck with one hand. "He already knows what I could tell him. And he's talked to Otto. I guess it isn't exactly the regular way to conduct a trial, but Wendell's been doing this for a long time. I trust him to make sense where all I can see is a muddled mess."

Creed felt a hand touch his shoulder. He twisted around and looked at the kids. Loyal—sitting right behind him—was the one who'd gotten his attention. He tilted his head to the side as though directing Creed's attention to the Westfall kids. Creed eyed the pair. Rebecca had tears standing in her eyes, and Michael looked like a man on the way to a firing squad. Well, shoot, of course they were scared.

"Judge Kline's one of the best, most honest men I've ever met," he said.

Virgil darted a look in the rearview mirror, and light dawned in his eyes. "Sure is. Nice fella too. Got eight or nine grandkids now. Takes 'em fishing every chance he gets."

Michael opened his mouth, and a squeak came out. He flushed and cleared his throat. "Will he put me in jail?" he asked.

"I don't know about that," Virgil said over his shoulder. "Mainly he just wants to get everyone together and see if he can't hash out what's going on. It's not every day people get in line to confess to shooting somebody."

"Will I have to get up in a courtroom and swear on a Bible?"

"Not today," Virgil said. "Wendell just wants to talk to you. Otto's trial was supposed to start today, but what with Earl raising a stink and witnesses going missing"—he shot the kids a hard look in the mirror—"he decided to delay it."

"Where's our father?" Rebecca asked.

Creed did his best to offer a comforting smile. "He'll meet us at the judge's office. Bud's driving him." The information didn't seem to put the kids at ease—if anything, it wound Michael tighter.

"Does he know . . . what I did?" the boy asked.

Creed rubbed his chin. "He does. Although I'm not sure he believes it." He'd meant the doubt to be comforting, but Michael's face twisted.

"Of course he doesn't. He doesn't think I can do anything."

"Except you can," Creed said. "I saw that camp you made. The way you taught your sister and Loyal how to tie knots and break camp. You did a real good job out there in the woods."

Michael appeared to grow before his eyes. The boy sat up straighter and lifted his chin. "You think so?"

"Sure do. Guess your dad just doesn't realize what all you know."

Michael slumped back down a notch. "He's too busy. Doesn't really care what I do so long as it doesn't make him look bad." He turned to stare out the window at the blur of green and spoke low. "Guess me shooting someone might make him look *real* bad."

Creed didn't know what to say to that. He'd wanted to comfort the boy—give him hope. Maybe he should tell about how Hadden slugged him when he heard Michael confessed. But if he really had killed a man . . . Even if that man had been doing something wrong, it wasn't the kind of wrong that justified killing and there was little comfort in death. He reached over the bench seat and patted Michael on the knee. It felt awkward, but the boy didn't pull away.

Turning back to look out the windshield as Elkins came into view, Creed felt anger against Hadden Westfall stir in his belly. The man had been too busy to give his son the attention he needed—the attention he *deserved*. What kind of father was he?

With a jolt, Creed realized exactly what kind of father Hadden was. The same kind as himself. He wanted to turn and look at Loyal but didn't dare. Instead he stared through the windshield until they reached the courthouse.

Loyal felt the strangest combination of fear and excitement as they walked toward the massive stone building with its towers and arched entrance. To the left of the steps, a column stretched to the second story with a carved statue of a woman standing on it. She wore some sort of draped dress and held scales high in the air. In her other hand she held a sword Loyal wished he could borrow. The building looked like a castle, and he felt like a knight riding in to face a dragon. He glanced at Rebecca and smiled. Maybe she felt like a princess. Michael? Well, Loyal had no idea how he might be feeling, other than scared.

Bud and Mr. Westfall joined them, and they passed through the double doors with stained glass above them. Inside, a short set of steps led to a wide marble entry hall. To their right, the stairs leading up to the second floor had a railing with a swirling gold design. The whole place was grand. It was also cool and dim inside, and Loyal sensed a stillness as though everyone were being extra careful as they moved around. Rebecca stepped closer and slipped her hand into his. He felt a jolt of surprise, then clasped her hand more firmly. It felt right and he smiled at her, trying to keep the fear and wonder out of his eyes.

The sheriff escorted them up the stairs, and Loyal ran his free hand along the smooth, glossy wood topping the railing. He wanted to lean down and press his palm against the floor to see if it was as cool as it looked but he didn't dare. Reaching the second floor, he caught a glimpse of a huge room with rows and rows of seats facing a massive desk sitting behind a short fence. He guessed that must be where they had trials. It sure looked fancy.

They entered a room with tall bookshelves lining the walls. It looked like this one room might have as many books as the library at school. A desk sat in front of a window. An old man in a white shirt with the cuffs folded back and his collar open sat there reading one of the books. He was holding a ruler against the page. He ignored them at first, then must have finished what he was reading because he looked up.

"At last." He picked up a cigar, thumbed open a heavy brass lighter, and flicked a flame to life. He held it to the cigar. His cheeks sucked in deeply as he puffed. Once he seemed satisfied with the pillar of smoke rising from the tip, he leaned back in his chair and looked at them like he was measuring them for new clothes. "So, these are the young rapscallions causing such a to-do in my court."

"The very ones," Virgil said.

Loyal released Rebecca's hand and rubbed his sweaty palm on the seat of his pants. He almost felt grateful that he'd have to talk to this white-haired man with the sharp eyes through an interpreter. Or maybe in writing. Everyone looked at him. He closed his eyes. He must have made a sound. Sometimes he did that when he was nervous or scared. Father's hand settled on his shoulder. Loyal shifted closer. He was still sorry Father had told about the gun, but right now he just wanted to feel safe.

A door Loyal hadn't seen before opened to his right, and a man in uniform brought Otto inside. The young German had handcuffs on his wrists and looked serious.

"Everyone take a seat." The old man—Loyal thought he must be Judge Kline—waved them toward a long table with eight chairs around it. They sat while the man in uniform stood behind Otto. Loyal tried smiling at the older boy, but he wouldn't meet his eyes.

The judge stood and unrolled his sleeves, working cuff links into place. He buttoned his top button and came to stand at the head of the table, behind the sheriff. He left his cigar in an ashtray on his desk—smoke curling in the stillness of the room. Loyal kind of liked the smell, earthy and pungent. Although it wasn't as nice as Father's sweet pipe smoke.

"It's rare that I'm in a position to pick and choose from a slate of murder suspects," the judge said. He looked at Loyal. "I understand you read lips. Can you tell what I'm saying?" Loyal nodded. He could, although it was wearing him out with all the big words the judge used. "Good. I've sent for someone who can use sign language, but he's been delayed. We'll make do in the meantime."

Loyal nodded again. He held up his flat left hand and made a motion with his right like scribbling on a piece of paper.

"Good idea," the judge said. He went back to his desk and returned with a long yellow notepad and a pen that felt as cool and heavy in Loyal's hand as the marble floor looked. He tried it out by drawing a line on the paper. It was wonderful. He added a swoop and a swirl just to feel the easy flow of ink. He smiled and nodded to show his appreciation and saw an answering smile flash in the old man's eyes.

"Take those handcuffs off that young man." Judge Kline gestured toward Otto. "I don't believe he's either dangerous or a flight risk."

The uniformed man did as he was told, and Otto rubbed his wrists. He glanced up then, and Loyal read confusion in his eyes. Well. He wasn't the only one wondering what was going to happen next.

The judge wore suspenders. He hooked his thumbs under them and stared at them all in silence for a few moments. "There's nothing regular about this situation," he began. "A man has been shot to death. Two men who aren't much more than boys claim to have pulled the trigger." He looked at them all until it began to feel uncomfortable, even to Loyal. "Someone is lying," he said at last. He unhooked his thumbs and leaned on the table. "Maybe more than one someone." Loyal wanted to scratch his nose but felt like he shouldn't. He glanced at the others and saw that they were getting twitchy, too. Hearing people often hated silence, and the judge seemed to use it like his own sword.

"Alright then." The judge clapped his hands, and Loyal saw Michael flinch. "Who wants to tell me the truth?"

twenty-five

Creed had heard about Judge Kline before. The old man had a reputation for being tough but fair. He also had a reputation for not always following the rules. Creed suspected this meeting wasn't how judges usually handled murder cases. He wondered if he should say anything—should explain how he'd failed to press Loyal about what he'd seen the day of the murder . . .

"I do not understand why Mr. Michael would say he shot that man." Otto was the first to break the silence. He lifted his chin higher and stopped rubbing his wrists. "It was I who pressed the trigger." He glared at Michael. "There is no need for a trial. You may punish me as the law demands."

"Well, that last statement is true," Judge Kline said. "I'm not so sanguine about the rest of it. Tell me again why you did it?"

"This man was trespassing. I thought to frighten him away. It was an accident, but I know I must be punished for this terrible thing."

"And what did you do with the gun after you shot the man?"

"I threw it away so no one would know."

The judge dragged a box across his desk and lifted a fancy pistol from it. "Is this the one?"

Otto paled and licked his lips. "I believe that might be the one, yes."

"And you threw it . . . where?"

Otto's eyes darted around the room from person to person as though one of them might give him the answer. "Where you found it!" he finally said with a note of triumph.

Judge Kline chuckled. "Remind me where that was?"

Otto shook his head slowly. "I was very distraught. I do not remember for certain."

"Can you narrow it down for me? Did you throw it in the water? Or maybe into the bushes? Or maybe you hid it somewhere?"

Otto closed his eyes. "There is no need to press me. I do not mind to take the blame." He opened his eyes and looked at the judge with something like desperation. "You must allow me to take the blame."

Judge Kline dropped the pistol back into the box. "Not unless you did it, son." He turned his attention to Michael. "How about you? Is your story any better than Otto's?"

Michael gripped his legs with his hands as if holding himself in place. He cleared his throat and began telling his story about planning to show his sister how to shoot, running into Eddie Minks who gave Rebecca a hard time, and how he fired the gun in anger without thinking. His voice gained strength as he spoke, and Creed had to admire the boy for how calm and steady he remained. Hadden's hands curled into fists and he bowed his head. Creed felt for the man. He looked at Loyal and tried not to imagine how he'd feel if his son were doing the confessing.

When the telling was finished, Judge Kline sat down behind his desk. "Now that story has the ring of truth to it." Michael looked almost proud. "Except for one thing . . ." Now Michael frowned and furrowed his brow. "Are you telling me you shot him *twice* without thinking?" He lifted the gun again. "We did some of that fancy new ballistics testing on this, and I'm told it's got a stiff trigger." He pointed it at the ceiling and pulled the trigger against an empty chamber. The click sounded like a cannon shot in the silence of the room. "You'd have to mean it if you did that twice."

Hadden stood, his chair screeching across the floor. "Are you suggesting my son shot that man in cold blood?"

Creed looked at Michael swaying in his seat. He laid a steadying hand on the boy's arm. Judge Kline narrowed his gaze at Michael. "Did you?"

"I . . . I . . ." Sweat popped out on the boy's forehead, and he lowered his gaze. "I guess I must have."

The judge laid the gun across his desk blotter and picked up a folder. "Now I'm going to share some actual truth with you all." He flipped the cover open, settled a pair of reading glasses on his nose, and peered at the paper. "These are the results of those ballistics tests. Seems we recovered two bullets. One retrieved from the victim—that would be the fatal shot—and one dug from a tree by the sheriff there." He looked over his glasses at Virgil. "Now here's the interesting thing." He let a pause swell and fill the room until Creed's ears hurt from trying to listen. "Those slugs were the same caliber, but they came from different guns."

It was as if a whoosh of air had been released by the room itself. Creed's mind scrambled to make sense of what the judge had said. Without planning to speak, he heard his own voice. "The one in the tree must have been a hunter's. Maybe from deer season. Or spring gobbler."

Judge Kline nodded. "A fine supposition. Except for one thing. The bullet in the tree came from this gun." He tapped the fancy pistol on the desk in front of him. "Which means the bullet that killed Eddie Minks did not."

This was better than reading *The Count of Monte Cristo*. Loyal held his breath. It was hard to keep up, but if he was following the story, it sounded like Michael couldn't have killed that man. At least not with the gun he took from his father. And Otto was getting all his answers wrong. Even Loyal could tell that. So, who was the killer?

Judge Kline turned his gaze on Loyal. "Alright, young man. Can you tell me exactly what you saw that day?"

Loyal chewed his lip. He picked up the weighty pen and tilted the notepad just so. He thought carefully before he started writing.

I saw Michael and Rebecca running along the path beside the river. Michael stopped and put something in a rotted stump. Then he told Rebecca to hurry. She saw me and I knew something bad had happened.

The judge came closer and picked up the notepad, reading the words aloud. "How do you know Michael said to hurry?" Loyal pointed at his mouth and silently shaped the word several times. The gray-haired man nodded and turned to Rebecca. "Had something bad happened?"

"Yes, sir."

"Can you describe what happened for me?"

Rebecca looked at Loyal, her big brown eyes wet and sad. She nodded. "That man was making fun of the way I talk, and Michael shot him." She twined her fingers together one way and then the other. "It was really loud, and the man stumbled. He fell down, and I looked away because he was bleeding and I didn't want to see it."

The judge waited, then said, "Alright. What happened next?"

"Michael started running. At first I didn't know if I should run or try to help the man." A tear escaped the corner of her eye. "But I looked at him again and got so scared I ran, too."

"Did you see your brother hide something in a stump?"

She nodded. "I didn't know what it was until later, when he didn't have the gun anymore."

"And did you see Loyal?"

"Yes, sir. I knew him from church, but he goes to a school somewhere else." A tiny smile curved her lips. "He's been showing me how to talk with my hands."

The judge nodded with kind eyes, and Loyal realized he looked more like a grandpa than a judge. "That's good. And you've done a fine job of telling me what happened that day." Rebecca thanked him as a second tear streaked her cheek. The judge fished out a handkerchief and offered it to her. "Now, I want you to close your eyes for just a moment." Loyal watched her eyelids flutter down, then focused on the judge's mouth. "Think back to when you heard that loud gunshot and see if you can tell me whether you heard more than one."

Rebecca squeezed her eyes tight, drew a deep breath, and let it out. A moment later, her eyes flew open again. "I did . . . but the second shot wasn't as loud."

"Like maybe it was farther away?"

"Yes, sir."

The judge clapped his hands and went back to his chair behind the big desk. "Right." He turned to Virgil. "Sheriff, I'm going to need you to find me that other gun, not to mention the person who fired it." He looked at Otto. "Son, unless you can produce a second weapon, I'm going to remain skeptical about your part in all of this."

Otto glanced from person to person around the table, finally resting his gaze on Hadden. Loyal thought the older man looked uneasy. "May I speak to Mr. Hadden alone?" Otto asked.

"No. You may not. While I'm not sure about holding you on a murder charge, you have surely made a mockery of my court. And until I'm clear on what's going on, I plan to keep you right here in Elkins." The judge blew out a puff of air. "I'm halfway inclined to give Hadden a room as well, but Virgil and I are going to have a private conversation before I decide about that." He indicated a door to the side of the room and raised his eyebrows at the sheriff. Virgil stood, rubbed his bald head, and followed the judge into the other room.

The remaining group sat almost motionless around the table. It seemed like no one wanted to look at anyone else. Michael stared at the table, a look of confusion on his face. Rebecca's eyes darted from person to person, and Mr. Westfall sat as though it was all he could do to keep from standing and stomping from the room. Then Father reached out to grasp Loyal's arm. A feeling of belonging washed through him. He and Father were in this together. And all would be well.

But Otto sat alone. Loyal could see the fear and uncertainty in the young man's face and posture. He was teetering on a rocky ledge not knowing whether he would fall or be pulled to safety. Loyal patted Father's hand and stood to go and sit next to the German boy. He laid his own hand on Otto's arm and hoped he could share even a little bit of the peace Father had just shared with him.

twenty-six

Durn if he was going to cry in front of this bunch. Creed fought to stay in control of his emotions. Michael hadn't killed a man in cold blood. He couldn't have. He was ashamed now that he'd ever believed the boy could have done it. Thank the Lord for Virgil's newfangled ballistics. The judge wasn't going to let Otto sacrifice himself. And his boy was wise enough to know Otto needed comfort. Of course, they all needed that. But until they knew who'd fired the second bullet, comfort was going to be hard to come by.

After what felt like an hour but was probably only ten minutes, Judge Kline and Virgil came back into the room. They looked serious, and why wouldn't they?

Virgil turned to the judge, who gave a small nod. "Alright. Here's what's going to happen next. Otto and Hadden are going to enjoy the hospitality of the Randolph County Jail until we can narrow down who fired the killing shot."

Creed flinched as Hadden leapt to his feet, knocking his chair backward. "Are you arresting me?"

Virgil frowned. "I'd rather you just agreed to stay over a few days until we can get this sorted out." Hadden turned red, while

Virgil narrowed his eyes. "But your cooperation can be enforced if need be. With the murder weapon missing, you make a mighty fine suspect."

Hadden sputtered until he got a handle on his emotions. "My attorney will have a few things to say about that."

"I imagine he will," Virgil said. "I expect your talking to him would be right smart."

"What about my children?" Hadden waved a hand toward Michael and Rebecca. "Roberta doesn't sleep in, and considering what's been going on, I don't think they should be alone at the house."

Virgil frowned. "I was about to get to that. They'll stay at my offices in Thurmond. Bud and I will take turns watching over 'em."

"That's ridiculous." Hadden's face started going red again. "I'd just as soon send them back to Clyde Hacker as leave them with you."

"They can stay with us." Everyone turned to look at Creed when he spoke. He cleared his throat. "Unless Virgil's planning to lock me up too, they can come back to the house in town and I'll keep them safe." He laid a hand on Loyal's arm again. "I'll keep them all safe."

Virgil cocked his head toward Hadden. "That suit you?"

Hadden threw his hands up in the air. "None of this suits me, but I suppose it's better than your plan." He eyed Creed. "If anything happens to my children . . ."

Creed nodded. "I understand." He tousled Loyal's hair. "Feel the same way as a matter of fact."

Hadden sank back down into his chair, a dark look in his eyes. "You two planning to lock up everyone involved with this? You'd better fetch Earl Westin, then. Seems to me we have some evidence pointing his direction."

"I've already sent an officer to take him into custody," Judge Kline said. "Virgil will be asking him some questions, as well."

Bud led Hadden and Otto to the jail while Virgil, Creed, and the kids crowded into the police car. The ride back to Beverly was quiet. Creed wanted to talk to Virgil but not in front of the kids. They'd heard enough for one day. Virgil, for his part, stared straight ahead through the windshield, both hands on the steering wheel. He took them straight to the white house with its picket fence and dropped them off. Creed leaned in through the passenger's side window. "You want any help, you know where to find me."

Virgil spared him little more than a glance. "That I do. But might be I've stood all the help I can from you."

Stung, Creed stepped back as Virgil pulled away. He guessed he deserved that comment, but even so he hadn't expected it from his friend.

The kids were watching so he shook off the bad feeling and led them to the front door. He grasped the knob thinking about how he usually came in the back door. Glancing at the Westfall kids, he guessed it was good to give them the best possible first impression of his home.

His home . . . But was it? His name was on the deed, but really it was Delphy's home—and Loyal's. He set his jaw and pulled the door open. Well, he sure enough wanted it to be his home and he was ready to do whatever it took to make that happen.

It was early afternoon. As he stepped into the front room, he could smell beans simmering on the stove, as well as the furniture polish Delphy used to keep the end tables gleaming. The windows were open, and gauzy white curtains tugged at their rods as a breeze followed them inside. Then Delphy was there, wearing an apron, tendrils coming loose from whatever she'd done to keep her hair out of the way while she worked.

She saw Loyal and gave a little cry, rushing forward to sweep him into her arms. The boy went gladly, and Creed smiled at the pair of them—his family. After burying her face in her son's hair, Delphy finally let her eyes meet Creed's. A tentative smile gave him hope.

"Brought your boy back, along with these two," he said, putting a hand on Rebecca's and Michael's shoulders as they stepped forward. "Their daddy is . . . uh, with Judge Kline up in Elkins, so these ones need a place to stay for a day or two."

Delphy, still holding on to Loyal, raised her eyebrows. Then she smiled at the children. "Do they now? Well, I've always enjoyed having company." She released Loyal and gave Rebecca a smile. "Especially the company of another lady." She poked Loyal. "All these boys leave me wanting for female companionship."

Rebecca beamed and settled against Delphy's side. Creed guessed the girl might be missing the company of a woman—of a mother. Roberta Tompkins was a fine lady, but no one had ever accused her of being motherly.

"Have you eaten?" Delphy asked the kids.

"No, ma'am," answered Michael. He lifted his chin a notch. "We hate to put you out, though."

"Not a bit of it," she said. "Feeding young people is one of my favorite things to do." She turned to Loyal, cupped her hand in front of her chest, and drew it down toward her belly. "Hungry?"

Loyal nodded enthusiastically and imitated the sign several times. Creed laughed. "Guess that means he's real hungry."

Delphy spared him a smile and led them all into the kitchen.

After eating bowls of beans with corn bread, followed by thick slices of pound cake, Loyal took Michael and Rebecca into the yard beyond the garden. His parents had made it clear that they were not to leave the property but seemed to understand that the kids wanted a little freedom. Loyal grabbed a ball and his glove in case the others wanted to play catch. But as they wandered past the rows of corn and runner beans, the massive cedar drew them into its shade. They settled on the ground soft from years of pine needles falling.

Loyal set his glove aside and rolled the baseball in his hands, eyes on the others to see what they might do. Michael leaned back against the tree trunk, and Loyal considered that he was probably going to get sap on his shirt but decided it was too hard to try to tell him.

"I really thought I killed that man."

Michael must have spoken the words softly because Rebecca leaned forward and spoke. "What did you say?"

"If it wasn't me that killed that man, who did?" Michael said. "And I did shoot him in the arm. Isn't that almost as bad?" He drew one knee to his chest and wrapped his arms around it. "I mean, I could have killed him."

"But you didn't," said Rebecca.

"Because of dumb luck."

Rebecca shrugged. "Still," she said. "You didn't want to kill him." She bit her lip. "Right?"

Michael hung his head, and Loyal missed what he said but could feel shame, frustration, and sorrow rolling off his friend. The older boy looked up. "And now that judge thinks Dad or maybe even Otto did it. Which I'm pretty sure they didn't. If we could just figure out who did, maybe everything would be okay again."

Rebecca shifted closer to Loyal as though needing his support. "But were things really all that okay before?" She let one shoulder lift and then drop. "I mean, Father was hardly ever around, and you . . . well, you were different." She twisted her fingers together. "I mean, you've been nicer since you decided to tell how you shot that man."

Michael's mouth hung open and he blinked slowly. "I have?" He looked to Loyal as if for confirmation. Loyal scrunched his face and nodded. "I guess I was so scared somebody was going to find out, telling the truth was a relief." Michael wore a look of surprise.

"And now the sheriff isn't even going to lock you up," Rebecca said. "At least I don't think he is."

Michael nodded slowly. "I guess he still might. It was surely wrong to shoot that man and I did lie about it for a long time."

"Maybe they'll figure out who killed him and forget about you," Rebecca suggested.

"Yeah. Maybe."

They sat for a long time not speaking or moving, until Loyal couldn't stand it any longer. He tossed the ball into Michael's lap. When the boy looked up in surprise, Loyal held up his mitt with a question in his eyes.

"Yeah. Sure. Why not," Michael said and climbed to his feet. Loyal gave Rebecca his glove, and they started a halfhearted game of three-way catch.

"He looks fine," Delphy said, standing on tiptoe to peer out the window to where Loyal tossed a ball with his friends. She was thrilled to have her boy home again and could hardly stand to have him out of her sight.

"He's fine. Better than fine—I'd say he's a marvel."

She looked at Creed over her shoulder. She was still stung by his sleeping on the floor the night before. She'd thought she was doing everything short of turning the covers back for him, and yet . . . "What do you mean by that?" She tried not to sound peevish.

"Our son is smart, kind, brave, and a good friend. I guess I've been getting to know him these past weeks." Creed stepped closer to look out the window with her. "I'm sorry I haven't taken the time to get to know him sooner."

Delphy held perfectly still, feeling the closeness of him. The heat of his body just inches from her own. He closed his eyes and breathed in deeply. When he opened his eyes, he looked right at her.

"What are you doing?" Her voice was whisper soft.

"You smell good," he said, his voice sounding gruff. He wet his lips and swallowed. "You look good, too." He reached out slowly and cupped her cheek. Delphy leaned into his hand—he might have missed her invitation, but she wasn't going to miss his.

He leaned forward, and when she didn't move away, he brushed his lips across hers. She sighed and laid one hand against his chest where she could feel the thrumming of his heart. He deepened the kiss and she welcomed it.

When he finally pulled away—not far—she felt flushed and breathless. "I've missed you," he said. "I've missed being a . . . proper husband."

"I've missed that, too," she whispered.

"Do you think . . . I mean, could we maybe . . . start again?"

She looked deep into his eyes and saw that, for the second time in their lives, he was choosing her. She glanced out the window, to where the kids were playing ball, and the ghost of a smile graced her lips. She took his hand and drew him away from the window. This time, he knew just what she meant.

When they finally trooped back inside for supper, Loyal sensed that something had changed in the house. There was a . . . lightness in the air. Mother and Father kept smiling at each other and seemed ready to laugh. Even Michael and Rebecca's spirits grew visibly lighter as they relaxed and smiled.

After supper they all sat on the front porch. Mother talked with Rebecca and Michael, signing for them all to make it easier for Loyal to follow along. Loyal even chimed in a few times since Mother could translate for him. Father just sat on the top porch step and watched, a look of deep satisfaction on his face.

When they went to bed, Michael bunked in Loyal's room while Rebecca got the guest bedroom all to herself. Loyal thought Father might sleep on the sofa like he usually did but was pleased to see him follow Mother to her room. Maybe his parents were finally going to act like real parents.

All in all, the evening had been so pleasant, and Loyal had such a good feeling about his family and friends that he almost changed his mind about what he planned to do. But he supposed that one good evening at home wasn't going to fix this situation. The sheriff still needed to know who had killed Eddie Minks, and until he did, none of them could really and truly relax.

Loyal feigned sleep for what felt like an hour. He'd given Michael his bed and was sleeping on a pallet on the floor. He cracked his eyes open and watched the older boy intently in the pale glow of moonlight. Michael lay flat on his back, one arm stretched over his head. His mouth was slack, his eyes closed. Loyal eased to a sitting position and leaned forward so he could see the steady rise and fall of the boy's chest. If he wasn't asleep, it was the best act Loyal had ever seen.

Gathering his feet beneath him, Loyal slowly stood. He tiptoed to the open window, shoes in his hand. Mother had let them go to bed in their clothes, so he didn't need to dress. He looked out to make sure no one was around, then swung out and into the night. He was down the trellis in short order and crept to the corner of the house. He halfway expected to see the sheriff or his deputy guarding the house, but the road was empty—except for a bright slash of moonlight glowing like an arrow pointing the way. Loyal slipped across the street, jogged past darkened buildings, and was soon headed for Rich Mountain, a pillar of moonlight urging him on.

twenty-seven

Creed whistled as he rose the next morning and set about shaving in the downstairs lavatory. He hadn't felt this fine since, well, since his wedding night. Delphy slipped up behind him and slid her arms around his waist, burying her face against his back. He splashed water on his cheeks and turned to wish her a proper good morning.

After a few moments, she murmured, "Those kids will be hungry."

"They aren't the only ones," he said softly in her ear before releasing her with a final squeeze and a kiss.

She began bustling around the kitchen while he finished setting his mustache and hair to rights. He found her at the stove and hooked one arm around her waist. He kissed the back of her neck where she'd hurriedly twisted her hair up. "It's good to be back," he said. "You, me, and Loyal. I'm sorry I stayed away so long."

She leaned into him and sighed. "I'm sorry, too. Do you think . . . ?" She turned to look at him, worry in her eyes. "Do you really think you'll stay?"

He didn't answer at first, just kissed her forehead, her

cheek, and finally her willing mouth. "I do," he said. And she smiled in a way that let him know she understood just what he meant.

Creed took the stairs two at a time and knocked on the kids' doors. He heard stirring in both rooms and called out that breakfast would be served in thirty minutes. Whistling again, he went downstairs to see what might need doing around the house. There were always little repair jobs and he wanted to make sure he did them before Delphy had to ask.

Fifteen minutes later, Creed relaxed at the kitchen table with a cup of coffee, trying to distract his wife from the eggs and bacon she was tending. Michael and Rebecca appeared in the doorway looking pale and frightened. He sat up straighter, fear piercing the happiness he'd been floating on. "What is it?" he asked .

Delphy spun around at the stove and seemed to notice the same change in the room's atmosphere. "Where's Loyal?" she asked, her voice sharp.

Michael swallowed convulsively, like he was choking on his words. "We don't know," he blurted.

"What do you mean?" Creed bolted from his chair and back up the stairs. He checked Loyal's room but only saw an empty bed and pallet on the floor. He quickly searched the other two rooms upstairs before bounding back down to the first floor.

Delphy met him at the front door. "I couldn't find him out-side. The kids say they don't know anything." Her shaking hand covered her mouth. "Could someone have taken him?"

Creed pulled her against him and looked at the Westfall kids standing in the doorway. "Did he tell you anything last night?" They shook their heads as though mute. "What did you talk about?" Creed demanded.

Michael stared at the floor as though he might read the an-swer there. "I guess we talked about how since I didn't kill that man, the sheriff would have to figure out who did. And how it was bad that Otto and Dad might get in trouble after all."

Creed closed his eyes and rubbed Delphy's back as she shed quiet tears. "He's a good boy. A kind and brave boy. Just the sort who would want to help his friends figure out the truth."

Delphy caught her breath. "You think he knows who the real killer is?"

"Probably not," Creed said, "but I'm betting he's decided to try and find out."

Loyal felt pretty proud of himself. Last summer he hadn't done anything but hang around the house and help Mother in the yard and garden. This year he was doing all sorts of things. He smiled and stuck his chest out. Being deaf sure wasn't slowing him down!

He headed for the bend in the river where Eddie Minks had been killed. He'd finally taken time to really think back to that day and what he'd seen beyond Michael and Rebecca running along a path. It might have been an animal, but the more he conjured the image the more he thought it was a person. Someone had been moving in the trees above the trail. He'd seen . . . what, a hat maybe? And sunlight glinting on bright metal. He wasn't sure what he expected to find now, but he was determined to do everything he possibly could.

The notion that the moonlight was leading him stayed with him until the sun peeked over the mountain and drowned out the moon. By then he was standing in the cold river, remembering how the mountain had looked the day his life changed. He found the path and the stump and let his eyes move up the slope of the mountain . . . there. A gap in the trees, perfect for exposing someone who didn't expect to be seen from the river. Loyal noted a pine nearby and began working his way toward the spot.

As the sun crept higher, the gnats got bad. There was practically a cloud of them in front of his face, and the infernal insects preceded him up the mountain. He swatted at them a few times but gave up when he realized they were mostly staying out in front of him. If he were a bullfrog, it would be his lucky day.

Reaching the tree, the cloud of insects finally lifted. He looked around until he found the gap he'd seen from the water. He began to search every inch of the ground and surrounding trees. He didn't know what he was looking for, but he figured . . . and then he saw it. It was just a twig, but the end of it was worn and frayed like it had been chewed on. Loyal picked it up and sniffed it. Sassafras. Just like the twigs he'd seen Sam chewing at the Hacker place. Just like the one he'd found in his room after Sam spent the night. He guessed it wasn't what the sheriff would call "hard evidence," but he was excited just the same.

Now all he had to do was find Sam and see what he knew about the day Eddie Minks got shot. Of course, Sam might even be the one who fired the second gun, so Loyal would need to be extra careful.

"Julia's been after me to quit sheriffing, and I think I just might go ahead and do that." Virgil looked like he hadn't caught up on any of the sleep he'd been missing. "I arrested Earl on suspicion of fraud and ran him up to Elkins last night. When I got back to the house, there was a quilt and a pillow on the sofa. I took the hint but can't say as I got much rest." He sighed. "Nor did I get much breakfast."

Creed could sympathize with him—even though he and Delphy were on the mend, Loyal running off was a setback all around. And telling the sheriff the boy was missing—again— had been worse than taking a beating. But Creed knew he didn't have a choice. "I think he's trying to figure out where that other bullet might have come from."

"Like father, like son," Virgil said, dragging his hands over his face. Creed tried not to show the spark of pride he felt in thinking that his son was taking after him. "Thing is, when I picked up Earl he finally talked. Turns out he and Eddie were supposed to meet somebody out there at the bend in the river. Except Earl was sick—hungover, if you ask me—and Eddie went by himself. Earl wouldn't tell me who they were meeting, just said it had to do with a land deal and he figured holding on to the name was the only leverage he had left. Says he'll tell us who it was if we cut him a deal."

Creed swallowed hard. "Any notion who it could be?"

"I went through that book of Eddie's with a fine-tooth comb and there are a couple of good candidates, but I keep circling back to Clyde Hacker. He talked like he might actually sell his land. I wonder if those boys of his think that's such a good idea?"

Creed stared at his shoes. "Clyde said something about giving Sam and Glen a way out of this place. But I guess I can see how they might prefer to keep the family business going rather than starting over somewhere else."

"What I was thinking. Those boys would never go against their daddy, but they might find another way around him." Virgil picked up a thick ceramic mug and slurped his coffee. It put some color in his cheeks. He stood and stretched his shoulders back like a bird stretching its wings. "Alright then. I'll get Bud to go over to your place and keep an eye on the Westfall kids. You and me are headed back out to the mountain. We'll start at Hadden's place and work our way to the Hackers."

Creed nodded. Though he was anxious to find Loyal, there was also a part of him that hoped the boy might actually find a clue. That maybe Loyal would crack this case wide open as they said in the detective stories. Wouldn't that be something?

He'd been so afraid of doing more damage to the boy for so long. Finally seeing how he could hold his own was liberating. Maybe it wasn't about pushing like his own father had done, but simply encouraging the boy's natural abilities. He thought maybe that was what a father ought to do and he was eager to try it out.

twenty-eight

Loyal sat in the dappled shade of the forest near a dancing stream. He was hot, tired, and maybe a little bit lost. He dipped a hand in the chilly flow and lifted it to his lips. The water tasted cool and delicious. He took off his shoes and waded into the shin-deep water, reaching down to scoop some up and splash his face. He wondered what the creek sounded like. He'd heard people describe water as being musical or roaring. He knew what music felt like. And he'd felt the roar of a storm or a train thrumming in his chest, but this wasn't like either of those. He sat on a rock and tried to feel what the water sounded like.

The current whispered across his skin, making gooseflesh rise on his arms and legs. He closed his eyes and . . .

His eyes flew open. He hadn't heard anything, but he'd felt a presence. Sam Hacker stood on the far side of the creek, twig twitching between his lips as he considered Loyal. He plucked out the bit of sassafras and tossed it in the water so that it sped away on the current.

"Seems like you're a fur piece from where you belong."

Loyal frowned, then realized Sam meant *far*. He held both

hands up and moved one away from the other, then pointed at Sam with his eyebrows raised.

"You asking if I'm far from where I'm supposed to be, too?" Loyal could see him jerk with a short laugh. "Farther than you know." Sam cocked his head to the side as he stared at Loyal. "What you huntin'?"

All at once, Loyal realized that if it had been Sam who'd fired the killing shot that made him dangerous. Loyal had imagined the shooting being an accident, but now, looking into the man's dark, piercing eyes, the notion that someone might do such a thing on purpose hit him full in the face, and he knew then and there that evil was a tangible thing.

Sam shook his head. "I been watching you. You're smarter than folks give you credit for." Loyal felt a spurt of pride. "Although maybe not as smart as you think." Then a bolt of fear hit Loyal and he felt deeply foolish. "Last I knew, you and the rest of 'em were headed to Elkins to talk to that judge." Sam narrowed his red-streaked eyes. "Hadden and that German boy didn't come home."

Loyal began to think that coming out here on his own had been stupid.

Sam rubbed his eyes. "Guess that means one of 'em did it."

Loyal released a pent-up breath. Maybe Sam wasn't suspicious of him after all.

"Come on then." Sam motioned for Loyal to follow. "Ma took a shine to you and them other two kids. I reckon she can feed you, and then I'll run you on home afore you get into trouble."

Loyal tried a smile, still uncertain as he waded out of the water to put his shoes back on. Maybe if Sam really was the killer, he could find another clue. Something that would take the heat off Mr. Westfall and Otto. He wasn't sure what that might be, yet that was how it went in the Hardy Boys books.

He trailed along after Sam while wracking his brain for a way to get the man to confess to shooting Eddie Minks. Sam wasn't even suspicious of him—probably because he was deaf—and if he could set everything to rights, he'd be a hero and Father would be proud of him. He smiled, picturing how good that would feel.

As they walked, he sniffed the air and noticed a sharp, stale smell rolling off of Sam. At school he'd once smelled something like that when a classmate's father showed up unexpectedly. There had been whispers about his being drunk. Loyal was so caught up in trying to tell if Sam had been drinking that he nearly stepped on a ginseng plant before he realized what it was. He stopped and must have made a noise because Sam turned back and looked almighty pleased when he saw the plant at Loyal's feet.

"That's a nice one," he said, leaning close and squinting. He found a stick and began working it around the plant to loosen the root. Loyal tried to remember if this was part of one of Father's patches. He thought it was but couldn't be sure. So many places in the woods looked a lot alike, and as familiar as this spot was, he couldn't say if it was where Father had shown him the plants he planned to harvest.

Sam tugged the root from the soil. He brushed off the bulbous growth that was as big around as his thumb and grinned. "You've got a good eye on ya there." He rubbed his own eyes. "I've always had puny sight. Say, you know where there are more of these?"

Loyal clenched his jaw. He wasn't supposed to lie, but Father also told him how important it was to keep the location of his plants a secret. And Sam clearly meant to dig them up. He settled for a shrug. Sam appeared to chew the inside of his cheek. "Tight-lipped, are ya?" Then he laughed. "Guess you are at that. Come on."

They continued on their way, and even though Loyal spotted another ginseng plant with its crown of berries, he made a point of not looking right at it. This must be Father's patch—the one where they'd found half a dozen plants that looked ready for harvest come fall. Sam hadn't even planted the seeds from the root in his pocket.

Sam didn't notice any more plants, and Loyal kept his head down so he wouldn't either. Because of that, he didn't realize that they'd come up on the Hacker place until they were standing at a door built into the side of a hill, with a small peaked roof over the door. He recognized it as a springhouse. Sam made a motion like taking a drink from a cup. Loyal nodded. He was definitely thirsty again after their hot tromp through the woods. Sam smiled and held the door open, making a sweeping gesture to invite Loyal inside.

Loyal nodded his gratitude and stepped through the doorway into the cool, dim interior. There was a trough in the back of the space, where the spring water would flow and they could keep things like milk and butter cool. And he could dip up a drink. But when he stepped closer and his eyes began to adjust, he saw that the trough was dry. He turned to see what Sam thought about it just in time to see the door shut out the light.

Clyde appeared to be napping on the front porch when the police car pulled up to his house. But based on the way he eased his hat back on his head and gave them both the once-over, Creed guessed it wasn't what you'd call a deep sleep.

"Sheriff, we live out here in the wilds of Rich Mountain because we're not partial to company. Seems like you're starting to make it a habit to call on us with some regularity." He stood and stretched. "I'm not sure how much longer I'm going to be able to extend my hospitality."

"Aw, Clyde, don't start talking fancy. You know good and well this isn't a social call."

Clyde snorted. "Is that supposed to make me glad to have you stop by?"

"No more than I'm glad to be here." Virgil stopped at the bottom of the steps and propped one booted foot there. "You seen Loyal?"

"The deaf boy?"

"That'd be the one."

"Nary a hide nor a hair since you took him out of here," Clyde answered. "Don't tell me you've misplaced him again?"

Creed flexed his fingers. He didn't like the way Clyde was talking about Loyal, yet he didn't want to alienate the man. He pinched his tongue between his front teeth in order to keep his thoughts to himself.

Virgil started up the steps. "Mind if I look inside? Maybe check with some other members of your family?"

"I do mind, but since it looks like you're coming in anyway, let's get it over with."

Creed followed Virgil through the door. He kept his lips pressed together and his hands in his pockets. He'd never had a reason to dislike the Hackers, but then he'd never had a reason to like them either. They kept to themselves, and so did Creed. At least he used to.

Clyde's wife, Bernie, sat at the kitchen table, threading beans on twine to dry into leather britches for winter storage. She nodded but didn't pause in her labor.

Sam walked in through the back door. He jerked, his eyes registering surprise. His left hand went to his pants pocket, then froze. He flexed his fingers and reached into his breast pocket instead, fetching out a twig that he stuck in his mouth. "You boys planning to lodge some more young'uns with us?"

"We're looking for Loyal. You seen him?" Virgil asked.

"Nope."

Creed couldn't stand this any longer. "You sure?" he said, pushing forward. "Not much happens out here without your bunch knowing about it."

"Maybe he ain't out here," Sam said. Creed was close enough

now to smell the sassafras twig clenched between Sam's teeth—along with the reek of alcohol. "Seems like whenever something bad happens, townsfolk figure a Hacker must be involved."

"Now, everybody just simmer down," Virgil said. "We're not accusing you of anything, just looking for help in finding Creed's boy. He was here not so long ago, and we figured there was a chance he might have come back."

Sam thumped into a chair opposite his mother and glared at them. "Too many people poking around out here. You'd think somebody dying would cut down on the traffic."

"Who else has been poking around?" Virgil asked. When Sam didn't answer, he looked at Clyde. "You see anybody other than the two of us and those kids?"

Clyde frowned at Sam. "Most everybody knows to steer clear or can't find their way out. Even them two government boys knew to send word about wanting our land by way of Glen when he was in town. Sam's just cranky."

Virgil nodded. "Speaking of those boys wanting your land, I was surprised to hear you say you were thinking about selling. Don't suppose a deal might've gone wrong?"

Clyde glanced at Sam, a thoughtful expression on his face. "They was supposed to come out and talk to me, but then one of 'em got killed before that happened. I figured that was the end of it."

"So, you really were going to sell your land." Virgil hooked his thumbs in his belt.

Clyde dropped into a chair next to Sam. "I was doing it for these hardheaded boys of mine. Time we got out of our"—he darted a look at the sheriff—"family business. It's gettin' more and more dangerous, and some folks"—now he speared Sam with a look—"have been mixing in products I don't much approve of."

Sam snorted. "Tired of you making my decisions for me, old man."

Clyde shook his head and turned tired eyes on Creed. "I'd have whipped him for talking like that back in the day. But now . . ." He sighed. "Guess there comes a day when you've gotta let 'em make their own bed and lie in it."

Creed watched Sam, who watched his father. "How about you, Sam? Did you have any more dealings with Earl or Eddie?" He felt Virgil elbow him but ignored it.

"Nope." He didn't take his eyes off his father, and the look was one that sent chills down Creed's spine.

"You sure?" Sam turned that cold stare on Creed and kept his peace.

Virgil stepped forward. "That'll do, Creed. We're not here to question these folks. We're just looking for Loyal, and it seems our time might be better spent getting out and hunting for him instead of troubling Clyde and his family."

Creed started to speak but snapped his mouth shut when he saw the warning in Virgil's eyes. Virgil herded him toward the door. "If you see or hear anything of Loyal, let us know."

"We'll do it," Clyde said. "He's a fine young fella. Wish I had a few like him."

Virgil almost shoved Creed out the front door and steered him toward the car. "Quit stirring up trouble and get in the car."

Creed did as he was told and managed to keep quiet until the Hackers' house disappeared behind a stand of pines. "I think Sam knew something about Loyal," he burst out. "He started to go for his pocket when he saw us, and there was fresh dirt on his pants and under his fingernails. He'd been scrabbling in the dirt, and I've got an awful feeling it has something to do with my son."

Virgil kept driving, eyes straight ahead. When Creed didn't think he could stand it another second, the sheriff pulled over and shut off the engine. "I agree."

Creed sputtered, "You do?"

"Sam was hiding something. Of course, the whole family's

hiding plenty in that barn out past the house, but it felt different today." He thumped his hand against the steering wheel. "They know that I know what's in the barn, and so long as they don't cause trouble, neither will I. Plus, you heard Clyde—he was ready to close up shop. Guess that's causing more than a little friction." He rubbed his temples and took a deep breath. "Alright. If Clyde was gonna sell but Sam didn't want him to . . . well, that'd give him motive to step in and try to change the situation."

Creed nodded. "What did he have in his pocket? And what did it have to do with Loyal?"

"Might not be Loyal," said Virgil. "Might be Eddie Minks."

"You think Sam's the one who shot him. But why?"

"Sam didn't want his daddy to sell the land. But Earl and Eddie didn't know that. Maybe Sam was the one they were supposed to meet, only no one expected two kids to show up." Virgil shrugged. "Or maybe Sam was just feeling ornery. He's not someone I'd want walking behind me if we were hunting together."

"And Loyal?"

"Like I say, Sam's jumpiness might not have anything to do with Loyal." He laid a steady hand on Creed's arm. "Although I can see how you'd want to think he might know something. When someone you love is missing, it's hard to see anything else."

Creed wanted to shake off the hand but figured he'd made Virgil mad enough the past few weeks. He needed his friend to stick by him, and letting his emotions have free rein wasn't going to help the situation. "I hear you," he said, "but I still want to know what's in the man's pocket."

twenty-nine

The panic he'd felt when first robbed of his sight by darkness had finally worn down to a tolerable level. Loyal's eyes had adjusted to the dark interior of the springhouse, reassuring him that he hadn't lost yet another of his senses. He could just make out the confines of what he guessed was his prison since he'd determined that the door would not open. Now he needed to breathe deep and consider his options.

There weren't any windows, but there were cracks where the walls met the roof and around the door that wasn't quite a perfect fit. He wondered if he could make one of those gaps bigger? Of course, it'd have to be a lot bigger for him to slip through. He kicked at the dirt floor. Maybe he could dig his way out. Looking around, he found an old metal dipper that must have been used to scoop water back when it flowed into the stone trough.

Boy, what he wouldn't give for a cool drink right now.

He felt the shape of the dipper, its rough edge and broken handle. He carried it to the door and tried using it to dig at the dirt there where the bottom edge wasn't even with the ground. But the soil was hard-packed, had likely been walked over a thousand times. He'd need a pickax rather than an old metal dipper if he was even going to make a decent start.

Pressing an eye to the narrow crack along the hinge edge of the door, Loyal could see the back of the Hacker house. He might even be able to holler loud enough for someone to hear him. But that probably wouldn't do him any good. Shoot, the whole family might be in on locking him up here. Maybe they'd all been in on killing Eddie and thought Loyal might've figured it out.

His stomach grumbled. Thirsty and hungry. He didn't feel nearly as fine as he had when he started out that morning. Finding clues didn't help much if he couldn't tell anyone about them. He looked down at the dipper he still held in his hand. The handle probably used to have a curl in it before it broke off. Now it was just a short, jagged piece of metal. He wedged it into the crack along the door and wiggled it back and forth. Surprised, he realized the wood was rotted and crumbling. The edge of the board in the wall gave way a little bit. He wiggled it some more and managed to widen the crack into more of a gap. He could actually work his fingers into the opening. It was a long shot, but maybe if he kept at it he could work open this spot wide enough for him to break free of the springhouse.

After what seemed like an hour, Loyal managed to open a gap big enough for maybe a cat to slink through. A skinny cat. He used his shirttail to wipe sweat from his face. Now he was even thirstier and hungrier and maybe not any closer to freedom. He dropped the dipper and sat back on his haunches to rest. Which was when he saw movement out in the yard. Falling to his belly, he held his face to the opening. He couldn't squeeze through, but he could sure enough see . . .

And what he saw were Sam and Glen. They weren't far from the springhouse, and they were arguing about something.

Loyal guessed they weren't much worried about his hearing them. But he could surely *see* most of what they were saying.

". . . turn him loose," Glen said, stabbing a finger in the air. "You're going to cause more trouble."

"He knows where his pa's sang patches are," Sam shot back. At least that was what Loyal thought he said. The way he shortened his words made it tough to read his lips. "And with Creed in town, we can . . . before he knows what happened." Though Loyal missed some words, he caught enough to get the overall meaning.

"Ain't you caused enough trouble?" The first word took a minute, but Loyal filled it in.

"You mean that government man? He was asking for trouble." Sam spit on the ground and swiped at his mouth.

"Why'd you have to kill him?" Glen looked disgusted.

Sam glanced toward the house, so Loyal missed the first part of what he said. ". . . cheat us. I wanted to get 'em both, but when that boy . . . think he did it."

"But they didn't. People kept . . . until the sheriff figured out it was somebody else. And they've already . . . around here. How long you think it'll take to figure it out?"

Sam gave his brother a push, and Loyal missed what he said.

Glen waved a hand toward the springhouse. "First, we turn that boy loose. Second, you take that rifle you used and head for . . . We'll say you're visiting . . ." Some of the details were lost to Loyal, but he saw Sam's lip curl. "I ain't running. Virgil White's a fool and . . . can't prove anything."

Glen ran a hand through his hair, making it stick up. "If Virgil's a fool, he's not the only one."

Loyal sucked in a breath when he saw Sam land a fist on his brother's jaw. Glen staggered, recovered his footing, and came back at Sam swinging. They must have been making plenty of noise, because Clyde came rushing out of the house carrying a sloshing pail. He flung water on the two men, who stopped their fighting and swiped at their faces. Loyal couldn't see if either of them said anything as they turned toward their father. He did catch Clyde's response, though.

"I don't care. If you two are gonna try to kill each other, have the kindness not to do it where your mother can see. And to think I wanted to give you a better life." Then he turned and stalked back toward the house.

The two men glared at each other for several beats. Glen spun on his heel and stomped off toward the barn. Sam lifted a hand to his chin and moved it around like it hurt. Loyal hoped it did. He'd definitely been rooting for Glen. Sam glanced at the springhouse, then looked all around. He started toward the door, and Loyal scrambled to his feet, moving to the rear of the small space.

He saw the crack around the door darken as Sam drew near, and he thought he saw the door move but then the light returned and nothing happened. He crept closer and lay back down to put his eye to the opening just in time to see Sam disappear around the house. He watched for a long time, hoping someone would come for him but no one did. Finally he fell asleep.

Creed and Virgil worked their way up the mountain well clear of the Hackers' homesite. They didn't use a trail, just pushed through as best they could, wading through poison ivy and stinging nettle and getting tangled up in more than one patch of shin rippers. Creed didn't care. He'd walk through fire for Loyal, and something in him said the Hackers knew more about his son than they were letting on.

"Remember, we're just going to watch. No busting in there to do anything crazy." Virgil wiped the back of his sweaty neck with a bandanna. "It's not like I have or could get a search warrant. We're trespassing as it is. Probably a waste of time, but there was something funny . . ." His voice tapered off, and he looked back at Creed with a finger pressed to his lips. He motioned ahead and pointed.

There was a rock outcropping on the side of the mountain that gave them a decent view of the house below. Virgil picked out a spot where he could sit behind a boulder and watch while Creed settled behind a massive oak tree that looked like it had sprouted from the stone. The sun was headed behind the mountain, leaving them in shade while illuminating the valley below. Even as worried as he was, Creed had to admire the spot Clyde and his family had carved from the mountain. This land was tough and unforgiving, but the Hackers had built a haven for themselves regardless.

After an hour or so of waiting that felt like a lifetime to Creed, he finally saw movement below. Bernie walked out the back door, carrying a pan of water to her small vegetable garden. She poured the water over what might have been hills of squash, then went back inside. Creed looked across at Virgil, who shrugged and patted the air with both hands. *Stay still and wait* was how Creed read it. He wondered how Loyal would read the motion. It was probably real sign language that meant something else altogether. He smiled thinking about his boy. He'd ask him when they were together again.

It was probably another twenty minutes before anyone else stirred. This time it was Sam stepping out the back door. He stretched and rolled a cigarette, then lit it, the match flaring in the gathering dusk. He strolled out into the yard in a way that looked intentionally casual to Creed. Like he was putting a show on for somebody. As he approached the slope of the hill, he flicked the cigarette butt into the dirt and ground it out with his boot. Then he disappeared below them, the outcropping blocking him from view. Creed crept forward, and Vigil hissed at him, motioning him back with his hand.

Creed frowned at him and lay down on his belly on the curved surface of the rock. He inched forward until he could see the peak of a roof on a small outbuilding. No sign of Sam or anyone else. He sighed and made his way back to cover. Virgil stared daggers at him.

Sam reappeared, walking with more purpose now. He headed straight for the barn and went inside. Creed nodded at Virgil and began easing around the oak tree.

"What are you doing?" hissed Virgil.

"I'm going to find my boy," Creed said, turning his back on his friend and working his way down the steep slope. It was a long shot, but if Loyal was in one of those outbuildings, Creed was going to find him.

Loyal knew what Sam wanted from him, but he acted like he didn't understand. Sam kept asking where his father's ginseng plants grew, but Loyal just kept shrugging and shaking his head. It hadn't been all that hard to seem convincing since he really was groggy from sleep. The man finally cursed and stomped back out the door, securing it behind him. Loyal figured he'd come back with paper and pencil pretty soon. Even though he didn't know what he'd do then, he'd at least bought himself a little time. And it was getting dark outside. Surely Sam wouldn't try to hunt ginseng at night.

Loyal perched on the edge of the trough. Of course, if he could get Sam to take him out into the woods to look for ginseng, maybe he could get away. His captor seemed fit and fast, but Loyal was smaller. He might be able to run into a rhododendron patch and wiggle through where Sam couldn't.

He was still trying to come up with a plan when he noticed the door ease open, letting in a spill of light only slightly brighter than the darkened interior of the springhouse. Loyal scooted to the far corner, as if he could hide from Sam. Shoot, if he opened the door wide enough, Loyal might be able to push past him and into the yard before Sam's "puny" eyes adjusted. He shifted to the hinge side of the door, hoping he wasn't making any noise.

Sam was sure taking his time coming in. He eased the door open like it was a contest to do it extra slow. Loyal saw his bulk there in the opening that was still just inches wide. He'd never get his chance at this rate. Maybe he should just grab the door, then try to shoot past Sam. He took two steps forward, trying to guess the right moment for his escape. Then Sam fished in his pocket, pulled out a match, and struck it.

Loyal figured it was now or never. He grabbed the door and jerked it, moving to run past the larger man, when an arm shot out and grabbed him, pulling him in tight. He grunted and twisted, then froze. What was that smell? It was familiar and comforting. The match had fallen to the ground in the struggle, but Loyal's eyes, adjusted to the dark, could make out the clean-shaven face of . . .

No. Not completely clean-shaven. It was Father's mustache and his warm tobacco smell that filled Loyal's senses.

Father grinned and stepped inside, hugging Loyal hard against his chest. They thumped each other on the back, and Loyal felt a couple of tears escape, making him grateful for the dim light.

Father held a finger to his lips and pointed outside. He looked around the edge of the door and peered all around the yard. Turning back to Loyal, he motioned for him to follow. They eased out and immediately pressed themselves to the side of the building facing away from the barn, but all too obvious to anyone looking out from the back of the house.

Loyal looked uphill into the trees and saw the shape of another man there where some rocks made a break in the brush. He jabbed Father and pointed, stabbing the air, his eyes wide. Father held up a hand to spell V-i-r . . . then stopped and frowned. Loyal nodded with relief, then finished for him g-i-l.

Father motioned for Loyal to move ahead of him, toward the sheriff who was crouched low, beckoning them forward in a *come on* gesture.

Loyal began working his way through the saplings and underbrush covering the steep hillside. It was rough going in the darkness, with vines and briars working together to slow him down. He sensed Father close behind him and turned to see that he was following. He was. Seconds later, Loyal stepped on a fallen branch that rolled under his foot and made him fall. He was pretty sure he made a noise and clapped a hand over his mouth. He could taste blood where he'd bitten his tongue, and his elbow stung. Father put out a hand to help him to his feet. As he stood, he saw movement near the barn. A man, his long arm stretched out to point at them. He punched Father in the shoulder and motioned behind them.

Before Father could turn, there was a burst of light and suddenly they were both falling. Then came another flash of light—maybe from where the sheriff was waiting. Confused and shaken, Loyal scrambled to his feet and tried to run up the hill, but his ankle throbbed and gave way beneath him. He glanced back toward the yard just as Father crashed into him, blocking yet another flash from below. The wind knocked from his lungs, Loyal froze trying to catch his breath. Air finally rushed back with a mighty whoosh and then all was still. He panted and waited to see what would happen next.

The sheriff appeared in his line of vision and began feeling his arms and legs. Loyal sat up and signed that he was all right, though the sheriff didn't know what he meant. Still, he seemed satisfied. Loyal climbed to his feet, limping only a little on the sore ankle. He saw that there were several people down below now, and light shone into the yard from the house and barn. But where was Father? He looked at the sheriff, who was waving his arms and likely yelling at someone below. Loyal could just make out what he was saying.

"Clyde, can you promise me no one's going to shoot?" He must have gotten a satisfactory answer because he nodded and pointed Loyal back down the hill. Which was when he saw Father, lying on the ground below them, eyes closed, face pale, and much, much too still.

thirty

There was so much blood. Loyal sat, wide-eyed, wishing he could do something to help. They were inside Clyde Hacker's house now. Bernie wiped more blood on her apron and moved a lamp closer to Father's still form. Her head bent forward, making it hard to see what she was saying, but he didn't really need to know. He could see more than he wanted to.

Father was curled on his side on top of the kitchen table, stripped to his waist. His eyes remained closed, his mustache a dark slash against his pale face. Bernie had boiled a kitchen knife that she was using to cut into Father's back where Sam shot him. Loyal wanted to look away with everything in him but couldn't tear his eyes from the woman's sure movements. Virgil stood nearby, his face serious.

Finally Bernie raised her head, a grim smile on her face, and held up a bloody bit of metal. The sheriff held out a handkerchief, and she dropped the bullet into it. She then reached for a needle and thread that she'd also boiled and began sewing up Father's wound. Loyal swallowed the sick feeling rising in his throat and squeezed his eyes shut. A wave of dizziness washed over him, and he must have swayed because Virgil was suddenly there, a hand on his shoulder. He wanted to ask if Father would be all right. The question must have shown in his eyes.

"He's lost some blood, but I think he'll be okay," the sheriff said. "We'll get him home to Delphy just as soon as he's stitched up."

Bernie filled a basin with clean water and began wiping away all traces of blood.

Clyde stepped into the room and approached Virgil. "Glen followed a blood trail a ways. Lost it in the dark." He shook his head. "Sam's always wanted more. Wanted what everybody else has. I don't think he meant to kill anybody."

The sheriff frowned. "Whether he meant to or not, he's in some pretty deep trouble. What was he doing with Loyal out there in that springhouse?"

"Glen said he was after Creed's sang patches. Thought the boy could show him where they are."

Virgil shot Loyal a look. "Is that right? Was Sam after your dad's ginseng?"

Loyal nodded. He wanted to tell the sheriff that Sam was also the one who'd shot Eddie Minks, but he was too exhausted, too wrung out to figure out how to tell him. And maybe he shouldn't do it in front of Sam's father anyway. He just wanted to go home. Tears rose up behind his eyes, but he fought them back. He wasn't going to look like a baby in front of the sheriff or Clyde Hacker. He went to Father, laying a hand on his chest to feel his heart beating and the rise and fall of his breathing.

A hand settled on his shoulder and it felt so like Father's that he had to squeeze his eyes shut again to keep the feelings bottled up inside. When he opened his eyes, Virgil said, "Let's get you two home."

Loyal nodded and held the door open for the sheriff and Mr.

Hacker as they carried Father out to Mr. Hacker's wagon for the slow, painful ride into town.

Creed could smell lavender. And he could hear someone singing a hymn, low and sweet. He started to open his eyes, then waited. Strong yet gentle fingers stroked his face, the shadow of his beard. It was so tender he felt tears prick his eyes. So he opened them.

And there she was. Delphy gazed down at him with a look of gladness that made his heart sing. "Hey," he said.

She pressed a fist to her mouth, tears filling her eyes. "Hey," she whispered back.

He lifted a hand to catch a tear as it reached the tip of her chin. "Don't cry."

"I'm not," she said, more tears wetting his fingers.

He tried to laugh, but pain stole his breath.

"Don't move. You've been shot." She pressed gently against his shoulder as if he was going to try to sit up. Which he wasn't.

"By cupid's arrow you mean," he said, managing a grin.

She choked on a laugh. "You're terrible. Nearly killed and still flirting with me."

He caught her hand in his. "I'll always flirt with you." He tugged her closer. Made her lean over him so that he could feel her breath against his cheek. "Kiss me, Delphy." She pressed her lips to his forehead. "That's not what I mean." He curled her hand against his bare chest and drew her closer until he could taste the sweetness of her lips. She let him, then drew away, flushed and a little breathless.

"Some invalid you are."

"Some nurse you are—I think I'm healed."

She laughed and turned as someone else entered the room. Virgil came into view, worry etching his brow. The wrinkles smoothed when he saw Creed with his eyes open and maybe a little color in his cheeks.

"Thought we might lose you," he said. "I've wanted to get shut of you a time or two, but not like this."

Creed grimaced as he pushed himself higher on the pillows in . . . glory be, he was in Delphy's bed. The bed that was his before . . . well, before he'd turned into such a fool. "I'm not that easy to get rid of."

"Don't I know it." Virgil laughed as he pulled a chair over to sit beside the bed. "Guess you're planning to live through this, then?"

Creed glanced at his wife, who now stood in the doorway. "I can think of a few reasons why I might want to live a long time yet. Guess I'll stick around." Delphy smiled and left the room, promising him she'd be back soon.

Virgil nodded. "Bud and a few others are tracking Sam Hacker this morning. Soon as it got light, they set out to follow last night's blood trail."

"Who shot him?" Creed asked.

"I did. Should've aimed to kill. My daddy always said if you're willing to shoot a man, you'd better be willing to kill him." He shook his head. "It's harder than it sounds."

Creed nodded, then groaned without meaning to. He felt like someone had tried to cut him in half with a rusty saw blade. "If Sam hurts as bad as I do, he might be wishing you'd done him that favor about now."

Virgil sat with his head down, hands clasped loosely between his knees. "I expect you saved Loyal's life." He paused. "I don't know who Sam was aiming at, but he sure enough would've struck down that boy if you hadn't jumped in the way." He lifted his head, and his eyes bore into Creed's. "I thought you were a fool to go down there on the off chance Loyal was in that springhouse. But I guess you were the right kind of fool." He shook his head. "I'm just glad you didn't let me stop you."

"So am I," Creed said. "About time being a fool worked out for me."

Mother wouldn't leave him alone. Loyal was used to her hovering and doting on him, but this was too much. Every time she drew near, she reached out to touch him—his hair, his shoulder—and he wanted to duck away but made himself tolerate the extra attention. Of course, when she wasn't hovering over him, she was tending to Father.

She hadn't let him venture up the stairs yet. He'd wrenched his ankle when he rolled his foot on that tree branch and it was swollen up now. He'd walked on it fine the night before, but by morning it looked like a plum had been tucked under the taut skin. Mother bathed it in witch hazel and wrapped strips of cloth snug around it. She made him sit on the sofa with the foot propped up on a pillow. He crossed his arms over his chest and glared at nothing in particular.

Rebecca slipped into the room. She smiled and handed him a book. It was *The Missing Chums*, a Hardy Boys mystery that had come out that spring. Loyal had already read the first three books in the series and had been hoping to get this one for Christmas. He smiled and made the sign for *thank you*. Rebecca lit up and signed *you're welcome*.

Loyal wanted to ask where she got the book, but it seemed like too complicated a question in sign language. While Rebecca had been quick to pick up what he'd shown her, they hadn't gotten that far. So instead he waved her into a chair near the sofa, where Mother had told him in no uncertain terms that he was to stay. *You okay?* he signed.

Rebecca's smile lit the room. "It's so neat that I know what you're saying. Yes, I'm okay. I'm sorry you got hurt, though." Her smile faded, her expression turning serious. "It was very brave of you to try to find out the truth." She made the sign for *brave*

246

without seeming to realize she'd done it. Loyal smiled and ran a hand over the cover of his new book. She really was turning out to be a wonderful friend.

He signed *Where's Michael?* She nodded, looking pleased that she understood. "He's doing your chores, I think. He said he wanted to help, so your mother sent him out to weed the garden." She grinned. "I gathered the eggs and fed the chickens. I help with that at home sometimes." She twisted her hands in the fabric of her skirt. "I like your mother. She's really nice."

Loyal smiled, chewed his lip deep in thought, and signed *Michael not kill.* The sign for *kill* was a sort of stabbing motion. He hadn't taught it to Rebecca, but he thought she might understand it anyway.

Rebecca cocked her head and considered his motion. "You're saying Michael . . . Oh!" She brightened. "Does that mean to kill someone?" Loyal nodded. "Michael didn't kill that man." She frowned. "But we knew that already."

Loyal looked around as if someone might be watching him in his own house, then signed *I know who.*

Rebecca leaned forward. "You do? Who is it?"

Loyal couldn't keep the grin from spreading across his face. Rebecca understood him so easily. He'd never met a hearing person who learned to communicate with him this fast. He sobered again. This was serious business. He spelled S-a-m.

Rebecca gasped. "Have you told the sheriff?" Loyal made the sign for no. "Are you going to?"

Movement drew Loyal's attention, and he saw the sheriff filling the doorway. He swallowed hard and read the words Virgil spoke. "Are you going to tell me what?"

thirty-one

The sheriff sat in a kitchen chair pulled up close to the
sofa. He leaned his elbows on his knees, hands clasped.
Rebecca moved to the end of the sofa where she was
careful not to touch Loyal's foot. He liked having her there. He
was worried that the sheriff might not believe him—or worse,
that he'd somehow messed up the evidence.

Fishing in his pocket, Loyal pulled out one of Sam's chewed-
up sassafras sticks and handed it over. Sheriff White looked
confused, then his expression cleared. "You're thinking Sam
is the killer," he said. Loyal blinked in surprise, then nodded.
The sheriff leaned closer as though he might be overheard. "I'm
thinking the same thing."

Loyal felt relief and disappointment wash through him in
equal parts. He was glad he didn't have to make himself understood, but at the same time it seemed like he'd gone to a lot
of trouble—*caused* a lot of trouble—for something that wasn't
coming as a surprise to the sheriff.

Sheriff White leaned back in his chair and crossed his legs.
"Between you, me, and the fence post, I'm expecting some hard
evidence that'll finally wrap all of this business up." He looked

at Rebecca. "And your family can get back to normal." He stood and nodded at Loyal. "Take care of that ankle."

Loyal watched him carry his chair back into the kitchen. The feeling of disappointment was definitely outweighing the relief he'd felt earlier. Had the sheriff already known what he'd set out to learn? Had he wasted his time and been responsible for Father getting shot? Now he wished Rebecca would just leave. He didn't want her to know what an idiot he'd been. He looked at her and saw that she was looking back at him intently.

"Normal," she repeated. "I'm not sure what that is. If it's what we were like before all of this happened, I'm not sure I want it."

Loyal frowned and signed *Why not?*

"Because *normal* meant we didn't talk to each other or do things together. Michael usually ignored me, and Daddy was always busy." Her chest rose and fell with a sigh. "At least I haven't been lonely the last few weeks." She smiled. "I like being here with your family. Your mom is nice, and she lets me help her in the kitchen. Mrs. Tompkins won't let me near the kitchen." She cocked her head to one side. "You sure are lucky." She turned her head as if she'd heard something, then flashed him a smile and left.

Loyal wiggled deeper into the sofa. His ankle throbbed with each beat of his heart, and he was pretty sure he'd made more of a mess instead of fixing anything. And yet . . . Rebecca thought he was lucky. She thought the deaf boy who'd managed to get himself kidnapped was lucky. He closed his eyes, still tired from the previous night's trouble. In Sunday school, his teacher liked to talk about the importance of counting blessings. Maybe he'd try counting a few right now.

Delphy hadn't felt this emotional since she'd been afraid Loyal's fever would do worse than leave him deaf. One moment she was mad that her son and husband had taken such risks, the next just thankful they were both on the mend. She went from thinking life had at least been simpler when she was estranged from her husband to wishing he'd hurry up and heal so they could . . . well. She was a mess. Which didn't help matters when she heard someone creeping down the stairs and saw that Creed had decided to get out of bed against the doctor's orders.

She never should have told him that Virgil was planning to come by. She'd assumed the sheriff would just talk to Creed while he was propped in their bed, but apparently her husband had a different idea. He'd even managed to dress himself. As he slipped into the kitchen, she gave him a look that he clearly understood.

"Woman, if I'm going to talk to Virgil, I'm going to have the conversation sitting up in a chair instead of lying in bed." He eased onto a chair as though it were made of glass. Or maybe as though *he* were made of glass. Beads of sweat popped out on his brow, and his hand strayed to his injured side. He forced a smile and leaned against the table. From the expression on his face, it didn't do much to lessen the pain he must be feeling.

"Virgil can walk up those stairs easier than you can walk down them," Delphy said. "I don't know why you're so determined to act like you weren't almost killed just a few days ago."

"I was a long way from death's doorstep," he said, swiping his forehead with the back of his hand. "Exercise will do me good." He grinned, but his lips were tight, and his eyes glittered. "Where's Loyal?"

"He and Michael are playing cards on the front porch. The swelling's gone down on that ankle, but I don't want him overdoing it."

She saw words taking shape on his lips, yet he bit down on them. Good. He wasn't in the best position to stick his oar in on her parenting right at that moment. She set a plate of tea cakes on the table and put out some of her nice china cups, along with a fresh pot of coffee.

"Virgil won't know what to make of all this. I don't think he's used to fancy."

Delphy made a *humph*ing sound. "Fancy. This is no more than I'd do for anyone else sitting down at my table. And Julia has plenty of nice things." Creed was right. It probably was silly, but lately she'd been feeling domestic.

Creed reached out and hooked an arm around her waist as she came near. He tugged at her until she stopped and let him draw her close. She knew it had to hurt, the stretching and pulling, so she went to him willingly and gently.

"You're acting like a hen caught in the rain." He settled his head against her side. "What's the matter?"

She didn't know how tense she was until she relaxed against him. She let her hand stray to the overlong hair at the nape of his neck. She felt him relax, as well. "I don't want to lose you." Her voice was small and quiet.

Creed stilled and seemed about to speak, but she pulled away when she saw Virgil coming in through the back door. He grinned. "Looks like you're recovering just fine."

"Wasn't much more than a scratch," Creed said.

Delphy thumped the coffeepot down on the worn table, glared at him, and leaned against the sink with her arms crossed. If he was going to act the fool, she was going to at least keep an eye on him.

Creed frowned at her but didn't suggest she leave. "What's happening with Judge Kline?"

The sheriff eyed her warily as if considering whether or not he could talk in front of her. She tightened her arms and stared him right in the eye. He gave his head a little shake and turned to Creed. "We got a rush on a ballistics report for that bullet Bernie dug out of your back. It matches the bullet that killed Eddie Minks."

Delphy's hand flew to her mouth, but she managed to keep quiet.

"So, Sam's the killer," Creed said, looking wilted.

"Most likely. Problem is, all that ballistics test proves is that Sam's gun killed Eddie. It doesn't tell us *who* pulled the trigger. And we have yet to run Sam to ground. But even if we do, he may have gotten rid of the rifle." Virgil poured coffee into a dainty china cup and then spent some time figuring out how to pick it up. He glanced at Delphy as he lifted the cup by its rim and took a slurp. She tried not to smile in spite of the sober topic. "Which is to say we have some important evidence, but it still doesn't tell us the whole story."

"Does it let Otto and Hadden off the hook at least?" Creed asked.

"While it's not what Judge Kline would call 'conclusive,' it sure as heck makes it hard to argue either one of 'em would've had access to Sam Hacker's fancy rifle."

Creed leaned on the table, and Delphy could see the sheen of perspiration across his face. She figured right about now he was wishing he'd taken her advice and stayed in bed. "So what now?" he asked.

"I was hoping to talk to Loyal."

Delphy took a step toward them. "About what?" she demanded.

"Anything he might've seen while he was with Sam Hacker."

Creed looked at her. "It sure would be easier for Virgil—and Loyal—if you'd translate."

She pinched her lips. "Is this official police business? Are you suggesting we go to your office or the courthouse?"

"No, I'd just like to talk to the boy—unofficially—to see if there's anything we need to make more official." He smiled and picked up a tea cake. "And I sure would be grateful for your assistance."

She rolled her eyes. "Don't try to butter me up, Virgil. I'll do it, but for Loyal's sake—not yours. Now, if you'll excuse me, I'll go fetch Loyal."

Virgil let out a low, almost-silent whistle she was pretty sure she wasn't meant to hear and gave Creed a look that she decided to take as a compliment.

Loyal was beating Michael at gin rummy when Mother stepped out onto the porch. He sensed the tension in the air before he realized she had joined them. She was smiling, but it didn't look right. He was on his guard immediately.

She began signing while speaking aloud for Michael's benefit. "The sheriff wants to talk to you."

Talk about what? he signed back.

She finger-spelled S-a-m H-a-c-k-e-r.

Loyal nodded. Finally the sheriff wanted to hear what he knew. He laid his cards facedown, shook a finger at Michael, and followed Mother inside, only limping a little.

In the kitchen, Father sat at the table with Sheriff White. Loyal smiled, glad to see his father up and around. *You okay?* he signed. Father smiled and made the sign for yes. Pleased, Loyal stood and waited for the sheriff's first question.

Sheriff White looked at Father and asked, "Can you talk with your hands now?"

"Not much," Father said. He smiled at Loyal. "But I'm learning."

Happiness swelled in Loyal's chest. Father was learning to sign, and the sheriff wanted to hear what he knew. The sheriff tapped his arm. Loyal gave him his full attention.

"How are you feeling?" the sheriff asked. "Looks like you're limping some."

Loyal furrowed his brow. He thought they were going to talk about Sam.

Fine, he signed, and Mother translated.

"Good, good. I guess you know why I want to ask you some questions?" Mother's hands flew as the sheriff spoke.

Loyal frowned. He wasn't a baby. He glanced at Mother and began signing. She translated, her lips not quite matching her hands as she shifted what he shaped into words that flowed smoothly for hearing people.

Sam told his brother he killed the man. I saw them talking.

Virgil's eyebrows shot up toward his naked scalp. "When did this happen?"

I could see through a crack in the door.

"When you were inside the springhouse?" Loyal was grateful for Mother's signing. The sheriff's lips were pretty easy to read, but it was much easier to follow Mother's hands.

Yes. They argued about it. Glen said Sam was only supposed to scare the man, but he shot him.

Mother's lips tightened. Loyal guessed she didn't like knowing how he'd spied.

Virgil licked his lips and looked toward Father. "Loyal's testimony combined with the ballistics and the way Sam's running should be enough to convict him if we can catch him."

"Testimony?" Loyal could tell the single word was a question.

"I expect Judge Kline will want Loyal to take the stand."

Mother frowned, and Father shifted in his chair. Maybe because he was hurting or maybe because he didn't like the idea of Loyal in a courtroom. Loyal stood straight and tall. "I'll testify." He spoke the words, hoping his voice didn't sound too rusty. It had been a while since he last spoke.

"Will that really be necessary?" Mother asked. Loyal had to read her lips—her hands had fallen into her lap like weary birds in a nest.

"Probably," Sheriff White said. "Why? That's not a problem, is it? Are you worried about the boy's safety?"

Father spoke then. "I expect we can keep him safe." He darted a look at Mother, who frowned more deeply. "Why can't he just talk to Judge Kline?" she asked.

"If Earl wasn't gumming up the works, we might could get

by with that. As it is, I expect we're going to have to put on a proper show." He glanced at Loyal and winked. "And I expect this young man will do a fine job."

Loyal felt his chest expand another notch. He smiled. Maybe he was going to get this right after all. Maybe he was going to make Father proud at long last.

thirty-two

I don't like it." Delphy said, trying to help Creed as he resettled himself in bed. He grunted and flinched. She felt certain the strain of walking and sitting at the table with Virgil had exhausted him. For her part, the conversation itself was causing her mother's heart pain and she could feel her patience thinning.

"What don't you like?" Creed settled against the propped pillows with a sigh and closed his eyes. He looked pale, but this was no time to spare him. Delphy folded the clothes he'd traded for a nightshirt and tucked them in a dresser drawer.

"I don't like the idea of Loyal having to testify in front of a courtroom full of people."

"Why not?" he asked, eyes still closed.

She frowned. "What do you mean 'why not'? Isn't it obvious?"

"Not to me." He patted the bed next to him. "Come sit and tell me what's got you riled."

Seeing him there in her bed, weak and tired, loosened something inside her. She eased down beside him, and he twined his hand with hers. "I've tried so hard to keep him safe," she said, and even she could hear the tears in her voice. "And this

256

summer he's been anything but. I just want to tuck him away where nothing can hurt him." She swallowed the tears. "Where no one can hurt him. People can be so cruel."

"Ain't that the truth." Creed squeezed her hand. "I don't know, Delphy. After all the time I've spent with that boy the last few weeks, I'm beginning to think he's a lot stronger and smarter than I ever knew." His eyes were open now, and Delphy felt almost as if she was being lectured. "Seems to me it might be time for us to let him grow up a bit—stretch his wings. I think he'll do fine."

Delphy jerked her hand away and stood abruptly, ignoring the flash of pain her sudden movement caused him. "*You* think? Time *we* let him grow up? Where have you been all these growing-up years? What makes you think you have the right to parent him now?" The anger and fear she'd felt when she didn't know where her son was bubbled up in her, and although she knew she should stop, she didn't. "Seems to me the last time you made a decision about what was best for our son, he ended up deaf."

The words dropped like stones. She froze as if she'd heard them strike the floor between them. The look on his face told her he'd felt them hit, as well. He seemed to be searching for something to say but she turned and fled the room before he could return her volley.

Delphy hid in the lavatory and closed the door. She caught a glimpse of herself in the glass hanging there and had to look away for shame. There was no excuse for her words, but she didn't know how to take them back. She buried her face in her hands and remembered how it was in the beginning.

Once they'd finally learned what was wrong with Loyal, it hadn't taken long for word to get around the community. People said things like "I'm praying for your family," or "At least he can see," or "Maybe he'll grow out of it." Each time someone commented, it felt like condolences, like there had been a death and people were offering cold comfort. Then Creed stopped spending time with neighbors or chatting with others at church and began spending more time in the old cabin up on the mountain. And eventually he stopped living with his family—with her—altogether.

She'd blamed other people for driving him up there. Had blamed his own guilt, which was palpable in those days after they knew Loyal would never regain his hearing. But hadn't she pushed him away, as well? Didn't she blame him more than she'd allowed herself to admit? The venom that had just poured out of her had taken her by surprise. She lifted her head and looked in the mirror. Perhaps it was past time she took a hard look at how she'd handled her marriage instead of lashing out at her husband.

"As much as I want Daddy to come home, I wish we could just stay here." Rebecca and Loyal sat under the cedar in the backyard that had become the place they gravitated to when Mother ran them out of the house. Loyal had been telling her how the sheriff had come by the day before to explain that he would get to testify. Honestly he was pretty excited about it.

Rebecca had begun to use a combination of words and signs. Loyal was continuing to teach both brother and sister his language, and Rebecca in particular took to it easily. Of course, she also had that knack for understanding him—knowing what it was he wanted to say even without words. Not even Mother understood him so well.

Good, signed Loyal. *I like you here.* She smiled radiantly at him. "I know two languages now," she said. "We can talk to each other, even if we're not close together." She made a movement that Loyal had learned was a giggle. "If you went to my school, we could talk in class or out on the playground and no one else would know what we're saying."

Loyal's smile faded. If only. He'd rather go to school with

regular kids. The school for the deaf was a good place, but he hated leaving home and it made him feel . . . different. Of course, he was different, but hadn't he proved this summer that he could get along just fine in the world of the hearing? *I want to go to school with you*, he signed.

Rebecca furrowed her brow. "What's this mean?" she asked, mimicking the sign for school. Loyal finger-spelled the word. "Oh." She repeated the sign. "Kind of like stacking books or pieces of paper. That makes sense." Then she looked at him with her head to one side. "Why can't you come to school here if you want to?"

He signed, *Mother, Father won't allow.* He made a face and rolled his eyes. Rebecca laughed. "That must mean your parents won't let you go." She looked serious. "Are they worried the other kids will make fun of you? Or that you'll have a hard time learning?" Loyal shrugged. "Why don't you ask them again? A lot has happened this summer—maybe they'll change their minds."

Loyal let his shoulders droop. Rebecca smiled. "Oh, come on. It can't hurt to ask." Loyal grinned. *You help*, he signed. "Help you ask your parents?" He nodded. Rebecca jumped to her feet. "Sure. Let's do it now!" Loyal scrambled to his feet beside her. She grabbed his hand and tugged him toward the house. He could see she was laughing and so he did, too. She didn't even flinch at the sound.

Inside, Mother and Father were drinking coffee at the kitchen table. They looked serious, and the air between them felt heavy—it had been ever since the sheriff talked to them the day before. Loyal hoped they hadn't been talking about him or the upcoming trial. He figured it would be one more way to prove he could get along fine in a hearing world. But it seemed to worry his parents.

Rebecca must have spoken. But he wasn't watching, so he missed whatever she said. Then she turned toward him and nodded. He realized his mouth was dry. He flexed his fingers and began signing to Mother, asking her to tell Father what he was saying. She nodded. Loyal worried the inside of his cheek as he thought how to phrase his request. Then he began signing, slowly, thinking through each gesture.

"I want to go to school here in Beverly with Rebecca and the other kids." Mother was frowning but her lips kept moving. "I've done a lot this summer, proven that I can get along fine. I want to be like the other kids." Mother's expression got wistful, and Loyal let himself hope.

He looked at Father, who was already shaking his head. "Sign for me, Delphy." He turned to Mother, only glancing at Loyal once he spoke. "That school teaches things Loyal can't learn anywhere else." Loyal wanted to tell Father he could talk to him rather than about him but didn't want to rock the boat. "Teachers in Beverly wouldn't know what to do with a deaf student. He probably wouldn't learn half as much, and it's not like the teachers would have the time to do extra to help him keep up."

Mother nodded and began signing her own words. "That's true. I think your father is right." Loyal felt his hope fade.

Father looked Loyal in the eyes. "Son, you *have* done a lot this summer. But much of it has been running off to take matters into your own hands without telling anyone." Father's whole body looked taut. "I've not taken you to task before this, but three times now you've gotten yourself into trouble by running off when you'd been told to stay put." Father made the sign for *stay.* Loyal was annoyed that he got it right. "You've caused your mother a whole lot of worry. I don't think you're ready yet for the real world." He paused and forced a smile. "Hey, the county fair's coming up soon—just before school starts. You can go to that with your friends this year instead of with your mother or me."

Loyal flinched. Not only was Father denying him what he wanted most but he was also confirming what Loyal had long suspected. Father didn't think his deaf world was "real." He didn't think Loyal or his way of speaking was good enough for regular folks beyond a silly county fair. He clenched his jaw and nodded, then turned and left the room.

Rebecca reached out to grasp his hand, but he shook her off. He could feel her sorrow hanging in the air behind him but ignored it. She probably didn't think his world was real either. She just thought it was *different* or *strange*. Well. He wasn't going to make a spectacle of himself anymore.

That night, Delphy slid into bed beside Creed. She'd been sleeping with Rebecca in the guest room but apparently thought him sufficiently improved for company. Her warmth and sweet scent made him wish he were more completely healed than he was. And that they hadn't had words earlier in the week. He took her hand and tugged it until she curled into his side.

"You still need to take it easy," she whispered.

"I know. I just want you near me."

She sighed and tucked her chin against his shoulder. "I'm sorry."

"So am I. And you were right—I haven't been here for Loyal." He stroked her hair as she ran her fingers absently over his chest, sending chills up and down the length of him. "Or for you." She stiffened, then relaxed. "Thing is, I want to be. I want to be his father." His voice deepened. "And your husband." She sighed, the puff of breath sliding across his skin. "As disappointed as Loyal was today, it felt good for the two of us to be in agreement."

"It did feel good," she said. "But I've been thinking. Maybe it would be good for Loyal to go to school here. There's still time to get him signed up. School's starting later this year, with times so hard and less money to pay the teachers." Her voice was so soft it took him a moment to register what she said.

He huffed a laugh. "Why would you suggest that?"

Her fingers hesitated and then resumed their gentle caress. "We can't protect him forever. I guess I realized that when I

. . . said what I did. It made me consider what part I've—" she stopped and took a deep breath—"I've played in making his safety more important than anything else. Even than . . . us."
Creed felt his breath catch and longed to roll over and wrap her in his arms. "Maybe it's time to let him start finding his own way."

Creed laid a hand over hers, stilling the distracting sensation of her soft fingers. "Maybe he's still too young. Has too much to learn."

"Let him learn it here. With us."

Creed sighed. "But like you said—people are cruel. They'll treat him like there's something wrong with him."

"There's nothing wrong with him," she said. "In some ways, I think he's stronger than people who can hear. Stronger than me. Maybe even stronger than you."

"I'm beginning to think you're right," he agreed. "But maybe it's enough that he's going to have to testify at this trial. Let's wait and send him to school here next year. Talk to his teacher about how that might work." Creed smiled into the darkness and squeezed her hand. "Besides, it might be nice for the two of us to have some time alone."

He thought he could feel her smile as she relaxed against him. He waited until he heard her breathing slow and even, then drifted off to sleep along with her.

thirty-three

I t's time to harvest the ginseng," Creed announced at the breakfast table on a crisp early September morning. Delphy had been more attentive since their bedtime talk. She touched him whenever she passed by, and Creed felt like he had when they were first seeing each other—happy and a little nervous at the same time. Loyal had been watching them intently, as if he noticed something was different between them. He looked interested in Creed's comment, eyebrows up.

"You're not well enough to go grubbing about in the woods," Delphy said, trailing a hand across his shoulders as she headed for the sink.

"Maybe not, but we need the money for Loyal's tuition." She sighed and slid a plate of eggs in front of him. He could guess what she was thinking. Still, he would not change his mind.

Loyal frowned at the mention of his school. He made a sign Creed remembered from the day they were working on Delphy's pie safe. "That means *help*, doesn't it?" Loyal nodded. "You want to help me dig ginseng?" Loyal gave a small smile that Creed hoped was pushing back the disappointment over his schooling. Creed smiled, too. "That's exactly what I was hoping." He glanced at Delphy. "Think you could pack us a lunch?"

"You'll be extra careful? Sam Hacker is still out there somewhere."

"You know I will," Creed said, trying to sound calm and confident. Sam Hacker's arrest was part of the reason Creed wanted to get Loyal out of town, though he couldn't say anything about it yet. Virgil had tipped him off about his plans and swore Creed to secrecy. Delphy nodded and went back to peeling the last of the summer tomatoes she'd scalded for canning. Creed started to tell her more but thought better of it. The last thing he needed to do was to make Virgil mad again. He reached out to ruffle Loyal's hair, but the boy ducked away. Creed let his hand drop. "It's a fine day for being in the woods," he said.

Excited to be digging ginseng with Father, Loyal tried not to hurry ahead. It was just the two of them going out to earn a living for the family. Mother hadn't seemed all that pleased, but she'd let him come and that was all that mattered. He might have to go back to boarding school soon, but until he did, he wanted to have as many adventures as he could squeeze in. And while he wasn't happy with Father's decision, he still liked being in the woods with him. He quelled his smile. Not that he'd let it show overmuch.

Loyal eyed the rifle slung over his father's shoulder. He'd said something about getting a squirrel for supper. Loyal guessed it had more to do with Sam Hacker still being missing. While Father wasn't completely healed, Loyal felt safe and watched over nonetheless. He also felt like he was part of a complete family for the first time in . . . well, maybe ever. His parents were even sleeping in the same room now, like real parents were supposed to. He darted ahead to get a closer look at what he thought might be a ginseng plant. He touched the leaves and looked back at Father, a question in his eyes.

"No, that's Virginia creeper. Looks a lot like it, though."

Loyal nodded and kept moving. Finally Father stopped and pointed to a plant with green leaves in clusters of five and its crown of red berries in the center. He knelt down, grimacing as he did so, and beckoned Loyal closer. He knelt too. Father gently loosened the soil at the base of the plant. Loyal leaned down, and Father showed him places where the stem narrowed and swelled.

"Stem scars," he said. Loyal motioned for him to repeat the phrase since it was new to him until he finally understood. "One for each year the plant's been growing. Don't dig unless there are at least four." Father held up four fingers. Loyal nodded. "How many do you see?" Loyal ran his fingers along the stem, counting. He held up five fingers. "Good. Do you remember the way I showed you to dig it?" Loyal nodded again, and they spent several hours finding and harvesting plants. Father looked pleased when Loyal remembered to plant the seeds without being told.

Around noon, with a fair number of roots in their gathering basket, Creed pointed toward some rocks along a stream and held up Delphy's lunch sack. Loyal made the sign for *hungry* that Creed had seen before. "Me too," he said, mimicking the sign.

They sat and Creed opened the sack, but before he could pull out the food, Loyal laid a hand on his arm. He put his palms together in a sign for *prayer.* "Right. Yes. We should give thanks." Loyal nodded solemnly. Creed licked his lips. At the table at home, Delphy would sign what he said. He'd just keep it short and wouldn't bow his head so Loyal could see his lips.

"Father, we thank you for this day, the beauty of your creation, and for this food we're about to eat. Amen." Loyal held up a finger, thrusting it toward Creed in what was clearly a *wait a minute* gesture. Then he turned his eyes toward the sky and began moving his hands in what looked like dancing. He made small sounds as he gestured, and Creed guessed Loyal had a few other things he wanted to talk to God about. He ended with a rolling hand motion that ended in the sign for *help*. As he made the motion, he spoke in that loud guttural voice of his. "Amen."

Creed was surprised to realize his throat felt thick and his eyes prickled. He'd never really thought about it, but God understood his son perfectly. Words, signs, or even just thoughts were something God understood without needing translation. Creed hadn't been the father Loyal deserved and yet he had a Father who was perfect. The thought was both comforting and intimidating. Maybe Loyal didn't need him.

The boy bit into his cold biscuit and watched leaves drift by in the stream at their feet. He saw a fish and made a sound of pleasure, thumping Creed on the knee and pointing. A huge smile spread across his face, and his expression made Creed think of laughter. He laughed too. Maybe Loyal didn't need him. Maybe he needed Loyal.

Suddenly that school for the deaf felt like it was awfully far away.

This had been the best day ever. While Loyal was still frustrated that Father was making him go away to school, he'd loved every moment they spent together tromping through the woods. And a couple of times he'd caught Father looking at him with what appeared to be pride. Which made Loyal feel taller and stronger than he had in a long time. Now they were crouching at the foot of the mountain, rinsing ginseng roots in the icy water of a stream with the wide valley spread at their feet. Loyal was looking forward to supper and yet he wanted these moments to stretch out longer, too. When would he get to do something like this again?

Placing the last root in the basket, Father touched his arm. "I need to tell you something." Loyal nodded. He'd gotten used to Father's way of speaking and following his lips was easier now. Still, he was tired, and if Father had a great deal to say, this was going to wear him out. He got comfortable and focused on his father's face.

"I talked to Virgil yesterday." Loyal nodded. "He knows where Sam is hiding out, and I expect he has him in a jail cell by now." Loyal's eyes grew big. Was that why Father wanted to hunt ginseng today? To keep him out of the way while the sheriff went after Sam? "Judge Kline is going to want to hold this trial as quick as he can. Are you ready?"

Loyal squared his shoulders and nodded. "Good," Father said. "Here's how it will work. When you take the stand, there will be an interpreter. Judge Kline is going to clear the courtroom." Loyal frowned in confusion. He wasn't sure how those words went together. His confusion must have shown. "That means there won't be an audience for your part of the trial. Virgil, Wendell, and I agreed there's no reason to put you on display for the whole town."

Loyal still didn't understand. He signed *Why not?* Father furrowed his brow. "Wait, I know that one." He snapped his fingers. "Why not. You're asking why we don't want an audience. Well, we want to make sure we keep you safe. The Hackers—" he paused, not wanting to worry Loyal unnecessarily about Earl—"and some other people might take issue with what you have to say." Father's face reddened, and he shifted like the rock he sat on was too hard. "It'll sure make your mother feel better."

Something unexpected rose up in Loyal's chest. He tried to tamp it back down, but it wouldn't go away. What was this feeling? His hands began moving as if he had no control. *No. I'm not afraid.* He stood and repeated the motions more emphatically.

Father stood, too. "Hold on there. I got the *no* part, but what else are you saying?" He held his hands out as if to quiet a child. Well, Loyal was no child. He worked his mouth, moved his tongue, and pushed out the words "not afraid." Then he turned and headed for the house.

Creed thumped back down and watched the boy walk away, his back stiff and his head held high. Did he think Creed was suggesting he was a coward? That was the last thing he wanted him to think. Loyal was smart and kind and brave. And yet he'd promised Delphy he'd do whatever he could to protect their son—to keep him out of the public eye and away from anyone who might wish him ill.

Creed hung his head. He never could seem to get things right with Loyal. He was a fumbling fool of a father. And now he'd hurt his son when all he'd wanted to do was protect him. He stood, stretching where his healing flesh had grown tight, and grimaced. Sometimes healing hurt. That was a fact. Maybe he wasn't trying to save Loyal from danger as much as he was trying to win his way back into Delphy's good graces.

Hooking the basket over one arm, Creed began the slow trudge back toward town. He'd go see Virgil—tell him to call Judge Kline and let him know it wouldn't be necessary to clear the courtroom for Loyal's testimony. It was almost certainly going to get him in trouble with his wife, but he knew in his gut it was the right thing to do.

Creed felt like he'd walked a hundred miles by the time he got to Virgil's office. He dragged himself inside and eased his tired body into the sheriff's desk chair. The room was empty, and he hoped Virgil was in the back and would come on out. After a minute or two, Bud came through the door from a back room, head down as he read from a piece of paper. Someone came behind him, and Creed jerked—which strained his back—when he saw that it was Loyal.

Realizing he wasn't alone, Bud stopped and looked Creed up and down. "You huntin' the sheriff?"

"I am." Creed tried to think how to ask what Loyal was doing there without sounding angry. He gave up. "Is he around?"

"Not back from Elkins yet. Today's arrest didn't go as smooth as he hoped."

Creed tensed. "Is Sam in jail?"

"No. He's in the hospital up in Elkins." Bud waved a hand toward Creed. "Sounds like he got it worse than you."

Now there were two issues Creed wanted to discuss. Bud didn't give him time to formulate his next question, though. "Seems your boy here is determined to testify in open court."

"What?"

Bud waved the piece of paper. Loyal looked uneasy but kept his chin up. "Wrote it out for Virgil." He held the paper up and read, "*I do not want the judge to clear the courtroom when I testify. Anyone who wants to should have the chance to see me when I tell the truth.*" Bud smiled. "I like that. Wants people to see him tell the truth." He looked from Loyal to Creed. "Sounds right to me." He turned to Loyal and spoke in a slow, exaggerated way. "I'll give this to the sheriff." Loyal frowned and made a sign like he wanted Bud to say it again.

"Speak normally," Creed snapped. "You make it harder for him when you draw the words out like that."

Bud looked surprised—as did Loyal—but he repeated his comment, and Loyal nodded. Creed felt as weary as he'd ever been. "Hand me that paper." Bud did, and Loyal stiffened with a suspicious look on his face. He watched intently as Creed found a pen on Virgil's desk and added his own note to the page. *This is fine with me*, he wrote and then signed his name.

Loyal drifted close and read over his shoulder. He looked at Creed with raised eyebrows. "You're braver than I ever was. I'm proud for folks to see that." Loyal grinned, and the look on his face was worth whatever this might cost Creed when Delphy found out.

Creed leaned heavily on the desk. "Now, what's this about Sam being in the hospital?"

Bud hooked his thumbs in his belt. "Apparently he decided he didn't want to come in easy. Barricaded himself in a shed out there on the property where they're putting in that Roosevelt community." He shook his head. "Took a couple of shots at Virgil before he realized Virgil had reinforcements. Those federal boys shot that shed full of holes and put a few in Sam, too."

"But he's still alive?" Creed wasn't sure what it would mean if their prime suspect was dead. "Last I heard he was." Bud looked disgusted. "I was headed up there to help, but Virgil told me to keep an eye on things around here." He frowned. "Probably meant you and your boy. Guess you've stirred things up pretty good."

Creed flushed. "Yeah, well, he can't blame me this time." He then held an arm out to Loyal, and the two of them headed for the house.

thirty-four

L oyal stared into the hall mirror as he signed. He wanted to try out some of the things he thought he might need to explain while on the stand in that fancy courtroom in Elkins. He felt equal parts excited and nervous. He wanted to make sure he didn't look strange. It had been a long time since he practiced signing in a mirror. A teacher had once suggested the idea as a way to see what the person he was trying to communicate with would see.

Rebecca sat on the stairs, watching. She got up and came closer so she could use her steadily improving sign language in combination with words he'd need to read from her lips. *Worry you?* she signed. He shrugged and made the sign for *a little*.

"I think you look . . . graceful." He liked the way her lips shaped the word. It made him flush and roll his eyes. "If you get nervous, just look for me." She grinned. "I can sign something to make you feel better." He grinned back. *What?* Her eyes danced, and she darted to the end of the hallway, turned and signed *I'm your friend*. But she did the sign for *friend* more emphatically in a way that Loyal knew meant *good friend*. Well, whether she realized it or not, he felt like that's what she was to him. And he was glad.

Loyal glimpsed movement and turned to see the sheriff standing on the porch beyond the screen door. He spoke, but Loyal had trouble reading his lips through the mesh. Rebecca bounced down the hall and flung the door open. Then Father came in from the family room where he'd been reading. He and the sheriff looked like they were talking. Father turned and motioned for Loyal to follow them into the kitchen. He guessed that was where everything important happened these days.

Mother was making grape jelly. Loyal felt the steam of the kitchen and smelled the sweetness of the sugared fruit. His mouth watered, even though he'd had lunch not an hour before. Few things were better than Mother's biscuits with butter and grape jelly.

Father spoke to Mother, who pulled the last two jars from the canner before joining them at the table. Everyone sat— even Rebecca—and the focus shifted to Sheriff White. Mother placed her hands on the table in front of her, ready to begin signing. And when she did, Loyal couldn't have been more surprised.

"Loyal won't have to take the stand after all." Sheriff White leaned his arms on the tabletop. Loyal noticed Mother looked pleased while Father's expression was hard to read. "Sam Hacker confessed."

Loyal had read the phrase "stunned silence" and suspected that's what was happening. Even though he couldn't hear, he could feel the stillness, the way the room held its breath. Then there was a mighty exhalation in the form of everyone's lips moving at once. Mother stopped signing, and Loyal couldn't keep up with the speed and flurry of movement. He closed his eyes so his mind would stop trying to snatch words from the air.

A touch. On his arm. He opened his eyes and Mother was patting him. She began signing. *Sam is hurt. He may die. He*

*told the sheriff he's the one who shot Eddie Minks. He said he's
sorry for what he did to you.*

Loyal frowned and looked from his parents to the sheriff. *No
trial?* Was it strange that he felt disappointed? Mother mimicked
his signing. *No trial.*

He glanced around the table. The sheriff looked like a weight
had been lifted off his shoulders. Mother was focusing on him
with a joyful expression, Rebecca sat wide-eyed, and Father was
trying not to grin. He told himself they were just glad that the
murderer had been caught. But Loyal felt twisted up inside,
like a spring wanting release.

Father and Sheriff White started talking again. Loyal didn't
even try to follow along. Mother squeezed his hand with a smile
and went back to her jelly. Loyal stood and slipped out the
screen door. He eased it shut behind him and then ran as hard
as he could down to the towering cedar, where he picked up a
stick and slammed it against the trunk. The force of the blow
ran along his arms and into his shoulders. He hit the trunk again
and this time was gratified when the stick snapped, the broken
end flying into the air. He stabbed the splintered end into the
soil and thumped down beside it, panting.

He jumped when something hit his arm. Whipping his head
up, he saw that Michael was perched high in the tree. He
worked his way down and dropped to the ground beside Loyal.
He formed his hands into claws against his stomach and jerked
them upward with a questioning look. Loyal nodded. Yes, he
was angry.

Why? Michael signed.

Loyal let his shoulders slump as Rebecca approached them
with a worried expression. *You okay?* she signed. He shrugged.

"What's eating Loyal?" Michael asked his sister.

"Sam Hacker said he killed that man. Now there won't be
a trial."

Michael's eyes went wide and his mouth dropped open. "Just

like that? It's over?" She nodded. Michael made a funny shape with his mouth and pumped a fist in the air. He slapped Loyal on the back. "Now that's good news!"

Loyal began to feel a loosening inside. He'd been so busy thinking that he needed to prove himself to his father that he'd forgotten what this would mean to his friend. For a long time, Michael believed he'd killed a man. And now he knew for a fact that someone else had done it. What a relief that must be! Loyal realized he was acting like a baby. Not so long ago he'd thought Michael was a jerk, but now he knew him better. And it was wrong of him to only consider himself.

Climbing to his feet, Loyal gave Michael a playful punch on the shoulder and managed to find a smile. The assurance of his friend's innocence—not to mention the innocence of his friend's father—was what really mattered.

"Does this mean Dad's coming home?" Michael asked. Loyal shrugged, and Rebecca looked back toward the house.

"We can ask the sheriff," she said, and the pair took off running.

Loyal watched them for a moment, then settled back under the tree to think. Maybe all three of them could get their fathers back.

Delphy hummed as she finished making jelly. The relief she felt that her son was safe and wouldn't have to point the finger at anyone made her want to wrap her arms around her husband and show him just how happy she was. But Virgil was still in the room and the kids were just outside. She glanced back at the man who was earning his way back into her heart and gave him the kind of smile that made his eyes go wide and hopeful.

Then the Westfall kids came barreling through the back door and started asking Virgil questions about their father. Creed left them to it and stepped up behind Delphy. He slipped an arm around her waist. She batted at his hand, glancing toward their guests. "Mind your manners," she said. She could feel her cheeks flush pink and hoped everyone would think it was from the steam of the jelly.

"I'm in a mood to mind more than my manners," he whispered in her ear. His breath sent chills up and down her body, already warm from the kitchen work.

She gave him a saucy smile, then sobered when she noticed they were missing one person in the room. "Where's Loyal?"

Creed stayed close, fingers fiddling with her apron strings. "Out back, I think."

She stilled his hand and tightened her lips. "You need to go talk to him."

"Why's that?"

"I think he was excited about the chance to testify." She began ladling hot jelly into clean jars. "If I had to guess, I'd say he thought it might be a way to impress you. To show you how grown up he is."

Creed frowned and stayed put as she stepped away to reach her jelly jars. "He doesn't need to show me anything."

"I'm not sure he knows that." She gave her head a little shake. She guessed Creed still had a few things to learn about his son.

Virgil stood, pushing his chair back from the table. "Time I got back to Elkins." He smiled at the kids. "There's the small matter of getting Hadden back home to his family." Rebecca beamed, and even Michael looked pleased. "Otto too."

"You need my help?" Creed asked.

"Nope. And for once it's not because you're more trouble than you're worth." Virgil said the words with a grin. "You just stay here and take it easy. Finish healing up."

Creed's hand went to the site of his wound. "Sure thing." Virgil slapped his hat on his head and left through the front door. Michael and Rebecca sat at the table, heads close together, talking over their father's homecoming.

Delphy elbowed Creed. "Quit stalling."

He sighed. "Alright. I'll go talk to him, although I think you're wrong."

"I hope so," she said and began pouring wax seals over her cooling jelly.

Creed could see Loyal sitting under the big cedar down at the bottom of the yard. He was stabbing at the ground with a stick, seemingly lost in thought. He saw Creed coming and sat up straighter but didn't smile. Creed squatted next to his son and nodded at him.

"Michael and Rebecca's father is coming home." He looked at the boy who was quickly becoming a man. Made sure he could see his lips easily. Loyal nodded and managed a weak smile. "Guess you'll miss them." He hadn't thought of that before. Maybe Delphy was wrong and Loyal was just upset his friends would be leaving. "Must get lonesome around here for you," he said. Loyal shrugged.

"I know what. Let's go up the mountain and fetch down that pie safe for your mother." Loyal looked mildly interested. "We could spend a day or two up there, just two men living off the land and doing some real work. Then, when we get back, it'll be time for the county fair." A slow smile crept over Loyal's face. He nodded. "You could even teach me some more signs."

Okay, Loyal signed with a proper smile. Creed gave him a one-armed hug and motioned back toward the house. They rose and walked the short distance. Creed did his best to ignore the fact that he had failed to take his wife's advice.

That night, Loyal slept alone in his room. He did miss having Michael and Rebecca around—mostly Rebecca—but it was also nice to be alone again. He was looking forward to spending time with Father up on Rich Mountain, but he was still sad that he would have to go back to school soon. Who would have thought the summer he found a dead body would leave him feeling so . . . normal.

In the past he'd spent summers with mostly just Mother for company. He did things at church sometimes, but even when the other kids tried to include him it was hard. They'd forget he couldn't hear. Rebecca was the first person to really try to use his own language to communicate with him. And now Michael knew some sign language, too.

And he was learning how to interact with hearing people better every day. He knew he could handle going to school with the kids in Beverly. Especially since he and Rebecca would be in the same class. That thought made him smile. He guessed if he was ever going to have a girlfriend, he'd want Rebecca to be the one. That sure wasn't going to happen if he went away to school.

The question was . . . how to convince Mother and Father? He'd hoped that doing well in the courtroom, showing how he could hold his own among hearing people, would help. But now he wasn't going to have that chance. Which meant he'd have to come up with something else. Father had said they could stop and visit Michael and Rebecca on their way up Rich Mountain. He'd see if they had any good ideas.

Father followed Mr. Westfall into his study when they arrived at the big brick house the next morning. Loyal went with Michael and Rebecca out onto the side porch, where Mrs. Tompkins gave them slices of freshly baked bread slathered with butter and sprinkled with sugar. They were too busy eating at first to say much, but once everyone swallowed the last bite and licked their fingers, Loyal made the sign for *father* and raised his eyebrows.

"The sheriff let him go," Rebecca said. "Brought all of us

home in his police car. I think Daddy's different now." She glanced at Michael as though looking for confirmation, yet her brother's expression stayed serious.

"I'm not so sure." He shrugged. "Seems like things are getting back to the way they used to be pretty fast."

Loyal bit his lip, glad for once that he wasn't expected to find the right words.

Rebecca jumped in as if trying to scoot past the uncomfortable moment. "I'm just glad he's home in time for the fair. I wasn't sure I wanted to be in the pageant with Daddy locked up." She gave her brother a playful shove. "Even Michael's going to be in it, although he said he didn't want to be David Hart, so Reverend Harriman has to find someone else."

Loyal perked up. He liked the annual fair well enough, but he'd always gone with Mother. Which wasn't all that much fun. He ended up looking at canned goods, quilts, and flower arrangements the ladies entered to win ribbons. Mother never let him visit the tents where the hawkers offered chances to see all kinds of wonderful and terrible things. And while he'd watched the annual pageant that told the story of the Civil War battle fought on Rich Mountain, he'd never paid much attention to who was in it. *Can I be in the pageant?* he signed.

"That would be great," Rebecca said, and he could see her enthusiasm. "You'd make a wonderful soldier." He finger-spelled D-a-v-i-d H-a-r-t. "Really? You want to do the main role? The only one with more lines is General McClellan." She wrinkled her forehead. "How's that going to work?"

Loyal grinned and elbowed Michael. *I sign. Michael talks.*

"Now wait just a minute." Michael held up both hands. "I already said I didn't want to do it. I hate memorizing stuff." *Read*, Loyal signed.

"Oh, I get it. Loyal will sign his part and you can just stand backstage and read what he's saying." Rebecca clapped her hands. "It'll be wonderful!"

"Reverend Harriman will never go for it," Michael grumbled. Loyal winked at Rebecca, and she laughed, knowing just what he had in mind. "We won't tell him. You'll say you're going to do the part after all and then Loyal will take over as soon as the pageant starts. By the time the pastor realizes what's happening, it'll be too late." She laughed harder. "And he'll be too embarrassed to stop the pageant."

Michael grinned. "It might be worth it just to see his face." He turned to Loyal. "But why do you want to do it?"

My father, Loyal signed, *thinks I can't.*

Michael nodded, his smile slipping away. "I know how that is." He gave Loyal a speculative look. "We'll just have to show him you *can*."

thirty-five

Creed was glad to have Loyal with him up on the mountain again. They finished the pie safe and dug the last of the ginseng for the season. Creed showed Loyal how to start drying the roots. He even planned to give his son part of the profits this year. But as much as he enjoyed the boy's company, there was a reserve that felt new. A holding back that he could swear hadn't been there before.

"If we can get this pie safe down to Hadden's place, he'll bring it on into town for us in his car." Loyal nodded and flexed an arm to show that he could help carry the small piece of furniture. "Glad there's a good trail and it's downhill all the way." Creed used his hands to talk more than he used to. It wasn't quite sign language, but then again it was in a way.

Loyal smiled without giving it his full attention. He'd been that way for two days now. Creed suspected the boy was dreading his return to school but that couldn't be helped. He needed to learn as much as he could for as long as he could. Shoot, that was why they'd dug all this ginseng—so there'd be money to pay for the schooling.

Creed wanted to tell his son how much he'd miss him. How

much he loved him and how proud he was of the man he was growing into. But the words felt awkward, and better words escaped him. Maybe Delphy could help him find the right ones. He warmed at the thought of his wife. This fall he wouldn't be living up on the mountain. He'd be at home with the woman he loved. And come Christmas, Loyal would join them and they'd truly be a family. And who knew? Maybe next year the boy could go to school in town.

Cheered by the thought, he pushed his son's moodiness away. He waved to get Loyal's attention. "I was thinking we'd stay one more night. If you want, though, we can head on down the mountain and surprise your mother." Loyal smiled and nodded.

Creed was glad but also felt a pang. Maybe Loyal didn't want to linger here alone with him. He'd noticed how the boy looked at Hadden's daughter. She was a pretty little thing and was always kind to Loyal. Did his son have a crush on the girl? Well, he'd be fourteen come spring. He guessed it was time.

"Want to see if the Westfall kids can come for Sunday supper?" he asked. This time Loyal's smile climbed all the way to his eyes. He nodded. "Say, they might like to come to the fair with us, too. It starts next week." He gave Loyal a playful punch on the arm. "Seems like I said something about you going around with your friends instead of old folks like your mom and me." Loyal flushed, and Creed figured he had it right about Rebecca.

"Alright then," he said, clapping his hands. "Let's get this pie safe down the mountain." Loyal leapt to his feet ready to go. Creed laughed. Maybe all his son was suffering from was the effects of his first case of puppy love.

While Father talked to Mr. Westfall, Loyal and his friends sat on the front steps. There was an amazing view from here all the way down to the Tygart River, but Loyal didn't have time for gazing at the lush mountain landscape. Michael told Reverend

Harriman that he would play the role of David Hart, the young man who'd led Union troops into Confederate-friendly Beverly in July of 1861 to gain control of the Staunton-Parkersburg Turnpike. The deciding battle had been fought on the farm where David's father lived, not far from where they sat. Although David hadn't been too popular at the time, he was a local hero now.

"Here's the script," Michael said, handing it to Loyal. "There really aren't that many lines—it's mostly just acted out." Loyal nodded as he scanned the pages. "We're practicing it tomorrow evening at church. Can you come and see how it goes?"

Loyal signed yes, then swallowed hard as he looked over the part he was going to have to act out without much practice. It wasn't too hard, but the magnitude of what he planned to do was becoming real for him. If this went wrong, Father would be embarrassed. As would Mother. And he might even get his friends in trouble. He looked at them with worried eyes.

Trouble? he signed. Rebecca watched and bit her lip. "You're asking if we . . . oh"—she lit up—"trouble. You want to know if we'll get into trouble."

Michael got a wicked grin on his face. "Maybe. But it'll be worth it." Loyal looked at Rebecca, who signed *don't worry* with a radiant smile. Loyal threw an arm around each of his friends and gave them a hug. He figured, whatever happened, it was already worth it.

Soon after Creed and Loyal got back to the house in town, Virgil turned up. Loyal had already disappeared into his room with a roll of paper that Creed suspected Rebecca had given him. Maybe his boy would have a pen pal while he was away at school this year. That would be good for him.

Virgil settled himself in a wing chair and jumped right into what he had to say. "Sam Hacker didn't make it." Virgil slid both hands over his shiny pate and flung them to the side like he was getting rid of something. "Bad ending, but I'm glad he decided to set the record straight before he died. Seems Clyde had it in mind to sell out to the government—thought he could give his boys a new start somewhere else. Sam didn't want to lose the 'family business.' Then on top of that, he learned Eddie and Earl were planning to cheat Clyde on the deal." He heaved a sigh. "He offered to meet those two boys and lead 'em out to the homeplace so that Clyde could sign on the dotted line. Guess if Eddie had turned up that morning, they'd both be dead and the bodies washed down the Tygart somewhere."

"How's Clyde taking it?"

"Who knows? He's tougher than mule hide and doesn't much yammer on about anything. Said they'd have a family burial out there on the mountain. I took that to mean I wasn't invited."

Delphy stood in the doorway to the kitchen. "I'll make a pound cake to take to Bernie."

Virgil laughed softly and shook his head. "Julia's taking a pot of chicken and dumplings. I never know what to do or say in a situation like this, but the women know, don't they?"

Creed nodded. "So, what happens now?"

"Well, there's no one to lock up for murder, but Judge Kline had more than enough evidence to throw Earl in jail for the scheme those two were running to skim money off the new community project. The federal boys are coming for him Monday." Virgil grunted. "Those fellers don't mess around. I'm betting that's the last we see of Earl for a long time. Maybe ever."

"Never did like the way he acted," Creed said. "Guess he'll pay for the trouble he caused, though."

"Eddie Minks sure as heck paid for it."

Creed sobered. "Yeah. I suppose we've all done some things we're not proud of after the fact. It's a wonder God lets us get away with it." He shifted on the sofa, thinking of the way he'd run from his family.

Virgil sighed and sank back into the chair. "In my experience,

God doesn't let us get away with anything. He just leaves us to make our own beds and then lets us lay in 'em . . . whether we like it or not."

The two men sat in silence for a few moments. Creed was busy pondering his own shortcomings, and maybe Virgil was doing the same.

Giving himself a shake, Virgil stood and turned to Creed. "Delphy entering anything in the fair?"

"She's got some preserves ready to go, and I think she's doing an apple pie." Creed stood as well.

"Julia gave up on the pie contest," Virgil said, "but she sewed a dress I think might win." He gave a wry smile. "'Course, I'm partial to just about anything that woman does."

Creed glanced toward the kitchen where he could hear Delphy making her cake for the Hackers. "Women are a wonder," he added.

"You finally figure that out?" Virgil slapped him on the back and saw himself out the door.

Creed watched his friend disappear down the street before grabbing his hat and heading for the Westfall place. He had an idea.

Loyal joined in with the rest of the kids on Friday afternoon as they practiced the pageant for the Battle of Rich Mountain. Reverend Harriman said he could be a Union soldier following Michael and his buddy Chuck, who were supposed to be David Hart and General McClellan. Rebecca and another girl were David's sister and mother, while most of the other kids were Union or Confederate soldiers. Loyal could tell they were being rowdy and likely giving the pastor a headache. At least that was what he figured from the way the older man kept rubbing his head. He'd taken Michael to task for not really knowing his lines and made him carry his script with him while they practiced.

Of course, Michael didn't care since he was going to switch places with Loyal, then hide behind the curtain to read the words out loud as Loyal signed them. Chuck was the only other one in on the scheme. He seemed to think pulling one over on the pastor was pure fun.

They finally finished their practice—or rather, Reverend Harriman finally gave up on them. He told them all to be at the town square in their costumes by six p.m. sharp on Saturday. The pageant would begin at six-thirty whether rain or shine. The reverend made some speech about how it was raining the night David Hart led the soldiers up the mountain to defeat the enemy, and if rain didn't stop their ancestors, then it wouldn't dampen their spirits either. Loyal could see the kids were giggling and elbowing each other instead of listening, so he didn't feel too badly about not being able to catch whatever else the pastor said.

Once released, kids scattered up and down the street to see the various fair displays. There would be a pancake supper at the Methodist church that evening. Loyal was supposed to meet his parents there, but they'd agreed he could see the fair's displays with Michael and Rebecca until then. The Presbyterian church offered quilts and handmade clothing that would be judged on Saturday. The old courthouse had all the food displays—preserves, fresh produce, baked goods—and Loyal had a mind to go there, but Michael said it was torture since they couldn't eat anything. Instead they decided to go to the Odd Fellows Hall where they could see woodwork, basketry, and ironwork while they waited for the arm-wrestling contest to get under way.

The warmth of the September sun gave way to the cool interior of the hall. Michael saw a few of his buddies, and they started talking and horsing around. Loyal and Rebecca made their way along the risers with their displays of handiwork. They didn't talk or sign, just pointed at items that seemed interesting.

Rebecca was excited about a gathering basket artfully arranged with fresh-cut flowers. While Loyal didn't much care about it, he feigned interest for the sake of his friend.

Then he spotted it. Father's pie safe with the tin inserts Loyal had punched was sitting on the middle riser between a side table and a fancy jewelry box. The judges had already come through, and the pie safe now wore a white ribbon. Loyal frowned. *Third place?* But it was beautiful. And it was a present for Mother. How could it have gotten less than first place? He felt a hand settle on his shoulder and turned to see Father.

He nodded at the piece of furniture. "We did alright, didn't we?" Loyal scowled and held up one finger. Father threw his head back with laughter. "You think it's worth first place?" He looked at the pie safe. "If your mother thinks so, that's good enough for me." He looked Loyal in the eye. "Mainly I wanted the whole town to see that I . . . that *we* had made something nice for your mom. Even if the judges didn't think it was the best, I'm proud of it." He gave Loyal a squeeze. When his father spoke next, his lip movement wasn't as pronounced, forcing Loyal to focus hard and fill in the blanks. "Things don't have to be perfect to get the job done." Then he winked at Loyal, tipped his hat to Rebecca, and left them to their own devices.

Loyal rolled his father's words around in his mind that night. He was tired. After eating a huge stack of pancakes along with sausage, he'd played stickball until dark. Michael made sure he was included and even got the other kids to learn a few signs for things like *out* and *home run*. Then there'd been a bonfire and baked apples with cinnamon and sugar. Mother had taken one look at him and made him take a bath before he went to bed. Now he had that pleasant feeling that comes with being well-fed and physically worn out. And happy.

Still, Father's comment kept returning to him. He wasn't

perfect. So why didn't Father see that he could get the job done? That while he might not come in first, he could do well enough to stay at home and go to school with the kids who, for the first time ever, were beginning to feel like friends?

As his eyes drifted shut, a sleepy prayer whispered through his mind, and he lifted lazy hands to echo the words. *Please let Father see that I'm good enough.*

thirty-six

Creed walked along the street with his wife's hand tucked in the crook of his arm. She fit perfectly beside him, and he finally felt like their troubles were behind them. The murder had been solved. He expected to get a good price for his ginseng. Loyal was safe and would soon be back at school. And once that happened, he'd be able to give his full attention to repairing the years of damage he'd done to his marriage. He patted Delphy's hand. Today would be a start.

"Let's see what's on display at Odd Fellows," he said. "Then we'll go see how many ribbons you've won for your preserves."

She laughed and jostled against him. "You're just dragging this out," she accused.

"Maybe, but we have time before the pageant." She smiled and let him guide her inside the hall. It smelled of popcorn and sugar. Creed bought a cone of sweet kettle corn, and they munched as they strolled past the displays.

"Oh, that's nice," Delphy said, stopping in front of the pie safe with its white ribbon fluttering in the breeze coming from the open door.

"You like it?" Creed asked. "It only got third place."

"That doesn't matter. I've always thought it would be nice to have a pie safe. And the design in the door is pretty." She started to move on, but Creed held her in place.

"I like it, too," he said as he reached over and plucked the ribbon. "Let's see whose name is on this."

Delphy swatted at his hand. "Leave that be."

Creed ignored her, making a show of examining the ribbon. "Let's see . . . it says Adelphia Raines." He looked at her, eyes wide. "Why, that's you."

She frowned and snatched the ribbon from his hand. "You're talking nonsense. Let me see that." She examined it, then turned wondering eyes on Creed. "It does have my name on it."

"Sure enough. Guess it must be yours."

"But . . . I don't understand."

Creed took the ribbon and hung it back over the button on the little door. "It's yours, Delphy. Loyal and I made it for you." He ducked his head. "I wanted to get a blue ribbon on it for you, but I guess third place will do." He coughed and cleared his thick throat. "The main thing is, I didn't just want to make you a pie safe, I wanted to make you a prizewinning pie safe. One with your name on it, so that everybody who sees it will know how special you are."

Delphy flung her arms around his neck and kissed him right there in front of everybody. Surprised, it took Creed a moment to respond. Then he wrapped his arms around his wife and kissed her like he meant it. Somebody whistled, but he didn't care who saw. It was high time the whole town knew how much he loved this woman.

Creed was still feeling the glow from kissing his wife in front of an audience as they found a spot to watch the pageant. He tucked Delphy close to his side where they stood in the street with a view of the park. Some of the men from church had hammered together a makeshift stage that the kids would use for their show. Creed smiled. He'd been in the same pageant when he was a kid. Always stuck to playing a soldier, although he'd changed from the Confederate to the Union side and back again depending on the year and who he wanted to aggravate. Now Loyal was playing the same part. He gave Delphy a squeeze and felt like his chest was expanding. He couldn't imagine being prouder or happier than he was at this precise moment.

Loyal felt like throwing up. Why did he think this would be a good idea? All the performers were gathered off to the side of the park, waiting for the pageant to begin. And while several of them looked nervous, Loyal didn't think anyone was as scared as he was. He moved his hands ever so slightly, rehearsing his lines again. Of course, if he forgot them, probably no one would know but Mother.

A wave of dizziness washed over him. Mother would be watching. He wanted to prove himself to Father, but the fact that Mother would be able to see if he got anything wrong suddenly chilled him. The whole point of this was to prove that he could fit in, even with his differences. What if he ended up proving just how different he really was?

Loyal began backing toward the edge of the park where some shrubs grew. Maybe if he just eased himself back into them, no one would know . . .

He yelped when he felt a hand slip into his own. He knew he'd yelped because several kids jerked their heads around to stare at him. Looking down, he saw Rebecca's hand firmly in his. She squeezed and shaped the words *You'll be wonderful.* Oh well, too late to back out now.

The plan was for Loyal to slip to the side of the stage and shed his soldier's coat just before Michael made his entrance as David Hart—telling General McClellan that he would lead him to the enemy. Chuck kept sniggering into his fist. He thought their plan sounded way more fun than doing the same routine they'd been following since the fair started decades before.

Loyal lifted up the sincerest prayer he'd ever mustered and watched for his cue.

"Where's Loyal?" Delphy shifted and craned her neck, trying to spot their son in the cluster of kids to the side of the stage.

"He'll be coming on with the rest of the Union Army." Creed laughed. "I have to say, this is the first time probably since I was up there myself that I've given this show much attention." He smiled and pulled Delphy closer. She let him. "Kind of nice to have our boy up there just like any other young'un growing up in Beverly."

She rested her head against his shoulder. "It is nice. I've always wanted him to be more a part of things when he's at home. Maybe . . ." She snuck a look at him from beneath her lashes. "Maybe we can tell him that next year he can try the local school? I talked to the woman who would be his teacher and she's already reading up about ways she could make learning easier for him."

Creed dipped down to give her a quick kiss and smiled. "You're mighty persuasive, woman. I've been thinking the same thing, and now we've got all winter to think it through." He let his hand drift to the curve of her waist and then a bit lower. "During the long, cold winter."

She giggled and captured his hand before he caused a scandal. The way her husband was wooing her was a delight. And the fact that they were already married made it even more fun than when they'd been courting the first time. She flushed and elbowed him. "Pay attention. It's almost time."

They turned their eyes to the stage, where Confederate troops huddled off to the side under a sign that read *Camp Garnett*. A painted sheet stretched across the opposite side represented the Joseph Hart homestead on the summit of Rich Mountain.

A road sign in the middle had the words *Staunton-Parkersburg Turnpike* painted in letters that started large and got progressively smaller as the artist realized he was running out of room.

A narrator stepped onto the stage and set the scene, explaining how General McClellan had been tasked with protecting the railroad and securing the counties of what was western Virginia in those days. Then Bud Corrick's boy Chuck climbed onto the stage and made a speech about the dangers of a frontal attack. He'd played General McClellan for several years, but Delphy noticed that he was showing unexpected energy this time. He had a twinkle in his eye and a bounce in his step.

Delphy knew Michael would come out next as young David Hart, who would offer to lead the general and his men through the dense rhododendron and laurel hells to flank the enemy on Rich Mountain. Then she'd get to see Loyal come out to follow Michael and Chuck all over the park as if it were the side of a mountain. Most years there were some kids who hammed it up, acting like they were clawing their way up steep hillsides and pushing through dense underbrush. One year, somebody decided to liven up the show by hollering that he'd been snake bit. Delphy hoped the kids would be more dignified for Loyal's sake.

Chuck said the line that was Michael's cue and Delphy looked to the group of kids waiting their turn as soldiers. Nothing happened. She felt Creed's hand in hers tighten. He must be nervous, too. Then there was a stir and a murmur and, instead of Michael, Loyal stepped up onto the stage. Delphy gasped and covered her mouth with her hand.

Loyal moved toward Chuck, his gait stiff and his hands clenched. He glanced at the crowd, blanched, and riveted his eyes on Chuck again. He lifted his hands, and as he began signing, a voice floated out over the park.

"I will gladly show you the way to Rich Mountain. My father's home is there, and although it will be hard going, the Confederates must be defeated." Loyal's movements were jerky at first, but then they smoothed into a continuous, fluid motion that was almost like a dance. Delphy couldn't take her eyes off him—he was doing it perfectly.

"He's signing the part," she murmured. Creed glanced down at her. She ignored the tears welling in her eyes. "Isn't he beautiful?"

In a stage whisper, someone said, "What's that boy doing?" And another answered, "It's that deaf boy, the Raineses' boy. He talks with his hands." Delphy wanted to defend her son—to protect him—then realized she didn't need to. People could see what he was doing and that he was doing it well. A surge of wonder and pride coursed through her. What had she imagined she needed to protect him from? Yes, people would misunderstand him. Yes, he would face challenges. But just look at him! All she'd been doing was holding him back.

Loyal was helping to lead the troops on a circuitous route around the park, behind the stage, back to where the crowd was gathered, and on to the waiting Rebels. His face was tense, lips tight, and skin pale. Delphy thought she could see sweat on her son's forehead, even though it was a pleasant evening, and the first hint of worry passed through her. Loyal kept his eyes glued to a particular tree, and she realized that Michael was there, reading from the script. Loyal watched him to make sure his signing was in sync with Michael's words.

"He's scared," Creed whispered.

Delphy tamped down her own fear. "And still he's carrying on. As if he thinks he has to prove something. Do you think . . . ?" She tore her eyes from her son to look at Creed. His expression was pained. "Do you think he's trying to prove to us that he can get along with hearing folks?" She looked back and her heart ached. She was afraid that was exactly what he thought, and as much as she wanted to blame Creed, she might be more to blame than him.

A woman to their left leaned closer to Creed and Delphy. "The way he talks with his hands is right purty. And it's peaceful." She smiled. "Do you'uns talk that way, too?"

Delphy could have hugged the woman. She signed as she spoke. "I enjoy signing. And I agree. It is pretty."

The woman beamed at her. "Maybe you can learn us some at church one evening."

"I'd like that," Delphy said, hands continuing to move.

Just as she turned her attention back to the stage, she heard a murmur. It was time for the big finish. The skirmish was wrapping up, and General McClellan would praise David Hart for his bravery and fortitude. There were just a few final lines, and then she could tell Loyal he didn't have anything to prove.

Except she didn't see Loyal. And there was a disruption among the kids that had nothing to do with the mock battle. Someone said, "Disgusting," and the group of kids parted to expose Loyal, who was losing his dinner in the bushes.

Rebecca rushed to his side and handed him a handkerchief. Loyal, looking paler than ever, straightened up, took one look at the crowd focused solely on him, and keeled over.

Delphy started running.

thirty-seven

"I thought it was the best pageant we've had in years." Turned out Virgil wasn't much good at giving pep talks. "Sure held folks' attention, and it's not like it was the first time someone threw up." He grinned. "Remember back in twenty-two? I think there was a stomach bug going around that year, and once the first one succumbed"—he chuckled—"it was a chain reaction."

The sheriff had taken it upon himself to "escort" the family home, and now he and Creed were sitting on the porch. Delphy had taken Loyal upstairs. The boy had clearly been humiliated, and from the look on his face, Creed guessed he'd been working hard to hold back tears. "I should go talk to him."

Virgil leaned forward, bracing his elbows on his knees. "Which speech did you have in mind?"

"Which what?" Creed was confused.

"Which speech. Will it be the 'get back on the horse' speech, or the 'it wasn't as bad as you think and you'll be gone soon anyway' speech?"

"I . . . well, I hadn't quite thought what I'd say."

"What I suspected." Virgil stood and stretched. "Pretty night.

Look at all those stars. Kind of night that gives a man room to think." He slapped Creed on the shoulder and sauntered off into the darkness.

Creed watched his friend go. Though Virgil wasn't one to meddle in family business, Creed thought he understood what he was saying. This was no time to go off half-cocked and make his son feel worse than he already did. So, what *should* he say?

Delphy slipped out onto the porch and stood next to Creed, leaning into him with her hip. He reached out, circled her waist, and urged her onto his lap. "Don't you try and start anything," she said, her breath light against his ear.

"How is he?"

She sighed and rested against him. "Upset. He wanted to prove that he could hold his own with the other kids. That he can do what they can do. That . . ." She trailed off.

"That he'd do just fine going to school right here in Beverly," Creed finished for her. She nodded, her hair tickling his chin. He reached up to smooth the stray wisps back into place. "Do you think he would? Do fine here, I mean?"

"I do. Although now I'm not sure he thinks so."

"I've been thinking about what I should say to him."

She raised up and looked at him, her eyes dark in the night. "I'm glad. Sometimes—" she hesitated, then picked up again— "I think sometimes you settle for what's good instead of taking the time to consider what's *best*."

"Is that how the ladies are talking to their husbands these days?" His tone was teasing, mostly because he didn't want her to know how deeply he felt her words.

"The ones who make the same mistakes as their husbands talk like that."

He caught the hiccup in her voice and drew her closer, pleased when she molded herself to him. "What do you think is best?"

She settled her head against his shoulder. "I think we shouldn't limit Loyal. For too many years I've tried to protect him, to insu-

late him from a world I thought would be dangerous for him."
She sighed. "But he's found a fair amount of trouble all the
same." She shivered, and Creed rubbed her arm, holding her
closer. "I think he should spend time with all sorts of people—
ones who can hear, and ones who can't. Kids his own age and
adults he can look up to. People from town and out on the farms.
People who come from different places—like Otto."

"Maybe even girlfriends," Creed teased.

She laughed and it echoed in his chest. "Yes, so long as they're
as sweet and kind as Rebecca Westfall."

Creed found her lips and kissed her long and slow, all the
tenderness he'd been denying for too many years singing between them. When they were both breathless, he pulled away.
"I'd better go talk to him before I forget how to talk," he said.

She laughed, low and husky. "Good idea. And then maybe
we can stop talking some more."

"Yes, ma'am."

Loyal buried his face in his pillow. Now he could neither
see nor hear. If only he could stop feeling. He'd been an idiot
to think he could pull off something like playing a lead role
in the town pageant. He'd been so nervous, and the greasy
sausage roll he'd eaten earlier had been a bad choice. When
he lost sight of Michael for a minute and didn't know if he was
supposed to be signing or not, he'd panicked. And the panic
had churned in his belly with the food and . . . humiliating.
What could be more humiliating than throwing up in front of
the whole town? Oh yeah. Fainting in front of the whole town.
He groaned, not caring if it made a sound or not. No one was
here to listen anyway.

The light switched on, and he felt the mattress shift. He
angled his head to peer out. He thought it would be Mother
trying to console him, but Father sat at the foot of his bed,

watching him. He sat up cross-legged and hugged his pillow to his chest. Was he in trouble? He probably should be.

"I've been thinking." Father made the sign for *thinking*. "You're going to be fourteen soon. Grown and a man before we know it." This was not what Loyal had been expecting. Was Father going to send him into the world on his own? He sure as shooting wasn't ready for that. "It's time you started making some of your own decisions." Loyal squeezed the pillow harder. "I'm leaving it up to you to decide whether you want to go back to the school for the deaf or go to school here in Beverly. The choice is yours, son."

Loyal just stared, not sure he'd read his father's lips right. He wet his own lips and found the words, "I decide?"

Father looked delighted. "Yes, you decide."

Loyal stared at the quilt on his bed. Mother had made it using lots of blue fabric, his favorite color. He had another one a lot like it at school. He'd stared at that one a hundred times, thinking about how much he wished he could stay home and go to school—be part of a real family. But now . . . he wasn't so sure. Here, everyone would know him as the deaf boy who threw up at the Civil War pageant. Back at the deaf school, no one would know about his embarrassing performance.

He pointed his index finger at his forehead and made little circles with a thoughtful look on his face. "You want to think about it?" Father asked. Loyal nodded. "That's wise. I knew you were smart." Father leaned forward and gave him a quick kiss on the forehead. It was something he hadn't done in years, and tears sprang to Loyal's eyes. Thankfully Father turned and left before he could see them.

By breakfast time, Loyal had made up his mind. He was going back to the school for the deaf. He was pretty sure it was what his parents wanted, and he wasn't ready to face the kids he'd embarrassed himself in front of. Although he thought Rebecca would still be his friend, he wasn't sure he wanted to see her either. Which made it that much worse when she waltzed into the kitchen while he was still eating. He'd gotten up late, and Father was cleaning out the shed in the backyard for some reason. Mother was hanging out laundry. Loyal stirred his oatmeal trying to make it look like he'd eaten some.

Rebecca skipped into the room, stopped, and frowned at him. "What's the matter with you?" He formed an o at his chin and flung his hand outward. "Well, you look like something's wrong. Is it because of yesterday?" Loyal shrugged and dug his spoon deeper into the bowl.

Rebecca slid into the chair nearest him and picked up the piece of toast he'd been ignoring. She began nibbling on it. "Some of the kids want to learn sign language. They thought yesterday was a pip." Loyal ate a bite of oatmeal for something to do.

Mother came inside and must have spoken to Rebecca. "No thank you, Mrs. Raines. I had breakfast." Then Father came in and ruffled Loyal's hair. He reached up and smoothed it back into place. Why couldn't everyone just leave him alone?

Mother sat across from him and lifted her hands with a smile to sign *Have you decided?* Loyal scowled. He didn't want to talk about this right now. He signed an emphatic *no*. Her face fell. *Don't you want to go to school here?* She was speaking as she signed, and Rebecca perked up.

"Are you coming to school with me?" She practically bounced in her chair.

They all watched him, eager, expectant. Even Father looked like he was trying not to smile. Loyal flung his spoon down, stood, and put everything he had behind speaking a single word. "No!" It must have been loud. They all froze and stared at him. He fled the room, banging out the front door.

Rebecca wanted to follow Loyal, but Creed persuaded her to go on home, assuring her that he would get to the root of what was troubling his son. But now, as he divided the lilies Delphy had planted in the front yard, he was mostly trying to tell himself he wasn't doing this just so he could keep an eye out for Loyal's return. He felt like he was messing this up no matter what he did. Had he been this changeable when he was a boy?

Delphy came out and sat on the front steps, watching him. "Thank you," she said.

"For what?"

"For doing my garden work for me."

"Oh. Sure. I imagine there are plenty of things you'd like me to do around here." He stomped on the top of the shovel, thrusting it deeper beneath a clump of roots.

"I could take offense at that, but I'm not going to." Creed stopped and looked at Delphy with a frown.

"Come. Sit." She patted the step next to her. He let his shoulders slump, leaned the shovel against the porch, and slouched down beside her.

"I've had to do some soul-searching," she began. Creed tried to jump in, but she held up her hand and even he knew what that sign meant. "I've been afraid for Loyal. Afraid he'd get hurt. Afraid he wouldn't fit in. Afraid people would be cruel because he's deaf." She sighed and laid a hand on his knee. "Afraid no one—not even his father—could be trusted to take care of him. And so I've been holding him back. Rebecca and Michael are the first real friends he's made away from his school and that's just wrong." She waved her hand toward the small cluster of buildings that made up their town. "This is his home, and I've been keeping him from it." She laughed. "I guess he finally got old enough—strong enough—to break free."

Creed took the words in, not rushing to respond. Loyal, old enough to make his own decisions. Even the bad ones. "He sure broke free in a big way. Can't say as I think all his decisions this

300

summer have been good ones." He felt righteousness rise up in his chest. "Like this morning. Yelling at us and then heading for the hills isn't exactly mature behavior."

She tightened her grip where her hand rested on his thigh. "Well now, I'd have to agree with you there."

"I . . ." Creed choked on his own words. He hung his head. "Walked right into that one, didn't I?"

"Like father, like son?" Her voice was soft, musical even. He wished Loyal could hear it.

"He's better than me in a lot of ways."

She patted his leg and leaned into him. "You're a good man, Creed Raines. Hardheaded and stubborn, but those can work to your advantage sometimes." She rested her head on his shoulder. "I think Loyal wants to please you more than anything. He wants to be like you, to do what you do, and believe what you believe. Maybe the problem is that you're still figuring out what that is." She stood and he instantly missed her touch. She looked down at him. "I think I forgot why I fell in love with you in the first place." His heart clenched, then eased when he saw a smile dancing around her lips. "But it's coming back to me."

The screen door slapped behind her as she went inside. Creed quelled the urge to follow her. He had something more pressing he needed to do.

thirty-eight

Loyal hadn't planned to come to this spot along the river, he just found himself here. *The scene of the crime*, he thought. He shucked off his shirt and shoes and waded out into the water. Although the September day was still plenty warm, the water felt icy cold. Goose pimples rose all over him, but he pushed ahead until he could dunk his whole body. The water was a shock against the heat of anger lingering in his face. He surfaced and inhaled a long, deep breath that reached all the way to his fingers and toes. It felt good—like he'd been suffocating and now could breathe at last.

He stood in the water and looked toward the place where Eddie Minks had died. It had changed since that midsummer day. A few leaves were starting to color, and the tangle of undergrowth was dying back. He didn't suppose there would be even a hint of the blood he'd seen there back in July. He moved closer and startled when he realized there was a man sitting under a tree, watching him. He lifted a hand, and Loyal saw it was Otto. Sloshing over to the riverbank, Loyal climbed out. Otto nodded once, and although he didn't smile exactly, he looked welcoming. So Loyal decided to go and sit down next to him—he had a question for Otto.

While Loyal was chewing his lip trying to think how to communicate, Otto touched him on the arm. *Thank you*, he signed. Surprised, Loyal signed back *Why?*

"This is my only sign," Otto said. It was a little hard to follow his lips since he spoke in a different way, but Loyal concentrated and thought he was getting most of the words. "Miss Rebecca showed me. In case I see you." Loyal lifted his shoulders, furrowed his brow, and gave his head a tiny shake. "Why do I thank you?" Loyal nodded. "It was you who, how do you say, got me off the hook." He hooked a finger in his mouth like a fish, and Loyal smiled.

The two sat in companionable silence for a while. A breeze stirred, drying Loyal's damp skin and making him shiver. He picked up a stick and smoothed a spot in the dirt. *Why did you confess?* he wrote.

Otto nodded, his expression serious. "It is difficult to explain." Loyal sat back to wait. Otto spoke carefully, as though plucking his words from the air one by one. Loyal was glad since it made it easier to follow him. "Mr. Hadden gave me a home when I had no home . . ." He paused, searching. "They do not like that I am different. I am German." He puffed his chest out as he said it. "My leg, it slows me down." He thumped the foot that Loyal could see was twisted. "But Mr. Hadden, he tell me he is different, too." He looked to the wind-stirred leaves above him as if they might whisper what he wanted to say. "He did not tell me how, but I see." Otto pointed to his eye. "His wife is gone. People want much from him but give little. He is lonely in a big house." Otto shrugged. "I could see a way to give him much."

Loyal considered the young man's words. He picked his stick up again, wiped out the earlier question, and wrote *sacrifice*. Otto smiled and picked up his own stick to write *opfern* in the dirt. "Now we have three languages between us," he said.

Loyal snuck back home expecting his parents to be angry. But neither of them was there. He'd missed lunch so he dug around and found a tin of cookies, then went out back to choose an apple from the tree. Mother would be making pies and apple butter soon, and she'd need his help. Maybe he should stay. Maybe he should be like Otto and figure out what the people he cared about needed. He'd been trying to impress Father and persuade Mother to let him stay in Beverly to attend school here. And he wanted to stay in Beverly so the three of them could be a real family—not just on Sundays or Christmas—but all the time.

Of course, that had changed when he made such an idiot of himself in front of the whole town. But if feeling embarrassed could change his mind . . . No. While he wanted to be part of a normal family, that wasn't what he'd really been after. He'd just wanted to be normal. Or at least to prove he could pass for normal.

He bit into the apple, the crisp, sweet flesh crunching between his teeth. Apples were always better right after you picked them. He took another bite and noticed there was a wormhole he needed to eat around. Even apples weren't perfect. God made the apple, and God made him. And neither of them was perfect. He took a bite from the opposite side of the fruit. Still good. Still sweet, even if there was a worm lurking on the other side.

Maybe he didn't have to be normal. Maybe all he needed to be was the person God made him.

Movement caught his eye, and he turned to see his parents walking around the house hand in hand. They were deep in conversation, and for just a moment Loyal felt like maybe they were complete without him. Then Mother looked up and saw him. Her mouth formed an o and she hurried to him, clasping him to her. He felt the rumble of her voice and then her laughter. She took a step back and began signing. *Funny that I forgot you can't hear me! I'm so glad you're home. I was worried.* Her expression changed. Grew serious. *I knew you would be fine. You are brave and smart. I know you can take care of yourself.*

Loyal didn't know what to do. He thought he'd be in trouble. He thought Mother would lecture him about not going off on his own, about how it wasn't safe for a boy who couldn't hear.

He looked to Father and saw that he had an expression of deep pleasure on his face. He lifted his hands and began signing. It was stilted and simplified and not altogether correct, but it was sign language nonetheless. *Happy me, you home. Proud me, you my son. You strong. You brave.* He paused and seemed to take a deep breath. He shook his fingers like it was hard work, this signing business, and he needed to loosen them up. *I hope you stay. Go school here.*

Loyal stared in shock. Father wanted him to stay in Beverly. And he was proud of him. Thought he was strong and brave. He realized he was shaping the words with his hands as they tumbled through his mind. He glanced at Mother, who was smiling and wiping at tears.

Then it really and truly hit him. Father was learning sign language. He'd learned a sign or two here and there, but now he was attempting full sentences. Complete thoughts. He didn't expect Loyal to be like him. He was trying to be like Loyal. Without thinking he ran as hard as he could and crashed into his father, wrapping his arms around him. He was sobbing, but it didn't matter. Father wasn't ashamed. Father loved him just the way he was.

Epilogue

Delphy watched Creed watch Loyal as he picked at his breakfast. Her son was nervous about his first day of school in Beverly—she could tell. She could also tell that her husband was even now delighting in their son, love shining in his eyes. Maybe all the time she'd spent with Loyal was teaching her to look deeper, beyond the words a person spoke. And maybe this summer had taught her to hold on a little more loosely than she had in the past, letting the people she loved live their lives without needing to lock them in her heart.

She heard Michael and Rebecca clatter onto the front porch and felt the tender moment fade. She'd hoped this summer might have taught Hadden to hold his children tighter, but she supposed he had his own struggles to contend with. While her husband had returned to her, Hadden's wife never would. And he had yet to learn what could ease that emptiness. Although, perhaps, his learning what wouldn't was a first step.

She touched Loyal's arm and pointed to the door, where his friends waved for him to join them. He let his spoon drop to the table, grabbed his books, and ran to meet them. Then he stopped and rushed back to give her a kiss on the cheek. He hesitated in front of his father, probably wanting to be more grown up with him. Creed reached out and squeezed the boy's shoulder and signed *Proud of you. Do good today.* Loyal's face lit like the sun appearing after a storm. He signed *I love you,* then turned and headed for the door.

Delphy watched as Michael made a *hurry up!* gesture, smiling at the sound of her son's laughter—loud and off-key—mingling with the other children's as they disappeared outside and down the street. Still smiling, she stood to gather the breakfast dishes when Creed hooked her with one callused hand and drew her down onto his lap. She pushed at him, but they both knew she didn't mean it.

"Worried about him?" Creed asked.

She reached up to muss his perfectly groomed hair, and he let her. "It's funny," she said, "but I'm not."

"Our boy can take care of himself. Guess we both know that now." A strand of hair fell across his forehead, making him look rakish. She pushed it back into place.

"He can," she agreed. "Still, isn't it wonderful he has you to take care of him, as well?"

"Not just me," Creed said while tracing her collarbone with a cool finger. "He has *us.*"

She sighed and dipped her face close until he could feel the heat of her breath against his ear. "That he does. And you know what?" She took Creed's murmur as answer enough. "I think Loyal might like to have someone to take care of too—maybe a little brother?" She brushed her lips along the line of his freshly shaved jaw. "Or sister?"

Creed wrapped her tighter and pressed his lips to hers, only pausing long enough to whisper, "That might could be arranged."

And with that, any last defenses she might have forgotten to take down melted away and she knew the long winter ahead wouldn't be nearly long enough.

Author's Note

I found the seed of this story in an account of the unsolved murder of Mamie Thurman. At first I thought I was going to write about this poor woman found murdered on a remote road in West Virginia in 1932. But there was a character in her story who kept calling out to me. In most accounts, the person who discovered the body was simply described as a "young deaf-mute." Intriguing. I did a bit of research and it turns out his name was Garland Davis and he was actually thirty-two—not SO young. Little else is known about him, however, beyond the one account that mentions he testified in the murder trial using "hand communication."

Well, if that won't spawn a story, I don't know what will! From that seed sprouted Loyal—a thirteen-year-old boy who's deaf but not altogether mute. And he does indeed use American Sign Language, something that must have been an oddity in a small town in 1930s West Virginia.

Special thanks go to author Jennifer Major, who has extensive experience with family members who are deaf and graciously read the manuscript to make sure I handled ASL and the deaf experience reasonably well.

Acknowledgments

My thanks for this story begins with my editor, Dave Long, who's never satisfied with the first version of any story I throw out (seriously, Dave, thank you for that!) but who has an amazing talent for weeding ideas down to the healthiest sprout with the strongest roots. I'm also so very grateful for the rest of the editorial team.

Then there's the marketing team at Bethany House, led by Noelle Chew and Amy Lokkesmoe. Not only are they smart cookies but they're also super fun to hang out with!

I couldn't do this work without the great team at Books & Such Literary Management. My agent, Wendy Lawton, is an encourager, a cheerleader, a prayer warrior, and a voice of wisdom when a story needs a little extra push.

Penultimate thanks go to my husband, Jim Thomas, who sometimes wonders if I prefer my laptop to him (I don't!). Thanks for putting the kettle on, hon.

And ultimate thanks go to God, who gave me the gift of words and the ability to wield them. May every story glorify Him.

Sarah Loudin Thomas is a fund-raiser for a children's ministry who has time to write because she doesn't have children of her own. She holds a bachelor's degree in English from Coastal Carolina University and is the author of the acclaimed novels *The Sound of Rain* and *Miracle in a Dry Season*—winner of the 2015 INSPY Award. Sarah has also been a finalist for the Christy Award, the ACFW Carol Award, and the Christian Book of the Year Award. She and her husband live near Asheville, North Carolina. Learn more at www.sarahloudinthomas.com.

Sign Up for Sarah's Newsletter

Keep up to date with Sarah's latest news on book releases and events by signing up for her email list at sarahloudinthomas.com.

More from Sarah Loudin Thomas

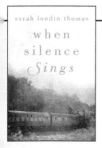

After the rival McLean clan guns down his cousin, Colman Harpe chooses peace over seeking revenge with his family. But when he hears God tell him to preach to the McLeans, he attempts to run away—and fails—leaving him sick and suffering in their territory. He soon learns that appearances can be deceiving, and the face of evil doesn't look like he expected.

When Silence Sings

BETHANYHOUSE

You May Also Like . . .

After a terrible mine accident in 1954, Judd Markley abandons his poor Appalachian town for Myrtle Beach. There he meets the beautiful and privileged Larkin Heyward, who dreams of helping people like those he left behind. Drawn together amid a hurricane, they wonder what tomorrow will bring—and realize that it may take a miracle for them to be together.

The Sound of Rain by Sarah Loudin Thomas
sarahloudinthomas.com

In this epistolary novel from the WWII home front, Johanna Berglund is forced to return to her small Midwestern town to become a translator at a German prisoner of war camp. There, amid old secrets and prejudice, she finds that the POWs have hidden depths. When the lines between compassion and treason are blurred, she must decide where her heart truly lies.

Things We Didn't Say by Amy Lynn Green
amygreenbooks.com

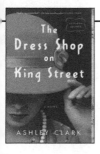

In 1946, Millie Middleton left home to keep her heritage hidden, carrying the dream of owning a dress store. Decades later, when Harper Dupree's future in fashion falls apart, she visits her mentor Millie. When the revelation of a family secret leads them to Charleston and a rare opportunity, can they overcome doubts and failures for a chance at their dreams?

The Dress Shop on King Street by Ashley Clark
HEIRLOOM SECRETS
ashleyclarkbooks.com

BETHANYHOUSE

More from Bethany House

Haunted by painful memories, Olivia Rosetti is singularly focused on running her maternity home for troubled women. Darius Reed is determined to protect his daughter from the prejudice that killed his wife by marrying a society darling. But when he's suddenly drawn to Olivia, they will learn if love can prove stronger than the secrets and hurts of the past.

A Haven for Her Heart by Susan Anne Mason
REDEMPTION'S LIGHT #1
susanannemason.net

Reeling from the loss of her parents, Lucy Claremont discovers an artifact under the floorboards of their London flat, leading her to an old seaside estate. Aided by her childhood friend Dashel, a renowned forensic astronomer, they start to unravel a history of heartbreak, sacrifice, and love begun 200 years prior— one that may offer the healing each seeks.

Set the Stars Alight by Amanda Dykes
amandadykes.com

Secretary to the first lady of the United States, Caroline Delacroix is at the pinnacle of high society— but is hiding a terrible secret. Immediately suspicious of Caroline, but also attracted to her, secret service agent Nathaniel Trask must battle his growing love for her as the threat to the president rises and they face adventure, heartbreak, and danger.

A Gilded Lady by Elizabeth Camden
HOPE AND GLORY #2
elizabethcamden.com

BETHANYHOUSE

CPSIA information can be obtained
at www.ICGtesting.com
Printed in the USA
LVHW042042231120
672479LV00004B/245

9 780764 237843